Garrets Lodge

D.W. Hitz

Fedowar Press, LLC

www.FedowarPress.com

ISBN-13 (Digital): 978-1-956492-53-8
ISBN-13 (Paperback): 978-1-956492-54-5
ISBN-13 (Hardback): 978-1-956492-55-2

Edited by Heather Ann Larson
Cover by Don Noble of Rooster Republic Press
Interior Design by D.W. Hitz

Also by D.W. Hitz

Adult Fiction

Judith's Prophecy (Big Sky Terror Book 1)
Judith's Blood (Big Sky Terror Book 2)
Judith's Fall (Big Sky Terror Book 3)
Gods are Born
Brady: A Novella
Bloodtooth
Cody Was Here and Other Stories
Our Trip Through Hell
Garrets Lodge

Extreme Horror

Larval Seeds
Stay Out of the Tub
You're Going to Die in Here
Santa vs. Satan
Custer Falls Extreme Horror Omnibus
It Came From Inside (August 2024)

GARRETS LODGE

D.W. HITZ

Part I

LITTLE LIFE REMAINED AROUND the cabin. Deadfall had taken most of the trees within fifty feet, disease the others.

It started with one tree soon after the Garrets died, and another followed. One dried-out husk of pine crashed into the next, and soon, what had been a lush homestead became a graveyard of ancient timber, broken and shattered in piles. Twigs of brambles and desiccated juniper littered the floor where unlucky seeds had dared to grow and found barren soil.

The life had been drained from it all.

1

*I*T'S ALL ABOUT AN *angel.*

That's what Mom always said when Angel was little. Angel Higgins didn't consider herself little anymore, even if the world disagreed. At ten years old, she was taller than the boys in her class, and that encouraged her as she stood up straight on the playground of North Custer Falls Elementary School during recess and shouted wholeheartedly at Allen Neddles.

"Give it back, you little turd!"

The boy just grinned, his freckled cheeks flushed from excitement and the chilly spring air. He held Theresa Holland's bow over his head like a trophy, a dozen strands of mahogany hair hanging from its clip.

Theresa was on her knees, crying. Her hands covered the sore spot on her head where her hair had been ripped away.

"I said give it back!" Angel fumed. She didn't know if she had ever been so angry; her fists were shaking. Theresa wasn't her best friend in school by any means, that was Marcy Graves, but this little turd had been at it all day. Before school, as they gathered, waiting for the bell, he was after Theresa, calling her ugly. In class, he shot spitballs at her. A few minutes ago, at the start of recess, he simply walked right up and jerked the bow from her head. And now he was laughing. Laughing!

Angel drew back her fist, aimed, and let it fly. If you asked

Angel at the moment, she wouldn't have been able to tell you the last time she hit anyone in anger. It just didn't happen. It had actually been four years earlier, in first grade, when Samantha West took her Melissa and Doug baby doll and ran its head through the mud puddle under the playground slide. She didn't remember that moment because she had seen red when her doll's hair dripped mud and brown water—a rage blackout. She didn't know how close to that she was right now.

Her knuckles landed to the right of Allen's Adam's apple. His eyes bulged as he quieted, his throat closing in. Angel could tell from the look on his face he wanted to scream, only, he lacked the ability. Instead, he dropped to his knees on a patch of half mud, half snow. The bow slipped from his fingers as he clutched his throat and tears raced from his eyes.

The other kids went immediately silent. Angel picked up the bow and scowled at him. His eyes were red, his neck glowed, and his lips pursed and pushed outward, trembling. Then her eyes teared as well.

Her rage flushed away, and as the pain on his face sank into her thoughts, her heart ached. She hadn't wanted to hurt him. She just wanted him to stop being mean to Theresa. The event replayed in her head, the muscle memory doing its job after the hours of self-defense practice with Mom. But it felt different as she looked into his weeping eyes. The fear in those eyes as he fought for breath was something she hadn't expected.

How was he afraid? He was the one that caused all this. He was the one laughing and taunting Theresa. How does the aggressor get scared? She supposed it didn't matter. He was. And she had caused it.

"I'm sorry," Angel said. So truly was. At that moment, if she could have taken her punch back, she would have. Maybe she could have found some other way to get through to him and make him stop?

He glared at her and coughed. He gazed at the other girls, at Theresa, and his expression shifted. It wasn't fear anymore. His teeth clamped down, and his eyes squinted. He sprang up and tackled Angel to the snowy ground. Allen could barely breathe, but he was sitting on her legs and pounding on her chest.

At first, all Angel could do was stare. None of this made any sense. He was attacking her now. She covered her face and shrieked. Her chest ached. The hits were softened by her puffy jacket, but they still hurt.

What was wrong with him?

The gathered circle of children yelled. Some shrieks, some cheers (Angel had no idea some of her friends could cheer for her getting pummeled); Marcy screamed for help. A moment later, a parent helper was lifting Allen from her legs, and Ms. Bates was kneeling over her with an outstretched hand.

When Angel thought about it later, this was the moment in time she blamed for starting it all. For everything going downhill. For all the blood to come. This was the pivotal moment none of them could have seen coming.

It's all about an angel.

Well, maybe.

She walked alongside Allen as the bell rang and everyone else ran to their classes. Ms. Bates led them through the first-grade hall, past the janitor's closet where the old custodian, Heath Williams, looked down on her with cloudy eyes, blood dripping from his temples. They went past the lobby, where her great-aunt, Joanne, lay in the middle of the floor, staring at the ceiling and silently wailing for someone to help. They stopped at the vice principal's office.

Allen took the chair on the left and Angel the one on the right. Once Ms. Bates sat, they each told their side of the story, and

Ms. Bates called two sets of parents to come and pick up their children.

It's all about an angel, her mother's voice repeated in her mind. Her head sank into her hands, and she hoped it wasn't true—that the bad feeling in her gut wasn't right for once.

Wanda Higgins cried in the front seat of her car, across from the house on West Hemlock where two of the worst events of her life happened. The pulsing sense of evil had faded from the charred pile of siding, wood, and shingles that had once been a home, but that didn't fool her. It was still in there. Maybe it was under the ash and rubble. Maybe it was buried under the tons of crushed lumber and debris. That kind of evil doesn't die; she knew that now. It still had designs on her, whether her rapist was still there or not.

The March sun had melted most of the snow, aside from the patches under hedges where light never reached and the shaded sides of homes the sun couldn't touch until late spring. The brown lawns, the lack of Christmas decorations, all should have helped her feel that the moment of terror was in her distant past, but it didn't seem to.

She trembled as badly as she had that day, after it was over.

(But would it really ever be over? Could it be as long as it lived in her recurring nightmares?)

The memories of his eyes, his stink (still tattooed inside her nose), his heavy breathing over her as he was inside her made her want to puke, just as it had every other time she had driven by this place.

Wanda never pictured herself as self-destructive, but she wondered if she had become that. At first, she looked at coming by this place as some sort of therapy—not that she would tell her therapist she was doing so—thinking it would help her to get over it, to make her stronger. But each time, it was the same: tears, flashbacks, nausea, and hating herself for being so stupid to go in there that day.

And here she was again.

She'd had the abortion and told no one. Other than the event itself, it was likely the hardest thing she had ever been through. But she couldn't let that evil grow inside her. She *couldn't.*

Another sheet of tears.

She had lost so much. She had been days from being approved to get back on the job as a patrol officer—having been off since the shooting—and then she just had to come back and check out the scene. She couldn't explain why she did it to anyone, explain the voice and the urge. Then that bastard raped her, and the house burned, and she was on suspension again, this time indefinitely.

She just wanted this chapter of her life to be over. She wanted to get back to being a cop. She may have been utterly green at the job, but she had been learning—it was the only job she ever wanted to do. She wanted to get back to being a mom who wasn't always crying in her bedroom. She knew her absence and shortness were straining the bond between her and Angel, and she hated herself for that. It was like everything she loved was falling away, and she just wanted the world back to the way it used to be.

She closed her eyes. Her heart throbbed. Her chest heaved, and her breath hitched.

Wanda's phone rang. The screen read: *Angel's School.*

Wanda sped to the school. She assured the vice principal she was coming, and she crossed her fingers that the woman wouldn't also call Henry to attend the *Emergency Meeting.* She wasn't sure exactly what she was walking into, but she knew she didn't want Henry there. The man always meant well when it came to Angel, but he was a walking beacon of dishonesty when it came to her.

"Angel's behavior" was all the woman would say on the phone. What was that supposed to mean? Angel was the most well-behaved kid she knew; maybe not that, but she was a dozen steps above where Wanda had been at her age.

She felt for her mother as she drove. How many times had Mom gotten the same call and had to leave the Police Department to come down to the old school and sit and listen to those windbags talk? She practically ran that station alone between the calls and the radio and the paperwork; there was no functionality without Rhonda Higgins. She had to have been so embarrassed having to leave work and deal with a kid in the principal's office.

Wanda was not embarrassed. She was irritated. What was wrong with those idiots to think her daughter could have done anything to require a disciplinary meeting? It was all some kind of misunderstanding, and they were putting Angel through it for no reason at all.

She was sure it was a mistake until sitting in the vice principal's office, where the Bates woman described what she saw her Angel do. And then Angel admitted it.

Wanda was flabbergasted. Shocked. She was proud.

"It sounds to me like Angel should get a medal." Wanda's voice was dry, and Bates stared down her nose at Wanda, and then back at Angel.

"I'm sorry?" The woman's forehead was scrunched up in an

unbelieving retraction. "She hit a child."

Wanda knew she was pushing the line. She knew she was walking into the conversation already frustrated with her own life, but she was speaking quite frankly. "What you've just explained to me is that your teachers are incompetent, and they failed to protect her friend Theresa. Then, when Angel tried to protect her friend and retrieve her stolen property, you treated *her* like the criminal."

"Mrs—"

"Yes, it sounds like she did exactly what needed to be done, and you want to punish her for it." The words felt good shooting from her lips. It wouldn't get her anywhere. Wanda knew that. There was nothing to be gained from the conversation other than her own satisfaction at releasing some venom. But she was happy to do it.

"We have a zero-tolerance policy—"

"Does that include that boy? Was he suspended for a week as well?"

"That's private information between his family and the school."

"He got detention," Angel said.

"Detention?" Wanda mocked. "A healthy punishment for the instigator of the entire event."

"Mrs. Higgins. He did not hit anyone."

Angel frowned. She couldn't believe none of the adults had seen Allen Neddles pounding on her chest. She didn't know if they were lying or blind to what they didn't want to see, as adults were prone to be.

"No," Wanda snapped. "He caused emotional abuse, and your system thinks that's less damaging than my daughter protecting a child that your staff failed."

"Mrs. Higgins—"

"Enough." Wanda stood and motioned for Angel to follow. "I've heard enough of this." She shook her head and pointed for Angel to go through the door. Lastly, she said, "You people should be ashamed of yourselves," and escorted Angel from the office.

Bates said nothing more. Her expression was sunken. Yes, she had failed them all, and she knew it. She wasn't half as good at this job as Hannah Gould had been. And she missed her old boss. Hannah would have made it all work. There would have been smiles around the room as the parents left, along with invitations to go get coffee sometime. She shook her head and sighed.

Angel followed her mother down the hall and into the school's entryway. She tried not to flinch as Mom sloshed through the pool of blood surrounding Aunt Joanne and gave it a wide berth, avoiding Joanne's grasping hands. It wasn't that the woman could touch her—she had seen the ghost try, her grip passing through dozens of kids every recess and morning and departure. It was the thought of those blood-stained fingers drifting through her body, maybe even through her soul. It made her shiver, and it made her sad.

They were outside when Angel shouted, "Daddy," and ran to give Henry a hug. Wanda gritted her teeth and approached him at the edge of the parking lot as Angel swung from his waist.

"Is everything okay here?" Henry was wearing his blue coveralls. They were newer and less stained than the others. His stubble was short today, as well, and the combed hair made Wanda wonder if the rumor she'd heard about him dating Sally Sheppard was true. Was she trying to clean him up?

Wanda wanted to snicker at that idea. Henry had been a mess since he was old enough to walk. The fact that he was a loving Dad was the only reason she was able to look at him these days.

"Yeah," Wanda said. "It's fine. She got in a little trouble for sticking up for her friend. So I thought I'd take her to get some ice cream."

"Ice cream!" Angel shouted. Her grip on her father faltered.

"Sounds like you." Henry smiled. It was an *ain't-I-charming* smile.

She didn't need that shit. Not the compliments, not now. It was not a good day for his come ons and praise or his whines about getting back together. He had fucked Mary Ralston while she was at work, and that was the end of it. One time was all it took, no matter how bad the woman had come on to him, how hard he'd had it as she cornered him in the shop and whipped those store-bought tits out and shoved them in his face. Of course, he'd tried the whole *she grabbed my dick* excuse, like that was some kind of man kryptonite, but Wanda wasn't buying it. He cheated. That was the end of it. And she didn't need to hear his crap now. She wasn't obligated to do a thing for him now.

"We gotta go." Wanda gestured Angel toward the car.

Angel gave her dad an extra hug, and he kissed the top of her head.

Wanda opened the driver's door and got in.

"Bye," Henry called, but it went unanswered by Wanda.

"Bye, Daddy." Angel climbed into the back, tossing her bag to the side. She buckled in and asked Mom, "You're still mad at Dad, aren't you?"

Tears ran down Wanda's cheeks as she started the engine. She couldn't speak. She couldn't tell Angel what she had been through. She would be damned if she was going to lay the weight of her pain on her daughter. She didn't know what she was going to do, but she knew she needed a break. She needed to get away from this goddamn place, this town, this shithole, and let her mind relax—release a little tension.

She needed to get away.

And maybe that was a good thing. She would plan a trip or something. Shit, she didn't have to go to work anytime soon. Angel had a week off. Why not get the hell out for a few days.

Yeah.

She wiped the tears away and pulled out of the lot. They had ice cream to get and packing to do.

2

STEVIE EVANS AND HONEY McCluskey drove through the industrial park on the east side of Custer Falls. Stevie squinted as they passed identical-looking warehouses, his frustration growing by the second. After barely escaping death the night before and the nearly-failed robbery yesterday, it felt like his entire life was turning into a shitshow. It didn't help that the heat barely worked in the rusted-out F250 they stole that morning.

"Where the fuck is it?" Stevie growled.

"Just call him," Honey whined.

He had avoided calling the man all morning and lied about the reason each time Honey suggested it. Yes, Shamus was the contact, but there were two problems: (one) he was actually Dad's contact—the man never really liked Stevie—and (two) they didn't have the loot.

"It's a bad idea to call Shamus. We're better off just showing up."

"Why? He's supposed to be this old family friend, according to your dad."

"Yeah, that was when we were supposed to be coming with bags full of jewelry. Now all we have is our hand out."

Her jaw was open as he jerked the wheel left.

"I think this is it."

The warehouse looked the same as the rest, but parked in front was a Dodge Ram with a black stripe down the side and a decal on the tailgate replacing the standard Ram emblem. Instead of the usual ram's head, this one was a four-horned goat skull.

"How do you know this is it?"

Stevie pointed at the truck.

"That's not subtle." She scowled.

"Yeah. He isn't a subtle guy." Stevie parked the rusted hunk of junk next to Shamus's truck. As they opened their doors and Stevie set foot on the ground, two men started toward them from the warehouse.

"Welcome wagon," Honey said. She recognized the type. Their eyes were fixed on her and Stevie, their clothes were cheap, ready to toss if they got blood on them, and their faces were overconfident yet blank: doers—goons paid to do what they're told and not ask questions. She tugged at her shirt, straightened her boobs, and walked to the front of the vehicle, where Stevie was waiting for her.

Stevie, Honey, and the two men met halfway between the parked vehicles and the warehouse door. Stevie didn't recognize either of them. While it was true he hadn't seen Shamus in a couple years, guys got around, did jobs for one crew and the next. Since the last time he was in Custer Falls with Dad for one of Shamus's jobs, he had run into three of Shamus's former guys back in South Dakota. Once you knew who was who in the racket, it started to feel like a small world.

The one on the right was bald and buff. He could have played a stunt double for The Rock if he wasn't as pale as an Irishman. The other was nearly as wide, but his bulk was more fat than muscle, and while thinning, he had a head of disheveled black hair.

Irish Rock sneered at Stevie and asked, "What do you want?"

Disheveled Hair crossed his arms and positioned himself in

front of Honey. For a half second, he held a firm face. After that, his eyes wandered up and down Honey, settling on her tits.

Honey didn't waste the opportunity. She stuck her hands in her pockets so her jacket opened a little wider and slowly swayed her hips left and right, her breasts following along.

Irish Rock glanced at the show and back at Stevie.

"I've got an appointment with Shamus." Stevie tilted his head left and squinted, wondering how big The Rock's balls were or if he just presented big.

The Rock didn't flinch. "So who the fuck are you?"

"Tell him Steve Evans is here. Like I said, he's expecting us."

The Irish Rock looked Stevie up and down and removed a two-way radio from his waistband. The gruff purse of his lips and the cords on his grip were obvious; he was praying this would go his way, because he really wanted to stomp the shit out of Stevie. It beeped as he pressed the *Mic* button and spoke. "*Steve Evans* says he has an appointment."

There were about thirty seconds of silence as Stevie's smiled widened and The Rock's tongue searched his teeth—the guy was nearly drooling for a fight, and Stevie wanted more than anything to point and laugh at him. But Dad wasn't here to back him up, so he really needed to win over Shamus before opening his mouth too big.

Disheveled Hair didn't move an inch other than to lick his lips at the hottest piece of ass he'd seen in weeks. Honey kept swaying back and forth. There was a practiced quarter smile on her lips, a tease she knew how to flaunt.

A white truck passed on the street, and somewhere to the west, a guy screamed at another guy—something about wiring and a yellow terminal. A bird's wings fluttered unseen on the rooftop.

The Irish Rock raised the two-way back toward his mouth

and was about to press the *Mic* button when it beeped.

"Bring 'em in," a guy said over the radio.

The Rock nodded and rolled his eyes as he motioned for Stevie to walk. "This way."

Stevie counted twelve cars and ten guys in the warehouse as they walked through open-hooded and disassembled vehicles toward the enclosed office in the back. Sparks flew, tools whirred, and eyes clung to them.

The place wasn't quite a chop shop, more of a prep station. Cars from the surrounding fifty miles—ones that thieves didn't want to drive to Missoula, Butte, Great Falls, or Billings—were brought in for some light touches to get them to their next stop with less detection. They switched plates, filed down or replaced VIN numbers, swapped out tires, or removed personalized items like decals and magnets. Things to make them blend in and look less noticeable. They also did some custom stuff on the cheap if you knew who to talk to.

The door to the office opened, and heat and cigarette smoke rushed to greet Stevie. They reminded him he was cold and that he hadn't had a smoke in way too long. He reached into his pocket, and The Irish Rock grabbed his hand.

"Easy, man," Stevie protested.

"Need to frisk you, *man*." The Rock pulled Stevie's hand from his pocket, and though Stevie rolled his eyes, he let it happen. Why not? He had left his piece in the truck, expecting this.

Disheveled Hair grinned from ear to ear as he began running his hands over Honey. He lingered on her breasts, and she slapped him.

"Enough, asshole." She was only going to give away so much

for free.

Disheveled Hair and Irish Rock chuckled then backed away, allowing Stevie and Honey to enter Shamus's office.

Again, Stevie went into his pants, this time successfully pulling his smokes free. He opened the box and counted five. The next stop better be the store or he'd be bumming smokes off these assholes.

He slid one into his mouth and lit it as Shamus shouted, "You motherfucker!"

Stevie turned, taking in the room for the first time in earnest. The right half, where they came in, had four desks. Three were covered in papers, while one was suspiciously clean. The left half of the room was dressed out into something of a lounge, and Stevie knew immediately this was where Shamus spent the majority of his time. Three black leather couches made a semicircle facing six large televisions mounted on the wall. Each displayed a different sport: horse racing, poker, football, baseball. Some were in foreign languages with writing on the screen that Stevie didn't get.

The screen that held Shamus's focus was the horse race.

"Motherfucker!" He balled up a sheet of paper and tossed it at the TV. Almost as soon as the trash hit the ground, one of three underlings snatched it from the aged linoleum and walked it to a corner shredder.

Shamus stood and turned to his guests, his eyes lingering on Honey.

Stevie almost lost his breath as he studied the man; he had forgotten how much Shamus looked like his dad. Both were mid-fifties, both built like stone demigods from some Greek play, both tall with salt and pepper hair. Only, Shamus spoke with a heavy Irish accent with no intention of losing it, even after the forty-plus years he'd been in the States. His father, on the other hand, was dead as far as he knew, and though he felt some sadness, the look of this man was more disturbing than Dad's death.

"Look at this fucker." Shamus opened his palm and gestured at Stevie. The boy had obviously gotten his size from his mother's side of the family, as he was half the width of his father.

"Look at me." Stevie half-grinned and gestured to himself.

Shamus walked around the couch and gave Stevie a hug with three hard pats on the back before he moved in on Honey. He had never met her, but Shamus wasn't one to pass up setting hands on a beautiful woman.

"Who is this lovely one?" He drenched his words with Irish twang, selling it hard.

She let him hug her and rolled her eyes. "Honey."

He stepped back, getting a nice feel of her ass as he backed away. "Why, you are, aren't you?" He smiled slyly, then turned back to Stevie. "Where's Big Steve? Haven't heard from him since last night, and he's not returnin' my texts."

Stevie took a drag from his smoke. He looked down and shook his head. All of a sudden, he was a caricature of a little kid being grilled by Mom. "Dead, Shamus."

"What the fuck?" Shamus went white. His eyes narrowed. He stared at Stevie with the harsh distrust of a prosecutor during cross-examination.

Stevie knew the man was tight with Dad, but Shamus seemed to freeze as if he'd been told his mother was just raped by a mule. Stevie's chest tightened. He would have to pull this off just right.

"What do you mean, dead?" Shamus leaned on the back of the couch. The entire room seemed to hush.

"Car accident." It was the easiest thing Stevie could think of. They happened every day, and there was no way Shamus would buy the real story. He sure wouldn't have—it was too insane.

"Car accident?" His entire face wrinkled with doubt.

"It's a little more than that, but yeah. During the job yesterday, the security guard got off a shot that nicked something in Dad's leg. We thought we stopped the bleeding, but it must have been worse than we thought. We were driving down the road in the middle of the night thinking all was good, and *BAM.*"

Stevie took a stuttering drag. "He must have drifted off at the wheel. Blood loss.

"The van flipped. Killed Mom and Dad." He paused for effect, taking a deep breath and quivering as he let it go. "Only Honey and me got out of it."

"Goddamn." Shamus shook his head. He walked to the bar by the wall and cracked open a bottle of whiskey. He took a long gulp from the neck, then filled three glasses which he carried back to Stevie and Honey. "To Big Steve." He took a deep breath and raised his glass, and Stevie and Honey joined him. They clinked. They drank. And, head bowed, Shamus lumbered back to the couches.

"God, what a shame." Shamus took another gulp from his glass, his eyes searching the screens, then, "Fuckin' hell!" A baseball player slid into home, and his team patted his back as he found his seat in the dugout.

Stevie finished off his glass and set it down on the bar. He tapped his ash in the tray, walked around the couch opposite Shamus, and sat.

"So, let me see the gems," the Irishman said, his eyes on the poker game now.

Stevie puffed on his cigarette and tapped it in the tray in the center of the seating area. Only a flake fell. "We don't have them. The job's a total loss. I was hoping—"

"What do you mean, *you don't have them?*" Shamus's eyes were back on him now. "Me and your dad picked that shop specifically, knowing how much they carried. It was the distribution point for all that chain's stores in the Dakotas. There should have been a half-mil in jewels alone once they were dismantled from the gold and silver."

"Yeah. It sucks. The security guard—he screwed it all up. We only got out of the store with a fraction of that. Then Dad put the loot in the glove box next to him, and when the van crashed... It was all a crumpled mess. There was no way to get to it without some jaws of life shit or some welding equipment."

"So why didn't you?" The question was low and firm.

Stevie was struck. He didn't expect that response. All of a sudden, it was his dad questioning him about the job back in Bismarck where he let Paul Hinderman choose the fence, and the douchebag only wanted to pay twenty-five cents on the dollar for each TV they boosted. "You should have gone to Freddy," Dad had said. It was a fuck up that cost them thousands. An obvious fuck up he should have seen before they even crashed the front window of that electronics shop.

Here he was again. In his made-up scenario, yeah, he should have figured a way to get those jewels. He'd have to play at this hard, hope for some sympathy.

"Why didn't I get welding equipment? The van was in the middle of the road. Cops were coming—they could have been there any second. Besides that—the front seat was drenched in Mom and Dad's blood.

"You think I should have welded through that for a few grand?"

"I would have. Your father would have." Shamus leaned back in his seat and lit a cigarette. "I hate to say it, seeing as he just died and all, but this right here is one of the reasons why he knew you were a shit criminal."

"What?" Stevie's heart thudded. His skin flushed. Yeah, he'd had arguments with his dad about jobs, but *a shit criminal?*

Would Dad have really said that?

"You think with your emotions. Your dad knew that. Shit. If you want to make something of yourself, you have to use your head. You should have been beating on that goddamn wreckage with your fists if you had to, up until the second cops showed on that scene." He shook his head and took a puff. His eyes beat down on Stevie with shame. "Too bad."

"Yeah." Stevie fought the heat rising in his chest. Who the fuck was this guy to tell him he was shit? That his dad thought he was shit. He wished he had his pistol at that moment, that he hadn't left it in the truck. He wanted to blow holes into that Irish asshole's eyes and piss inside his head. Shamus didn't know shit—fuck him.

"So, where'll you two be headin' now, then?" Shamus's eyes were back on the screens. He puffed on his cigarette and flicked the ash aimlessly into the air.

"I was hoping you might be able to help us out. Give us a job or two so we can get back on our feet. You know, as a favor for Dad."

Shamus cracked half a smile. "Your dad would go out and find the work. Even with as much heat as that last job caused, he'd go find another score. Then he'd bring the work here, and I'd fence it for him. He wouldn't expect me to drop a job into his lap."

"Yeah, I guess. But since I don't know the area..."

"You are not your father. That's for sure."

Stevie's fists wanted to clench. Oh, he wanted to let them and then beat this man with his own bottle of whiskey. He wanted to see blood run down and soak that couch, to splatter those TVs in red so every sport they showed in the future was stained.

"I—"

Shouting in the warehouse.

One of Shamus's men flew through the door. "Cops! The cops are here!"

3

ABIGAIL SPENCER STARED AT her computer screen, dreading the hours to come. The graphic design work was done and the layouts were complete. The copy was mostly in her inbox, though clients always slacked on the details—she knew she would be emailing them back for clarification on a dozen pages before this stage of the website build was complete. But now, it was time for what she thought was the monotonous part of the job: putting it all together into a functional site.

She yawned and sipped her coffee.

Some loved this part. To them, it was like the home stretch, taking all the pieces and assembling them, seeing it all come together into a finished product. To her, it was mindless and robotic.

Abby liked the brainstorming. She liked pulling together the abstract ideas that made the site shine with inventive layouts and graphic styles. She liked imagining where it could all go and digging into the tools in Photoshop and Illustrator and making the visuals come to life.

With the creative parts out of the way, what she saw in front of her now made her sigh. It pulled the energy from her soul and made her want to hit the bed.

She could do that, she supposed. She was a few days ahead on the project, and the next check-in with the client wasn't for two weeks. She could take a nap or watch some Netflix and come back to it this afternoon.

But what if she found something good, something binge-worthy? She wouldn't want to walk away. And if she didn't find a time suck, she would have the same sensation when sitting down again this afternoon.

It just wasn't her favorite part of the job, and that was no different than any other commission.

"Fuck." She took another sip.

She leaned over the keyboard, preparing to launch Dreamweaver, and her phone dinged.

Thank God.

She glanced at the spot under her monitor where she habitually set the thing, where she could read any notifications without taking her hands off the keyboard and mouse. It was a text from Wanda.

A smile crossed her face.

Wanda seemed nice. She was a new friend—well, each of her three friends in Custer Falls was new. She only just moved there in the fall. But the meeting with Wanda always stuck out to her.

She had been sitting in the 406 Bean, a local Starbucks knockoff, and working through some ideas for a plumbing website on her laptop. She wasn't really planning on using any of those, just playing around for shits and giggles. The plumber was local, and his last name was Beavers, so of course, her mind went to a beaver on a toilet, then a beaver in a toilet, a beaver in bib overalls fixing a toilet. But it all felt too derivative. One thing she took away from design school and leaned on was that the first five ideas you come up with are always crap. They were so surface level that anyone could come up with those. You have to dig deeper.

So here she was, reimagining a beaver in a sewer system with a wrench and tool belt and shit floating by in the water and a dumbfounded look on the beaver's face—and this woman behind her started laughing.

Abby spun, eyes sharp, embarrassment widening her gaze, and the smile on this woman's face was just infections.

"Sorry." Wanda covered her mouth, trying to stifle her laughter, but she just couldn't. "I know it's rude to look at someone's screen, but I just love that."

Abby looked back down at the ridiculousness and couldn't help laughing as well. The shapes of turds in the underground river, the goofy beaver's smile, his raised shoulders, it was just so bonkers.

"Wanda?" the barista called, and Wanda leaned in and grabbed her white mocha.

"Can I ask what it's for?" Wanda asked. "Are you a web-comic-artists? I'm sorry, I don't even know if that's what it's called."

That started it. Within another minute, they were sitting and laughing and sharing their life stories. It was refreshing for Abby. She had only met her neighbors at that point, and being the only black woman in public most places she went, she had started to feel somewhat isolated in this new town. She'd known that might happen. Coming from Georgia, where her friends were a mix of all kinds of people, to a place where she was the exception, the one to cause heads to turn when she walked in—this was new. She knew most of them didn't mean anything by it—she was an anomaly to them. But it was taking some getting used to. Now, after six months there, she had settled in quite well, but seeing Wanda's name still made her smile.

She unlocked the phone and read: "Hey! Call me when you're free. Drama at the kiddo's school *rolls eyes* I'm thinking of doing something and wanted to invite you"

"Well?" She glanced at the computer screen again. This could let her procrastinate a little longer. She tapped *Call*, and the phone rang.

Wanda picked up after the first ring. "Hi! That was quick. I thought you'd be busy."

"Ugh, it's one of those days." Abby scowled at the computer.

"Yeah. Don't I know it."

They chatted about the warming weather and other small talk before Wanda explained what happened to Angel and how pissed she was at the school. That led into the invitation.

"I know it's early in the year, so it might be too cold for you—being you're a southern girl—but I was curious if you wanted to go on a hiking trip with me and Angel?"

"When? Like, today?"

"Yeah. She's suspended for a week, and I'm not going back to work any time soon. So I thought we'd go check out some trails."

Abby's mind shifted from the onslaught of coding in front of her to excitement. "So, this is an overnight thing?"

"Yeah... which is why I said it could be too cold for you. I have all the gear, though—I even have Henry's stuff here, too, so you could use that. We can share a tent to make it a little warmer, but I have zero-degree sleeping bags and a little propane heater if it absolutely gets *too* cold."

"What do you mean by *too* cold?"

"I doubt it'll get below freezing, but you never know in the mountains."

Abby hesitated. Yes, she wanted to take a break from this job, and yes, she wanted to get out there and see some of the nature she moved here for, but it was only March—there were still snowy clumps in the apartment complex's yard.

"It's totally cool if you're not interested," Wanda said. "I just remember us talking about camping and you said you wanted to get some outdoor time in. But if it's too cold, I get it. We'll hit it again this summer, I'm sure."

"I'm coming." Abby didn't know what part of her made the decision, but it had been made. She had plenty of time to get this job done, and this was a valuable friendship they were forming. It was best to nurture it. "What do I need to bring?"

Angel's bag was nearly packed by the time she heard Mom say, "Perfect. See you there."

She ran from her room into Mom's, where Mom sat on the bed beside her backpack. Angel jumped and bounced on the mattress, belly-flopped, then rolled onto her back, where she was face to face with her mother.

Mom frowned down at her. Angel burst into giggles.

"She's coming?" Angel asked.

Mom nodded. "She was a little reluctant, but I made sure she knew it was going to be cold and told her to pack layers."

"And she's going to use Dad's stuff?"

"Yup."

Angel was disappointed Dad couldn't come, but she knew Mom and him were on the outs right now. She really hoped it was just temporary, though she supposed all kids thought that when their parents split up.

But it was okay. She'd go camping with Dad later. This was going to be a girls' trip, and they were going to help introduce their new friend to proper Montana outdoor life. At least, that's what Mom and she had decided when they talked about it earlier.

She had only met Abby a few times, actually, and she thought it was pretty neat that now they would get the chance to become better acquainted. Abby was from the east, like way east, farther than Angel had been her entire life, and the way she talked about that side of the country made it sound amazing. There were Walmarts that never closed and fast-food places she had never heard of. Places that only sold chicken, some with only spicy chicken, and stores that specialized in clothes for girls, and stores that only sold toys, and others that only had games, and the people... It sounded like they were everywhere. That had to be so much fun.

She tried to imagine what it would be like and just couldn't fathom it on her own. But she could when talking to Abby. The woman described the beach, and it was like Angel was there. She had seen the beach at the lake, but not like this. Abby told her about the golden sands and the greenish waters and the people everywhere on towels, and Angel could smell the saltwater.

She could smell it now as she went back to those thoughts. It was like seeing through Abby's eyes, back when they talked about it. She saw swimmers in every color suit, kids on floating boards, others with pails making buildings out of sand, and girls lying on their backs all shiny from oils. Those smelled like coconuts for some reason. She could feel the sand between her toes, and it was hot and gritty, and she wanted to rush into the water and let the warm wetness rinse it off.

Mom snapped her fingers over Angel's head. "Hello? You in there?"

Angel laughed. "Of course!"

"Okay. You kind of blanked out there."

"Just thinking."

Mom nodded. "You done packing?"

"Yeah, just need to pick a stuffy."

"Long underwear?"

"Check."

"Extra winter socks, underwear, pants?"

"Check, check, check."

Mom gave Angel a look, and Angel could see right through it. Mom did that look sometimes—it was a longing, like she missed Angel even though she was sitting right next to her. There was love in there, but there was also a sadness, like Angel was going to grow up and move out tomorrow and Mom only had the weekend to fit in all the love she had for her.

"I love you," Mom said.

"I *know!*"

Mom frowned and her fingers found Angel's tickle spots. Angel screamed.

"You little booger!"

Angel ran.

"Get your stuffy and pack it up. We leave in thirty minutes!"

Mom's phone rang, and Angel couldn't have cared less who was on the other end. She had an important question to answer.

She scanned the wall across from her bed. Along the floor were the bigger ones, every stuffy bigger than her arm that she had been given since she was a baby. On the shelf above that were the smaller ones. They were stacked, piled high, one over the other over the other.

She sat on her bed, wondering. "Who would make the best camping pal?"

There was Taxi Duck, Colorado the Husky, Momma, Sister, Baby, and plain ol' Bouncy the Rabbit. There were buffaloes, meerkats, tigers, and unicorns, both with and without wings, some with black eyes, some with blue, and some big and sparkly.

Such a choice was so important.

She had a thought. "Mom! Can I bring two?" *That would make it much easier.*

Mom was talking on the phone, a low mumble through the wall. "One!" she shouted and went back to her call.

"Shit," Angel whispered.

She closed her eyes and wandered forward. She would let them decide. She imagined the next few days and invited the stuffy that would be best. She pictured the woods. She imagined the smells of trees and wind and campfire. She thought of her tent and her sleeping bag and cuddling with something soft and cozy at night.

Angel held out her hand and took a step. She felt an urge to lean right and went with it. A coldness crept at her back, and she took another step.

Her skin grew icy. She didn't like that. It was a feeling she recognized from when some (dead) people got too close. Most recently, she had been going down the main hall with Marcy and laughing and lost track of where she was. She brushed past Heath Williams, his bloody grasp stretching from his closet. It was like ice cubes ran over her back when he touched her. It had taken all day for her to warm up after that.

She tried to ignore it now, though. Her house was safe—at least it always had been. She kept moving forward.

The cold crept around her, coming from the sides as well. It snuck in low and traveled up her legs, like walking through a snowy field.

She blocked that out. It wasn't really there. She was sure. It was just memories, or her wild imagination, or her mind was wandering to thoughts of other places, which happened some-times. Angel told herself it would be fine.

The cold passed over her hips, and she noticed as it tickled her neck and gave her goosebumps, there was a smell to it. It was old and musty, like logs in the woods from a darkened place. From an abandoned, moldering place. She didn't like that smell.

But forward was warm. She could feel the difference and pinched her eyes tighter as she moved. Her stuffy called her, and she would listen.

She stepped and reached, and through her closed eyes, she saw it glow—the stuffy volunteering to her.

She was about to grab it, and the creeping coldness burned. It stung her back like the subzero ice fishing trip with Dad a year ago when water somehow spilled down the rear of her coat. The water could have been boiling; it hurt so badly. She had to spend the next two hours in the truck warming up as her jacket dried. But this icy burn was walking up her ankles. It was pinching her skin and scraping as it climbed. It had claws that pierced and prickled. It called to her, too, just as the stuffy did. It was demanding she stop.

She didn't like that. Whatever was calling her from down there was hurtful. It wasn't just the coldness; she felt more than that. There was an anger and a sickness. It had terrible things in mind and mean, awful thoughts.

The cold rose. The smell became wet, almost dripping into her nose. It was a scent like spoiled food—no—it was that scent when there was a dead deer on the side of the road, and Mom said the county was being lazy and not picking it up like they should. It was a pungent, slimy smell, and it also spoke. *Come.*

She didn't want that either.

Angel jumped forward, fingers grasping; the glowing warmth she wanted was just ahead. She felt its furriness in her hand, and the call from below howled. It was anger, but there was pain too. It implored, and though she didn't want to, she had to at least look.

So Angel did.

She froze.

She saw a gaping, frozen void beneath her feet and a hundred furious things staring up. They were horrible things, nightmare things, eyes without lids, shadowed faces without lips, open mouths hollering in agony and reaching for her.

Reaching for her.

Reaching for her.

It struck her in her soul. She had almost gotten used to seeing the macabre. Dead things were just about everywhere; that was how the world worked. But this view—it was like someone had opened a window into Hell. The bloody, gory faces. The mangled limbs and damaged flesh. It was... It was too much. She was going to scream if she didn't look away. She just couldn't take it anymore.

Angel's eyes flew open, and she yanked the stuffy to her chest, squeezing. She felt the soft, fluffy coat. It was Betty Bobcat, and as it touched her body and the fur brushed her skin, she was instantly warmer, instantly better in so many ways.

She held her breath and looked at the floor to verify she was safe, that those nasty things had gone.

They were. She sighed and backed away anyway. Just off-white carpet down there—but five red scratches ran down each of her shins.

4

S TEVIE DIDN'T KNOW WHO fired first. He saw a cop, his body halfway into the warehouse. His gun swung right, smoking, the back of his head popping open while his bloodied brains splashed the inner wall. Almost simultaneously, one of Shamus's men dropped behind a silver Camaro as an arc of crimson sprang from his chest.

Bullets swarmed through the door, and cops shouted outside. The door's spring tried to pull it shut, but it caught on the officer, half his arm inside and his dead, crumpled body leaning into the frame. Holes pierced the metal. Bullet-sized windows of sunlight circled the entrance. Blood ran down the dead man's arm, and his body seized. The arm repeatedly slapped against the floor flicking blood across the concrete.

Stevie turned to Shamus. The man pulled a case from under the center couch, flipped the top open, and lifted a black AK-47 to his shoulder. His three subordinates stared at the office door, pistols in hand.

Shamus saw Stevie watching. "You want one of these?" He gestured at the couch to the right. "You might as well make yourself useful."

"Fuck yeah." Stevie was always ready to shoot something, but right this second, what he really wanted was to have his hands on a piece of hardware. He also needed to know they had a way out of this, that it wasn't some sort of Alamo situation. And before he planned an escape route, he wanted a gun in his hands.

Shamus's men fired in the main warehouse. Muffled gunshots sounded from out front. Shamus stood at the entrance to his office, Irish Rock on one side, Disheveled Hair on the other, and another guy behind him in a gray tracksuit looking like he was about to try out for a role on the Sopranos.

Honey followed Stevie to the couch as he searched beneath it. Another long, black case, and inside it, another shiny, black AK along with three mags, and a SIG Sauer 9mm. He picked up the AK and stuffed the mags in his pockets. His jeans were too tight, but he made them fit with just a little tearing, two in front and one in the rear. Honey took the Sig and checked the chamber and the safety.

"What do we do?" Honey asked in a hushed tone.

Stevie waved her off. He had to think, and he didn't need her distractions right now.

He looked for the exit.

There was no back door within the inner office. Stevie quelled the rising panic in his gut. There had to be one. He was going to get out of this. He didn't just survive a botched robbery and travel across two states to get caught now.

There had to be a back door in the main warehouse. And he needed to get to it now, before the cops surrounded them. And God help Shamus if he got in the way, because Stevie was ready to put him and every one of his dogs down if they caused him trouble.

He sidled up beside Shamus. "What's the plan? Back door?"

There was a gleam in Shamus's eyes as he grinned at Stevie. "My boy, we're just gettin' to the good part."

On any other day, Stevie would have loved the man for that. He had a fire in his soul that was captivating, and even now, part of Stevie wanted to jump right into the fire with him and let both feet blaze. Shamus was definitely as stone willed as Dad, but more than that, there was a fantastic streak of lunacy that Stevie respected. He remembered Dad telling him how Shamus was raised by what he called the Irish Folk Warriors of the IRA, men so hardened and dedicated to their cause they didn't care who they killed if it meant a free Ireland. At least, that was true for some of them—those like Shamus's pa used the rebellion as an excuse to practice their hand at death under the shroud of moral justification. And the man was good at it. Big Steve always said Shamus would have been at home on a medieval battlefield with mushrooms in his veins and bloodshot eyes, going berserk for the Norse on their way through Northern Europe. Dad always got his European cultures scrambled, but as Stevie saw that glint in Shamus's eyes, he knew exactly what Dad was referring to.

"We charge them." Shamus smiled.

He pushed past his guards into the main warehouse, his chest heaving and his grin widening. He waved his guys over toward him.

"Now's the time, men." He spoke with ferocity, sharp words with sincerity in every syllable. "We go out there, and we take every one of them. We drop them where they stand, and we scatter to Kalispell, Anaconda, and Coeur d'Alene. We do it now before their backup gets here, and we vanish like we were never here."

He looked each man in the eye, his confidence fueling theirs, filling them up, imparting his gas into their engines.

"Are you ready?"

There were grins over grinding teeth and hands flexing over weapons. They shouted back, "Yeah!" "Yes, sir!" "Fuck those cops!"

Shamus pointed to the two men nearest the rear of the warehouse. "You two go out the back. Split up and come around the front and flank them. When we hear you firing, we'll spill out the front.

"Everyone got it?"

"Yeah!"

There was a tension in the room that Stevie had only felt twice in his life: once as a teen in a high-speed chase with the South Dakota Highway Patrol, and once in a bank robbery in Utah. It was a rush he reveled in. It was a spike of power in his veins that made his hair stand on end and his finger hover over the trigger, ready to squeeze.

But still, he wasn't stupid. He wasn't going to rush out there like a madman for Shamus. He was ready to shoot, sure—he'd even enjoy the fun—but he was going to wait and see how this played out first before he poked his head into the line of fire.

Officer Frank Wazowski held his M4 rifle steady behind the suspect's pickup, aiming at the warehouse's front door. He tried not to stare at Officer Braden's corpse as it leaked onto the concrete walk, but it was hard not to.

The firing had subsided for the moment, and Harris and Mc-Neil covered the sides of the building. Frank prayed that would be enough.

He hated himself right now. It was a stupid mistake to let Braden go in there. He knew it was a stupid idea at the time—why didn't he stop the kid?

He had spotted the truck and called it in. He'd waited for backup, and three vehicles came. It should have been enough—would have been enough most days—but that feeling, he should have trusted it. It was an alarm bell he ignored in favor of machismo and fear of looking foolish to the others. He should have demanded more backup.

Who was he fooling? They wouldn't have sent anyone else. This was half the officers on duty right now—well, was. Supposedly, now everyone was being mobilized. The state was sending in troopers, and the county was digging their riot gear out of mothballs. There was no SWAT team in Custer Falls, so that would have to do.

The three of them just had to hold out until the rest arrived.

Frank's radio crackled, then there was McNeil. "I've got movement on the right." Following that, McNeil was shouting, "Stop there!"

Gunshots rang on the left.

"Drop the weapon!" Harris screamed.

More shots. Then, from the right.

Frank saw Harris fall behind a blue Subaru as sparks flew from the hood. He was clutching his arm—*Where was his rifle?*

He couldn't see McNeil, but there was a flurry of rifle shots, then, "Got one!" over the radio.

Frank peeked around the truck bed and saw McNeil. He saw a body by the warehouse corner. A shot ricocheted off the ground, and pebbles flew past his face. A rock chip sliced a line from his cheekbone to the corner of his eye. Frank dropped and heard the worst news of the day.

Harris was on the radio. "Front door! Front Door! Front—" There was a gagging sound, then static.

Gunshots—loud shots, no longer pistols but rifles. AKs—he knew that sound from Iraq; it was unmistakable. He saw himself behind tan walls, sand in his eyes—hell, in every orifice. He saw dozens of ill-trained kids running at him just to get mowed down. And he heard the same joke a million times. "Wazowski, like the green eyeball monster? You look like him!"

Shit!

Gravel and sparks flew past. His fingers twitched over his M4.

He was back at home; this shit wasn't supposed to happen here. It was supposed to be boring, small-town policing. Rousting drunks from bars, helping wives with domestic disputes, giving goddamn tickets.

Get yourself together, Wazowski!

He peered around the edge of the truck, saw McNeil fire three shots before a 7.62mm round ripped a ravine through his face. The back of McNeil's skull exploded into mush, and his M4 fired three wild shots over the warehouse roof as the man went down.

Fuck no! Fuck no!

Frank held his rifle to his chest and crawled away as fast as his knees would take him. The butt of his rifle dragged over dirt and gravel, and shouting issued from the warehouse. Cheers. And then, "There's one more! Find him!"

Rocks crunched under feet. Frank's ears rang with the sounds of gunfire.

"Over here," one said. "Look over there!"

Panic seized Frank's chest. There emerged a pressure in his bowls and a fire under his legs that made his scurry faster, his heart heavier, and his lungs hotter. He clutched at the stony ground, his fingers aching as hard rocks jutted into his skin, and he spotted a darkened place, the shadowy underbelly of another truck.

He scrambled beneath it. His hands, his shoulders, his waist were all under as something clawed into his foot.

"I got him," a man called.

"Let go!" Frank squealed as the scum pulled him from his gloomy hideout. His fingers clawed at the earth, and the unmistakable presence of Death hovered over him. He knew what it was. He knew the scent, the way the air became metallic when it was near, when that other plane was expecting a new arrival.

And he just knew this time it would be him.

He shook his feet and kicked as another set of footfalls came. He grabbed at the frame under the vehicle and tried to pull himself from their grips, and a stabbing pain tore through his calf.

"Come on out, big boy!" one of the men said.

There was another stab, this time in the other leg.

"My knife don't care," the man said. "It can keep doing this all day."

Another blast of pain, and Frank screamed. He couldn't take this. He didn't want to let go—he knew they were going to shoot him, or worse—but he couldn't stand more stabbing. It was just delaying the inevitable.

A gash in his leg. Blinding, hot agony.

"Stop! Stop!" He released his hold on the vehicle. "I'll come out!" His voice was breaking. The sound sickened him.

He didn't know if they stopped stabbing him or if he just couldn't feel his lower legs any longer. They were cold, throbbing zones, and he knew his blood was rushing from him. But he couldn't just let himself die!

They chuckled and dragged him until his head was clear of the car. They rolled him over.

There was only a split second for Frank to think, and during that time, he wasn't sure if his thoughts were real or from some imaginary hell he'd created in his head as the world grew fainter and fainter. He saw three men standing over him. One was screaming as Frank moved, not even sure what he was doing.

But some part of him knew. Some part of him wanted to live, and that part remembered the M4 strapped to his chest.

.223 rounds sprayed as he rolled. One man then another burst with fountains of blood, across the first man's chest and the second one's face.

Frank couldn't even tell the second man had a face as the gun clicked empty and the dead men sank. He saw a mound of red and tan, hairy meat, and then he heard the third man's shots. He felt the wetness in his groin and his neck and the soreness in his chest below his vest.

His view went white as he understood: his neck was bleeding. Yes, Death was here.

Stevie heard the last gunshot and stepped outside. Honey was right behind him. Four of Shamus's men were on the ground, along with three more cops, and sirens were in the air.

Shamus's thugs shook their weapons in the air like bandits until Shamus held his hands up and shouted, "Good job, all. Now get to your safe houses and get back to work. I'll be in touch soon."

The group began to disband with huffs and chuckles when Shamus raised his hand once more. "And each of you gets a four grand bonus, a grand for each dead pig."

They cheered and loaded into pickups and SUVs. The warehouse's garage opened, and three of the stolen vehicles they had been working on drove out. Others sat abandoned. One thug got into the SUV above a dead cop and rolled forward over his body, crunching the corpse's chest before backing out.

"Shamus," Stevie ran up to the man. "We'd like to tag along to your safe house so we can get to work too." He didn't really care so much about the work as much as he wanted money and a bed for the night until the heat died down. He didn't know this town, and the last thing he wanted to do was hole up in the wrong motel or take the wrong homeowner hostage for a place to stay. He didn't need any more risk right now. Not after the last forty-eight hours.

Shamus glanced at The Irish Rock and Disheveled Hair. "He rides with you." He turned to Stevie. "We'll get you set up with something when we get to Coeur d'Alene." He climbed into his pickup, and a skinny guy who Stevie couldn't believe he hadn't noticed yet climbed into the passenger seat. It wasn't that the guy was that skinny or that short, though he was both of those, but the general appearance of the guy stuck out in his mind. His mouth and chin and nose all seemed to come to a point at the front and made him look rat faced. He had heard the term before, but never had he seen someone fit the description so well. And more than that, when the guy glanced at Stevie, he could swear he could hear the guy squeak.

"Move it, asshole," Disheveled Hair called to Stevie. He was hanging from the driver's seat of a dark blue Suburban. The Irish Rock was in the passenger seat, and Honey watched him from the back door with urging eyes.

"Yeah."

Under the shrieking howl of incoming sirens, Disheveled Hair followed Shamus east out of the lot. Stevie set the AK on the floor and felt the swell of an uneasy feeling. He wondered then if he and Honey should have taken their chances alone.

5

S IRENS WAILED AS A city cruiser, two county pickups, and a state trooper screamed past the Wesker Pump. Wanda got out of the car, her heart jumping inside her chest. Something big was going on, and she was missing it. Something that seemed to have the whole local law enforcement community rushing somewhere, and goddamn if she didn't want to be following along to see what was happening.

She took a deep breath and fought the urge to call Kacy in dispatch and ask questions.

Angel got out and joined her mother, gazing down the street at the kaleidoscope of lights. "That was nuts, Mom! What's going on?"

"I don't know." She shook her head and tried to hide the sadness with a smile. "Let's head in and grab the snacks."

"Okay." Angel shut her door, and her entire body seemed to bob with playfulness as she navigated her way to the front of the car. Wanda joined her on the sidewalk as Abby pulled up in her compact SUV.

Angel hugged Wanda as they waited for Abby to join them. Wanda tried to block her discomfort. She had been a hugger since childhood, and she assumed Angel got it from her. But since the day after Christmas, since it happened (the rape), any physical touch made her flinch. Any hand on her body made her shiver. But she couldn't turn Angel away, no matter how it made her feel. That just wasn't in her. She would bear it as much as she could, and she'd bear it even longer if she had to.

"I'm here!" Abby was layered in a winter coat, a thick hoodie, and a flannel. Wanda didn't want to know what else she was wearing underneath. She had told Abby to dress in layers, not like she was going to Antarctica.

"So glad!" Wanda smiled.

"Yay!" Angel detached from her mother and hugged Abby. Abby smiled and hugged her back. It was a genuine smile.

"All right." Wanda pointed to the doors. "We're burning daylight. Let's get our supplies."

Angel released and led the way. Once she was inside, she headed straight to the snack aisles.

Abby walked with Wanda. "What are we doing again? You said you had all the supplies covered on the phone."

"Oh, I do. The meals, that is. This is a last-minute stop for any of those luxuries you know you won't be able to live without for a few days."

Angel walked from the snacks, holding a giant bag of gummy bears, and headed to the drink wall.

"Gotcha." Abby nodded and started her own perusal of the snack aisle.

Wanda grabbed a few bags of jerky, which most times she *could* live without but would be a nice snack while hiking over the next few days. She snagged four Caramello bars, one for each day she expected to be gone—those she couldn't live without.

She saw herself and the girls sitting around a crackling fire with hot cocoa and chocolate after a day of nature, laughing and sharing the way she used to with her friends back in high school. There was a sense of joy and also a sense of loss. She didn't speak much to Janel or Terry these days—hadn't in a while. It hadn't even occurred to her. They didn't have a falling out, just kind of drifted apart as high school ended and they went about their lives. She wondered if she should give them a call and arrange a meetup with some wine or coffee to catch up.

Yeah, she thought, *I'd like that*. She made a mental note to make the calls once they were back in town.

Wanda's thoughts went back to that fire, saw the smile on Angel's face. She wanted to see that tonight, every night they were out there if she could. Angel deserved it after everything that had happened over the past year: dealing with her mom and dad breaking up, the off hours of Wanda's new job with the police department, and now this whole thing at school.

She pictured the surprise she had coming—she had told Abby another mom and daughter would meet them there but so far had managed to keep the secret from Angel. That didn't happen often—the kid seemed to have a sixth sense for secrets—but she thought she was doing well with the surprise right now. She actually wanted to giggle at the thought of how happy it was going to make the girls. She pictured chocolate in Angel's hand; Lins's too.

Wanda grabbed a few more bars. The girls had the uncanny ability to hone in when Wanda had something good in her hand—it would happen, she was sure.

She also picked up a large bag of trail mix and met Abby by the beer.

"What should we take?" Abby pondered.

"Well, you can grab beer if you have a favorite or something, but if you can stomach it, we'd actually be better off with a small bottle of liquor." She pointed to a door where the gas station ended and a small casino with electronic gaming started. "More of a punch and less weight to carry."

Abby nodded. "Makes sense. I'm down for that."

"Nothing like having warm hands and a warm chest at a campfire." Wanda grinned.

"I could use someone to warm my chest these days." Abby laughed.

"Whoa, whoa, not that kind of trip." Wanda laughed back.

Angel popped up with a handful of Ring Pops and a variety of gummy things. "What's so funny?"

"Nothing." Wanda shook her head and guided them all to the register.

They paid and grabbed two bottles from the casino, whiskey and tequila. Wanda had said it was overkill, but Abby argued. "Weren't you like a scout or something? Isn't there a saying about being prepared?" Wanda had thrown up her hands and acquiesced.

It was too much stuff. Wanda knew she always packed too much stuff. But she wasn't going to let it bring her down. She had enough trying to bring her down. This trip was about letting go of some of those things and enjoying some time away with a new friend and some people she cared about. They would deal with the extra baggage, and they'd have a good time.

They piled into their vehicles and headed west out of town. It would be okay.

Angel sat her Nintendo Switch on the seat beside her as the view from her window widened from houses to woods and the countryside came into focus. She had planned to use up the time in the car with a little Minecraft and maybe a few laps in Mario Kart. She would have to leave the games in the car once they got there—that was always the rule; nature was for nature, not electronics—but her plan was falling apart. Her mind was too active to concentrate on the screen.

She had been thinking about her confrontation with Allen Neddles and the image of Theresa Holland holding her head where a chunk of hair was missing. It bothered her, but more than that, what was swirling in her mind was her vision of those dark things. She shuddered, thinking of what could have happened if they had gotten a hold of her. The stinging scratches on her legs were bad enough. Could it have been worse? She didn't know, but she worried about such things.

The images she saw in her mind weren't always pleasant; it depended on what she was concentrating on, but she didn't think she had seen anything quite like that—not since Halloween when Mom hurt her head and went to the hospital.

Halloween was supposed to be a spooky night, a night where being a little afraid was good. But there she was, walking between houses, and the October night became as cold as the dead of winter. Her Nezuko Kamado costume was suddenly not enough to keep in her warmth, and all she could think of (beyond the freezing wind no one else seemed to be bothered by) was her mother, knocking on a stranger's door and being beaten unconscious.

Angel dropped her bag of candy on the sidewalk and screamed. Marcy Graves spun next to her, looking around for an adult to help. Dad came running from a half block away, breaking his conversation with Mary Ralston, whose skimpy witch's costume must have made her the coldest one on the block—at least where her boobs were showing.

Angel hovered over her mother, watching things around her that should not have been, but she knew they were real: monstrous things charging, the faces of the dead, a hole into another place she was pretty sure some would have called Hell.

Then Dad was holding her on the street, shaking her, and she stopped screaming for him. She couldn't stand his worried face. That made her sad.

But sometimes Angel saw nice things. Like the Thursday after Grandma Rhonda died. The house was full of people, and there were so many tears in the living room and kitchen it was like swimming in sadness. So many memories were good, and they were shared by one after the other after the other, and Mom couldn't stop the tears.

Angel walked toward her room, past the counter of baked goods and casseroles and the nicely dressed adults. She could still hear it through the walls, the low murmur of voices and the sense of loss within everyone. It was like a swamp, and the sadness was so deep and so thick it threatened to seize her feet and drag her into the mire.

She went to her stuffies and grabbed Betty the Bobcat. She wasn't sure why she took that one. It was as if her hand was guided to it, and she didn't argue. She carried the fluffy thing to her bed and curled up on top of the covers, pressing it into her face.

Her eyes burned as they grew damp. She closed them and wished she could make it all go away, bring Grandma back and ease all the suffering under her roof. She wanted to hug her grandma one more time, to be hugged with those soft, strong arms, and to hear that voice promise her that it was all going to be okay.

That was when the humming came. It was an old country song she had never heard anyone sing other than Grandma, and as the tune met her ears, someone rubbed her back in extended swooping circles the way Grandma always would.

For a half second, Angel thought of leaping to her feet and running. But it was nice—unexpected, but nice. The strokes on her back, the lovely tune, and as she breathed deeply, she felt the swamp fade. Her sadness waned. Her fear and longing gave way to a soft concern that Grandma Rhonda would be out of her life now, but she would see her again. It was just a temporary thing, a blink of an eye in the age of the universe. And eventually, they'd be together once more. Then they would laugh and sing, and none of this sadness would matter anymore.

That made her smile, and the smell of baby powder and flowers, her grandmother's scent, filled her nose.

Angel jumped to her feet, an imperative in her mind. She ran across the house until she found Mom and wrapped her arms so tightly around Mom's waist she was sure it would hurt just a little—but she had to. This was important, and it was wonderful, and she had to tell.

"What is it, sugarplum?" Mom's voice was tired. It was pleasant but strained, and her red, puffy eyes struggled to stay open and dry.

"It's going to be okay, Mom," Angel promised. "We'll see her again."

She smiled at Mom, and Mom burst back into tears.

Angel wasn't quite sure why. She tried to explain, but Dad shuffled her back to her room. Eventually, the house emptied and the tears stopped, and Angel learned that sometimes it was better to keep quiet about certain things. Like what she saw when her eyes were closed and there were people there but weren't quite there.

But she was thankful for Grandma that day. And thinking about it now, she realized why she had brought her Betty Bobcat with her on this trip. She loved that thing. It reminded her of Grandma and all the joy they had together. In some ways, she thought, Grandma was part of that toy.

As Mom drove, she ran her fingers through Angel's hair, and Angel turned to her. She wished she could help Mom with her current sadness as much as she wanted to the day of the funeral. But she knew she couldn't. Mom had to do it herself, just like last time.

She glanced back into the trees, the clouds, the vast wilderness ahead, and a distinct feeling came to her that those scary things from this morning weren't entirely done with her. Again, she was glad she brought Betty Bobcat. Again, she wished she could talk to Mom about it.

6

Detective Mark Rand wandered through the bloodbath in front of Shamus Betty's warehouse—well, not quite Shamus's he found out after doing just a few minutes worth of investigation. The place actually belonged to an elderly man, Scott Neighbors, whom no one had seen for a few months. The workers in the warehouse next door said the man just stopped coming in one day, and Shamus showed up the next. Rand made a note to himself to have some cadaver dogs do a search around the property once the scene was cleaned up.

He leaned over a pool of Frank Wazowski's blood. It had mostly soaked into the gravel, leaving a large, red, man-shaped stain, except for the three offshoots where crimson had filled grooves in the ground, making the outline look like Wazowski had tentacles sprouting from his neck.

The bullet casings scattered across the lot still shined; CSI hadn't picked them up yet, and they told a story that Rand didn't want to hear. His hands clenched into fists—these men were slaughtered like animals. Simultaneously, and he would never admit it, he was glad as hell he hadn't been there. The amount of brass, the story he was told, the number of holes in Wazowski, Braden, McNeil, and Harris—their last few minutes must have been terrifying. Even if ten more cops were on the scene, Rand didn't think it would have gone much better. There likely would have been ten more bodies.

Rand walked around the bullet-ridden cruisers to the warehouse door. Braden's fluids were split between inside and out, and the interior still shined, while most of the outside had dried. He didn't want to go through that door. It had already been documented and photographed, but as he looked at the doorway, remembering the image the CSI photographer had shown him, the feeling of utter helplessness the man must have faced hung in his mind. Trapped within the door, bleeding out, unable to move, and knowing death was only minutes away... He had been pinned there until those bastards walked right over him, trailing bloody footprints into the lot as they hunted down the others.

He couldn't bring himself to go through. He headed around and entered through the back door.

The inside of the warehouse answered a lot of questions Custer Falls police had had over the past few years. Questions regarding stolen cars that sporadically led the highway patrol on chases around the county. Questions about influxes of strangers and rises in drug traffic and prostitution around the warehouse district.

These were all numbers that would have been insignificant in any metropolis, even small enough that most residents likely hadn't noticed, but to a numbers guy like Rand, it was something that had been bugging him, even if he hadn't been sure why. And here it was, some kind of stolen car way station, with eight vehicles in varied states of work to prove it.

Rand moved into the office, where a handful of cops were staring at the television screens. He had to stare as well when he realized these were probably bigger than the ones at Hardy's Bar, where he found himself if he was ever free during a Broncos game.

"Some setup, huh?" one of the patrol officers asked.

Rand was embarrassed to admit he didn't know the guy. He

read his badge: McKinney. He must have been a night shift guy, like a few of the faces here were, brought in to cover the gap. "Sure is."

He took a breath, realizing that gap would need to be covered for a while—they were now four guys short in the department.

One of the screens showed a tennis match somewhere in Europe. Another showed a horse race. Another a pair of talking heads with Spanish crawling over the bottom of the screen.

"Some kind of a bookie ran this place, huh?" McKinney asked.

"Too early to say." Rand turned and reexamined the room. A bar with some damn-expensive booze. A few desks. Black-and-white pictures on the wall of old-school boxers. It was a strange mishmash of objects, but out of it all, Rand spotted something interesting on the uncluttered desk: a coaster that said Boulders. It was brightly colored with an illustration he was fairly certain would be called anime. A woman was pole dancing, the silver tube between her breasts and pasties over her nipples in the shapes of tiny boulders.

It wasn't a place he had heard of before, though he got the idea. And the address at the bottom, Pierre, South Dakota, struck a nerve. The reports of the jewelry store robbery and the BOLOs regarding the fugitives whose truck was parked out-side—the one that caused this whole mess—came out of South Dakota.

Rand turned to ask McKinney if anyone had run the plates on the other vehicles in the parking lot yet, and Stafford, the other detective this shift (who was supposed to be investigating a string of cattle mutilations on the other side of town), rushed into the room.

"It's them," Stafford blurted. He was out of breath. "Just ran the F250 out there."

"Stafford?" Rand frowned. "What are you doing here?"

"Really?" Stafford mocked Rand with a frown of his own. "You expect me to stare at cattle corpses instead of helping with the biggest shootout this town's seen since '96?"

All Rand could do was shake his head. He guessed the detective was right. The cows weren't going anywhere.

Rand sighed. "We know that's the F250. That's what started this whole deal."

Stafford nodded, happy to have them both on the same page. "Yeah, but that's not the whole story. That truck wasn't in the robbery, you see; it belongs to a guy named Terrance Cambridge, outside of Hauser. Turns out, the crew wanted for that robbery in South Dakota—well, they took a family hostage overnight in Hauser and fled this morning with the old man's truck."

Rand scanned the office again, letting all the information sort itself into place. "They left the family alive?"

"Not entirely sure, the story's a bit odd. The father—Terrance—is missing. The mother and daughter reported it and said Terrence is dead, along with three or four members of the crew, but there's no bodies to prove any of it. They said two of them fled in Dad's 250—" he held up his notepad and flipped a few pages back. "A *Stevie* and a woman named *Honey*."

"No bodies?"

"That's what their dispatch told me."

Rand stared at the coaster. The illustrated woman stared back at him, smiling while licking her lips.

"I wonder if the family's covering for them? Maybe they were paid off?"

"Don't know."

"Well, it's best we assume we have the whole crew in town until we can prove otherwise. And if Dad's 250 is here and they aren't, it means they likely fled with our friends who ran this place.

"We need fingerprints off everything here, and," he pointed at the coaster, "I want a rush on whatever they pull off of this thing."

7

NGEL'S HEART SKIPPED A beat when Mom pulled into the parking lot for Laurel Trailhead, their most commonly used entrance into the eastern side of Custer Falls National Forest. Three cars were in the lot, though there was only one she cared about: a red Toyota RAV4, with who was without question her best friend in the whole, entire world.

Sure, she usually thought of Marcy Graves as her BFF, but if she was going to be 100% honest with herself—and seeing that RAV4 made it impossible not to be—her true BFF was Lindsay Roberts.

If life really worked as it should have, Angel and Lins would have shared the same womb, lived in the same house, and the rest of society would have called them sisters. As it stood, their mothers were friends who saw each other almost daily until Kathy (Lins's mom) got a divorce and had to move in with her mother to financially recover. Angel and Lins called themselves sisters no matter who might argue with it.

"It's Lins! It's Lins!" Angel bounced in her seat. "You didn't tell me."

Lins cupped her hands around her eyes against the window of the RAV4, and her mouth stretched into a braces-packed grin.

Angel didn't know how long it had been since she had seen her friend, only that it was way too long. It was actually during the summer, almost seven months prior, a night in the park, the music and a projector set up by the City Council in the amphitheater for "Classics Under the Stars." Mom and Miss Kathy had shared a blanket, and Angel and Lins had their own. The music was okay. The company was fantastic, and the high school boys and girls walking in endless circles around the park, pretending not to notice each other, provided a near-endless supply of entertainment for the night.

And here she was, curly red hair bouncing up and down inside the Toyota, matching Angel to a T.

"Park! Park!" Angel screamed. Why was mom taking the longest cruise in the history of the world just to pull into the space and stop the vehicle?

"Okay! Okay!" Wanda found herself grinning as well. She was regretting the inevitable, the conversation around the campfire where she was sure she would break down and cry, telling Kathy about the rape and the abortion. She would have had that conversation long ago if Kathy still lived in the city; but now, things were different with her farther away. It would have been a *phone* conversation—one that she couldn't have had. But for now, yes, it was a happy reunion. And seeing Angel smile the way she was gave her the best feeling she'd had today. In a lot of days.

Wanda stared into the woods as she set the vehicle into *Park* and Angel burst from the car and crossed the parking lot. The wooded sight instantly depleted every ounce of joy. Wanda saw darkness deep inside those trees. She saw shadows and an overcast blanket of canopy making the ground look almost sad in a way she hadn't noticed before. It was an alien look, something she didn't recognize even after having set off from this trailhead what seemed like a thousand times before. That canopy had always filled her with comfort in the past. It made her feel enveloped by a giant green hug, as if the mountains, nature, and the trees were all welcoming her inside to take part in their joy. But this looked different. Ominous, almost like a warning.

The house on West Hemlock came to mind, and Wanda shoved at it like an intruder. *No.* Now was not the time for that. *No.* It was time to be happy and enjoy those around her.

There was squealing from outside the car as Angel and Lins hugged and giggled. Wanda heard Abby's car stop and the door open.

Wanda pulled her gaze away from the forest and shook her head. It had to be her, not the woods. The woods were eternal, always welcoming like a timeless friend. Whatever she was feeling was inside her, not out there. It was her subconscious digesting the horrors in her life and projecting them outward.

Yeah. That's it. She pushed the door open and forced herself out.

Abby watched the pair of ten-year-olds giggle and scream. It put a smile on her face as she brought her bag of treats and bag of clothes and met Wanda at the trunk of Wanda's car. A woman, Kathy, she assumed, got out of the RAV4 and met her and Wanda.

There was a smirk on Kathy's face, a devilish sign she was ready to cause some trouble. It was endearing the way she aimed it at Wanda and squinted. It was the type of genuine expression that grabbed hold of you and made sure you saw it.

"Come here right this minute!" she demanded, her arms extended.

Abby watched the absolute love inside each of their four faces, the brightness of smiles, the nuances in their expressions that told the difference between the smile of polite greeting and the joy of long-missed family and friends. It made Abby a little joyful—and a little jealous. Not so much to drive her away, but enough to remind her she was the stranger in the group. She was the one not reuniting. Again, she was the outsider.

Kathy and Wanda hugged. Wanda introduced Abby to Kathy. Kathy introduced Lins. They shook hands and looked into the forest together, past the trailhead. The scents of cold pine and earth hung below a light breeze, and the path ahead stood in an ominous gray light. Each of them had a second thought just then, doubting if this was indeed where they wanted to go, though none of them opened their mouths to give the feeling a voice. Instead, Abby took the discomfort as her nerves growing uneasy within the silence.

"So, what's next?" Abby turned to Wanda.

"Yeah." Wanda broke her gaze and guided Abby and Angel to her trunk. They consolidated Abby's bags and helped each other get strapped into their hiking packs. Wanda made sure the bell on Angel's pack jingled, and an old adage fluttered in her mind—something she couldn't remember fully but reminded her of Goldilocks and the Three Bears—either way, the bell would ring as they hiked, making sure the kids alerted any wildlife far in advance instead of potentially startling any bears by stumbling right into them.

Abby walked to the wooden display board by the edge of the parking lot. It stood beside the gate into the trail, which was more symbolic than anything. She imagined anyone could just climb through the rail fence, and small animals would scurry under it, and deer would leap over it. Yet here it was, a barrier between the civilized world and nature. As her eyes went to the sun-bleached map on the corkboard, she wondered if the fence was supposed to keep the wild things at bay or keep the civilized world out of the wilderness.

It was a silly thought, she knew, yet the idea lingered as she passed through the gate and wandered the next few feet over compressed dirt and reached out to the first tree. Her fingers ran over the rough, dark bark of the ponderosa pine. She touched a dried trail of golden sap that ran down its eastern side.

It was real. Abby was here. She was standing inside what had once been her dream: to come out west to Montana and create the life she wanted.

The idea gave her chills.

It had been years that she dreamed about making this happen, years where her family called her crazy, her friends said she would freeze to death in Montana, and they each repeated that black folk weren't made for the cold. "We're a tropical people," her brother Miles had said. "We need the sun." She had told him he sounded as dumb as the rednecks in the Appalachian foothills that scared the shit out of them when they took trips into South Carolina to see their cousins on holidays. That didn't stop Miles. It encouraged him to slap on his Joe-Bob accent and bounce left and right as if he was leading a hoedown.

Thinking of Miles made her smile. As much as he teased, she knew he would enjoy the view here—for a minute or two before the cold forced him inside.

"Ready?" Wanda's words made Abby jump. She didn't realize the rest of the group had joined her at the forest's precipice.

Abby nodded. "Let's do it."

The adults led the way, the kids right behind. Kathy asked Abby questions, the usual get-to-know-you stuff. The kids giggled, still high from their euphoric reunion. None of them mentioned the feeling of dread as their eyes searched the trees, the ground, and the distant gloom for the cause. None of them spoke of the creeping unease below their skin.

8

S TEVIE WASN'T ONE TO be paranoid, usually, but as they rode through Custer Falls, there seemed to be a nonstop cascade of sirens. As soon as one faded into the distance, another started. Surely they didn't have that many cops in this sleepy little town, though he imagined the slaughter of four members of its police department was likely monumental in this shithole of a burg. They were probably mobilizing every member of the law enforcement community, calling in the county and state as well.

It sent shivers down his spine. The idea projected an image over his mind of a net shrinking, closing in over him, over the town, over every escape route they could take.

"Where are we going?" he demanded of The Irish Rock and Disheveled Hair.

Irish glanced at Disheveled. His expression was a shallow shield over worry, a hard frown and squinting eyes. He was likely having the same thoughts as Stevie. The net was going to tighten if they didn't have a plan—that was if the man they were following didn't have a plan—and execute it quickly.

"Just sit tight," Disheveled said. "The boss'll know what to do." His voice was firm but lacking the confidence Stevie would have liked in this situation. They turned north, passing a sign that signified they were crossing the city limits.

To Stevie, it was déjà vu, back to yesterday, fleeing the jewelry store with Dad at the wheel. It was so similar, it was uncanny, and Dad had had a plan. Dad knew what to do and was on top of it, confident. But Dad was dead now. No matter how confident he had been, it didn't help. Still, he wished the old man was there.

Honey's gaze shot back and forth from Stevie to the unfamiliar road, then behind them in search of blue lights. She tried to hold Stevie's hand, and Stevie shooed her away. She glanced at Shamus's idiot minions in the front seats, Shamus's vehicle ahead—fuck, this was a shitshow. She wished they hadn't stopped in this stupid town. So what if they were broke. So what if the heat didn't work in that ratty F250. They would have been better off just taking their chances and driving on through.

She shouldn't have trusted Stevie's judgment. She knew that now. It wasn't like when Big Steve was there. Big Steve always knew what to do, had backup plans, kept Little Stevie in line. It seemed like Stevie thought Shamus would take over for his father and lead them to safety. Dumb idea.

She would have to think for herself now that Big Steve wasn't in the picture. Back to the old days, before she met Stevie and he pulled her into the crew.

Honey thought for a moment about sidling up to Shamus, that maybe he could get them through this. She quickly tossed the idea away. The man was single from what she knew. A man that age in this business was only single if they got their kicks from hurting girls like her. Sure, she could probably get him to fuck her, but she wouldn't be able to hold it over him. He wasn't like Big Steve, where she had power keeping it from his wife and he would help her when she got in jams with Stevie.

No, she would have to play this just right. She'd stay close to Stevie while it looked advantageous, and when it wasn't any longer, she'd look for the door.

Shamus's vehicle took a hard turn onto a dirt road surrounded by trees. There were wide residential lots, at least an acre or more each, and each had a log cabin or timber-frame house, something that looked rustic and blended into the forested lots. They passed six or seven and turned down a long driveway. They stopped in front of something that couldn't be called a log cabin but more of a log palace.

Shamus stepped out of his pickup and waved his pistol, gesturing for everyone to get their asses out of the SUV and hurry inside.

Shamus had chosen his home for several specific reasons, few of which he shared with underlings unless he needed them to perform job functions there.

The house was at the end of a dirt road, and though he had neighbors, they were all what he considered either hicks who wanted their privacy or city people from the last migration of west coasters who knew nothing about how things worked in the country. And little did any of them realize, over the past year, Shamus had placed wireless video cameras and Wi-Fi repeaters along the road to make sure he knew every coming and going that occurred on his street.

His house backed up against public lands. There were a few thousand-acre trusts some idiots had created to keep hunting and conservation lands wild—like Montana didn't already have plenty of that—and beyond those was Custer Falls National Forest, where he had placed a stash of guns, cash, and other necessities if there ever came a need. He just hoped he had left a small enough footprint at the warehouse that that time wasn't now. He doubted it, though.

Shamus led the group through his living room and down into

the basement. They turned a corner and entered a large room with a bar, several couches, and cabinets. It was obviously set up for entertaining, but what kind of entertaining wasn't readily apparent.

"This is a nice place," Stevie commented, holding tightly onto his AK. The rest of the group was smart enough to keep their mouths shut as Shamus scowled and closed the door, then opened the cabinets on the neighboring wall.

Screens mounted within the cupboards illuminated the dim room. The salt-and-pepper shag rug lit with cast-off flickering from rotating camera views. The black leather sofas squeaked as Tony (Rat Face), Perry (Irish Rock), and Nick (Disheveled Hair) sat. Honey tugged Stevie toward a matching leather love seat, leaving a pair of recliners empty.

Stevie obliged his girlfriend, and all eyes watched the shifting images on the monitors. There were four of them: the two on the left rotated among several images of Shamus's street, and the two on the right showed views surrounding the house.

"You got it all covered, huh?" Stevie said.

Shamus scowled again. It was like the kid couldn't keep his mouth shut. Either that or he was too stupid to know when to be quiet. This was an important moment to Shamus, to all of them. The next few minutes could determine their entire future. These seconds would tell whether they had hours or seconds to prepare for the safe house in Idaho. He needed to know if the cops were right on their tails or if it was going to take the idiot pricks time to figure out that he was the one running that warehouse.

The stubble on the back of his neck from yesterday's haircut itched. He ignored it. The sofa creaked as Tony, Perry, and Nick shifted in their seats. He ignored it. There was a click and a hum as the furnace started and a low hiss of air rushed through the vents. He ignored it.

The breeze outside pushed through needles in the tall conifers, making the monitors' images shift. Shadows swayed in the road and on the driveway. A delivery truck passed on the cross street.

It was calm out there, and the stillness, the absence of cops should have made Shamus calmer; it didn't. It should have reassured him they had a little time to load up the vehicles and head out, but instead, the hairs on his neck rose at the quiet. It was deceiving; he knew that. It was a false calm. It was a sniper in a ghillie suit, hiding in plain sight and readying himself to take the shot. It was trying to lull him into a false sense of security so when the hordes of cops came rushing up the street, he wouldn't be ready.

He wasn't going to fall for that. They needed to go now—shit, he shouldn't have even come back here. That was a mistake, a stupid choice driven by simple greed. And though he knew that, he couldn't change his mind about what he had to do.

"You all wait here." Shamus didn't wait for a response.

He left the room and headed down the hall, turning into the second room on the right. It was made up to look like a spare guest room, though there was no way he would have let a guest use it.

Shamus pulled the left nightstand from the wall and kneeled. He pressed on the surface, and a small door opened, revealing his safe.

His fingers were cold, almost numb. He knew what was coming and had to hurry, and the fear—

So strange was the fear. He wasn't afraid of men with guns or walking into a fight. He wasn't afraid of cops themselves; he was happy to take them out one at a time or in mobs. But this was a fear of something else he couldn't put his finger on. It wasn't even for the money. He didn't want to lose that, he could make it again if needed—

There was something distant driving him now, beyond the assholes in this dinky little town, and it was leading to a growing terror in his gut. It told him to get his damn money and run—run fast, or he wasn't going to get out of this.

He punched in the code—4050, his mother's birthday in reverse—and yanked open the door.

There it was—a little over two hundred grand, everything he had skimmed off the top over the past year. It shouldn't have been here, he knew that, but it had given him some comfort knowing it was under his roof and not a thousand miles away in some offshore bank. But now he regretted that. In this moment, it would have been safer there than under threat of raid and seizure.

"Fuck."

He reached under the bed and grabbed the duffel stored there for this specific occasion. It was heavy, with a Glock in the side pocket and a sawed-off shotgun in the main compartment. Shamus set the shotgun to the side and loaded in the cash, then he put the sawed-off on top and zipped it up.

Shamus closed the safe and the door, then set the nightstand back where it belonged. He grabbed the bag and started back toward the others. He made it as far as the door before he stopped.

He stood there, one hand on the bag, one on the doorknob. His heart was pounding. His fingers were trembling around the knob, around the bag's handle.

No. He couldn't go out there like this. He couldn't let them see him like this. He was the boss, goddammit. He was the one in charge. He was the roughest son of a bitch in three states, and he wasn't going to let some irrational fear shake him. He had been in jail before. He had been shot at by cops before. None of this was new. Whatever way this all turned out, he could handle it.

Shamus clamped his teeth together and flexed his hands tight. There was a growl from within as he yanked the door open and headed down the hallway. He was about to grab the knob to his surveillance room when it flew open in front of him.

"Boss." Perry stared, his eyes wide. He pointed at the monitors. One after another, small SUVs with Custer Falls Police rolled up the street. Behind them were two black Montana State Trooper Chargers, then two pickups with Custer Falls County Sheriff on the door. "Cops. They're coming."

Tony Hallenger may have tried to look the part to the other members of Shamus's crew, but the fact was he wasn't nearly as experienced at being a criminal as the rest of the room. He wasn't even supposed to be here—that was, if you were to ask the rest of his family.

It wasn't well known to Shamus's crew that the reason Shamus was even in Montana was to make sure he was near his sister, who also happened to be Tony's mother. Shamus didn't really have much to do with Claire's life; she had actually asked him to stay away after he nearly beat her husband to death at their wedding eleven years prior, but that didn't mean he wasn't keeping tabs on her. It also didn't mean Tony was staying away from his favorite uncle after he watched the man pummel the loser his mother had married.

Claire had warned him to stay away from Shamus, as had his real dad, who had disappeared years ago. But Tony always thought they were exaggerating—until today.

He had been working for Shamus for almost a year, mostly running errands. He was more of an assistant than anything; at least, that's how he thought of himself. But he had to blend in with the rest of the crew, so he made up a bunch of stories (most of which were inspired by comic books) and hyped himself up to be a bad guy, always figuring Shamus was there to protect him if things ran off the rails too severely.

He never expected things to go as batshit crazy as they had today, and he was still hiding the fact that he'd pissed his pants just a little at the warehouse. More than anything, he wanted to go home and change, then hide under his covers for a few weeks and pray this was all a dream.

But none of those things seemed likely right now. As he followed Shamus up the stairs and toward the back door, he was just hoping not to get shot. As they crossed the back yard and approached a shed that looked more like a large garage, he was biting his lip and imagining he looked more like a rat than ever.

Yeah, he knew people saw him as the rat-faced kid. He had been called Rat Boy and Rodent Face in school. He hated those names, but he understood them. Shit, he figured he would have made fun of someone that looked like him if it wasn't him. He'd gone as far as looking into plastic surgery to change himself. He even had a secret savings account slowly building to pay for it.

He wondered if he would ever get to use it. He heard when you go to jail, cops try to take all your money. He hoped that wasn't true.

They crossed Shamus's backyard, and Tony wondered why there were no sirens. *Shouldn't there be sirens?* It made his stomach clench worse—they were sneaking up on them for chrissake.

Shamus flung open the doors to the shed and grabbed something from a box on the inner wall. Inside, there were two vehicles: a four-seater side-by-side and a hefty four-wheeler. The view boggled Tony as Shamus slung his duffel bag on his back, the strap across his chest, and climbed onto the four-wheeler.

Shamus turned the key on the quad and tossed Nick another key. "Follow me, and be quick. They'll be here any second."

He drove the ATV out of the shed and waited about ten seconds as the others climbed into the side-by-side. Nick and Perry got in the front, Honey and Stevie in the back with Tony. Honey sat on Stevie's lap and held tight as Nick gunned the motor.

Tony couldn't see, but he imagined the cops pulling up to the house and crashing through the front door as they vanished into the wooded trails of public land behind Shamus's house.

Part II

9

T HE CONVERSATION LULLED. IT was an odd thing, especially so early in the reunion between Kathy and Wanda. They usually enjoyed a fountain of unending topics, questions, and quips, and when the wine flowed, the fountain exploded. But there was something different here, now, as they hiked uphill along the wooded path, the overcast sky casting blue-gray light over the forest's undergrowth. There was a disconnect from the past, a feeling that this trip was destined to be something different than what Kathy and Wanda had experienced before, and Kathy was a little scared to question why.

Snow clung to the wells around trees and hid in the shadowy recesses below logs and north-facing boulders. The gritty clumps of white, half-thawed and refrozen, clawed into the coldest patches of the land, desperate for even a few more days of winter. Kathy recognized the desperation, and her jaw clenched.

Just a little more, she thought.

It took her back to the final days of her marriage, as badly as she wished she could forget them. The daily attempts to pacify Bill with whatever she could muster: making him coffee before he headed to work even though it made her late; sending Lins to her mother's house on Friday nights so they could spend some time alone; even getting down on her knees and putting him in her mouth as he watched sports. He seemed to appreciate none of it. He accepted her offerings, sure, but it made no difference in the end. He still told her he was leaving, just as she saw it coming. And once that happened, she did what she had sworn she would never do; she begged.

Not in her wildest dreams did she think she would do that. She wasn't a beggar. She had never begged for anything in her life. But as the words came out of his mouth, all she could think about was the cold absence in the bed beside her, the empty seat at the dinner table, and Lins's tear-lined face as she would undoubtedly ask, "What did I do wrong?"

She begged with a gaping hole in her heart and cried as he packed. She looked like a fool; she knew that now. She looked like a spineless weakling, and she was grateful Lins didn't see it. She would remember forever how hopeless she felt that day, and she would regret the vulnerability she allowed him to hold over her—the look of disgust on his face as he glanced at her while emptying his sock drawer into his suitcase.

Kathy watched Lins walk with Angel ahead of the adults, the bell jingling with every other step Angel took. They giggled, their voices low, deep in their own world and defending it from anyone over ten. The sight drew a smile over Kathy's sullen face, one that she needed.

It wasn't enough to be out with her best friend; she needed Lins to have hers as well. Kathy needed more than to take her mind off the divorce and losing her home and feeling like she had to start her entire life over again at her mother's place. She needed to feel like the joy wasn't dead. And yes, it was usually her who instigated that spark in her conversations with Wanda—not that she didn't love Wanda, but the woman was very down to earth and usually needed a kick in the ass to lighten up and have some fun. What Kathy found as the darkened woods pressed into her thoughts was that she might need someone else to give her the kick in the ass.

She was thankful she packed some booze. It would make things go a lot easier when she revealed the real reason she had decided to come—she had found a lump in her breast this week.

The doctor said it was probably caught early enough, though the tests weren't scheduled for another week. He said if it was cancer, she would likely get away with a mastectomy—but it could take a double—and she cried every moment she was alone for the next two days.

She cried for herself, and she cried for Lins. This could kill her—she was barely thirty; she shouldn't be planning her own funeral right now. She should have another fifty years for that. And Lins—God, she was only ten—ten-year-olds shouldn't be worried about losing their mothers. It was a waking nightmare, a bad dream that seemed to be going on for days, and there was no end in sight.

But as horrifying as the news was, telling her friend about her potential diagnosis wasn't the biggest topic. What she needed to tell Wanda was she wanted her to take Lins, God forbid, if it came to it. Mom was getting too old to handle a young kid, and as close as Lins was to Angel, as close as Lins was to her—

Kathy teared as she walked, and she wiped her eyes hoping she wasn't noticed—

She needed Wanda to say yes to this. She needed to know Lins would be in good hands if the worst came to be. Wanda had to say yes because, in the pit of her stomach, she knew something terrible was coming.

Wanda tried not to let the silence between herself and Kathy bother her. She tried not to think it was a result of her lack of presence in Kathy's life and tried to ignore the idea it was a reflection on their relationship as a whole. She tried, but it was hard.

Kathy didn't quite seem like herself today. She was her, not like she had been replaced by the Pod People, but there was definitely something off. Her vitality felt... suppressed, maybe?

Wanda knew her friend had been through a lot, maybe nearly as much as herself. They were reflections of each other in some ways: both recently divorced or separated; both having some problems with their kids (over the phone, Kathy mentioned that Lins had been lashing out around the house since the divorce); both of them were going through a lot of pain.

She probably wouldn't be the only one baring her soul around the campfire tonight.

She glanced at Abby, who was deep in examination of the forest around her. She hoped the poor woman wasn't going to get bored or, more than that, disgusted by some pity party that may ensue once they had a few drinks inside them and let it all go. That wasn't why she invited Abby.

And Wanda had to question herself—exactly why had she invited Abby? She told herself it was an act of kindness, that she was trying to show the newbie what life was like in these woods, to share the majesty she had known and loved her whole life. But there was more to it below the surface.

Yes, she was trying to be nice, but she had her own motives too. Shit, didn't everyone? She wasn't exactly sure what they were yet, though. Was it a chance to live vicariously through Abby as she showed her awe-inspiring sights? A way to see it all again with another's fresh eyes? Was the invitation a way to commiserate? To be able to share her woes and add one more soul to her sympathetic audience? Wanda didn't think she was that shallow. She didn't think she needed external validation to know she was on the right track—but she had to wonder if she really was. Especially after the past six months.

She would have to wait and see and hope she hadn't become an asshole for taking advantage of a woman who was just looking for new friends and experiences. She would hate to think she'd become that person.

Wanda glanced at her cell. There was no longer any service, but she had downloaded a map of the forest onto her phone. As long as she had access to GPS satellites, it was supposed to still work—or so she'd been told. This was actually her first trip in without a paper map. Sure, she knew most of the forest's major trails by heart, but there were smaller ones she wasn't as familiar with, and there was a small set of falls she had never visited which she was hoping to lead everyone to tomorrow if everything worked out as planned.

"Are we on track?" Abby asked. She was looking at Wanda's app in an exaggerated gesture of being nosy, her eyes squinted and her body leaning.

"Oh, yeah." Wanda nodded. "I know where we are, anyway. I was just checking it out to see if it was working."

"Yeah?"

"Yeah. A friend told me he always uses this app for hunting. It's supposed to work even without a cell signal. Thought I'd give it a try."

Abby opened her mouth to say something, but her eyes jerked to the left as a loud crack echoed through the forest.

They all stopped and turned, and a deep groan reverberated through the trees. Hearts sped up. It was loud but distant while being much closer than any of them would have liked.

Kathy jerked like she had been awakened from a dream and met Wanda's gaze. She whispered, "Was that a grizzly?"

Wanda nodded. She didn't say a word, only shooed everyone up the trail, faster this time.

The girls covered their mouths and held in laughter. As frightening as a run-in with a grizzly might be, it was almost no match for ten-year-old horseplay. They moved ahead at double-time, and everyone else followed, their eyes on the left wall of trees.

While everyone hurried, Abby looked like she was about to pop with fear. Her eyes were strained on the forest wall, her forehead wore a deep set of lines, and her mouth was sealed with pinched lips.

A call came from ahead on the right. It wasn't the same as the last, though it was similar. It was higher, and Wanda knew precisely what that one was as well. There was only a second before a crash of limbs roared from behind them, and Wanda grabbed Abby and Angel by the shoulder and dragged them both into the woods to her right.

"Come on!" she hissed, and Kathy seized Lins and followed her into the bush.

"What—" Abby tried to talk.

Wanda shushed her and pointed deeper into the woods, away from the crash, away from the calls.

The ground shook as a galloping sound plodded up the trail. It reverberated through soil and wood and flesh and bone. It was an eight-hundred-pound beast stomping behind them, and they felt it move. It was unseen, but it was real, as solid as a thing in their grasp.

Abby led the way as they rushed into the dark gaps between ponderosas. She jumped over a creeping juniper and dodged an oncoming cedar branch. A smell filled her nose, reminding her of her hamster's cage when she was younger, and she glanced back at the rest. They were all right behind her, and Wanda waved her on yet again.

Abby's chest heaved with burning breath. She trembled as she ran, growing more confident in her steps but envisioning massive claws ripping through the pine boughs at any second. She knew she had to get away; her eyes had adjusted to the heavier canopy and she was feeling a steadiness in her stride. She would run as far as she had to, and she could do this. At least she thought she could—a fact arose in her mind, a trivia tidbit that stated bears could sprint up to thirty miles per hour. She doubted she was as quick. It made her heart leap inside her chest, and she pushed herself harder.

10

S TEVIE HELD HONEY TIGHTLY as the side-by-side jostled the five of them up and down and left and right. He smelled the strawberry and lemon still clinging to her hair and, through her clothes, the growing scent of body odor from her lack of shower and deodorant since before the jewelry store. He would tell her to get cleaned up once they stopped somewhere. The next time they fucked he wanted her to smell good. He wasn't going to put up with this for longer than he had to.

Trees flew past on the side of the trail. Occasional pine boughs swatted the vehicle frame. The rat-faced guy they called Tony looked scared as shit as he stared at Perry, then Nick, then Stevie and Honey—Stevie had learned to recognize that look and prey on it. Tony was definitely going on his list.

The noise from the two ATV engines was deafening, and Stevie wished he had brought earplugs. The day seemed to be mutating from shitshow to shitshow, everything had been since yesterday, and he couldn't help but think for a split-second he was doomed—only a split-second, though. He liked to think he was like his dad, that he would always come out on top. He had never really been tested that way, sure—Dad had always been there to guide him—but he was growing more confident now as the day moved on, and Shamus seemed to keep fucking up. He was going to have to be the one to get himself and Honey out of this. He was mistaken to trust this Irish prick.

Shamus led the off-road vehicles around a turn into a clearing with a worn-down campsite and small stream. They blew past the campsite and drove down and then up the stream's banks and stopped where the forest's edge met the clearing.

"What is it?" Tony looked around, desperately trying to identify anything he could, whether it was a car, a house, a plane, anything to get him out of this situation. Seeing none of those things, his eyes widened. "Is it cops? Have they caught up to us?"

"Shut up, kid," Perry snapped from the front seat. Nick chuckled and ran his hands through his hair. It didn't fix it. It still pointed in every direction like a scattered rat's nest.

"What's going on?" Honey whispered to Stevie.

He didn't answer. He didn't know and wasn't about to say that. Better to just wait and see what the hell Shamus was up to.

Shamus climbed from his four-wheeler and pointed at Perry, then to the ground. Perry nodded at the command and waited like a loyal dog as Shamus disappeared into the woods. After a minute of waiting and Tony whispering how fucked they were, Shamus emerged from the trees with a second duffel bag that matched his first.

He lay the bag across his ATV's seat and unzipped it. After digging through its contents, first some smaller bags, then something that looked like a folded shovel, he came up with a satellite phone.

Stevie nodded as if he understood what Shamus was up to the entire time.

Shamus powered on the phone and dialed.

"Here we go," Perry mumbled.

"Boss always has a plan," Nick agreed.

"Yeah," Shamus grumbled, "it's me. How's it look over there?" He nodded, then his jaw clenched and his face flushed. "You're fuckin' kiddin' me. It can't be that bad." Cords bulged from his wrist, and he looked ready to pitch the phone as far as he could, then he took a breath. "Just drive by there in an hour and see how it looks. I'll call you back." He powered off the phone before the other person could have possibly answered.

Shamus shook his head and breathed deeply before putting the sat phone back in the bag and zipping it closed. He stretched a pair of bungees up from the ATV's rear rack and secured the second duffel. The first still hung from his back, and Stevie knew that one wouldn't leave its place any time soon—he was pretty sure what was in there.

Perry and Nick waited patiently as Shamus walked over. Stevie thought they looked like chihuahuas waiting for a bonbon. He could see the frustration on Shamus's face as he formed his words then looked at the five in the side-by-side.

"The cops are all over the roads outside the public lands. There's some kind of bulletin on the radio and TV saying to look out for us in this area. I was hoping we could meet someone at the trailhead north of here, but it looks like the police have that covered right now. We're going to have to keep moving and check back with our ride in a bit."

"Shit, shit," Tony moaned.

Shamus stared at him with a half-regretful, half-despising glance. "We're just going to head deeper into the woods for now. Until I hear it's clear."

"Yeah, boss," Perry agreed. Stevie pictured him panting and licking his lips.

Shivers ran through Stevie's nerves as he heard the worst sound imaginable from the east: the low, rhythmic hum of a helicopter's blades.

Shamus immediately turned east, and his eyes sharpened. He recognized it too. "Come on!" he screamed, and ran to his quad.

Stevie thought that was the fastest he'd ever seen Shamus

move.

Mark Rand slid his hand over the hood of Shamus Betty's pickup when he got to the scene. The uniforms ran through the house clearing room after room. He felt silly, like a tracker on *Gunsmoke*. But it worked. The hood was still warm. He wasn't far behind them.

Then the uniforms reported in. Their quarry had fled.

Officers searched the house, finding cocaine, not much but enough for a fun night or two, some Cuban cigars, and various other items to add to Betty's growing tab—but there was nothing that would break the case open and really let Rand into the details behind what was going on in that warehouse. Who was Betty working for? Where did the cars come from? Where did they take them? Who controlled the flow? The network? And how was it related to a jewelry heist in South Dakota and a stolen pickup after a home invasion in Hauser?

He had almost thought Betty had gotten away clean until Officer Scott grabbed him from the kitchen and showed him the setup in the basement. After rewinding the feed, it was all on the video surveillance system—and they had just fucking missed them.

There they were in brightly colored pixels. Car after car came up the street as Betty and his group of thugs—and one lady; he wasn't sure how she fit into this—got on ATVs and sped off into the neighboring wilderness.

They had just fucking missed them!

His hands clenched at his sides and he tried to slow his breathing. Anger wasn't going to help this. But as he rewound the footage and let it play again, as he watched the ogre of a man climb onto the four-wheeler, he couldn't help the pool of Officer Braden's blood from coming to mind. He couldn't help seeing where blood had spattered against the walls and ran down in streaks as the man had nowhere to go and no ability to escape. And that fucker was responsible for it all.

He studied the footage, noting the direction they drove, and rushed outside. He stood by the shed, radio in hand, judging the tracks of flattened grass stalks as they led into the woods.

He pressed his radio's *Mic* button and said, "Dispatch, we're going to need the state. Tell them to gas up the chopper."

11

ANGEL GLANCED OVER HER shoulder as Mom pulled her past a pair of spruces and over a dead log. She dinged as the ball inside her bell rolled and chimed. She saw trees and only trees, though the clumps of cedar and the distant gloom threatened to hide so much.

"What is it?" Lins cried. "Why are we running?"

"Quiet!" Kathy whispered.

The five ran another hundred feet, dodging tree trunks and ducking under branches. Wanda finally stopped, finger over her lips in a desperate sign for quiet. She grabbed the bell on Angel's pack tightly so the little ball could no longer vibrate.

She looked back.

The sounds of heavy breathing circled through five mouths. Lins trembled. Abby scanned everywhere, her eyes darting. Kathy watched Wanda—all eyes found Wanda and waited for her to say anything.

Another moment passed.

"I think we're safe." Wanda's voice was hushed and raw. "I don't think she's following."

"She?" Lins asked.

Wanda put a hand on her shoulder. "There was a momma bear and a baby bear, and we were right in the middle."

Lins's eyes grew wide, and Kathy pulled her into a hug. Angel seized her mother between her arms. Lins whimpered.

"It's okay," Kathy said.

"I want to go home," Lins squeaked. Her voice was muffled by Kathy's coat.

Kathy frowned.

Angel closed her eyes and felt the forest. There was a darkness out there; she could sense that. She could feel a swath of animals going about their business, foraging (and migrating?), but none of it hostile; the bears weren't coming.

The darkness, though. That was cold. It crept through the branches and under roots. It was a thing she hadn't felt when they were out here before. Was it new? Where had it come from? And why were the bears—

It made sense then. The bears—all the migrating animals—were moving away from it, and Angel and her party must have gotten in the way. She hoped whatever direction Mom was leading them was out of its way too.

Angel put a hand on Lins's shoulder. "We're okay now." Lins turned to her, and Angel smiled. "Don't worry about that bear. She doesn't care about us."

They waited another few minutes as the adults listened to the distant wilderness, reassuring themselves they weren't on the edge of a grizzly attack. Wanda and Kathy had seen the results of those at one time or another. The clawed flesh, split and puckered outward, the exposed muscle and bone, the blood. It was a horror that everyone who lived so close to the forest was familiar with and, unless they were crazy, respected. Grizzlies stood taller than a human, weighed as much as four, and had claws and power that could rip a man to shreds. They were not to be taken lightly.

When everyone had caught their breath and pulses had calmed, they began hiking again. Wanda directed them west, first gauging where they had been heading and where she thought the trail had been leading, then checking her instincts against her map.

She was right. They didn't have the luxury of a worn-down path to follow, but they had a direction to go. If they kept a good pace, she thought they would rejoin the trail in an hour or so, and that was fine with everyone. No one wanted to be on that trail again, not until they put some distance between themselves and that momma bear.

The kids walked in front, and Kathy swung her pack around as she walked. She pulled out a shiny pink flask and slipped the pack back where it belonged. After a few breathy gulps, she passed it to Wanda.

Wanda smirked and accepted.

"I was going to save it for tonight, but I think we deserve a swig after that." Kathy looked up into the canopy and shook her head.

"I'll take it," Wanda chuckled. It felt good to laugh. She squinted as she swallowed two gulps of her own and passed the flask to Abby.

Abby looked at the container cautiously. There was a cursive engraving across the front reading *Glitter Juice*. "What is it?" she chuckled.

"Just something to calm the nerves," Kathy said.

Abby smelled the flask. The alcohol in the air nearly burned her nose, but the scent also held a sweet hint of apple. She wasn't sure she had smelled anything like that before, and though she wasn't really a drinker at home, she figured, *why not?* She was here to explore new places and have new experiences. She might as well try it.

The taste instantly burned her throat as sweetness lit up her tongue. It was like she had swallowed an apple pie coated in acid then set on fire. She got it down just in time to cough.

"Whew!" Her eyes watered, and Kathy chuckled.

"You okay?" Wanda asked.

Abby flashed a wrinkled face and an exasperated smile.

They navigated their way through a cluster of trees, and Abby nodded, then repeated to herself, *why not?* and took another swig. It burned a little less, but the heat rose from her chest and warmed her veins, and the thoughts of momma bears ripping her apart settled, wading from the front to the back of her mind.

She passed the flask. Wanda took a swig and handed it to Kathy. Kathy had another as well and slid the container into her jacket's inner pocket.

Abby took a long, deep breath. She gazed into the treetops all around them. She glanced at the girls, the moms, and back to the surrounding nature. She didn't know if it was the alcohol or the place, but she felt overwhelmed with the reality of where she was. She had done it. She had gotten out of Georgia, something ninety-five percent of her friends had never done. She'd followed a dream to leave the urban sprawl of the metro area and live in a beautiful, faraway place, and now she was exploring it with new friends.

It brought tears to her eyes.

The smells of pine and cedar enveloped her. The silence of all things manmade other than their voices and the crunch under their feet was awe-inspiring. She heard the wind rustle in the boughs of evergreens. She saw green and brown, growth that only nature could perform, and rolling land shaped by eons of geology, and the culmination of her senses nearly made her laugh.

Abby wasn't sure about too many things: if Wanda was really going to be a good friend as the years passed; if it was going to end up so cold on this trip that she'd never want to hike again; or if she would look back in ten years and see her move here as a wise or horrible choice. What she was sure of at the moment, though, was that she was glad to be here right now. She was glad to be with this small group of people, experiencing a new thrill and taking in an opportunity she would never have had if she'd stayed in her comfort zone back in Georgia. She was going to soak it all in and take it as it came. There was time to figure out the rest, to learn from it and make the next call.

There was a chatter in the trees and a flapping of wings. The girls giggled.

"Shit," Kathy said. "This trip is off to one hell of a start, Wanda dear."

"I try to keep you on your toes," Wanda said.

The wind blew across Abby's neck, and all her heat dipped for just a moment as she thought she heard a whisper. But it was immediately gone, and her eagerness returned. She pushed aside the words she thought she heard—because, really, that couldn't have happened. It was just the wind playing tricks on her. No one was around.

She couldn't have heard someone whisper *delicious*.

Nick VanSyke piloted the side-by-side—the wind mussing his hair even more—listening to twigs snap and the engines of the ATVs roar. Perry sat quietly in the passenger seat, as did the three in the back.

The three in the back... Jesus.

What a bunch of bullshit this was, chauffeuring those assholes around. The girl he could see holding onto, she could be fun to have around once they reached the night's hideout. But the boyfriend was worthless; Nick had listened to the conversation back at the warehouse, and he could tell the guy was just looking for a free ride. So what if Shamus and his old man were friends? That didn't mean shit. If the kid couldn't pull his weight, he was no good.

Just like Tony.

That rat-faced little fuck's only good use was being bossed around. Oh, he had seen the kid go on runs, pickups that an elementary school kid should have been able to handle, but he had never seen the guy do anything that actually required a little muscle, a little out-of-the-box beating like Nick knew was coming.

Nick had been on the run before. He knew the types of decisions that had to be made when the cops were just steps behind and a wrong choice could make the difference between seeing daylight tomorrow or seeing cell walls. He didn't have faith that anyone in the backseat had the guts—or the balls—to make those choices.

The bag on Shamus's back shifted as the boss rode over a bump in the trail, and Nick wondered just how much money was in that bag. Not that he had any plans to take the boss out—not right now, anyway. They still had a long road to go, and for now, Shamus seemed to have a plan to get them out of this. If that fell through, though, who knew. Nick always had friends in Chicago who would welcome him back, especially if he walked in with a giant bag of loot like the one dangling from Shamus's back.

He wondered about that bag. The green of the duffel looked exactly like the ones they used on the job in Phoenix.

It was hot that day, like ninety-nine percent of the days out there were. The empty bags were strapped to each of their four backs, a lot like Shamus was doing now only they were on the way to fill them.

Shamus was in the lead as they ran into the condemned building that used to be apartments. It was shady, and even in the dry heat, it smelled like mold.

Behind Shamus was Danny, then himself, then Cheeks. They passed the block of metal boxes where residents used to get their mail, doors open or ripped off, and Shamus entered the stairs. They had to take the stairs, of course, there was no power to the building, but fuck did that suck.

The concrete-enclosed space was like a cement oven. They had gone up half a flight, were turning at the first landing, when sweat started streaming from Nick's face—each of their faces—and the grip of the shotgun in his hands began to feel wet and slick to the touch. He made sure his hands were centered on the pump and the grip, both surfaces that were grooved, but it barely helped. By the first floor there was so much sweat, so much heat, his brain was starting to swim.

Shamus stopped them all there. He slapped himself in the face, made each of them do it to themselves to regain their focus, and they kept moving up. But it was on the third floor where their focus really mattered.

Shamus crossed from the last step onto the third-floor landing as the door to the level opened and a cartel member stepped through.

Nick's ass clenched, and he raised his weapon, but by the time his sweaty finger rested on the trigger, Shamus had handled it. He swung the stock of his rifle up, crashing into the guy's temple. There was a grunt and a crack, and the cartel member hit the floor like a sack of meat, then started to twitch and piss himself.

Shamus grabbed him, pulling him into the stairwell and shutting the door quietly. There was another groan, and Shamus lifted his massive boot and crushed the man's face into something barely recognizable as human. He shoved the body to the side, and one by one, they slipped through the door into the hallway.

The stench instantly grabbed Nick by the gut and twisted.

There was a loud noise a few doors down, the rumble of a small engine running. Electrical cords ran from the doorway into the next apartment, and it made sense to Nick. The cartel was running a generator in one unit, feeding the next.

They passed an open door, and Shamus glanced in and kept moving. When Nick went by, the smell was unmistakable, shit in buckets and piss on the walls. What he smelled, though, was worse than just excrement. That was coming from the next room.

Nick thought he was going to puke as they passed the cracked door. Dried blood soaked the carpet; it had solidified into thousands of tiny crimson spikes. A table held knives and pliers stained in a thick, reddish film. That would have been enough to make Nick think twice about this job, but as he took in the last sight through the sliver of door, it took all he had not to turn and get the hell out of there.

Nick was a seasoned guy. In Chicago, where he started, he had done his share of muggings, robberies, even a hit or two when it was required. He'd come down to Arizona as a favor to his buddy, Joey Treet, a year earlier and decided to stay when the money kept flowing. But as that year went on and the jobs got heavier, as he worked more and more for Shamus, one thing he had learned—and this stuck in his head—do not get caught fucking with these goddamn cartel guys.

In a chair was evidence of why you didn't fuck with them—something that would have convinced him had he not already known Shamus's plan; after this job, he'd be on the road out of town, no matter what the boss wanted. No matter how good Deloris's, his favorite girl at the west-side strip club, pussy was. He wasn't going to let what happened to this guy happen to him.

It was worse than a Columbian necktie—an execution

method he heard of where the throat was cut and the tongue was pulled down and out over the chest. It was that and more. This guy's tongue was hanging from his throat, but his pants were also down. His cock and balls had been removed; the dick's severed end protruded from his mouth, and a testicle floated in each sunken socket where his eyes should have been.

All Nick could think when he saw that was how he hoped the necktie was first, because the other way around... he couldn't imagine.

Luckily for Nick, he didn't have time to ponder the order of events that poor soul had been forced to endure because the next door was the target.

The opening was cracked just enough for the electrical cords from the generator to pass through. A cold rush of air exited the crack, and a hum followed it, blending with the chatter of several Spanish-speaking voices. Then, a round of laughter.

It occurred to Nick they were in there just hanging out and bullshitting. There was a dead, tortured guy across the hall, and they were chilling in the AC and laughing it up. Nick would have laughed had it not been sending shivers down his spine. He and his crew were usually the bad guys; right now, he was about to do the world a favor with some heroic shit.

Shamus glanced each man in the eyes—Nick, then Danny, then Cheeks. He nodded, then kicked in the door.

The sounds of gunfire and screams, the cold air, the acrid smell of gun smoke and incense all rushed over Nick like a wave of unrecognizable static. It blended into a blur of blood and noise as one cartel member after another splattered into gobs of tissue, bone, and then corpse at the end of each of their guns.

When the chaos stopped and Nick could focus, he saw the bodies of five men and one woman pooling blood onto the floor. Some twitched while vomit expelled; some pissed as their muscles relaxed. And then he saw the table of blood-spattered cocaine, the thing that would buy their ticket out of Phoenix and Shamus's job in the syndicate.

Nick wondered if the bag shifting on Shamus's back as he turned down trails and went over bumps was worth as much as that coke. He wondered if Shamus really had a plan good enough to get them out of this shit. Because if not, he had a plan that would get him to someplace warm, and he could sure as shit make it happen with that bag.

12

R and's television was showing a screensaver as he walked inside his Huckleberry Avenue home. He tried to remember what he had been watching before he was rushed out of the house. A picture of snow-capped Mount Custer faded from the high-definition display, replaced by an image of Janeen in her bikini on the side of the river.

Shit.

When was he going to change the settings so he didn't have to look at that slideshow anymore? That was three years ago, back when the marriage was good, back before the town seemed to be cursed again, before she opened that damned envelope and its powder forced her into a coma.

People like to say that time heals all wounds. That may have been true, but how long did it take to heal grief? How many years? What did it take to make the rage go away after your wife died from such a stupid thing as opening the wrong goddamn envelope?

Because his rage was still there.

Others say it's love that heals, and Rand had had at least a chuckle or two over that. How does one find love after it's ripped from your chest beside a hospital bed? Ripped as hard and as painfully as your own beating heart. Rand figured that if love healed, the lack of it tore a gaping hole in a person, the kind of chasm that might just be impossible to climb out of. How do you find love to heal if all you have is anger and sadness?

Rand sighed and dropped his keys in the artisan bowl on the entryway table. Now he was rushed. He had to get to the remote and kill those images before he could take off his jacket and gun. That goddamn slideshow had to end before he saw another picture, and... He didn't want to spend tonight like that.

On the way home, he had toyed with the idea of calling Officer Torres over to relieve a little tension, but now that idea was wrecked. He wanted nothing more than a beer and maybe a slice of the cold pizza he knew was in the fridge.

TV awake, Rand walked into the kitchen. He patted his pocket, making sure he brought his phone in from the car—the last thing he wanted was to miss the call once they picked up the trail of those bastards in the woods. He felt it there. *Good.*

He opened the fridge and saw two beers, a pizza box, and a ribeye steak still in the styrofoam, waiting to be cooked. The thought of tossing the hunk of meat into a pan of olive oil with some salt and pepper came at the same time as the memory of a sticky warehouse floor pooled with blood, crumbs of Officer Braden's flesh still adhering to the concrete and wall.

He grabbed a bottle and closed the door, but not before sliding the steak into the vegetable crisper. Maybe he would have the stomach to grab a slice after the beer, but he didn't want to see that again and ruin his appetite when he came back.

The living room was a web of memories which he waded through with blinders on. Past the art Janeen had chosen for the walls, horses and ranches, some framed ancient rope from the oldest cattle ranch in the county. Past the furniture, a port wine-colored leather couch and loveseat and a rough-sawn Douglas fir coffee table. He sat in a black leather recliner, the color meant to offset the other pieces and ground the room—she picked that too. She had an eye for home design, at least in her style. Her friends frequently pulled her into shopping trips to aid their searches for that special piece to cap off their space—though they never actually finished; there always seemed to be a need for one more item.

It wasn't exactly the opposite of what Rand would have chosen on his own; he liked the style, it was just he would have been too lazy to go to so much effort. He was the type to go to a furniture store, stumble upon a set of items designed to match each other, trusting the store and the designer, and just buy the set.

But this—yes, it was a reservoir of memories, a place where he essentially lived inside his dead wife's choices—was a place that felt like home. Even if it practically brought him to tears more often than he would admit.

Rand sipped his beer and rescued himself from the TV before it faded back into screensaver mode. Part of him wanted to drift away and sleep, to forget the horrors of the day and find a comforting place inside his head for the night. He couldn't do that in his bed anymore. As much as this room reminded him of Janeen, the bed was worse. Her smell had long gone, but still, he imagined it in his nose as soon as his body touched those sheets. He would have to be drunk and ready to pass out before lying on that mattress.

The other part of him hoped he'd get a call once his beer was done. That part was anxious after the helicopter had flown back to refuel, finding nothing in the vast acreage of public lands it had scanned. It was supposed to return for one more sweep tonight, and if it didn't find anything, they would all start over at dawn.

"Dawn," he grumbled, and clicked play on a western, *Gunsmoke*. He sipped his beer and faded as the black-and-white images of cowboys rode across the California backcountry, pretending to be in Kansas. His thoughts ranged from the warehouse, to Shamus Betty's home, to the stolen vehicles, to the woods. He let his brain wander; it was sometimes the best way to work, to let his subconscious do its thing and freely associate the events of the day.

But he came up with nothing. No leads, no ideas of where to look next. What he had was a fading mind that took him to a world of dreams where Janeen was alive and they sat on a blanket on the outskirts of Dodge City, both in black and white, as they ate a picnic and laughed at the ridiculous joke someone had told him of her having died. It was astonishing how wrong someone could be. She was right there with him, as alive and as wonderful as ever. She even led him on a walk into the woods.

They passed a field of deadfall, piles of decayed wood resembling ghostly tepees and mounds of rotting pine. They approached a cabin in the mountains, and he thought how this looked more like Montana than either California or Kansas. It was old; he could see that from the simple trapper style to the crumbling edges and sinking right corner. Janeen pushed on the door, and it opened with a rusted-hinge squeal, and—she led him inside. He hesitated, but only for an instant. He knew this was odd, that there was something off here, but he would follow her wherever she led, no matter what his intuition warned. He felt a chill, not just a lack of heat but a solemness he hadn't felt since her hand had gone cold in his at the hospital.

But no, that had happened in a dream. She wasn't dead. She was here with him, guiding him into a group of others, a woman and a man, in clothes people hadn't worn in a hundred and fifty years, through a crowd of children who all looked up at him with smirks and grins as if he was the only one not in on their joke. Through a crowd of hairy, rough-looking fellows dressed in the same era's clothing as the rest, these with desperate looks on their faces, some wincing in pain. And they found a room with a single bed, a dresser, a wash bowl, and a dark shadow that hovered across each wall, rising as she sat him down and mounted his lap, placing her lips onto his.

They were cold. And she didn't smell like her. And as she pushed him down against the bed, he wanted to scream. But instead, he cried. And he knew this was just the beginning.

13

T HE FIRE CRACKLED, AND the smell of burning pine filled Wanda with joy she wasn't expecting. The tents were up, the bags down, the group back on the trail and at their first planned stop—a small primitive campground eleven miles into the forest and eight hundred feet higher in elevation. There had been no more sightings of bears, only the flutter of birds and the scurry of squirrels. The smiling faces around the growing fire gave Wanda the feeling of being not eleven miles but eleven thousand miles from the rest of the world and all its hassles along with it.

This was the reason she came. This was the feeling she was hoping for. As she looked across the fire into Angel's eyes, saw her laughing at something Lins had whispered in her ear, she knew Angel felt the same way. Their troubles with Allen Neddles and Vice Principal Bates, the fear and violation of West Hemlock, the breakup with Dad and ex-boyfriend Henry were all as distant as they could have been. Regardless of the scares they had encountered on the trail today, Wanda knew this was the place for them to be.

Kathy passed her flask and dug in her bag. Wanda took it and happily chugged two swallows and passed it to Abby.

Abby took a single sip and passed it back. She had nearly gotten drunk from the two sips on the trail and didn't want to rush things tonight or have a hangover tomorrow morning.

"So, what are the dinner plans?" Kathy said, and brought the flask to her lips. Before Wanda could answer, she raised the liquor and asked, "Or is this it?"

Wanda shook her head. "No—well, that's the side course. I have some dehydrated stuff in my bag. I'll get some water from the stream in a little bit, and we'll be all set."

Kathy nodded.

Abby took a breath and leaned away from the other adults. She rubbed her hands together, preparing herself for what could be an awkward situation. When she leaned back in, her eyes squinted as she spoke. "So, tell me about this—I mean, you guys have lived here forever, right? What's the deal with this town?"

Kathy smirked. "Girl, there's a lot of weird in this town. You're going to have to be more specific."

Abby winced. Her whole face seemed to tighten. "I wasn't trying to be disrespectful or nothing—"

"It's okay," Wanda interrupted. "I'm sure an outsider would have a lot of questions, especially one completely new to the northwest. What is it?"

Abby's expression loosened. "Like, I've met some nice people and all, but why does it seem like most people keep to themselves here? Other than you two, I haven't really met many outgoing people."

Wanda and Kathy glanced at each other.

Kathy leaned in. "Let me ask you a question. How did you pick Custer Falls? Did you just throw a dart at a map or something? Tell me you did some research first."

Abby hissed through closed teeth and a smile. "Honestly, I kind of just picked it from the location. I always wanted to live in the mountains, and a small town seemed perfect. I mean, I work online, so I could live anywhere."

"Girl." Kathy shook her head as she spoke, then laughed. "You picked what some call the murder capital of Montana to set up shop."

Abby's eyes widened.

Wanda raised her hand. "Hold on, it's not like that. We don't have roaming bands of murderers or anything. Jesus, Kathy. It—it seems to come in waves. I only really know as much as I do 'cause when it happened in the 90s, my mother was a dispatcher. And I'm a cop now. But—" she paused and looked into the woods. "Per capita, over like a fifty-year period, we've had the highest murder rate. But like I said, it came in spurts. There was a wave in '92 and another in 2022. But other than that, we're pretty normal. But still, it keeps the town on edge. People don't tend to socialize with people they don't know. They don't go out as much as they might in other places—especially since '22. Give it a few years, though, and I think things will lighten up again."

"Is that why it seems like the whole town goes to sleep every night at, like, nine o'clock?"

Wanda wasn't sure if she was helping calm Abby or not, and she definitely didn't want to share the story of how she got put on her current leave. But at the same time, she also thought the woman deserved to know the place she lived in.

"That's probably one reason. But there's more. I mean, you're in a state where the settlers had to depend on themselves for everything. The winters were so bad that people had to be prepared and know that if they got into trouble, no one was going to come rescue them. That kind of thinking is hereditary. People here are still pretty independent because of that. And they expect others to be the same. There's a mindset that only the tough can survive here, and you have to be ready for the worst."

Abby nodded. "I guess I can see that."

"And it's an early culture." Kathy sipped her flask. "The ranching life, I mean. People had to get up early to tend to things, and that means going to bed early. A lot of that is still in the veins of people around here. Not many late-night parties other than Saint Paddy's Day or New Year's Eve."

"So it's not just the murders?" Abby said.

Wanda glanced across the fire—the kids were listening now.

"It's *totally* the murders too." Kathy snickered.

Wand raised her hands as if to tamp down the topic. "Let me get some water, and I'll start working on dinner." She rose to her feet.

"Need help?" Abby stood with her. "I'd love to learn how to do it."

"Come on," Wanda said. She was happy to see the conversation didn't completely weird the woman out.

She led Abby to the tent they were sharing, where she pulled out two bags of dehydrated food and set them on the ground. One read *Lasagna*, while the other read *Beef Stroganoff*. Each had bold letters that said their package fed three.

"That's it?" Abby said. "Just add water?"

"Yup." Wanda pointed toward the stream. "This way." She carried a large, clear bag and stuffed some gadget into her pocket.

They hiked the few dozen yards and kneeled by the stream, and Wanda was about to dip the bag in the water when Abby said, "Can I?"

"Yeah." She handed Abby the bag.

It was about a foot wide and two feet long with something like a Ziploc top and a cap at the bottom. "I figure I should learn this if I'm going to do it myself." She examined the bag, guessing what to do but waiting for instruction.

"Definitely. Just open the top and dip it in the stream. Try not to get any debris if you can. And when it's mostly full, you pull it out and close it."

Abby nodded and opened the top of the bag. She leaned over the stream, shifting herself several times hoping not to fall in—the idea of being wet in this weather was frightening—and she let the lip of the bag lower into the current.

There was a noise far beyond the stream, a branch cracking and a shifting sound in the brush. Wanda didn't look at first, not concerned with the normal woodland noises, until she remembered the bear. It wasn't likely the momma bear would track them down after this long, but it wasn't a possibility she could ignore, not after being the one to invite all these friends into the woods. In a way, they were her responsibility.

She glanced into the darkness and scanned the gloom. Not much stood out, just ominous shapes of black tree trunks and dark bushes over an onyx canvas. It was an unknown space that stretched all around, and she imagined it going for miles. Darkness. Unrelenting darkness.

There was a feeling within that gloom that she hadn't sensed since she was a child, a fear of an unseen, unknown world she was blind to, yet it could have been peeking in on her as she stood helpless. It could have been watching her from any direction, studying her and Abby, waiting for its chance. The fear of night had taken hold.

This was a moment where she wanted nothing more than to flick on the lights and cast some glorious rays of illumination upon the Earth. This was a primal fear from deep within her DNA, the fear that drove humans to crowd around the fire at night for safety.

Wanda thought of camping as a kid, shuddering at the distant dark from the fire, knowing that whatever loomed in the night was hidden from her. And it was there. Many *its* were there.

But like so many other discredited truths from that time of innocence, from what adults treat as ignorance, that feeling was more accurate than anyone would have given her credit for. There had been things out there. There *were* things out there now.

She knew it. There *was* someone—some-*thing*—out in the blackness, staring back at her. It studied her wantingly, and she felt its icy stare moving over her skin. Its desire seized her stomach and pulled her back from the water's edge.

There was a whisper in the night as the breeze pushed needley boughs over one another. There was no voice behind it, but words hung in the disembodied hush, and Wanda was sure it said, "*Come.*"

Her heart pounded at the sound, at the unseen, and she wanted to go grab Angel and run back to the car. She wanted to scream as they took off, and no matter how silly it looked or how crazy it sounded, she wanted to get out now.

"*Come.*"

She had never felt this way out here. Not at this campsite and not at this stream. If she had tried, she wouldn't have been able to count the number of times she had camped at this exact spot, and none of those times had yielded the feeling eating at her insides right now. There was something new here. Something evil. And she wanted nothing to do with it.

If only she knew which way was the safest to run.

Wanda's mind flashed to the rape, to the grimy, disgusting man hovering over her, thrusting. Her helplessness in that moment. His reek of garbage and spoiled meat. Her lips wanting to scream but not responding. His grunting. Her disgust and fear and rage at herself, at her inability to defend herself, and the knowledge that once he was done, he could slice her throat and abandon her there like nothing but a discarded piece of trash.

Wanda was about to turn back to the camp. She assumed it was the safest path out of there. She had completely forgotten her friend was even with her until Abby stood, lifting the bag. It hung three-quarters full of water.

"Is that good?" Abby was plastered with a childlike grin.

Wanda took a breath. She looked at the bag, at Abby's smile, and stood awed for a moment. Abby had heard none of that—felt none of that. How could it be? Her gaze went back to the woods, to the quiet, empty darkness, and she felt nothing. Whatever had been there was no more.

Or... her idiotic paranoia had passed.

But why? She had no reason to be paranoid. As she kept telling herself, she had been here so many times.

A gnawing voice in the back of her mind said, "It's the rape. It's never going to leave you. You're broken now, traumatized. You can't trust yourself."

Was that true? Had her senses been ruined? How could she go back to work without clearly being able to determine what was dangerous and what wasn't? That was a necessity for a cop. A necessity for a parent.

Was she worthless now when it came to protecting Angel as well as herself?

No. It couldn't be.

She looked again at Abby, who was gazing at her with curiosity. She was about to talk, and Wanda said, "Perfect. Just what we need." She intended her voice to be calm, but it was tight, high-strung. "Close the top and bring it back to camp."

She wanted to run there. Yes, the feeling had waned, the forest no longer felt like a hungering beast, but she wanted nothing more than to be back by the safety of the fire. It wasn't a real thing, she knew that—sitting by the fire was no shelter, provided no barrier to fierce beasts or creeping evil—but there was something primal in the desire to be by the light, as if it could cast away the evils of the world in the same way it pushed back the darkness. And as she moved, she was ashamed.

Wanda snagged a small bowl and the dehydrated food bags as she hurried past her tent. She guided Abby through attaching the filter to the small end of the bag and filling the bowl. They waited for the water to boil and poured it into the bags, shook it up, and let it sit. And when it was done, they ate.

The usual remarks circled the fire. "I can't believe this was dehydrated." "They didn't have this when I was a kid." Finally, from the kids, "Can we do s'mores now?"

Wanda got through it, but she barely ate. Only Angel seemed to notice, though she didn't say anything. Angel always seemed to know when something was wrong, and later, when the kids crawled into their tent and the adults drank around the fire, staring at what stars they could make out in the sparse cavities of the overcast night, Angel surprised her mother by placing Betty Bobcat in her lap. There were hugs, and neither said a word more than *Goodnight*, but Wanda was grateful.

Though Angel would have been better off keeping it.

14

O VER THE COURSE OF the afternoon, Stevie's ass had grown progressively more sore from the hard seat, the rocky ground, and the weight of Honey on his lap. Even though they had stopped several times and he'd gotten out to stretch his legs, each time he retook the seat, less and less time passed before he was numb and aching again.

Shamus had called his contact with each stop, and each time, the answer had been the same: cops were manning the forest exits and the bird was in the air. But now, with the sun down and the sound of helicopter blades nowhere to be heard, they stopped again. This time, they were told the chopper had been sent to refuel, but even more cops were at the trailheads.

None of them would be getting out of these woods any time soon, and definitely not through the eastern or northern exits.

Stevie could tell Honey was feeling the strain as well. She was shifting in his lap constantly. She gripped the roof, then the seat in front of them, then the roof again. She practically whined when they stopped, then got pissy when Stevie didn't have answers about when this trip would be over.

He was just about ready to put a bullet in her head, leave her behind a dead log, and call the trip done. At least his ass would be a little less sore.

The whole day had worn out its charm. It started with them running, with having zero sleep, and that was bad enough. They had made it safely, he'd thought, to Custer Falls, and here they were on the run again. He wasn't a superstitious guy, but at this point, he was starting to wonder if the day was cursed.

And the novelty of Shamus's antics was gone. Stevie was ready to get off the damn side-by-side and say fuck it. He could walk from there, find a road, carjack someone, and be on the way. Besides, he didn't know if these cops were even after him. Sure, some cops were, but possibly not the locals. They were probably just after Shamus for shooting their own.

Stevie was about to tap Disheveled Hair on the shoulder and tell him to stop the vehicle—he knew now the guy's name was Nick but didn't give a shit—when Shamus halted at the edge of a stream and killed his ATV.

Nick parked the side-by-side and cut the lights and engine as Shamus waved. Stevie was ready to throw Honey from his lap so he could stand, but she hopped down before he could. The entire group climbed from the vehicles and stretched and groaned.

Shamus spoke on his satellite phone again, and Stevie was ready for him to tell everyone to get back on, and ready to tell Shamus to go fuck himself, when Shamus instead said, "Gather some firewood, guys. Looks like we're going to be here a while."

"What does *a while* mean?" Stevie asked.

Nick and Perry, the Irish Rock, stared at Stevie, then at Shamus, wondering if they would get their chance to tune this guy up finally for asking stupid questions. But Shamus shooed them away.

"Couple hours," Shamus said. "Maybe morning. Now get the fucking wood."

Honey took a seat on a giant boulder by the water. She was wearing her jacket, but the night was cooling. She rubbed her arms until Shamus turned to her.

"What, you didn't hear?" He shook his head as she stood and wandered into the woods, clueless about what she was supposed to do.

Shamus stared into the stream, the dim light reflecting on the babbling rise and fall of water over river rock. He ground his teeth, holding on to his temper as best he could. Losing it wasn't going to help him here. Beating that little shit Stevie into the ground might make him feel a bit better—he was pretty sure the only reason that cop showed up on his warehouse doorstep was because he was looking for him—but that would only aggravate matters. It would mean he would have to kill the girl, too, probably, and two deaths might throw the other three even more on edge.

He didn't need that shit.

What he needed was for everyone to calm the fuck down so they could think better. They needed to rest, maybe even sleep a little, because it was hard to see the trails and lead the way at night. In the morning, he would actually be able to track where he was going, not just navigate by the ATV's compass and shitty headlights, hoping the trail was going in the direction he needed.

He exhaled slowly, hearing the others tromp through the forest, looking for wood. He wondered if they'd all come back or if some would get eaten by a bear. He doubted any of them had any wilderness training. He sure as shit didn't. He was a city boy, had been his whole life, and that wasn't going to change. All he knew was that if he built a fire, they could stay warm—and it felt like tonight was going to be a cold one. If they could just hold their shit together until morning, when he could see the way again, he was positive he could lead them out the western side of the forest and they could get a ride the hell out of there.

As long as they were as far into this forest as he thought. They had been going for hours, after all. They had to be deep enough into the woods that the helicopter wouldn't find them tomorrow. Had to be.

Shamus watched the water move, watched small bits of grass and debris float over the rocks and swirl before slipping to the center of the current and flowing downstream. It was a calming sight, an entrancing sight where he found himself not only focused on the view and sound of the river but the sounds of nature around him. The wind through the trees. The crickets in the distance. The scurry of a squirrel or chipmunk or some other furry little shit he couldn't name.

The scene lulled him into deeper thoughts, where he began to see himself in another place, a cabin someplace out in these woods. A log building where he saw himself resting. It was a place where he could be at home, relaxing while this whole thing blew over. He saw himself warm there, full there, his face with a smile and his men at his sides. It was out there; he just had to find it. Maybe if he started walking now, he could make it before dawn? Before the chase started again. He could be—

"*Come*," the wind called.

He took a step, and a hand rested on his shoulder.

"Shamus?" It was Tony. The little shit had the nerve to touch him. He spun and backhanded the kid, sending him hard into the rocky earth. Tony looked up, blood rushing from his rat-faced nose and a split in his lip. "S—sorry. You—you weren't answering."

Perry ran his hands over his bald head, feeling the stubble on the sides and back and wondering how he had been reduced to gathering wood. He wasn't an outdoorsman, not unless you counted burying bodies. He was a city dweller, and he had no idea how you were supposed to *gather firewood.*

He saw some sticks on the ground here and there but no logs. Weren't you supposed to burn logs? He damn sure wasn't a lumberjack and had nothing to chop a tree down with or even cut up the dead ones he was seeing on the ground.

It was like he was sent out here to fail. Or just to make him look stupid. He despised looking stupid.

The breeze whispered as he ducked below a tree for a stick. *"He thinks you're stupid."*

Perry spun. He stared into the surrounding night, hearing the others in the distance as they foraged in their own directions.

He saw no one. But someone had said that, didn't they?

The wind shook a pine cone loose from the tree to his left, and he jumped as it patted the ground.

"Is someone there?" His voice was low. There was no one there. He had to have imagined the voice, and he didn't want anyone to hear him ask. Yet... he had to. Whether it was his disbelief in himself or his distrust for his associates, he had to ask to know for sure. "Hello?"

"Fucking bullshit." He picked up another stick.

The trees rustled. *"Nick hates you,"* the whisper said.

Perry pivoted right and left, his eyes scanning every shadow, every gap between trees, every conceivable place someone could be hiding to mess with him.

This was bullshit. He didn't need this. He could go back east and work for Big Freddy in Tampa. It was warm there, and he wouldn't have to deal with all this nature shit. He wouldn't have to deal with the same three hookers either—they had plenty of broads there, enough to have a different one every night of the week.

"*They're scheming on you,*" the wind said. "*They'll take you out.*"

"That's it." He was done. He had a dozen sticks, small or not, and that would have to be enough. And when this goddamn ordeal was finished, he was hopping on a flight to Florida.

Fuck Shamus. Fuck Nick. Fuck this whole goddamn place.

He stomped back toward the ATVs. His brow furrowed in anger, and the thoughts repeated in his head. *They think I'm stupid. They hate me. They're scheming on me.*

Honey muttered under her breath as she picked up a twig. She wasn't about to lift anything heavy, and she sure as fuck wasn't going to pick up anything dirty. She figured she would wander around for a few minutes before heading back—just long enough for the men to gather what they needed.

The wind blew, and she stopped and hugged her arms close to her chest.

"Fuck," she hissed.

She wasn't supposed to be out here right now. She was supposed to be in a warm cabin with a bag of jewelry, sorting and deciding what to fence and what to keep for herself. She was supposed to be laying low without a care as the rest of the world forgot about the robbery.

Why was she here?

She growled.

She was here because of Stevie. She had kept her mouth shut since the jewelry store, but she knew as well as the rest of their crew it was his goddamn fault. First he screwed up the robbery by starting a gunfight, and then he couldn't handle his own shit and had to stop at that prick Shamus's place. She was here because of Big Steve, because he couldn't pick a getaway car worth a damn. She was here because she had been coasting and hadn't insisted on doing better. That was going to stop now. When they got out of these woods, she was done coasting. She'd get the hell away from all these idiots and get back to the old grift. A little bit of leg could get her to the next state, a little blowjob if she absolutely had to, but she was going her own way.

Beside the next tree, Honey spotted another twig and crouched to pick it up. The wind blew, and something scraped the back of a tree behind her.

Honey wasn't one to be startled, but after the previous twenty-four hours, there was little holding her upright beyond a few minutes of sleep and adrenaline. And the noise alone wasn't the thing—there was a feeling that tickled the back of her neck as it happened, and there wasn't much Honey could have done to stop herself.

She spun, her eyes rushing to focus on the dim woods ahead. She hoped to see nothing, that is, see just a branch against another tree and know that there was nothing to be startled by.

The burning sensation rising in her gut argued. It demanded there was something there, hidden in the gloom. So she stared, hoping to God she was mistaken.

The first tree, black bark, gobs of leaking sap. The second wearing short needles over its tiny branches. Her eyes darted to the next, skipping over the darkness between, and as she settled on what could have been the perfect little Christmas tree, the shadows she had skimmed past moved.

Tiny prickles ran over her entire being as she rotated toward the shadows. Her heart pounded inside her chest as if it were a caged animal struggling for freedom.

The woods seemed lighter now. It was like a shadow had

consumed the gap, and now it was gone. But there couldn't be shadows without something to cause them. Even a kindergartener would know that. Someone had to have been there.

"Hel—*hello?*" Her voice was shaky. It would have been embarrassing if fear wasn't bubbling in her gut. "Is someone there?"

No one answered, and her gaze again bounced from tree to tree, this time scrutinizing the gaps between trunks.

"Who's there?"

Nothing but evergreens and the blackened void—until the darkness in the corner of her eye lapsed again.

"*Shit.*" She spun to get a better look, watched the trees around it. Nothing else moved. Nothing made a sound. Was it—someone—playing with her? "This isn't funny."

There was another scrape behind her, something against wood, and the wind wasn't even blowing.

Honey rotated. Her foot slipped on the layered needles and debris. She teetered and jolted upright. The thing—she didn't know any other way to describe it as it both was and wasn't in front of her. It both had and didn't have a shape. She could see it, yet see through it, and it was completely without form other than the vague outline of a large, bulging man. It was like the outline of some gigantic person, a lumberjack or a pro wrestler, and it was filled with darkness. A shadow of a man with no man there to make it.

Her throat closed as she opened her mouth to scream. The only noise she could muster was the click of her tongue against the back of her palate.

A second passed where she thought she should run, but it seemed planted, like a thought that wasn't her own, like it wanted to chase her, and it was going to kill her regardless, so why not enjoy her fear. She could stand. She could go to it. She could run and find her voice and scream. And no matter her choice, it would have her.

Tears ran down Honey's cheeks. She turned back toward the ATVs, and the twigs dropped from her grip as she burst into a sprint. She darted through the woods, looking back after three steps, convinced it would be right behind her.

It wasn't. It wasn't between the trees where she had seen it. It wasn't chasing after her.

It didn't matter at this moment because she wasn't stopping for shit. Not until she reached the others. Not until there were men there to die first.

15

ANGEL DRIFTED THROUGH THE woods without walking. It was dark, much like her camp, back where her tent and her sleeping body lay. But the darkness didn't bother her, and even in the gloom, she found that she could see—or rather sense—enough to make her way without trouble.

She wasn't sure where she was going. That happened sometimes. She would find herself wandering, drifting in the ether as if carried by the wind. While the real wind couldn't touch her here, there was something, another force, she had come to respect. It showed her things. It allowed her to see things that little girls wouldn't—or couldn't or shouldn't—normally see, like it was trying to teach her or give her some piece of knowledge that a living person needed to know. So, while she wasn't sure what was going to happen tonight, she was confident to explore.

Ahead, Angel heard growling engines that settled then died, then the stern words of a man with an accent. He was their boss, she could tell from the tone alone, and a bad boss from the way he snapped at them. He was tense and angry, as were the others. There were red strands of fear, a frayed web that stretched between them all as he commanded. Then, the others dispersed.

Angel slipped through the brush, wisping over the stream, and she saw him more clearly, the boss, and the backs of the others as they left in search of firewood. When the whispers called to him, she heard them. They spoke in a voice below the rest of the scene before her, in a tone most people only heard when it wanted them to. And she knew something bad was happening here. How bad, she wasn't sure.

She watched him look into the trees, searching for the speaker. He wouldn't see them. She could barely see them as dark, elusive, cloudy shapes hovering in the gloom. She could sense them, though. And while she usually had no fears, no worries around beings like these—they had never been able to touch her, only stare and shriek through mouths that failed to make words, or if they did occupy the same space, they would pass through with only an eerie, cold sensation—these, though, seemed different. As much as she trusted the guiding force that led her here, she questioned whether these entities might hurt her. There was a blackness radiating from them, a dark power that made her very uneasy.

Angel moved to the base of a tree, blending into the energy around its trunk. She pressed up against it as more whispers traveled over the wind.

She didn't like this. She didn't like the words or the ones speaking. She didn't like the feeling as the sounds dripped over her like the drool of a starving dog.

Angel saw it like that in her mind. These things were hungry, and though she didn't think she would like these people—they felt bad, mean—these other things were worse. She didn't want any part of them. She wanted to be back in her tent, back in her sleeping bag, back near Mom—and right now.

She spun to return down the path she'd come from, and freezing cold jolted through her. It was like ice attacking her heart and spreading, and there was no doubt in her mind what had happened. One had seen her.

It was behind her. It was charging at her.

Angel took off. She had no feet to carry her, but she moved across the brush with will alone.

She darted between trees and over a dead log, and she was forced to stop as she came face to face with a woman running toward her. Behind the woman was something *else*.

It wasn't like the others. The others were one and the same while acting like many. They were parts of a single darkness that was hungry. This thing was angry. It was malevolent. It was something that wanted to hurt for its own pleasure.

Angel only saw it for an instant. It was a shadow of a man with no substance—it had left that behind somewhere. What was here was only his essence—dark, bleak, bloodthirsty energy.

The shadow vanished from view, but that didn't mean it was gone. Angel could feel its stare on her chest. Her heart, back in her tent, was pounding. She had to get out of there now. She was done with this walk. They weren't supposed to go this way. She prayed to be back in her head and prayed these things wouldn't follow her—not to Mom and Lins and Kathy and Abby.

She spun to her right, and the first entity was there. Its edges were hazy and erratic, and it was moving in her direction. She turned again and took off into the woods. It was away from her camp, and that was okay. What she needed more than anything was just to get away from all of them, to put some space between herself and those things.

The woods crowded around her. The trees closed in, and the brambles shrouded the ground with tight branches and sharp needles. The boughs of pines and spruces descended as they swept toward her like arms. Behind her, those things neared.

"Go away!" Angel screamed. Her mouth opened and closed back in her tent. "Leave me alone!" She spoke it in this astral place and from her own flesh.

Branches passed through her. She felt the needles scrape her insides. The entities whispered at her, but not words—screeches. They reached, the shadows growing fingers, the haze turning to claws.

Her panic was making the connection stronger. She could feel the nylon of her sleeping bag against her skin. She felt the cool air inside her tent.

Angel stopped in the center of a spruce and focused as the forest moved around her. She clenched her body tight and demanded to be back in her tent.

The change wasn't instant, but it happened before they touched her—she thought, at least. When she opened her eyes, she wasn't so sure.

She wasn't in her tent, but she wasn't in the same place either. It was something more like a regular dream than her usual dreamwalks—or was this a memory?

It was cold, colder than it had been since January. A man in a fur jacket knocked on a wooden door as snow was carried by the wind. It wasn't a regular door like Angel was used to; it was constructed more like a barn door or a gate, with slabs of wood nailed to each other, supported by a central crossbeam. Beside the door, a wood carving hung, a cursive G beside a sleeping bear with a roof and the top of a chimney above them.

Angel puzzled over the man as he waited for someone to answer. His beard was long and bushy and speckled with snow. His mustache was frozen. Snow topped his shoulders and his head, and it blew between him and the door as a latch clinked and scraped, and it opened to the warm, flickering firelight within.

A man stepped into the doorway, and Angel wanted to

scream. She couldn't see his face or his features, but what she saw was more than enough—

She wanted her Betty Bobcat. She wanted Mom or Dad. She wanted someone she trusted to get her out of there and tell her it was all going to be all right.

The shape in the door was all she could make out through the blowing snow and the light inside. She saw his silhouette surrounded by the firelight, and she recognized it. It was the shadow person from the woods. It was the thing that liked to hurt.

"Garret?" the bearded man said.

The shadow man nodded. He wasn't Garret; Angel knew that. His name was Eustace... something.

"Bed for the night?" the bearded man said.

The shadow man spread the door wider, and firelight showed the side of his face as he gestured for his visitor to enter. It was a rough, pitted face. His skin was scarred though closely shaven. His nose was bulbous and his lips were cracked, and his massive girth seemed to move effortlessly.

The bearded man followed, and Angel found herself forced to come with him. She hovered over his shoulder as he closed the door and latched it, then rubbed his hands together to thaw them.

There was a mixture of smells in the room, some that Angel couldn't pick out. What she could discern was cinnamon, baking bread, and body odor. Below it all, there was a scent of something sour, maybe molding; she wasn't sure. Whatever it was, she didn't like it.

"We have some biscuits tonight," the shadow man said. His voice was low and rumbled as he spoke. "Bacon and coffee in the morning."

Beard Man nodded.

"Two bits for the bed, two more for the grub if you wan' it."

"Yup," Beard Man said. He lowered his pack to the floor and took a pouch from inside his jacket. He opened it and showed Shadow Man the inside. It was filled with small, shiny nuggets over a bed of golden powder. "We good?"

"Yessir," Shadow Man said. He pointed to a door on the left side of the cabin. "You're the only roomer tonight, so pick what bed you like. There's wood and a stove in there, so go 'head and start it."

Beard Man nodded and picked up his pack, then he headed toward the door, lumbering but favoring his left side. He stopped. "Biscuits?"

"I'll get 'em. Just go on and get settled."

Something was wrong here. Angel could tell. Yes, it was freezing out and this man needed warmth, but this place—this hotel? She wasn't sure what to call it—was off, and she didn't understand how the bearded man couldn't feel that. There was a fragility in the air. It was a sensation that something was going to break. She felt as if a glass had been dropped, and she was holding her breath while it raced toward the floor. There may have been heat and a bed for this man, but there was no safety here.

The traveler set his pack by the third of six beds. Each was covered in grayish sheets, a thick wool blanket at the foot. Shelves lined the walls with small trinkets: stuffed animals, a jar of white marbles, a tiny painting on a tanned canvas.

He kneeled by the stove, not much more than an old wash bin that had been beaten and folded and made to fit an iron chimney, and he stacked sticks inside. He fished a box of matches from his pocket and lit it as Shadow Man walked in with four biscuits on a tray.

He set the tray on the bed as Beard Man lit the smallest shard of wood and watched the rest crackle and suck the flame into their dry fibers. The traveler sat beside the tray, watching the fire. He lifted a biscuit and raised it to his face.

"No!" Angel screamed. But it seemed only she could hear her voice. Neither man moved as a result.

He placed the biscuit between his lips and bit. His lip curled, and his face contorted in disgust. A glob of wet, rock-hard bread tumbled from his mouth as he turned toward Shadow Man.

Eustace's hand swung from behind his back as his mouth twisted into a wide grin. In his grip was a hammer. It made a wet cracking sound as it met the side of the bearded man's head.

Angel screamed again, though this time she wasn't the only one to hear.

The traveler's eyes rolled back into his head, and his body went limp. It slumped as Eustace recoiled his hammer and brought it down on top of the man's head. Blood arced over the third bed, and Eustace's eyes rose and rested on Angel.

She didn't make another peep. His stare was like a river of ice, and she felt it cut through her and freeze her flesh. She expected him to lunge toward her and grab her. She didn't know how he would since she wasn't there physically, but the logic of that question didn't matter. Terror wrapped around her mind so hard she thought he might be able to do it.

His only action was in his arm.

His stare remained. His grin remained. But the hammer raised and came back down. And again. And he chuckled as blood spattered his face, refusing to take his eyes from Angel's.

"Eustace!" a woman screeched from the other room.

He didn't answer. He only shifted slightly as Beard Man's body slumped onto the bed so he could continue bringing his hammer down on the dead man's skull—though now the tool was over the man's face. Now, as the hammer fell, it was nose and lips and eyeballs being crushed. It was wetness from eyes and mouth that splashed the bed, sprayed the wood stove, and made it sizzle with the rising heat.

"Eustace!" A woman came in screaming. She held a cleaver in her hand, glanced at the mess her husband was making, and then locked eyes with Angel. Florence smiled and licked her lips.

Angel sat up in her tent, tears streaming from her eyes. Lins quietly snored in the sleeping bag beside her. Mom laughed from outside by the fire. Then Ms. Kathy laughed, along with Ms. Abby.

She was safe. It had all been a dream. She knew it wasn't just a dream, but she had to believe that for now. Her dreamwalks were usually real, not that she understood exactly what they were. Yes, she'd had some visions in her dreams that turned out not to be true, but most of the time they were. So this one probably was... she thought. But she couldn't be sure, and she couldn't run outside and cry to Mom about it. She was ten now, after all. She wasn't a kid. She couldn't just go crying to Mom about everything. And she really didn't want to ruin this hike for her—Mom needed it. So, it couldn't be real.

She listened to the laughter. It made her happy. Mom had been so down lately. She tried to hide it from Angel, but Angel knew. And whatever happened after Christmas, when Angel was at her dad's, was the worst of it. There were moments when Mom just started crying, and all Angel wanted to do was fix her. But how?

Angel lay back down and stared at the roof. She forced herself to smile as the next wave of laughter infiltrated the tent.

"It was all a dream," she whispered to herself. "Nothing to

worry about."

She didn't know how many times she repeated it to herself before she fell asleep. She didn't know how badly she would wish that lie was true tomorrow.

123

16

THERE WAS A GRAYNESS to the morning as Wanda broke down her tent and packed her things. The air was dense and the world somewhat less colorful, as if the life around them was being muted.

The morning fire heated the air in a constant ring, but it was too far away to keep back the cold. She flexed her fingers and rubbed her hands together as she attached her tent to her bag, helped Angel do the same, then met the others around the communal flames.

Abby continuously yawned and rubbed her eyes. She stared at the pot of coffee on the side of the fire, waiting patiently for it to boil. Angel and Lins sat across from her, munching on dry cereal and yawning almost in time with Abby. Kathy still lay in her sleeping bag. She was awake but moaning and cursing the sun behind the clouds while covering her eyes.

"Lord Jesus, why'd you let me drink that much?" Kathy moaned.

Abby snickered to herself. The pot bubbled over, and Wanda filled three steel cups, taking one to Kathy.

Kathy sat up and took the cup. "You earned your spot in heaven, girl." She gave a slight nod and stopped as the throbbing inside her head commanded.

"I'll get you some Advil too." Wanda smirked.

While they weren't in a rush, there was a push behind each

of them as they finished coffee and breakfast and loaded their things onto their backs. There was an urge to move on to the next camp, empowered by a feeling that this one wasn't quite right.

Wanda thought it was the lingering fear of the momma bear. For Angel, it was the dream. Kathy and Abby felt a dread associated with the trees around them with no way to describe it other than a general unease telling them to get moving.

None of them understood that they chose the wrong direction when they set off.

The map showed them heading north, the way toward the waterfall. It didn't look right to Wanda. She had been there a dozen times, but she decided to let the map lead—maybe she would learn a new route.

It wasn't north. It was northwest.

Wanda listened to the crunch of debris underfoot. Five pairs of feet on dry needles and twigs, on random dry grasses and weeds. She heard through the silence of their steps that none were talking, and she thought how odd that was. She wanted to say something, to break the quiet, but when she opened her mouth, she found no words. There was something else on her lips instead—the want to moan. It was a rush of grief for the life she had lost, and if she made a single sound, she knew it would come out in sobs.

She couldn't do it. Not with Angel there. And the embarrassment of not being able to keep herself together? What kind of crazy person just breaks out in tears in the middle of a hike?

Her mind betrayed her, showing her images of *him* hovering over her. She smelled the filth and decay as he thrust and heaved sour exhales over her. The helplessness was a tidal wave across her bare chest, and she clamped her mouth shut, her teeth clacking together and her fists clenching.

Abby had thought she was fully awake when they started hiking, but as her steps moved her forward, her mind drifted into the trees. Bough by bough, needle by needle, she found herself remembering fights back in high school. Malcolm had hit on her at lunch, and Tianna, who she had no idea was fucking Malcolm, slapped her in the middle of the hallway on her way to sixth period.

"You fucking bitch! How dare you!" Tianna's earrings were off, and she was ready.

Abby had no idea what was even happening until the burn on her cheek set in, and she saw Malcolm smiling by the lockers. That son of a bitch had set her up.

She pushed the thought away, still feeling the sting on her face, recentering herself in the woods with the smells and the cold and the sounds of the girls around her. Then, the images from College Park a year ago came to mind. The shine of the chrome barrel in her face. The shadow inside it, where fear may have been what drew the picture, but she was sure she could see a bullet in the chamber.

They had only wanted her money, but that fact didn't stop them from appearing in her nightmares night after night for months, even now revisiting her on occasion.

But why that memory was looping in her mind during this hike, she couldn't explain.

Angel saw the shadow man around so many trees. He blinked within the silhouettes of pines and firs. He waved from within the blackness of rocky hollows on the sides of boulders. He was there, watching from cover, and she could feel him, his sight boring into her like a frozen laser.

Lins walked beside Angel as quietly as the rest. She tried not thinking about the faces that hovered over her inside the tent when she awoke during the night, but they refused to leave her mind. They were only kids' faces—some older, some younger—but all of them made her want to cry. To scream at their sadness. If only they had let her, her mom could have rushed in and sent them away—if they were real, that was. Because as much as she knew they were, she didn't want to believe that. She couldn't. Mom had told her a dozen times things like that weren't real, just leftovers from bad dreams. She had to believe that, even if she couldn't shake their faces from her thoughts. Even if, more than anything, she wanted to go home and hide under her sheets.

The wind picked up, and the group offered a collective shiver. They kept hiking in the wrong direction, rising in elevation as the sky darkened and the distant clouds rumbled.

For Shamus, the night was less a continuous streak of uninterrupted darkness than it was a cold, stuttered series of moments where his eyes were closed, then open, then closed again, each iteration showing a lighter and lighter sky.

The group of fleeing fugitives had no tents and no sleeping bags. They had no blankets other than a few thin, aluminum foil-like emergency blankets that were packed in Shamus's go bag, which he reluctantly lent to the others. It was a night of sitting on the cold, hard ground, feeding the fire with handfuls of twigs at a time, and praying morning and the sun's light would bring enough warmth to raise their temperatures above freezing.

After false dawn gave way to the real thing through gray, overcast fog, and Shamus could no longer force his eyes to stay closed, he had no choice but to stretch, grumble, and begin kicking the others, rousing them from their own fitful slumbers.

Shamus begrudgingly shared the few protein bars from his go bag, telling himself they would be out of this forest soon and on their way to Coeur d'Alene for a steak dinner and some good ol' Irish whiskey. They just had to keep moving and find an exit that wasn't covered by the cops.

If he was a man who had regrets, this would have been where he wished they hadn't killed those cops, that they would have found a better way to escape. The pigs weren't going to stop looking for cop killers any time soon. But he wasn't one to walk away from a challenge and definitely wasn't one to want a cop to live. If he could have had the choice, he would have wanted more there to kill. It wasn't often that he had the pleasure.

It didn't make this excursion any easier, though.

With silver blankets folded and packed away, protein bar wrappers charred in the ashes of their fire, and a failed call made to Shamus's contact, they loaded back onto the ATVs. Shamus didn't know why his man wasn't answering, only that he better pick up the next time he called or the man was going to bleed when they met up.

The vehicles started with hesitation. Shamus didn't put much thought into it, but it was odd. The things were only a year or so old, stolen right off a truck bound for bumblefuck central Montana. They barely had a few hours of ride time and were practically full of gas.

He shook his head and led the way toward what he thought was the north exit. It was actually northwest.

The trail grew thinner and less traveled as they went. Brush closed in on their sides, and twists and turns forced Shamus to go slower than he wanted. As the forest grew more dense and the path narrowed, he nearly blew his top when a downed tree blocked their way.

Shamus killed his four-wheeler three feet from the obstacle, and Nick turned off the side-by-side. Shamus got off, and the rest followed, stretching limbs and rubbing their sore asses, all tired and grumbling, all growing more and more irritable by the second.

The forest was packed all around them, foiling Shamus's first thought to just go around. Trees, mature and young, thickets, and dead, decaying trunks made sure the vehicles weren't leaving the trail.

Shamus kneeled, taking in the fallen tree. It had to be three feet thick and fifty feet tall. He'd need either an army or a chainsaw to get the thing out of the way. The ATVs couldn't climb over it. He had a flash of an idea. There was so much debris all around them. That was it.

"All of you." He pointed at his crew and the two newcomers. "We need to build a ramp to get over this. Start searching the woods and bring any logs or sticks you can carry. We'll lay them beside this goddamn tree and make a slope up this side and down the other."

The already worn faces of Nick, Perry, and Tony formed clenched jaws and pinched lips. Stevie shook his head, studying the situation himself as if he could come up with a better plan. Honey rolled her eyes and started walking down the trail the way they had come—Shamus assumed it was another attempt to get out of any work. That bitch was really starting to get on his nerves, no matter how much he liked looking at her ass.

"Before we get started," Shamus told Nick, "let's move the vehicles back, out of the way."

"Yeah, boss." Nick nodded and sat.

Shamus climbed on the four-wheeler and pressed the start button. The starter clicked, and nothing happened. No gears spinning, no spark, no rumble. He checked the key, the starter switch. The LED was lit green. The goddamn thing should have been revving. It's 800ccs should have been rumbling. They weren't. He checked the gas tank, still more than half full. He checked the choke, right where it should have been.

"What the fuck," Shamus mumbled to himself.

"This thing's dead," Nick called from the side-by-side. "I don't get it."

Shamus's fists clenched as he looked back at Nick. The asshole's blank expression made him want to walk over, grab the idiot by that fuzzy mop, and smash his skull into the steering wheel. He had the urge to rub Nick's face up and down one of these fucking trees until the bark took his skin off like a cheese grater. What the hell did he mean, *dead*?

"Try again." Shamus's voice was low, controlled—barely.

Both flipped switches and checked their engines, their gas tanks, and their batteries. The others stood in a circle around them, watching.

As they inspected every item, as each second ticked by without resolution, without the ramp being built, without them making progress in getting the fuck out of these woods, Shamus felt his chest tightening harder and harder.

This wasn't happening. It couldn't be. He'd had bad deals before and had to work them out, but this made no fucking sense whatsoever. Both machines doing this at the same time?

He wanted to lift the four-wheeler over his head and toss it. Instead, he sat, pulled out the sat phone, and pressed power.

The mother fucking thing wouldn't turn on!

Shamus opened the back, took out the battery, re-seated it, and tried again.

His heart pounded. Blood flushed his ears; he could hear it moving around his head. His breathing was almost a roar. He was debating about whose throat he should cram the defective phone down when a whisper overrode every other noise.

"*Come*," it said. It rode on the wind. It called from the other side of the log.

Shamus dropped the phone on the ground and stared up the trail. No one was there. Had he expected there to be? He knew the voice wasn't there as soon as he heard it, but at the same time, he also knew it was real. As much as he could chalk such a thing up to mishearing the wind on some other day, today he didn't have a doubt it was real. He didn't know what it was, but it was real.

And he wanted to follow it.

Shamus stood. The bag of money on his back swayed as he unstrapped the other bag from his ATV and tossed it at Nick. "Carry that." He glanced at the others. "This way."

He climbed over the log and continued up the path. Thunder echoed through the woods.

Angel tried to keep upbeat, but it was getting more challenging as the morning progressed. It was getting colder. It was getting darker. The distant sound of thunder seemed to be moving closer. She knew the rest of her group was getting concerned, but no one seemed to say anything, not until the lightning strike.

A flash of white lit what had gradually grown to resemble a sky near twilight. Angel wasn't sure if it had been the slow darkening of the sky or if some other event was at work here, but the flash was so bright, and the immediate darkness that followed so blinding that she screamed.

It cracked so loudly there was no sound for a solid two seconds after. The hairs on Angel's body stood on end, and she felt a static pull between her body and the ground.

They all screamed.

A branch creaked behind them. There was a crash in the trees, needles rained, more crashed, and one after another, hunks of smoldering and broken limbs rained on the trail floor behind Abby and Kathy.

They screamed again and ran forward. They all ran up the trail. Mom shouted words; so did Kathy. The girls squealed. None of it was clear. It was a strange auditory blur that blended into the lightning's aftermath like a smudge being wiped across a page.

They all stopped a hundred feet up the path. Mom patted Angel down and looked her over. Kathy examined Lins. Abby looked back, breathing heavily.

"Are you okay?" Mom asked.

Angel looked into her eyes. They were fragile eyes. She saw her mother's hurt. She saw a guilt for having brought them here, and before the next words left Mom's mouth, she knew what they would be.

"I think we should head back, guys," Mom said, her gaze still searching over Angel's body as if some new wound would appear out of nowhere.

"I'm okay, Mom," Angel said. She didn't feel like it, but she faked a smile. She didn't want Mom to lead them home out of guilt, even if she knew leaving was the best idea. But it was time to say it. "I think we should leave, though."

Mom stood and checked on Abby, Kathy, and Lins. "What do you guys think?"

"Yeah," Kathy nodded, holding Lins tightly to her belly. "I think that's best."

It was more than this scare, more than the momma bear; this was a gut reaction from the entire forest bearing down on them.

"I don't want to admit it," Abby said, "but I think so too. Honestly, I could have left this morning, but I didn't want to be the sissy from back east ruining the fun."

They all nodded in agreement. They would head back. This just wasn't the right time for this trip. They could return another time. Maybe they'd even go back to Angel's house for hot chocolate for the kids and wine for the adults. That could be fun.

The idea of home brought a smile to Angel's face. The snow that began to fall yanked it away.

<h1 style="text-align:center">17</h1>

WANDA HUFFED. IN MERE minutes, there was a white blanket on the ground. The trail was more of a wish than a real thing as white filled the air and her sight was limited to only a few feet.

She pushed forward, though, as the sky dumped and the path ahead became thicker by the minute.

Wanda checked her phone. Maybe if she couldn't see the trail, the GPS map would still guide her. If there was one good thing about that map, the GPS would have to be it. But as she pressed the power button, nothing happened. She pressed harder. She held it. After a few seconds, an icon appeared of an empty battery.

Shit. She shoved it back in her pocket. She would have to figure this out the old-fashioned way, and hopefully it would work. It had to, right?

She wanted to believe that, that people didn't get stuck and freeze to death in the mountains like they did in the old days, but unfortunately, that wasn't the case. People did go into the wilderness and freeze to death, even in these modern times. Nature didn't care if it was 2024 or 1824. Snow was cold, and cold could kill. And this group was her responsibility. She brought them here. She had to get them out.

Wanda looked back. She saw Angel at her heels, followed by Lins, followed by Kathy. She could barely see Abby, only a flash of her gloves as they swung forward with her stride.

Snow blew down Wanda's shirt and chilled her instantly. She wondered how long they could do this, how long the storm would last. It seemed to have crashed down upon them—maybe it would just stop? She couldn't count on that. She decided for the group, she would lead them as far as she thought was safe, then they would have to pitch a tent, all get in the same one for warmth, and wait it out. Then pray it ended soon.

Wanda's chest burned. She didn't think they had been going that long, but there had to be eight inches on the ground. *So much so fast?* She knew the deeper it got, the more tiring it would be.

Why did she do this? Sure, she had checked the weather before they left; sure, it said overcast, not snow, but she knew you couldn't trust the weather in the mountains. She knew it could switch on a dime.

But this—she couldn't have predicted this.

Images passed through Wanda's mind: Angel frozen beside a tree, her arms wrapped around the child; Lins, blue, encircled by Kathy; Abby frozen solid, her mouth open in the middle of a scream. It was going to happen if she didn't keep her wits.

Maybe it was time to stop and get the tent set up? There were miles to go, and she wasn't even sure they were going in the right direction. She thought she was, but miles in this stuff? The adults might be able to do that, but the kids couldn't. She needed to just admit defeat and do the safest thing.

Wanda stopped. She was about to open her mouth and call to the others when something caught her eye through the white fog. It looked like a fire. Not a full-on blaze, but a twinkling, like a candle.

Surely she could go a little further.

It wasn't a candle, couldn't have been in this weather, but if it was something, some kind of fire or shelter...

She led them onward, wondering. She probably got off the trail. They hadn't passed anyone the way they had come, so if there was fire or shelter ahead, they were definitely off trail. She hoped they were at this point. Shelter and fire were what they needed. Shelter and fire could make the difference in them surviving this storm.

The snow was up to a foot. Every lift of Wanda's boot was heavy. Every swing to put it back down was a chore. She checked on Angel and the others. They waded through it, lumbering, leaning forward and back, each step with visible exhaustion. She prayed the light was real.

But as she moved forward by feet, she only seemed to gain inches toward the flame.

Her head ached. Her chest burned. Her fingers and toes were numb, and her layers were dripping with sweat.

The light flickered, and she thought she could see it behind a pane of foggy glass.

It *was* shelter! It was a structure, and as much as she worried that she was delusional at this point, it had to be real.

"Come on!" Wanda shouted. She waved them all forward. She peeked and saw them moving, and she drove them on. "I see shelter!"

It seemed she was actually gaining on it now. She pushed ahead and moved nearer to the light. It was a warm glow. It was, inviting her with heat and safety. She could feel it on her skin from dozens of yards away.

And then it went out.

A cold shock, harsher than ice, ran down Wanda's spine. It ran into her guts, and she felt instantly sick. Had she been a fool? Had she imagined it all? *No.* It had to have just blown out. She would get there and use her lighter, help whoever was at the shelter by getting it going again. *Yes*. They would make it.

"Almost there!" she called back.

There was a break in the white, and she saw what was ahead. It was a dozen things at once: it was salvation; it was shelter; it was a way out of this storm; and below that, something screamed in the back of her mind—it was death.

Wanda reached back and grabbed Angel by the hand. There was no time for doubt or suspicion, no time to let nagging worry slow her down. The kids were probably already on their way to hypothermia. She and the other adults weren't far behind them.

She saw Kathy's gaze. Kathy had seen it, too, and put a hand on Lins's shoulder, guiding her forward. Abby's face was shrouded in white, but Wanda saw the vague shape of her through the snow.

Cold pressed into Wanda's eyes. They watered, tears rolling over her numbed cheeks. She reached ahead as if the building would vanish if she didn't get her grip on it and hold on. She touched a log, and the shape of what she could see made some sense.

It was old, at least a hundred years old or more. The logs were thick, rough, old trees, and the flat design of the roof ahead was like ones she had seen a hundred times in history books and ghost towns across the state. That made sense as she saw it. There had been no new construction in Custer Falls National Forest since the 1930s other than signs and trail markers. Whatever this place was, it was old. And she was grateful to find it.

No light shined within the window. In fact, nothing at all was visible through the clouded, dirt-smudged pane of glass. There was a tarnished brass handle nailed to the door, though, and Wanda took hold and pushed.

Her gaze passed a carved G and sleeping bear beside the frame, and she watched as the inside unveiled itself.

Everything was as old as she suspected. A wooden table in the far corner. A wood stove on the right. A few chairs on the left, and doors at the far left and right corners. There was an old-time, though likely very expensive for its day, wallpaper on the walls—roses with intertwined vines. Everything was draped in dust, spiderwebs, and graffiti, and each piece of wood was cracked and dried with splinters extending and waiting to be snagged. Other than the obvious visits from teenage vandals, the place could have stood empty for a hundred years based on the level of grime and decay.

But its appearance didn't matter right now. Its dryness and lack of snow and wind did.

Wanda pulled Angel inside, and the rest of the group flowed in behind them. Abby closed the door. It was a tight, squeaky squeeze, the locking mechanism long gone, but the swollen door crunched neatly into its frame.

There was instant quiet. The lack of wind, the cease of snow on their faces, and the absence of crunching frozen earth beneath their feet made their own sounds scream in their ears. Heavy breaths. Angel's jingling bell. A whimper from Lins as she examined the room.

A draft cut across Wanda's cheek, and she spotted a gap in the far wall's logs. She smiled. That was nothing in comparison to what they had just faced, and if they could get through the rest of the storm only dealing with that, it would be a godsend.

The inside was bigger than she expected, but of course, she couldn't see the whole thing through the storm. Her nose was running from the cold, but she could smell a dingy must and assumed animals must use the place for shelter as well. But she didn't see any. In fact, other than a slight trace of graffiti, some beer bottles, and a little bit of trash on the floor, it didn't look like anyone had been there in years. There was even a pile of logs beside the wood stove, as if someone had left the place ready for a storm just like this. She had a thought that made no sense as she approached the wood, eager to start a fire and warm them all up—what if it had been left for them?

The layer of dust on the wood wasn't nearly as thick as the dust on the table and chairs. But that didn't mean anything—it was wood. Dust doesn't cling to all surfaces the same way, right?

"Oh, start a fire!" Lins shouted as she saw where Wanda was walking.

Wanda glanced at the rest. "Yeah. Let's warm it up in here."

Abby examined the furniture, the graffiti, and the trash.

"Thank God we found this place," Kathy said. She came toward Wanda, grinning as she picked up a piece of wood and handed it to Wanda to place in the stove.

Angel was the only one not moving. There was a moment where Wanda worried something serious had happened, that her daughter may have been injured. Angel's eyes were wide, taking in every inch of the cabin. Her mouth was frozen, partially opened. She made no sound.

The door flew open behind her.

Part III

18

S TEVIE'S TEETH CHATTERED UNDER his tight-lipped grimace. He hugged himself, one arm over his chest, the other on top of that. He had thought the day started off horrible, but he had no idea it was going to turn into this. A blizzard. A goddamn blizzard! He wasn't dressed for this. None of them were. Sure, they had jackets, but not winter parkas. No snow boots. No long underwear or even a pair of gloves.

And he was starved. He hadn't felt this hungry in years, maybe ever. His stomach walls were grinding on each other, and the story of the Donner Party eating each other kept recurring in his mind.

He growled to himself, walking behind Honey over a ten-inch-deep snow-covered path. She trembled, hugging herself as well. Nick, Perry, and Shamus were ahead, though he could only really see Perry's back. Tony was behind them all. He thought he could hear Tony weeping, and it made his stomach turn. It was bad enough the little shit was there—Stevie had decided the kid was pretty much worthless—but now he had to listen to this as well. It was disgusting to hear a man sound like that.

Honey turned back and met his gaze, then spun forward again. She wasn't crying, but Stevie could tell she was worried. She had been giving him cold stares and keeping more to herself today, but now that she was scared, he was pretty sure her tune would change. She needed him, after all. He was the man. He was there to protect her from the other four, and if this day got any colder, he might just have to shoot the others and layer their coats on top of himself and Honey. She'd be thankful for that.

He had shifted the rifle to his back quite a bit ago. The cold metal on his hands was freezing, and he was sure if he didn't do something, he was going to get frostbite by keeping them exposed. Luckily, his pants stayed up just fine without a belt, so he used his as a sling for the weapon. But he was starting to wonder how much longer until he would need to swing it around and—

"There." Stevie heard Shamus below the blowing wind. The man's voice ground on his nerves. He didn't know what Shamus thought he saw up there—it was a whiteout. All he knew was that it better be good: an exit from these woods, a vehicle they could use for shelter, something to fucking eat. If it wasn't, he was sure it would be time to swing that rifle around. If nothing else, Stevie was positive there was more food in one of those bags, and he would be happy to relieve Shamus of the money in the other one.

Besides, Stevie was pretty sure Shamus was losing it. As far as he could tell, it wouldn't be long before they had to get rid of him anyway. Ever since the vehicles died, there was this strange look in his eyes—like he was staring at something just beyond the rest of them, just out of reach, and he was the only one who could see it.

Stevie had seen that look before, but it was on a job in St Louis, a warehouse robbery. They'd gotten inside, loaded the trucks with printers and TVs and a bunch of computer shit that he couldn't tell you what they did, but was definitely worth a hefty pile of cash. That was when Scott heard noises from the other side of the warehouse and swore it was a security guard they had missed. Maybe he was right, maybe he wasn't. When he started being weird and yelling, Dad dropped him on the pile of dead guards by the loading dock. Stevie was happy to do the same to Shamus, but he knew he better be ready to do the others at the same time.

"Fuck yeah." That was Perry. Now Stevie was getting interested. What was making them so excited up there? What had they found?

The pace at the front of the line increased. Honey followed, then said, "Yes!" She glanced at Stevie and pointed forward. "Look."

He could make out a wall of wooden logs through the snow.

Angel screamed.

Wanda watched as snow and wind rushed into the cabin ahead of five men and one woman. All the men were armed, and all their faces were frozen and angry.

Wanda grabbed Angel and pulled her back. Kathy grabbed Lins by the shoulders and jerked her close. Abby backed against the far wall.

Thoughts rushed through Wanda's head. What did these people want? She had yet to replace her gun since her rapist stole it. Even if she had one, this group had overwhelming numbers. Was there a back door to this cabin? Would she be fast enough to make it before they decided to fire? If they made it outside, how far could they get in this blizzard? They had already tried that once.

The one in front, a huge man, pointed at the wood stove, then to Kathy. "What are you waiting for?" His accent was distinctly Irish, and he raised his gun as he spoke. "Let's get a fire going in here."

Kathy just stood, watching, saying and doing nothing, either too scared or confused to move.

Lins looked up at her mom. Her eyes squinted, her fingers clenched into balls. "Mom, start the fire."

The last one in the door slammed it shut. The entire cabin echoed with the thud.

"I asked you to start the fire." The big man glanced at Wanda, Angel, Abby, and back to Kathy. His gun followed his eyes from person to person. "I won't ask again."

Abby, hands up, walked to the wood stove. She unlatched and opened the door, then not knowing what to do next, she placed a hand on Kathy's shoulder. She had seen these things in Westerns and the odd home-improvement show on TV but had never used one. She felt the adrenaline rushing and was able to move—shaking, but able—and hoped to God she could keep the guy from firing. But goddammit, she needed some directions. "Help me out here, girl." She begged with her eyes. "Show me what to do."

Wanda backed toward her friends, pulling Angel along. Two of the intruders leaned against the wall and watched. One smirked. The woman gazed around the room, locked onto a chair, and strutted toward it.

"Y-yeah," Kathy said.

Wanda pulled Lins from Kathy and guided both kids behind her. Kathy dug into the woodpile and transferred four or five pieces into the stove, arranging them something like a lean-to before pulling a lighter from her pocket and setting the corner of the smallest piece ablaze. It was so dry, flames spread instantly.

Kathy and Abby gave each other a nod then turned to the large man for approval. He was nodding also as he raised the pistol higher, aimed, and blasted a hole through Kathy's right eye.

The organ didn't seem so much to explode as it did implode. The socket became a tunnel, and the rear of Kathy's head gushed in an instant spray of flesh over the ancient wooden walls, floor, and stove.

The room was immediately frozen in time as Kathy stood there, not knowing what had happened. Her body drifted down, her good eye finding Wanda. No words came out—that part of her brain no longer worked—but there was a solid lock onto her friend's gaze before every part of Kathy lost control and flopped against the dust and dry lumber.

That gaze froze in Wanda's mind even after passing. Within it, there had been shock. There had been sadness. There was a message attached of pain and grief and a bundle of cries for help. Help for her, as if she wasn't irrevocably doomed. Help for Lins—the girl was Wanda's responsibility now, without a single word being uttered. All of these thoughts were instantaneous and took an eternity to ponder as Kathy's body went limp and settled.

The room was still, silent for that eternity. Wanda knew she was about to burst into tears. It was coming, and she had to hold it back.

The new arrivals watched the girls as if eager to see their reactions. Wanda, Angel, Abby, and Lins held in place, praying this wasn't real and too scared to move. It was Lins who spoke first as she rushed from behind Wanda. She screamed as she kneeled and reached for her dead mother.

Abby backed out of the way. She didn't know what else to do. Wanda went after Lins, with one hand on Angel, pulling her along. She knew she wouldn't get there in time.

Lins grabbed her mother's arm. Her scream was now a wail, and her eyes were pumping tears. Blood gushed from Kathy's eye as Lins leaned closer to her mother's face, determined to get a response.

She shook her mother. "Mom! Wake up!" Waves of blood fell from the back of Kathy's head and leaked through the cracks in the floorboards.

Wanda took Lins by the arm and pulled her away. For a moment, Lins refused to release her mother, and the body lifted, flopped, and a gasping, burping sound erupted from her mouth. Lins screamed and released, then buried her head in Wanda's chest.

The laughing started small but then bellowed from three of the men in the back. The shooter didn't laugh. He just watched. He waited for a gap in Lins's screams while pivoting his pistol from one female to another. Then he spoke.

"This is what happens when I have to wait. I asked twice. You all saw it. I expect your cooperation in the future."

Again, Wanda pushed the children behind her. She couldn't help glancing down at her friend. But still, she didn't cry. Not yet.

"We'll cooperate," Wanda said. "We'll cooperate."

"Y-yeah," Abby said. "We'll cooperate."

The large man seemed to chuckle to himself, though the look on his face was not jovial. It was absent, and Wanda didn't want to see his attention fully return.

He pointed to the door on the left as if he knew what was in there. "Perry, Nick, take the bags and tie up the girls in there."

Two of the laughing men looked at each other, then stormed on Wanda and Abby. They ripped the packs from their backs, dropped them on the floor, and shoved the girls toward the door.

Wanda, Abby, Angel, and Lins moved without speaking. Angel and Lins cried quietly. Abby was tense, her feet moving as she was told to, her eyes darting from the floor to their captors' guns.

Wanda watched the kids. Her breathing was rushed; she wanted to react decisively, to fight back—but the kids... Lins had lost her mother. What would Angel do if she lost hers? What would they do to the kids if she wasn't there to stand up for them, to lead them out of this?

Her heart was a thudding drum in her chest, but Wanda had to keep control. So she obeyed.

She followed instructions as the men sat them on the floor in front of hundred-year-old rotting beds. They ripped the blankets and sheets into shredded, makeshift rope and tied them up. She was patient as they finished. Her heart slowed, and electrifying fear crept over her. It chilled her beneath her skin as they backed out of the room and closed the door. It warned her that she may have been better off dead—they all may have been.

When the tears came, they were a mix of terror for her daughter and friends and hate for herself. This was all her fault. The evil from West Hemlock had followed her, and she had led people she loved right into its grasp.

There was a sliding, clawing sound in the wall between this room and the main one. There were eyes on her, on them all. She noticed none of it through her tears.

19

STEVIE WASN'T SURE WHAT to think about this. Dead woman on the floor, okay. It was a nice shot, he'd give Shamus that, and it may have helped get the message through to the others that he was in charge, but right in the middle of the room? With the snow blowing and the temperature dropping the way it had been, and the police on them (chopper and all), who knew how long they would have to hide here—with the floor soaked in blood.

He wasn't cleaning that shit up. That was for sure.

A draft blew across Stevie's neck, urging him forward. He walked, examining the room.

Old, old shit. Decaying everywhere. Every piece of wood seemed to be splintering. Every fabric was covered in holes. Every surface was layered with dust.

He brushed by the table, and a wave of nausea passed over him. It felt colder there, and he had to look back and see if the fire had gone out. Not that the flames had done much to heat the room in the few minutes since they had been lit, but until he stepped here, he had felt them going. Here though, it was like a vortex existed, sucking the heat from his body.

Stevie shivered and stepped past the table. It must have been another draft, a hole in the roof, something. He moved on.

On the right wall, he approached a closed door. He reached for the handle, and the brass, like the table, seemed to radiate cold.

Whatever, he told himself and lifted the latch, pushing the door open.

Behind him, the other door shut. Nick and Perry were back in the main room. They picked up the girls' bags and started dumping the contents onto the floor. Honey and Tony had moved over to the stove and were hovering their hands above the warming metal.

Shamus stood over the dead woman. He seemed to be staring into her deflated eye.

Stevie shook his head and continued into the next room.

The final space of the three-room cabin was darker than the rest. There was no window and no fire. There were no holes in the wall for light to pass, which seemed odd since it felt even colder than the outside. He expected it should be snowing in here, or coated in ice, some frozen hellscape—but as he took out his lighter and pack of cigarettes (noting to himself he only had two left) and set the smoke ablaze, he saw no frozen hell.

What he saw looked like it had been taken from some exhibit in a regional museum on settler life.

He puffed and held the lighter's flame out to guide his way.

There was another wood stove with a pile of wood ready to burn. He saw a large bed in the corner of the room. There was something odd about it that he couldn't place. The bedding didn't look like the ripped and moth-eaten fabrics in the other room. It was almost like there was some kind of leather over it, and though everything in the main room had looked decayed, he was discovering that other than a layer of dust, every item in this room was preserved like a time capsule.

He spotted an oil lamp on the table beside the bed and lit it. It burned with an odd smell, almost like someone was cooking with lard.

There were paintings on the walls. They were crude—home-made—and the canvas shined along with the dark, muted pallet of reds, browns, and grays. They depicted scenes in the mountains, creatures Stevie didn't recognize, and large bonfires. If he didn't know any better, he would have thought they were depictions of Hell. But that didn't make sense. People back—it occurred to him that he didn't know when this place was used, but regardless, they didn't have devil worshipers back then like they did today.

Beside the stove, Stevie found cookery, another table, and a series of shelves stacked with jars. He couldn't tell what was in the jars, but he assumed it was rations for whoever used to live here, food he was sure wasn't good anymore.

Still, though. He felt his stomach growl. With the action in the other room, he had momentarily forgotten how hungry he was. The stuff in those jars was dark, a deep brown in the lantern light, but some part of him wanted to twist the tops off and dig in.

"No." He huffed and looked away.

Another glance at the bed. The blanket was definitely leather. How odd. Who sleeps with a leather blanket?

Above the headboard, there was something hanging that reminded him of a dreamcatcher, though this was made of bones and shaped unlike any dreamcatcher he had ever seen.

There was a tall dresser topped with photos. He gladly walked from the pantry and studied the images. One was an elderly couple standing outside of what he thought was this cabin. The woman was shriveled and bony. The man held a shotgun in one hand and what Stevie assumed was a pelt of some kind in the other. He somehow knew the couple had built this place. The next photo was of a woman and a large man with a kid between them. The kid leaned on the woman, his eyes closed.

"Why didn't they wake him for the picture?"

The woman had dark, distant eyes. She was somewhat pretty, though a bit plump and mean looking for his taste. The man was a monster of a fellow. He could have been twice her size if they were standing by the way the photo looked. It was then that two things caught Stevie's attention. One, there was wallpaper on the walls, some kind of roses with intertwined vines, and he was sure he had seen that before. In the other room—this photo was taken here. Two, as the expressions on their faces and the position of the boy sank in, it became apparent what he was looking at wasn't a family portrait—it was a death photo.

Stevie unconsciously took a step backward. He stared at the image of the child, and a sadness fell over him. It was as if he could feel what that mother was feeling. It was like her dark eyes were peering into him, and the despair was drilling into his mind.

She was telling him things. This was her second child. She had lost (given up, maybe?) the first. This was one she was desperately hoping to keep, and yet she couldn't. And below that sadness was anger. Below that anger was hatred. She deserved better. She was promised—

He shook his head and lost it. *Weird ideas...*

The sensation had been bizarre. He wasn't one to sympathize with people. His attitude was always *better you than me*. So why now—why this? Was it hunger?

He glanced at the man. A wave of rage flowed over him. He wanted to pick up the dresser and throw it across the room. He wanted to smash the jars and burn down the cabin. The rage was so blinding that as he looked around, he found he was no longer in the darkened bedroom of the lonely cabin.

He was there, standing in the main room, the wallpaper new, the fire blazing, the couple and their dead child in front of him on the couch, and around him—he had seen nothing like it before.

He was spinning, taking it all in.

Piles, more than he could count, mounds of blood-soaked bodies lay around the room. And not just bodies. These were naked, opened, and butchered. Skin was missing. Organs had been removed and placed in their own heaps by the stove—a stack for livers, one for hearts, a gleaming mound of snake-like intestines.

This was not a home. This was a slaughterhouse. This was a factory for human meat, and he was standing over the bloody killing room floor.

Stevie's gaze fell upon the couple. Their eyes were focused on him, and for the first time in his life, he felt what his own victims must have felt: he was prey. Both of their eyes burned into him, and he felt both of their emotions at once. He was sad, he was angry—and as the dead child lifted its head and opened its eyes, its empty, black eyes—fear crashed through his being.

As if they didn't even exist, Stevie's legs failed him and he dropped to the floor. The hard, dusty bedroom wood knocked on the back of his head, and the lantern's light flickered across the room.

He was back, but it didn't feel like it. He spotted the pictures on the dresser and scurried across the floor. It was all a delusion. Hunger and cold and fear, they had let his mind run away with itself—that was the logical answer to what he had just seen, but... even that didn't make sense.

His eyes remained on the photo while keeping it out of focus, refusing to let the image back in, but it was already there. He may have been back, but those people were still in his mind. The sadness, the rage, the fear, the need for motherhood, and the hunger for revenge; they all danced below his thoughts. They ran through his insides like slithering snakes within his organs. He could feel the disease of their emotions squirming through him, and as he rose to his feet and ran toward the door, he wanted nothing more than to get the hell out of this cabin.

He didn't care if outside was death by cold. He was ready to embrace that if it meant getting out of here.

Stevie grabbed the door handle and yanked it open. He burst into the next room and ran toward the exit.

<h1 style="text-align:center">20</h1>

Detective Mark Rand watched from the Laurel Trailhead command point as the search helicopter passed overhead for the third time that day. For the third time, he was confused and frustrated about why this was taking so goddamn long.

Custer Falls National Forest was big, thousands of acres big, but it wasn't Yellowstone big. It was a cold day, by no means the coldest day of the year but cold enough that this group of criminals should light up like Christmas trees under the search copter's infrared cameras.

But no.

They had spotted hundreds of deer and elk, enough that Rand was ready to change his hunting plans for next season. They had seen a few dozen bear families, both black bear and grizzly. It was like the entire forest had been abandoned by humans—other than the vehicles.

With the last pass, the Search and Rescue flight had found the fugitives' ATVs. A small CSI team was getting prepped to head out there and confirm it was them, and the search chopper was supposed to do another widening loop from that spot. After the last one, though, Rand was growing more irritated by the minute. It was a half-dozen fugitives, after all—not one or two, not a couple that could easily duck behind a tree or below a log—they should have spotted them by now.

A park ranger who had been pulled into the operation suggested they could be hiding out in one of the hundreds of undocumented caves in the area. That would have kept them out of the chopper's view. Rand doubted it—these guys were thugs, not mountain men. He didn't expect them to be able to hide out in such a place for more than a few hours before getting back on the run.

So why hadn't the chopper spotted them?

Rand stared into the overcast sky, wishing he had a beer. After dealing with this shit, after the bodies yesterday, after a lack of progress, his mouth was so dry. It wasn't a need; he just really wanted it. Ever since Janeen was gone, it had become a habit. Bad day, tough case, dreamless night (or worse, one with dreams), have a beer. But that's what people did, right? They dealt with their problems in whatever way they were able to. He was no different. Not as long as he could wait until quitting time. Which he did, most days.

If he wasn't on the edge of the forest with an array of cops and agencies surrounding him, today would have been one of those exceptions. As it was, there were state troopers, his fellow city officers, county cops, rangers, the state CSI team, and even a few FBI guys in suits. He couldn't walk fifteen feet in any direction without walking into someone chomping at the bit to get these fugitives.

It was the standing around and waiting. He wasn't built for that. He needed to do something, to be more involved.

He scanned the area, debating. Uniforms chatted far to the right; state guys and liaisons from the FBI drank coffee outside an old army tent someone had brought from their cub scout pack to use as a command center. Local paper and radio outlets chatted behind the barricade in the road.

Rand's fingers flexed and his jaw clenched, until he heard a bark.

Officer Andrew Marshall was far on the right side of the parking area, a ball in hand and his K9 partner, Ivan, a six-year-old German Shepard, panting in front of him. Ivan's face was hard while concentrating on the red rubber sphere as Marshall cranked back his arm and rocketed the ball into the adjacent field.

Ivan shot like a bullet between the top and middle beams of a wooden rail fence, swallowed into the tall brown grasses. It was mere seconds before he came back through, his eyes proud and his tail wagging, red rubber wet and glossy between his jaws.

Rand nodded to himself and marched over to the officer.

Ivan dropped the ball at Marshall's feet, sat pretty, and stared into Marshall's eyes, waiting.

Marshall bent down and grabbed the ball. He was about to crank his arm back again as the crunch of gravel under Rand's shoes caught his ear. He turned. Ivan's eyes kept focus on the ball.

"Detective." Marshall let the ball rip across the field, and Ivan became a blur.

"Marshall, you look busy."

Marshall smirked. "I do what they tell me."

They both watched the grass part as Ivan sharked his way through the stalks, then returned victoriously.

"I'm making a trip into the park following the CSI team," Rand said.

Marshall picked up the ball at his feet. "Yeah?"

"I want you and your partner to join us. See if we can find a trail."

Marshall looked around, pausing on the meeting of state and FBI agents. "They in on this?"

"I'm told they have their own tracking team coming over from Missoula, but that'll be another hour. After losing four officers yesterday, I don't think waiting is the appropriate response."

Marshall gazed into the field, ball in hand, then glanced at the woods. "I was on a bowling team with Braden and McNeil. Played poker with them" He tossed the ball. The throw lacked speed and distance compared to the last two. "They didn't deserve that. Neither did their families."

They both stared quietly into the tall grass. Ivan returned and waited patiently as Marshall hesitated before retrieving the toy.

"We could get reprimanded for this," Marshall said.

"We could."

Marshall chewed on his lip for a moment. "We couldn't—if we went—follow the CSI guys."

"No?" Rand's brow furrowed.

"They'd stop us—either that or report us. And they wouldn't let us close enough to anything to let Ivan catch the scent—not until they were done with their tweezers and cameras and test tubes. We'd need to beat them there."

"Yeah?"

There was silence between them. Ivan whined softly, his gaze fixated on the ball. Gears turned, and the overcast sky brightened for a few seconds before returning to the ominous gray it had been all morning.

Marshall spoke firmly yet softly. "Let's go by my place. I'm only about three miles from here. We can grab my four-wheelers and head in from Rodger's Trailhead. If we're quick, we should beat them. Those guys aren't familiar enough with these woods; they're from Helena, for fuck's sake."

"You sure about this?"

Marshall led Ivan to his vehicle and opened the rear door. Ivan hopped in and waited patiently. "Give me two minutes before you follow."

21

PERRY RAN HIS COLD fingers over his bald head. The room was slowly warming, but not enough to thaw his digits just yet, and not enough to make this fucked up day more normal.

He scanned over the items they had dumped on the floor and immediately locked onto a bag of Cheetos and an unopened fifth of whiskey.

"Jackpot." He grabbed the whiskey.

Nick scooped up the snack. "Boss, look."

Shamus didn't turn. His gaze was on the bloody floor, the crimson fluid soaking into the wood and leaking through the floorboard cracks. Tony lifted the woman, scooping his hands under her armpits and dragging her to the front door.

"Pass it around," Shamus said. His voice was low and wet. "Keep searching."

Perry twisted off the whiskey's cap, wrapped his lips around the opening, and upended the bottle over his mouth. Four fast gulps, and he sucked in a lungful of air and breathed out a little bit of unease.

"Oh, yeah. That's better." He traded Nick the bottle for the Cheetos and ripped them open. The smell made his mouth water, and before he knew it, he had a jaw full of snacks. Honey drifted over from the fire, sliding her hand in the bag for her own portion.

Nick gasped, three gulps down, and the three of them

watched Tony open the door and drag the woman's corpse into the blizzard.

"Close the fucking door," Perry shouted. Tony hadn't even pulled the lady's legs through, but snow and cold were racing in, and goddamn if Perry hadn't dealt with enough cold.

Tony dropped the corpse right outside the door and raced back in. He slammed it shut, shivering, and zeroed in on the snacks.

"Yes." Tony's hand led the way to the bag. He was about to seize a handful when Perry snatched the Cheetos away.

"Anything with cheese, huh?" Perry held the bag high, as if he was playing keep-away from the nerdy kid on the playground.

"Fuck you," Tony snapped. He didn't reach. He wasn't about to give Perry that satisfaction.

Perry smirked with the left half of his mouth and lowered the bag for Tony to reach. He chuckled and went back to the pile of supplies.

"Shit, look at this." Perry kicked a stack of garments over, revealing a dozen plastic packages of dehydrated food. "They got lasagna, oatmeal, some kind of meat macaroni—all kinds of shit. We could hide out here for like a week with this shit."

"Shit," Honey said, her words muffled from the mashed glob of food in her mouth.

Nick leaned in and came back with one of the packages. He skimmed over the directions. "Needs water." He scanned the cabin. "Ain't no water in here."

"What?" Perry looked around to verify. "The fuck?"

"I don't think this place has indoor plumbing," Honey said, and took another handful from the bag.

"Shit."

"Snow," Tony said. "We could melt snow for the water."

Honey smiled at him. "Good idea."

Perry rolled his eyes and went back to the pile.

An ear-piercing scream blasted from the right corner of the room. It was somewhere between the sound of terror and madness. Perry barely had time to recognize that douchebag Stevie's face as the howling bastard burst through the bedroom door and crossed the room, headed for the front door.

Shamus spoke. It wasn't a scream, didn't even sound loud enough to be heard over the manic idiot, but they all caught it. "Stop him."

Honey stood motionless. All she could do was watch, her face barely registering the shock from seeing Stevie's petrified expression. Tony crunched on a Cheeto, his eyes glued to the action. Perry moved, but he was way too slow and nowhere near Stevie as he darted past. Nick somehow seized one of the rifles and swung it as Stevie's hand grasped the door handle.

There was a crack, and Stevie collapsed. Honey bit her lip and watched the men surround him.

"Put him with the others," Shamus said. He was finally looking at the rest of the gang, and his demeanor had completely changed. He wasn't dry and detached. He was locked in on each and every person in the room. One at a time, he checked in, eyes secured on theirs, making sure they knew he was there. The sides of his lips curled into a grin as if the world was suddenly a sunny place and he was ready to catch the rays.

"He just needs to settle in," Shamus said. "Make him comfortable with the ladies."

"Yeah, boss," Perry and Nick said in unison. Neither was sure what the boss's change in mood was all about, but there was no second-guessing him. Nick took Stevie's legs, Perry his arms, and they lifted him like a sack of meat, like any other job they would perform for the boss.

It took all Angel had inside herself not to scream. This place—it was like she had been dropped into Hell. Not that she knew what that would be like, but she was sure it couldn't be worse than what was before her.

The others sat in it. They smeared it around, and it soaked their clothes, and though they were scared for their lives, they didn't react. Angel was used to that on the city streets and at school. People didn't react to what they couldn't see.

No one was bothered when they walked through the blood-stained floor in the entryway of North Custer Falls Elementary School. They stepped on Joanne every day and tracked her blood across the entryway and down the halls. Feet dripping and squeaking. Into their classrooms. On their shoes and, god forbid, their bags if they paused in the front of the building and set their bookbag down to talk.

On the streets and avenues of Custer Falls, tires were streaked with blood. It was never fully cleaned from the roads; the rain never washed it all away. The dead writhed in the roads, bleeding, victims of accidents, hit and runs, and bicycle collisions. She had seen a one-legged body by the old mill that wasn't much more than a skeleton with eyes and rotting muscle—it was in a constant state of crawling though it never seemed to move. She was happy they rarely traveled to that side of town.

But nothing she had seen could have prepared her for this room.

The ceiling dripped red. The beams above were drenched, hunks of flesh glued to the splintery pine. The walls were pained with layer over layer of crimson fans that, in any other color or medium, may have looked lovely, but here they told of a splatter-fueled past that refused to let go.

The beds were dripping. Angel could tell without touching. They were blood-soaked sponges, waiting to paint, waiting to seep into anything that came close to them.

But maybe worse than anywhere else in the room was where Angel, Mom, Abby, and Lins were forced to be: the floor. A puddle reached from the bottom of the door across the room, below her rump, and lapped the walls with any slight movement. Crumbs of flesh bulged from below the scarlet murk. Chips of bone. Fragments of limbs, fingers, organs. Clumps of hair. Roots of teeth. The image of a red-filled blender occurred to her.

She could have puked from that alone, but holding her still and refusing to let Angel go were the stares of more eyes than she could count.

People who were no longer people hugged the walls. They sat on the beds. They were plastered to the ceilings. One sat on the wood stove. They sat in rows on the floor, several near her mother and friends.

None of them were whole; all of them had been mutilated in some way, and they all stared at her. Adults, children, babies. So many that, as strange as it sounded, Angel felt like they were sucking away all the room's oxygen—that there was none left for her, that at any moment...

Spots filled her vision.

"Baby?" Mom was looking at her. Her face was broken between tears and worry as she pulled at the strips of bedding around her wrists. "Angel? Are you okay?"

There were no words in Angel's mind, only an influx of pressure and a lack of understanding as the colors faded and lights flashed.

"Angel!"

Her eyes fell shut.

Abby could tell Angel was barely holding on from the moment they entered this place, but the look on her face now—it was beyond fear. It wasn't a fact that she was proud of, but Abby always thought she had done well when her life was threatened. It was something she had learned early in life, when she was five and she and her mother were carjacked on their way home from Lenox Square. She didn't cry. She didn't wet herself or scream. Mom grabbed her hand and pulled her from the car as the men with guns jumped in and took off.

When she was in high school and dragged by friends to the south side of Atlanta to buy some Molly for a party, she didn't make a peep when the robbery happened. She handed over her money, her heart beating like an electro song on fast forward. Sure, later that night she had cornered Dwayne Meyers in the bathroom and forced him to sit on the edge of the tub as she went down on him and then sat on it, but she refused to believe that was in any way a reaction to that event. She had taken control of her feelings in that robbery and her body at that party. That was again what she had done in the other room.

But in Angel's short life, Abby had doubts the girl had ever been confronted with such stress, let alone had to see a person she knew shot.

Jesus, the blood.

And then there was Lins. The girl had lost her mother right in front of her and, since then had only stared at the floor and wept quietly. She wanted to hug the child and comfort her. She wanted to tell her something that would make this feel better, but what was there?

The fact was, none of them had anything to say. Between tears, fear, and shock, no one had opened their mouths much beyond heavy breathing and Wanda trying to get Angel to respond.

Wanda pulled at her bonds. They creaked and made tiny tearing sounds, but they weren't letting go.

Abby had to accept that whatever this was, whatever their captors wanted, they were in this for the long haul. She was going to have to wait and see what happened next. And when the time came, she would have to be ready.

A scream penetrated the wall, followed by a thud. The door flew open, and two goons carried in an unconscious third. They dropped their cargo by the farthest bed and tied him to the frame the same way they had Abby and the others.

"Why are you doing this?" Wanda asked. Her voice was calm and non-threatening.

They didn't answer.

"We can leave. We don't want any trouble. We were just trying to get out of the storm."

The bald one looked at her with an indifferent gaze. "Shut up." He glanced at Lins, still crying, still looking down, and averted his eyes as quickly as he could.

"That's it," the other man said, running his hand through his wild hair. "He's good."

The one with hair walked by each female, grabbing their restraints and double-checking the tightness. Lins whimpered, and he rolled his eyes. He was the first one out of the room.

The bald one looked them over as he stood by the door. "I'm not going to lie to you and tell you that you'll be okay. You're going to die in here. Unfortunately, that's just how it is."

"The fuck'd you say that for?" the other said from outside the door.

"It's the truth." He stepped out, pulling the door shut.

"Fucking idiot."

"Fuck you."

The door ground closed inside its frame, and a new wave of shivers crawled over Abby. They admitted it. How could they... They said they were going to kill them. Every time she had been in danger, every time she'd lived through something, she had never even thought that she could die. It just wasn't a possibility, not as long as she kept her wits and behaved rationally.

But this? To be told specifically that they were going to kill her? And after they'd already killed Kathy.

Her entire body trembled. She wanted to believe it was the cold, but it wasn't.

22

E VER SINCE THE ENGINES stopped, since the snow began to fall, a tingling sensation had been growing in Shamus's chest. It was fuzzy, something like a tickle, except when it wasn't. When he shot the woman, it wasn't tickling—it was throbbing, enticing, spiking his veins in a way that reminded him of doing blow back in the 90s. Once she was gone, though, it settled as if an orgasm had passed and his entire being needed to rest. Now, it was back to a tickle, and it brushed against his back, urging him toward the bedroom on the right.

"I'm going to rest," he told the others. "Don't bother me."

"Yeah, boss," Nick and then Perry said.

"Okay," Tony muttered, digging through the provisions on the floor.

Honey was back by the fire. She said nothing, but her expression told Shamus she was thinking, gauging the place and him, and figuring out her plan. She had said nothing when her man went down, which was as he'd expected. She was going to play it cool. She knew how things worked. But what she would try later, he wasn't quite sure of.

It didn't matter, though, because they'd all be dead eventually.

He grunted and passed into the room, tugging the door shut behind him. The lantern was still lit and flickered across a room that felt like home way more than it should have.

Shamus dropped his bags at the foot of the bed and looked at the photos on the dresser. They made him smile. It was like the mom and dad he wished he'd had. Then, the dead grandparents who deserved what they got.

He glanced at the floorboards and chuckled, then returned to the bed. He peeled back the leather blanket and the human-hair-stuffed quilt below. He dropped his shoes on the floor, stripped naked, and slid beneath the covers. His breath fogged above him, and he watched it disappear into nothing.

He was home. As the walls' scratching and tapping slithering sounds filled his ears, he closed his eyes with a smile.

Summer in these mountains was supposed to be tame; at least, that was what Samuel and Marie-Beth Arlen had been told. That was why they had chosen this time and this path to go west. Some had told them they should go through Colorado, that the passes were easier, especially for a family of four with eight orphans in tow, but Samuel made the choice to come through Montana on their way to California.

"There's less savages and more beautiful country," he had said. "The orphans'll never get to see something like it again once they find families in California."

Marie-Beth didn't like the idea. There were trains through Colorado now, with barely any trouble with the savages and few robberies these days. It would have been safer, in her mind, and so much faster. But Samuel made the decisions, and that was that. Even when the claims of temperate summer weather proved distinctly unreliable.

It was only a breeze when they followed the path into the woods. Rain didn't start patting lightly on the wagon's roof until the second day, once they had packed up camp and went on their way ever higher into the mountains. Then, the wind turned malignant, ripping their wagon's sides, and the rain turned to sheets of snow. They tried to move on, but Samuel proved useless at determining direction.

They thought they were saved when they came across the lodge.

Maire-Beth grabbed Samuel's arm when she spotted the flickering lantern in the window. "There! There!"

"I see it!" Samuel shouted.

Under the ripped wagon roof, Marie-Beth pulled the snow-covered blanket tightly over John and Daniel, their sons, and called to the orphans farther back. "We found a place."

They said nothing. They had learned not to speak without there being a question. The group of four- to ten-year-olds simply huddled under their horse blankets, snug against each other.

Samuel stopped the wagon in front of the door. He paused for a moment before getting down from his seat. As much as he knew they needed to get indoors, out of this cold, there was a hesitation in his belly. It was a shameful pause, he told himself. He needed to get Marie-Beth, John, and Daniel inside—and, of course, the orphans, assuming they had room. There was no reason not to make that happen, but he hesitated still. He didn't know what it was, but something was wrong with this place, even if he couldn't articulate what it was. Even with the snow and wind, something told him they might be better off continuing on along the trail.

"Samuel!" Marie-Beth called. "What are you doing? We're going to catch our death in this mess. Go to the door."

He took a breath and climbed down. She was right. They needed to get indoors.

His nose burned in the wind. His fingers were numb as they

held his coat hard against his body. His nose ran, and ice had frozen in his short, brown beard.

He knocked.

The door opened to the shadowed outline of a giant of a man. He towered over Samuel, and Samuel watched his eyes find the wagon.

"Hello, sir," Samuel began, "might you have room for a traveling family this—"

The giant's eyes darted back to Samuel as his arm swung something from behind his back. Samuel didn't know what it was, only that it was hard. When it crashed into his temple and his legs released him to the snowy ground, he found himself remembering the postcard he carried in his pocket from his friend Reginald, who was already in San Francisco awaiting them. It was a drawing of the hilly streets and a tram running down them. He thought about how nice it was going to be to ride with Marie-Beth during the day and to find the cat house Reginald had mentioned at night. He had been told they had oriental girls, and he really wanted to try one of those.

Samuel didn't move as the man stepped over him toward the wagon. He thought of the cleaners back in Ohio and the oriental woman who washed his clothes there. He had always wanted to push her into the back room and force her onto the table but never had. California would be different.

Marie-Beth watched as Samuel twitched in the snow. Blood bubbled through his nose and mouth as he stared at the falling snow like a halfwit.

She couldn't believe what just happened. It was not logical. People didn't beat you to the ground for knocking on their door. But here it was. She must have misunderstood something. She must have seen it wrong. She was sure when Samuel got up, he would be laughing, and they would straighten it all out and go inside for something warm to eat and drink.

The giant reached the side of the wagon and looked her over. Steam poured from his nose like a raging bull.

"Sir—" Marie-Beth could only say the single word before he raised a hand the size of her head and gripped her right braid. He turned and walked without a word, and her head and then body followed with him. She howled as her hips slammed the ground. Her head burned as hair ripped free. She slid over the snow, trying to get her footing and not realizing she was chasing him now, walking as fast as she could to keep her head from hurting.

She passed over Samuel as the giant dragged her inside. Samuel's eyes were wide and unblinking. Blood had frozen to his face beside his nose and lips.

"How many?" a woman asked from beside the wood stove.

"Wagon full of kids," the giant muttered, and threw Marie-Beth at the woman's feet.

"You best get 'em." The woman came toward Marie-Beth with a hammer as the giant turned back toward the door.

Marie-Beth closed her eyes and held the burning side of her head. There was a cracking sound on the opposite side, and then some kids screamed. She couldn't tell whom the screams came from. She hoped it was the orphans and not her John and Daniel, but more than that, she hoped the new throbbing in her skull would stop. When the next crack sounded, it did.

23

M ARSHALL'S HOUSE WAS NOTHING like Rand expected. Most officers lived in town, where they were close to the station and all the conveniences town has to offer, like grocery stores and fast food, shops and neighbors. Even doctors and firefighters were nowhere near this place. He could tell from the drive it would take forty-five minutes for an ambulance to reach this place—good luck if you were injured or had a heart attack. But at the same time, he could see the charm.

The old farmhouse and detached garage were surrounded by several acres of grass. Beyond that were fields of wild sage, juniper, and ponderosas. Through one edge of that, Rand could see the valley that led toward town; on the other, the land grew thick with trees overshadowed by the snow-capped mountains beyond—their destination.

Rand spotted Marshall by the garage, where a trailer was already attached to a pickup. Marshall had loaded a pair of four-wheelers. He was in the process of strapping them down as Rand parked.

Ivan ran from the grassy field as Rand approached. He stopped a dozen feet from the detective, scanned him and sniffed, and ran back to Marshall, who was climbing down from the trailer.

"You got a lot done quickly," Rand said.

"Clock's ticking." Marshall opened the cab's rear door and

made a clicking sound with his mouth. Ivan jumped inside and took his spot on the rear seat. "If we want to get there ahead of everyone else, we need to get moving. Right?"

"Right."

Marshall gestured at the passenger door and headed to the driver's side. Rand patted down his gun and phone, shuffled his backpack's weight on his shoulder, reassuring himself he was ready, and climbed into the cab. Marshall's handheld radio stood upright in the cup holder, and his department-issued AR-15 lay on the back seat beside Ivan.

"Ready?" Marshall asked.

"Let's go."

Rodger's Trailhead was only a few turns away. Though less popular with hikers than the Laurel entrance, its trails crisscrossed the same paths leading to falls, the lake, and several mountain destinations.

Marshall parked on the left side of the lot and tried not to think about Braden and McNeil as he unchained the ATVs and let down the ramp. It was hard to make his brain listen.

Braden was an idiot. He was young and eager and a good guy. His family was from some minuscule town in southeast Montana that even natives had never heard of, and he had looked at the small city of Custer Falls as landing on a big-time police force. When they played poker, the kid always lost, but that idiotic smile never left his face. Marshall wondered if anyone had gone by his apartment and fed his cat.

McNeil was also a hard case to ignore, but for different reasons. He had a wife and daughter, and Marshall thought he remembered McNeil saying his wife was pregnant again the last time they played—it was late at night, though, and Marshall was pretty drunk at that point, so he wasn't totally sure that happened. Either way, the idea of McNeil's wife and daughter crying at the door when the sergeant delivered the news gutted him. Because he knew what that was like.

It was 1992 when they knocked on his door and he had to watch his mother collapse in the doorway when she was told. He comforted Mom, but it didn't sink in for a few days that Dad was really gone. How could he have been? Dad was invincible in his mind back then, like some Greek demigod, a superman. The idea that he was actually dead, that he wasn't coming home—ever—was such an unbelievable concept that when it finally hit him, when he finally accepted it was true several days later, it made him so sick that he puked all over the backyard.

He had just fed the horses and was taking a few minutes to himself. He had thrown his model airplane into the wind. Dad had helped him build that plane a few weeks prior. They'd sat in his room with the cheap wood and glue and pinched their noses and laughed at the smell. Dad was supposed to be there for the maiden flight. He was supposed to use his unfathomable Daddy strength to thrust it up onto the wind and make it glide across the yard, while little Drew imagined it was a combat pilot sneaking into enemy territory to rescue captured POWs.

But Dad wasn't there. It was at that moment he understood, that he let the fact sink in: Dad was never going to be there again. It was just him and Mom now, and that wasn't ever going to change.

The plane crashed into the grass, and little Drew dropped to his knees. It was a long time before he got up and wiped his face. He picked up his plane and went inside after. His eyes were red but dried from his shirt. He gave his mother a hug but didn't say a word, and he went about his chores. He didn't have a choice anymore; it was just what he had to do, whether Dad was there to remind him or not.

He wondered if McNeil's kid had figured it out yet, if someone was helping them out. Not that he knew them personally, but still, he would need to stop by and check on them later.

Ivan growled at something in the woods, and Rand let down the ramp. It hit the ground with a loud clunk, snapping the dog's attention back toward them.

Marshall tossed Rand the key for the machine closest to the ramp. "You know how to drive one?"

Rand was by no means a pro, but he had ridden ATVs a dozen times or so. He deduced by the pink band on the key that this one belonged to Marshall's wife. He nodded and slid in the key. "I think I got it." With the flip of a switch and the push of a button, the machine growled to life, and Rand reversed it down the trailer ramp.

Marshall followed Rand down, stopping beside the truck. As Rand raised the ramp and locked it, Marshall grabbed his radio and his backpack from the back seat and slung his rifle over his shoulder.

"You know the way?" Rand asked.

Marshall pulled his phone from his coat pocket and tapped the screen. "All programmed and ready to go." He squeezed the throttle, and the four-wheeler lurched onto the trail. Ivan gave a brief growl and trotted off after him.

Rand scanned the trees as a feeling shifted through his nerves. There was confidence there—he was sure they would find these guys—but there was a lingering concern whether they brought enough manpower. They were only two guys and a dog, after all, and these criminals had taken out three cops. Had he started them down a road they couldn't handle? Or was he just getting the jitters because he'd soon come face to face with these scumbags?

It didn't matter. They were on the way now. And Marshall had a radio; they could call for backup once they found their men—if they needed it.

He hit the gas and raced to catch up, paying little attention to the growing darkness within the trees.

24

Honey came back inside for the third time, carrying three camping cups filled with snow and dumping them into the pot on the stove. The pot instantly stopped steaming as the icy white clumps melted. She figured this would finally be enough, but who knew. She would have guessed all that snow would have made more liquid, but it was like the stuff was made of air and not water.

She was ready for it to work. Even after Cheetos, she was goddamn hungry, and those bags of dehydrated meals were calling her. But just as much as feeding herself, she wanted the men to eat. Men are a lot easier to control when they're fed—and a lot more dangerous when they're not. Tempers were already short, and the entire gang was nervous. That wasn't a good situation for an attractive woman such as herself. She was too aware that when men were hungry, little things set them off, emotions ran wild, and there were certain emotions she wasn't about to share with these scumbags.

"How's it coming?" Nick approached the stove, standing way too close, and inhaled a deep breath. He wasn't smelling the food, whether or not that was what he was implying.

Honey played nice. "I think this'll be enough water. The bag said to let it boil, but then I think we'll be ready for the buffet." *But you're a sicko if you expect me to start cooking all your meals.*

He licked his lips and nodded, then smacked her ass as he turned and walked away.

In her mind, Honey calculated how far she was from the rifles leaning against the far wall, how long it would take her to reach them, and how many shots she could get off before they were able to shoot back with their pistols. She reminded herself she was under scrutiny right now, and if she didn't at least play a little nice, they'd tie her up in the other room with Stevie—or worse.

She let the slap go—for now. Nick had obviously been dreaming about it since they met.

The snow melted, the water steamed, and Honey found herself thinking of hot springs and hot tubs. Standing next to the fire had warmed her a bit—she would have guessed the cabin was up to the fifties by now—but it wasn't enough. She wanted to be warm, tropical warm, warm enough to strut in her bathing suit, so warm she would beg for AC. She was sick of this. It had been days at this point of not having any heat, and for what? She wasn't any richer, wasn't any safer. But that steam made her feel warm inside, just watching it rise.

Small bubbles appeared in the bottom of the pot. It wouldn't be long now, and the taste of hot food in her stomach would heat up her core—it had to.

She watched the bubbles form and multiply. Tiny bubbles ringed the pot. She closed her eyes, letting the steam bathe her face, and when she opened them, fear gripped the back of her neck and chilled her from shoulders to toes.

There was no longer a small camping pot on the wood stove. It was a deep iron pot, and this one was at full boil. The water rolled over what she was sure was a hand. The skin was puffy and peeling away from the digits, but it was most definitely a hand. She tried to close her eyes, thinking maybe if she could look away, this vision would vanish, but her eyes were peeled, her lids stuck like glue. She was forced to see more.

In the murk below the hand was a bulbous shape she was unfamiliar with. The bubbles rushed past, and the thing moved, and she knew the reddish, triangular blob with lumps and four nubs on the thick end was a heart.

Her stomach felt like that water, dirty and rumbling, bubbling and rising.

Rising.

Small crumbs floated to the top. Hunks of fat. Shreds of what she thought could be skin. A fingernail stained with blood.

Her stomach no longer held, her eyelids clamped shut, and vomit poured from her lips.

"What the fuck?" someone shouted.

Honey opened her eyes. Her camp pot was boiling, though floating inside were strings of yellow bile and mashed Cheetos chunks.

"What did you do?" Nick shouted.

Tears streamed down her face as she stumbled backward. This was bad. They'd tie her up. Hot tingles ran down her flesh as she saw the anger in Nick's eyes. She had to fix it.

"It's okay." She grabbed the pot and raced to the door. "I can clean it. Just hold on." She scrambled outside.

"Fuck. Did you see that?" Nick shouted at Perry.

Perry looked up from the table, where he was amusing himself with a game of solitaire. "What?"

"The girl. She just puked in the pot of water."

"Gross." His gaze went back to the game.

Snow enveloped Honey as she stepped from the cabin. It seemed to instantly pile on her shoulders and head. She tossed the pot's steaming contents into the air, and it instantly vanished into the storm. She scooped a new pot full of snow from the ground and watched it start to melt. She was about to carry it back inside when she saw the hole she just created in the snow.

It looked back at her, not frozen, not dead, but somewhere in between. Eyes glassy but not solid, as if they were made of Jello. Its skin was pale, almost blue. Its hair was frayed and dirty, wild and half-clumped with snow. The face in the white hole looked upon her; it was something that should have been dead but wasn't yet allowed to go, a thing left to rot but kept prisoner by a never-ending winter that refused to let nature take hold.

She knew that if it was just a body, it wouldn't have bothered her. But this was more than the almost-frozen corpse beside the cabin that was recently a live redhead. This was something that wanted to die yet hungered. It was lying in that snow and it was waiting—she didn't know for what, and she didn't want to find out.

Honey glanced up the snowy path they had come from into the falling blanket of white. She stared back at the cabin, where Tony was walking toward the door—she had left it open, not sure how or why. She knew then that she'd rather die in the storm than wait for this thing to emerge from its hole when it was ready.

The pot slipped from her fingers, its newly melted water sloshing out. She ran into the shower, her mouth sealed and her heart racing. She would make it. She would find another shelter, and she'd get out of these woods. These local cops weren't looking for her; they were looking for the guys. No one knew who she was around here.

She just had to run.

Tony watched Honey fade into the wall of white, and several

thoughts conflicted with each other. Should he tell Shamus? His uncle would want to know. Should he get Nick and Perry to help bring her back? Should he go and see if she needed help? She was really hot, after all. But as he thought of these things, another thought overwhelmed him, *Just let her go*. It didn't fit with any of the others, and if he was to think a little bit harder, he may have disagreed. But he didn't.

He glanced at the pot on the ground and went outside to grab it, scooping up and pressing into it as much snow as would fit. He brought it in, shut the door, and set it on the stove. He was hungry. The Cheetos were nice, but they only delayed his appetite, they didn't satiate it.

Tony was on his way outside to get more snow with the camping cups when Nick asked, "Where's the girl?"

Tony continued on his way as he answered, "She left."

There was a brief snarl of anger on Nick's face, but as if someone had whispered in his ear, he nodded in agreement then sat back down beside Perry.

The falling snow seemed somehow prettier when Tony made this trip outside. He took a moment to watch it fall, to admire the flakes as they spun and danced with each other. He looked up into the everlasting downpour, streaks coming at his face from an infinite height and fanning around him in a hypnotizing, alluring call. He knew he was staring. He knew he didn't want to look away, even as his face felt the cold crystals land and flakes slipped down his shirt. He thought this must be what sailors felt like when seeing mermaids or hearing a siren's song.

And as quickly as the draw had begun, Tony looked down, scooped up his snow, and turned back toward the door.

The window was yellowish and dim, and he wondered if the stove needed more wood. He took a step toward the cabin, and the firelight faded as a dark shape filled the pane. It was a large man's shape, a shadow over the glass, and it struck Tony that this man was even larger than Shamus, and that was rare to see.

He walked inside and dumped the new snow into the pot and considered if he would have the beef and macaroni or the lasagna. He thought the beef and mac sounded good.

The shadow moved across the wall, hovering in the corner. It hovered in the corner of Tony's vision as he watched the water and drooled.

25

WANDA'S SHOULDERS WERE SORE. Her wrists burned. Having her hands tied behind her back to the bed frame was more painful than she thought it would have been, and despite yanking and pulling and twisting, the only thing she had been able to do was make her wrists hurt more. She would have expected the old fabric to rip or at least give somewhat, but all she got was creaking and whining as if it would break—and it didn't.

Some of the panic had faded. She had covered it with the cool facade she learned from her mother, but it was there, and the grief was mounting no matter how much she tried to tamp it down and tell herself she needed to wait for later, she needed to think clearly for the kids and for Abby.

But how do you do that?

Every time she looked at Angel, she wanted to burst into tears. Her little head was slumped down over her chest as she rested—rested? She was in shock, passed out, but *rested* sounded so much better in Wanda's mind. She needed that, just a little, because if she dwelled on the pain her daughter was in, on the fact that she was helpless to protect her right now, on the reality that she had no way to keep her alive if those psychos wanted to shoot her like they had Kathy—she was going to lose it.

It shouldn't have been easier to look at Lins, but somehow it was. The girl had sobbed herself to sleep after a horror Wanda couldn't imagine and could barely bring herself to think of. Because if she did, she would find herself cycling again and again—what could she have done differently? How could she have saved her friend? She was a police officer! She should have had tactics to confront those men. She should have known how to talk to them, to resolve the situation peacefully without anyone getting hurt. She had failed in so many ways.

Wanda turned to Abby, the farthest from the door, against the wall, tied to the last bed in the room. Abby was staring at the ceiling, her breath puffing upward like the exhaust from a cartoon steam engine. She lowered her gaze and locked eyes with Wanda.

"We're going to die here, aren't we?" Abby said. Her voice was low, calm in an unsettling way. "Just like that guy said."

"No. We're not going to die here." Wanda wasn't as sure as she made her voice sound, but she couldn't admit her fears right now. That Angel was going to die. That she and Lins and Abby had no chance to get out of this. How could she have any hope at this point, when they couldn't get free, had no heat, and a group of maniacs were in charge?

Abby shook her head. "I wish I was as sure as you. You know, I don't talk about it. Hell, who would want to relive it? But I've had criminals pull guns on me."

"You have?"

"Part of living in the city, I guess. That, and making dumb decisions. But yeah."

"You made it, though."

"I did. But every time it happened, I knew I was going to be okay. I knew they just wanted money. They may have threatened to kill me, but that guy..." She gestured toward the door with her head. "He flat-out said they were going to kill us. I believe him."

Wanda clenched her teeth and swallowed hard. "That asshole

may try, but I won't let him. They're not killing anyone else." Abby flashed a gentle smile as Wanda went on. "Not you, not me, and especially not these kids. *We're going to find a way out of this.*"

The guy tied to the farthest bed moaned.

"What about him?" Abby said.

"They can kill him. He's one of theirs."

"No, I mean, what do you think his story is? Why's he in here with us?"

The smell of pasta sauce reached Wanda's nose, and she instantly recognized what it was. "They're cooking our food. Those bastards are eating our food."

"Forget the food. We have to get out of here." Abby yanked at her bonds. "We can eat when we get back to town."

She was right, only there was the problem of their restraints not coming loose, and then there was the weather. "Yeah. It just pissed me off; that's all. We have to keep trying to rip these ropes. They have to be a hundred years old; they should break for chrissake."

"Wait. You know where we are?"

A chill washed over Wanda as the parts of the story she remembered came to mind. It was like a cold tap had been opened down her back. She had to take a breath before she spoke. But there was also a sense that these words needed to be said—that something more than just Abby wanted to hear them.

"I've never been here, but I'm pretty sure what this is. Garrets Lodge."

There was a skittering sound in the far corner of the room, something moving in the darkness. Wanda heard it this time and told herself it was a mouse—just a harmless little field mouse that had made this place its home.

Abby pulled and writhed. She tried rubbing her restraints

against the bed in a sawing motion. "Well, I think we have time. So why don't you fill me in?"

Wanda glanced at the kids, hoping they wouldn't have to hear this, then she continued working on her own bonds. "The story goes that this place used to belong to an old couple, the Garrets. This was a long time ago, like before statehood, when Custer Falls was still little more than a mining camp and no one dared to come out here but trappers, and even they would only travel the mountain passes in the summertime. Winters were just too harsh. You get trapped up here in the winter, and—"

"I think I see how that could be a problem."

"Yeah. Well, at some point, that old couple disappeared—no one knows what happened to them, but the townspeople and the travelers that happened by knew their name, so even without them here, the place was known as Garrets Lodge. Anyway—at some point, another couple moved in. They'd rent out the beds—" Wanda motioned behind her, "—to any travelers or trappers or people that found out that these woods were harsher than they expected. Only—after a while, rumors started to circulate in town that some of the people that came here never made it to their destinations."

"Shit." Abby paused as the idea sank in.

The sound of tiny feet rained from above, through the ceiling. It echoed from the woodpile by the stove.

"Yeah. Trappers never reached the other side of the trail. People headed west toward the pass never made it to the other side. Stuff like that." Wanda heard the faint sound of children whimpering. There was a vibration as a gust of wind rattled the roof.

"What—How could that happen?"

"You know, it was the old days. There were no records, no dash cams or GPS. People just went missing sometimes."

"But you said people suspected?"

"Sure, but that doesn't mean they did anything other than warn each other to stay the hell away. If you came up here to investigate—this kind of remote area—you could disappear too."

A faint hiss, then a slithering sound. Something could have been running down the walls and dripping on the floor. The far, obsidian side of the room revealed nothing.

"So what happened?"

"Time moved on. Trappers found other places; the mines in town went dry; people used the train more for traveling. It all just kind of stopped. And then, when the government started making national parks in the 30s, the whole area became a national forest. All that was left of this place were rumors."

Whispers crisscrossed the room, all too faint to understand, all too quiet for either woman to insist the sounds were more than their racing imaginations and the ambient sounds of the raging storm outside.

Abby looked around the room with new eyes. Wanda could see her gears turning, imagining the history within these walls, the death that could have happened right where they sat. She went back to pulling at her bonds.

"This is creepy," Abby said.

"Yeah." Wanda's wrists felt like they were on fire. She tugged anyway. The nagging, cold sensation of someone breathing down her neck only seemed to intensify the longer she was here—and telling the story, both to Abby and herself, had made it worse.

Angel was floating again. It wasn't a dreamwalk—or at least it wasn't like the others she had experienced. Dreamwalks were always *now*—this was more like a *then*. Someone was sharing this with her, and as she looked down on the group of kids in the snowy covered wagon, she suspected it was one of them.

A giant grabbed both boys in the front of the wagon. They screamed as they hung by their arms. Legs dangling, unable to reach the ground. They swung, their feet unable to kick the massive man.

"Daddy!" one boy screamed.

"Momma!" the other boy screamed.

The giant looked one at a time into each captive's gaze. Angel stared alongside the boys. She saw no shine in that man's eyes. It was as if the light couldn't find him and didn't dare reflect. She had heard the term soulless eyes before, but this didn't feel like that. It felt like his soul was dark, dangerous. And she knew, then, this was the thing she'd met last night. This was the enormous shadow in the forest. This was the killer in the cabin. It was Eustace.

There was no warning. The giant thrust his head forward, cracking it into the forehead of the boy on his left. That was John. His eyes shut, and he fell limp. Daniel screamed, and the giant slammed their skulls together. It went quiet again, and Eustace lowered both kids until his arms were relaxed and their feet were buried in the snow.

The orphans said nothing. The younger ones whimpered, a boy and a girl, but the rest covered their mouths. When the giant leaned into the wagon and spoke, their eyes were glued to his.

"In the house," was all he said, and each boy and girl came from under their blankets and walked in a single file line into the cabin. The cabin Angel was in now.

Angel wanted to scream at them and yell at them to stop. They shouldn't be going in there. But this was a memory; she couldn't stop them, and that giant—she was just glad he wasn't staring at her.

One by one, they sifted through the door. As the last one entered and the door closed behind them, Angel felt the world slip around her. She would have grabbed hold of something if she could have, but there was no use. The falling snow slid from around her, the sky warped away, she blinked and was inside. Again, inside this horrible, evil place—

Angel tried not looking at the walls and floor and chairs. There was blood—not as bad as the other room, but it was there. She saw a large pot with rising steam on the wood stove. There was a woman facing away on the far side of the room. She swung a cleaver. It slammed into the table with a thud and slurped as she raised it.

There was a naked man on the table.

Thud. Slurp.

There was a naked woman on the floor at the lady's feet.

Thud. Slurp.

Angel knew the man on the table was dead, he had to be—but she didn't understand why the lady was hitting him with the cleaver.

Thud. Slurp.

Angel wanted to puke. She was cold, so cold. The inside of the cabin was warm; the fire was blazing. But she was just so cold.

Thud. Slurp.

Angel wondered where the kids had gone. She had been sure she was watching one of their memories, but they were nowhere to be seen.

Thud. Slurp.

She heard crying. Whoever it was was close. They could have been in the same room. But she couldn't spot them.

Thud. Slurp.

The lady put down the cleaver and scooped up what lay in front of her. She turned, and Angel saw it all. She carried what must have been a dozen pounds of flesh. There was a hand, sections of an arm, things that Angel couldn't place other than the fact they were wet, red, and bloody.

The lady carried them to the stove and let them slowly drop into the boiling water. There was a sizzle as blood dripped onto the stove's hot surface. More as the pot splashed.

Angel knew where her eyes were going next and prayed for them not to move, but they did. They were drawn by something irresistible, something that needed a witness, and she was powerless to ignore it.

She knew the naked man on the table to be the father. His arm was missing, and strings of muscle and skin hung from the socket, over the edge of the table. His stomach was opened up. She could see through his abdomen, where the side and belly muscles had been sliced free and a cavern now existed. The organs were gone, and she stared at the inside of his ribs and spine. And the blood. The blood rained from the table to the floor.

It tapped. It puddled. It ran into the floorboard cracks.

She wanted to cover her eyes, but it was impossible. She tried to scream, "Let me go home!" She heard it in her mind but nowhere else.

She wanted to cry, to vomit, to turn and run.

She could smell the blood, the stew warming, its salty, savory mist, the must of the home, and the decayed breath of the woman—it all filled her nose like some kind of hellish potpourri.

The only hint of relief Angel had was knowing that this was the past and everyone here was long gone. They couldn't touch her, couldn't hurt her. As bad as it was, she was only a witness—until the woman turned, her eyes wide and wild, her mouth curling into a maddened grin, her large, mischievous face peering straight at Angel's.

This can't be happening. It can't—

The woman, Florence, reached forward, and Angel felt heat around her neck. It grew hotter by the second, burning her skin.

The mumbling and whimpering got louder. The pot roared to a boil, splashing and sizzling on the stovetop.

Florence leaned in, bringing herself nose to nose with Angel. The heat rose over Angel's jaw to her ears. To her scalp. To her eyes.

The woman sniffed. Her harsh breath made Angel's gut twist and turn.

She ached inside and out and screamed, "Let me go!"

Florence chuckled and yanked Angel from her hovering plane. In an instant, she was no longer in a dreamwalk, but there physically, her body in the insane woman's grasp and her throat closing as this maniac squeezed.

Angel gagged. It hurt like Florence's fingers were blades. It burned like their tips were on fire. Her view became a cloudy, red haze. She grabbed the woman's arm. Her feet flailed as she was lifted over the pot.

"No!" Angel's words were a wet, garbled mess. She did the only thing she could think of; she rammed her fingers as hard as she could into the old witch's eyes.

There was a soft, wet squish and a scream. Angel didn't get to see what she hit, but she felt what happened next.

Florence dropped Angel, and her feet were instantly wet. Then her shins and her thighs and her hips. As her waist entered the pot, she felt the heat, the burning, the indescribable pain that locked her body in place as hard as an iron cast.

She could feel her skin splitting from her flesh, her muscles tightening, trying to escape into her body and having nowhere to go. She saw floating sections of the dead man in the pot beside her and understood this was just a first step in her death, because when that woman recovered and returned, she was going to eat her.

Angel's scream halted only for a second so she could suck in more air. When it resumed, the rest of her sank into the pot until boiling broth ran down her throat and steaming bubbles rose.

26

R AND HAD TO TRUST that Marshall knew the way. He had done his share of hiking and was secure in his knowledge of the county geography, but he was by no means an outdoorsman. Put him in a car, and he was confident and able. Out here, it was an entirely different thing.

The trees whipped by. The four-wheelers bounced on their shocks, letting Rand know he was going to feel this in his back and shoulders tomorrow. His hands were getting sore from the constant vibration, but he was happy he was wearing gloves—he feared they would be nothing but blisters without them. He didn't understand how people did this sort of thing for fun. ATVs seemed like capable vehicles for an outdoor job, but he had friends who would go riding as a pastime. He just didn't get it.

Ivan sat on the rear of Marshall's machine. The dog had run alongside for the first mile or two, but when he started slowing down, Marshall put him on back and strapped his vest to the seat. The dog looked like he was having a blast.

Marshall and Ivan together reminded him of his cousin, Trevor, and his dog, Sicko, and a week that changed the way he looked at dogs altogether. Rand spent a lot of vacations at Trevor's place when he was younger. Having a single mother with a meager income meant their vacations had to be cheap, so visiting Aunt Gloria and Cousin Trevor on the edge of the national forest was as lavish and exciting as it got, even if they were only a few dozen miles from home.

The summer of his twelfth birthday, Rand had been at Trevor's house, sharing his cousin's room with Sicko. Trevor's family, Aunt Gloria and Uncle Charlie, lived in Uncle Charlie's childhood home. It was a forty-acre lot, chopped down over the years from the initial several hundred his family had ranched until subdividing it and selling parcels during the depression to keep their heads above water. The part they kept was mostly forested, and that was the way Trevor liked it.

The first day there, they spent their waking hours in Trevor's treehouse. It was on the eastern side of the property, next to a thousand acres of Bureau of Land Management property, a good five-minute walk from the house and the only sign of human civilization as far as they could see. That meant when Trevor went out there, he had to take Sicko every time.

It wasn't just because he loved the dog, and he did; Sicko was protection. He was a hundred and thirty pounds of black Labrador Retriever because when you lived next to unbound wilderness, you needed protection. Mountain lions, bears, bobcats, and foxes all lived either just beyond or on his land, which meant there were times of the year when Trevor would have been the one hunted if he didn't have a big, active dog at his side as a deterrent.

The interesting thing about Trevor's treehouse, at least to twelve-year-old Mark Rand, was that it had a hole in the floor on one side where Uncle Charlie had installed a type of dumbwaiter. It was huge, in fact, made specifically to be large enough for the dog to climb in and ride the twenty feet up to the treehouse. Rand thought it was so cool, he even made Trevor bring him up inside it a few times, even though they weren't supposed to.

"Dad says it's just for the dog, and not a toy," Trevor said that morning. Of course, he had an arch in the corner of his mouth as he said it... So, after the dog was up, Rand climbed in. They took turns going up and down, eventually making Sicko nervous enough about it that he wouldn't stop barking his head off and they had to either knock it off or risk someone coming out from the house and catching them.

They read comics and played cards in the morning, then ate hot sandwiches they had carried out there in lunchboxes. In the afternoon, Trevor got up the nerve to ask Rand if he'd ever seen a Playboy, after which he pulled three of his father's magazines from a hiding place he had built between the outer wall and the tree, behind an old footlocker.

The twelve- and thirteen-year-old spent an hour flipping through the pages, barely containing their hormones and trying to decipher the meanings of adult phrases in the articles.

Trevor unfolded a three-page spread of a blonde on a bed, her rump in the air. "You like these?"

Rand glanced over from his haze of Ms. July's nipples peeking out from the holes in what must have been her boyfriend's basketball jersey. "Blondes?"

"No. These pictures with their butts out. I mean, aren't these magazines made for boob pictures?"

"Oh." Rand felt himself flush. "I guess so. She has a nice one."

"Huh." He looked the image over again, considering. "I guess I just like the boob pictures more. She just looks weird, crawling like a dog." He showed the picture to Sicko. "You like her, bud?"

Sicko started to whine. He sniffed at the air and walked to the window.

"What's he doing?" Rand ask.

"He's prob'ly gotta poop," Trevor said. "That's the sound he makes when he wants to go down."

Trevor commanded the dog into the dumbwaiter and lowered him to the ground. Sure enough, Sicko walked five feet, sniffed, and dropped a load right there. The boys watched from above, and Trevor called him back into the dog-sized elevator once he was done. But Sicko didn't listen.

"Get in the box, boy," Trevor shouted down.

Sicko's mind was locked on something, though. He stared into the woods to the east, hackles up toward the sky.

"Sicko! In the box!"

The dog growled, then barked. It was a deep, thunderous noise that Rand could feel all the way up in the treehouse. He watched on his knees and felt it vibrate up into his chest.

"He's barking at *something*," Rand said.

"Prob'ly a rabbit or something." Trevor shook his head. "Sicko!"

After another minute, Sicko calmed down enough to listen, and Trevor brought him back up, where he sat quietly in the corner for the rest of the afternoon. It was around five when they started to get hungry again and climbed down, and they finally understood what had happened.

East of the treehouse, maybe twenty feet away, Sicko sniffed a bloody hoof extending from the bottom of a leafy bush.

"What's that?" Rand asked. A moment passed where his mind tried to reconcile the leg-shaped stick on the ground, trying to understand why it looked like an animal's limb. Was it an animal? Animals didn't lay in bushes like that. They didn't sleep like that.

It clicked inside Rand's mind. He was struck by a cold wave of fear. Something inside him recognized what he was seeing wasn't right, whatever it was, and they should get back up in the treehouse or run back to Trevor's.

It took Trevor a minute to spot what Sicko was sniffing before he said, "Shit. Let's see."

Sicko's nose jutted up into the air again and again. He heard Trevor coming and darted in front of him, rounding the bush and sniffing at the prize. When Trevor and Rand got there, they were both speechless.

Something had been interrupted having lunch.

A large doe lay spread out over a bed of flattened pine needles. Its belly had been ripped open, and its entrails stretched for three feet before coming to a gnarled end. Its head had been stripped of half its flesh, and its neck was sliced from jaw to shoulder in four long, jagged tears.

"That was a lion," Trevor said.

"What was a lion?" Rand asked. More than the grossness of what he was looking at, a heavier unease took hold. It was an ice-like jolt of realization that there was real danger here. "Shit! You mean earlier? That Sicko was barking at?"

"Yeah."

Rand's eyes searched the surrounding trees, shadows, and canopy. If a mountain lion had been there, it would be back, especially if it left its dinner behind. It could have been anywhere around them at that moment. Hiding in a bush, in a shadow, up in a tree. It could have been waiting for them to come by its feeding spot to bag another meal.

What the hell had they gotten themselves into?

He didn't want to be eaten. The very thought, not just of the pain but of his flesh going down the throat of an animal, never to be seen again, rocked his nerves. That idea made his legs tremble. Losing part of himself... and then death.

"Let's go," Rand said.

Trevor leaned over the carcass. He picked up a stick and poked at the intestines, stretching them out and gazing at what was beneath, above, and to the side in the open cavity.

"Come on," Rand said. "It's gonna come back."

Trevor scowled. "Wuss." He poked into the deer's empty eye socket, rocking the skull back and forth and watching as hide draped from the head and neck.

"I'm going back," Rand said. His eyes continued to scan the surroundings. Maybe he was being a wuss? Maybe the thing was long gone? There was just no way to really know. So why push their luck?

"Go if you want. This is my place. I come here every day." He pointed at Sicko. "Besides, he chased it away before. If it comes back, he'll do it again."

That kind of made sense, but not enough to risk it. "Yeah. I'm still going in. I'm thirsty, you know, so. I'll see you at the house."

"Whatever."

Rand really wished his cousin would come. He didn't want to walk back alone where there could be more lions hiding out of sight. More than that, though, he didn't want to remain by the treehouse where he knew one had been.

"Okay. Bye." Rand turned and walked. His gaze ran 360s over the ground as he moved, then he did the same through the trees. He was slow at first, then gradually picked up his pace—until he heard the barking.

Sicko's deep, heaving bark echoed through the woods. It stopped Rand in his tracks, both startling him and, for an instant, making him think the dog was after *him*.

Then Trevor screamed.

Rand knew he should run to the house, maybe try to find Uncle Charlie and tell him to bring a rifle and hurry. That would have been the safest thing to do. He even took a step toward the house, thinking, *I need to get help*. But it was only one step.

It didn't matter if running away was the safest thing. His cousin was back there, possibly in danger. How could he run away?

It only took a dozen steps before Rand was under the treehouse once again.

"No!" Trevor screamed. "Go away!" He was behind the bush,

but Rand couldn't see him. He screamed again, but his voice was buried below an unearthly growl and a howl of pain.

Rand ran closer. He slowed to a walk and gave the bush a wide berth as he came around.

Trevor lay on the ground a few feet from the deer carcass, tears coursing down his face. Ten feet farther, what must have been a two-hundred-pound mountain lion squared off with Sicko.

Sicko's massive mouth sank into the lion's rear leg. The lion swiped at the dog, ripping a chasm over Sicko's ribs. The dog let loose and chomped down again into the cat's belly. Its tan fur went brown as blood shot out, and the dog came away with a mouthful of meat and hair.

"Sicko! Run!" Trevor screamed. Tears ran like rivers. He had no grasp on why the dog was doing what it was doing, he only knew he didn't want this to happen—that his best friend was in a fight to the death and he had no control over the outcome.

Rand grabbed Trevor by the arm and dragged him. Trevor shook his cousin free, turning back to his dog.

"Come on, Trevor!" Rand grabbed the arm again. "He's trying to protect you."

Trevor screamed as the lion sank its fangs into Sicko's front paw. There was a crunch as Sicko howled, releasing the lion's belly.

"Sicko!" Trevor howled as loud as his dog, and the lion's eyes turned to meet his.

Trevor went quiet as he looked into the beast's shining stare, and the lion leaped toward him.

Rand tripped backward. Sicko lunged on wounded paw. The lion spread its jaws, and Sicko clamped down on the cat's spine, ripping him from the air.

Dog and cat rolled over one another. Teeth and claw tore

flesh. Blood sprayed the dead needles and forest debris until both animals stopped and Trevor's weeping was the only sound within the woods.

That smell, pine and spilled blood, stuck with Rand through the years. As he watched Ivan and Marshall ahead, he smelled it like he was right in front of that lion. It sent a chill down his spine, and Trevor's cries echoed in his mind. He hated to think of something like that happening to Marshall and Ivan, but for some reason, there was a lingering feeling that it would.

They crossed over another trail, and Rand looked right and left, the driving habit hard to escape. He was about to look forward again when the shape of a man in the trees caught his eye. It wasn't specifically a man, but more of a shadow between a pair of tall spruces.

Then he was past the intersection, his heart thumping. *That could have been them. They could have doubled back.*

Rand slammed on the brakes, studied the transmission for a moment, and threw the ATV in reverse. He stopped in the center of the intersection, hand over his gun, and searched for the suspects.

He saw no one. The pair of trees held nothing between them. He heard no one. The only sound was the roar of Marshall's four-wheeler and the putter of his own.

"Shit." He was mistaken. He had to be. It was a trick of the shadows or something.

He shook his head and drove on, trying to convince himself it was nothing but knowing he couldn't.

27

PERRY POLISHED OFF THE package of hamburger macaroni meant for two all by himself. It wasn't good. Not that he was some kind of foodie, he was far from it. His idea of spaghetti and meatballs came from a can. Even so, he would have eaten another package of that garbage if he wasn't concerned about how little there was left: seven bags.

He wasn't the one in charge, but he had to assume they would be rationing the food. They were on the run in a snowstorm in the middle of the woods. Who knew when they'd get out of there? When they'd get more food? There were other odds and ends in the women's stuff, some chocolate and snacks, some booze, but not enough to feed everyone in the cabin for more than another day or so.

His eyes ran over the pile of stuff by the wall, things they'd decided weren't worth anything. It was mostly clothes; the sleeping bags, tents, and food had been sorted and stacked by the stove. But in the junk pile, Perry's eyes came to a fuzzy little face.

He wasn't sure why, but the kid's toy held his gaze. Its fluffy, speckled face and sparkling hazel eyes were almost alive. They were watching him, and unlike the strange shapes he had seen in the woods and in his dreams, this thing was... *nice*. There was something like a motherly smile to it. It was warm and positive, and it made him remember his own mother, from the days before she died after falling down the stairs of their shitty apartment building. It brought thoughts of her loving embrace and her smell of baby powder and flowers.

That thought, his missing mother, was something that came to him seldom these days. He cried himself to sleep a thousand times in foster homes thinking of her, missing her. Then high school started, he dropped out, and he pushed all that kid stuff away. But now, he liked it—how that little stuffed animal made him feel—and he imagined what the kids in the next room must feel.

They had murdered one of their mothers. On most days that might not bother him, but usually he wouldn't have seen the kid's reaction. There weren't many kids present at the crimes they typically committed. And at this point, they were going to have to kill those kids. There was no way around it. He imagined Shamus was only keeping them alive in case they needed hostages, but, man, kids...

He had never killed a kid. He didn't know if it was a code of some sort or just that he'd never had to. He had never thought about the idea until now. He imagined he could do it if he needed to, but as he saw that girl's crying face in his mind, he realized he didn't want to. He really didn't want to.

The shot was nice; he had to admit that. Shamus plugged that broad through the eye in textbook style. He thought he saw her brain through the hole in her face as she was dragged outside, and, man, it was stellar work.

But the way that kid bawled afterward...

Perry found himself staring into the eyes of the stuffed cat. The sparkle over its glassy pupils took him back to his mother's lap, her caressing his hair and rubbing his head. It reminded him of the tears, the never-ending tears, and he wished she was there right now. Sitting next to him. Telling him this was all going to be okay.

In his daze, he saw her there, telling him that it could, in fact, be okay, but he needed to be on the right side. Her hair swayed as she leaned toward him. Dimples sank into her smiling cheeks. He needed to stop with the crazy lawlessness and stop the horror in this cabin before it got even more out of control. There was a warmth on his head where she used to rub so many years ago. Her scent rose inside his nostrils. He needed to take that bobcat and give it to the child it belonged to.

He nodded. "Yeah." That was what he had to do. Get right. Help the kids.

"Yeah, what?" Nick said. He sat at the table, shuffling the deck of cards.

"What?" Perry's mother vanished from beside him as he turned to Nick.

"You said *yeah*, I said *what*. What the fuck?"

Perry shook his head. He searched the room.

Did he really just see his mother—here? It couldn't have been.

His eyes landed on Nick, who was staring at him curiously. "You okay, man?" Nick's hair somehow seemed even wilder in this place, bulging in every direction.

"Ye—yeah, man. I was just thinking about something."

"*Okay*." He shuffled the cards, arching them into a high bridge as they slid back together. "Why don't you come take your mind off of it with a game?"

"That's a good idea." Perry stood, then glanced at the stuffed animal one more time. "Let me just check on the girls first." He bent over and swiped the stuffy into his grip, and a high-pitched scream burst from the next room.

Angel awoke to the sound of her own terrified shriek. Her arms wouldn't move, so she yanked. Her heart pounded as she took in the room: the blood, the dripping viscera, the jagged bone, and then—it was Mom. And Mom was talking.

"It's okay, Angel. I'm here."

But it wasn't okay. She was tied down. The room looked like a massacre. Mom, Lins, Abby, and some man were also tied. She didn't like this place. She stopped screaming, but her eyes didn't stop searching. She wanted to leave before the man and his wife came back. He was terrible. She was a maniac. That pot of—she didn't even know what to call it—cannibal soup? Thank God she was out!

"Angel," Mom was talking. "I'm here, baby."

But Mom was sitting in a pool of blood. They all were. It was the most—the horrible—the disgusting—her mind couldn't understand how to deal with this. It was like the janitor's closet or the entryway at school, but it was everywhere. She could avoid those other things, but not this. She was sitting in it. She was splashing it as she writhed and tried to slip her hands through wet, sticky ropes.

"Angel, sweetie, breathe. I don't want you to pass out again."

Pass out? Maybe that was better—the soup—*no, it wasn't.*

"Calm, sweetie. Take a slow, easy breath."

Angel's eyes stung as tears ran.

Lins stared at her, her own face red and irritated. "It's going to be okay."

No, Angel thought, and the shot came to mind: Ms. Kathy, shot in the face. And here Lins was, trying to help her, saying it would be okay. How was *she* so strong?

Angel tried not looking at the blood and gore. She focused on Lins and breathed. If Lins could be calm, so could she. If Lins could see hope somewhere, so could she.

Across the room, the door swung open and the large, bald bad guy came in. His face struck Angel in a different way than before. His expression was flat, but he was hiding something. There was worry below his tight lips and cold eyes, and when he saw Angel and the tears on her cheeks, his mouth parted as if to talk, and his brow loosened.

"What's going on in here?" he asked Mom.

"You have children tied up like animals," Mom said. "That's what's going on."

The big man sighed.

Abby watched quietly.

"They haven't eaten," Mom said. "It's cold in here. They're scared. What do you think's going to happen?"

Angel could tell Mom was hiding something. She could tell Mom knew she saw something. Mom always seemed to know. She couldn't see things the way Angel did, but it seemed like every time Angel was face to face with something and Mom was there, she made sure Angel could walk out of the way or avoid the mess. She never asked questions, but Mom knew.

"Yeah, yeah." He turned back to Angel and brought Betty Bobcat out from behind him.

Angel gasped at the sight. There was a smear of blood on her back left paw she was sure none of them could see, but she wanted Betty so badly. She tried to reach for it, forgetting her bonds.

"This yours?" the man said. He leaned down toward her.

Mom shot daggers with her eyes. "Keep your distance, buddy."

He scowled at Mom and kneeled. He held the toy over Angel and set it gently in her lap. He glanced at her wrists, then at the door.

"I can't untie you, so this'll have to do."

"A toy?" Wanda said. Her voice was stiff. "How about some

heat? There's wood next to the stove. How about some food, since you've taken all of ours?"

The hulking man stood. "Maybe. Let me think about it." He walked to the door and stepped through. He paused for a second, looking Angel over, then closed the door.

"What the hell was that?" Mom said.

"Creepy." Abby shook her head.

Angel stared into Betty Bobcat's large, glassy eyes and calmed. There was a warmth in its gaze that took her back to younger, happier days. She couldn't explain exactly what she was feeling, only that it was like someone she loved was holding her and stroking her head.

The blood on the floor below her legs, the crimson caked on the walls, all the attached panic and disgust shrank away. It didn't vanish, but it became more like just another thing, more like a layer of dust than the putrid liquid she knew it was.

Angel saw eyes in the distant crevices and shadows, and images from the wagon came to her. Those frightened kids that were ordered inside—was that them?

She realized at that moment she wasn't going to get out of this right now and maybe not any time soon, and her revulsion at the environment was only going to hurt. She had to control her reaction. She couldn't allow this place to sway her.

The memory of those kids, the soup, Kathy, the things in the woods, those criminals—there was a connection, she was sure of it. If she was going to get through this, to help Mom and Lins and Abby through this, she needed to control herself.

Angel looked back into Betty Bobcat's eyes. She was amazed at how their warm hazel reflection looked so much like Grandma's.

28

THOUGH RAND'S FACE WAS growing numb from the rush of cold wind, the increased stuffiness in his nose was readily apparent. His chapping lips were too. But he ignored those as he did his sore, vibrating ass and his aching back and hands. This trip was more important than minor inconveniences. Those officers' lives were worth more. And they were going to find out where these criminals were no matter what.

They had taken two breaks, mainly so Ivan could lay on solid ground for a few minutes. The dog was like a superhero the way he did what he was told without issue. Rand knew humans who couldn't do that well. Marshall wasn't going to take advantage of the dog's good will, though, so they stopped for him to rest. Rand was pretty sure they were still ahead of the CSI team.

Marshall waved his right hand in the air, signifying a stop and double-checking his GPS. Rand felt his heart flutter. This was it; he was sure. The ATVs had to be just up ahead.

They slowed, and the afternoon air seemed to thicken around them. There was still no sun, only clouds above, and the smell made Rand think of snow. That wouldn't have made sense—at least when he checked the weather this morning, there was no mention of snow—but they were in the mountains. When it came to the mountains, the weather did what it liked. Especially when the sky was dimming and dusk was growing ever nearer.

Marshall stopped, and Ivan hopped down. Marshall pointed

at the ground and said, "Sedět." The dog sat and waited for his next order.

Rand parked his ATV and joined Marshall. "Don't get close. We don't want to contaminate the scene."

"Yeah."

"Let's make a wide circle around them and see what we can spot."

Rand went right, and Marshall went left.

In the center of the path were the two ATVs. Rand recognized them from the video at Shamus Betty's house, one side-by-side and one four-wheeler, parked in a line. The weird thing was there was no indication of why they were abandoned.

Rand couldn't see the gas gauges without starting them up, but the idea that both would have run out of gas at the exact same time didn't make sense. There was nothing in the road. The vehicles didn't look physically damaged, at least as far as Rand could tell with his untrained eye.

There were no clues in the woods, either. The side of the trail looked exactly the same as the entire path they had been riding down. No trash or human items, no destruction of the trees or bushes.

It didn't make sense.

Rand and Marshall met in the center of the trail, ahead of the first vehicle.

"What do you think?" Marshall stared down the front ATV as if a hard look could make it talk.

"I don't see a damn thing," Rand said. "They look fine. Why would they have abandoned them?"

"I know this would be a long shot, but could they have called in a helicopter? Could they have been airlifted?"

"I doubt it. Our chopper's been up there. I would assume it would have been seen. Plus, the money that would take? I mean,

I think it's as likely as them getting beamed up by aliens."

Marshall cracked a smile. "I said *long shot*."

"Yeah, yeah. But, no, I think they must have gone on foot."

"That would be better for us. We can have Ivan sniff 'em out. But first, we need to get our four-wheelers on this side, then we can see what Ivan can do."

"Let's do it."

It took a good five minutes for Marshall and Rand to find a way around what was soon to become a CSI investigation. They worked through trees and shrubs back to the main trail, and Marshall carefully guided Ivan to the front ATV, where the dog could sniff.

"He's got it," Marshall said, and with the dog ahead on a thirty-foot lead, they headed down the path on their quads.

The first hundred yards led directly down the trail, past two turns, until they reached a switchback where the land rose sharply and the path narrowed. They took it slow, irritating Ivan, who wanted to run.

From the incline, Rand could see over the lower ridges across a thousand trees. They were going toward the pass. That made some sense—maybe their fugitives thought they could escape more easily from the west side of the forest. But those exits were guarded, too, and he was sure the chopper had scanned this whole area with infrared. Regardless, they climbed the trail, past another switchback and over a wide ridge, where the trees moved closer and the clouded sunlight dimmed.

It was there the path ended and only dense forest remained. Trees stretched to the sky, thick and tall, resembling a paleolithic forest where mammoths or dinosaurs reigned and no human had ever fallen a tree. It was there that the ATVs were now useless as the thick undergrowth refused a wide enough space for them to pass.

"Where the hell are we?" Rand said, killing his vehicle behind Marshall's.

Marshall had already turned his off and was staring into the gaps between spruces and holding Ivan tightly. He glanced at the GPS, which he had mounted to the four-wheeler. "I don't know. I've lost connection to the satellite."

A map still showed on his screen, but there was no pointer, and a message complained: *Signal lost.*

"What does that mean?" Rand sat straight up in his seat, and though he knew the answer, he wanted to hear it out loud.

"Ivan's still got a scent. I guess it means we do it the old-fashioned way from here." He depressed the power button on the GPS unit, and the screen went blank. He climbed off the ATV.

Rand dismounted his as well.

Ivan barked in the night-like foliage ahead, pulling at his lead, and the three of them ventured on.

Rand watched the world grow darker, unsure if it was the clouds or the canopy or the oncoming night. His phone showed no service and five o'clock one minute, then seemed to tell him it was six the next. The passage of time and the decrease in light fueled his growing unease; adding to that was a noticeable drop in temperature.

The positive, the thing that kept them moving, was Ivan. He sniffed and navigated between trees. He paused only seconds here or there, then growled and darted ahead. He was fast, and he was determined. He was exhausting, but they kept going.

Marshall called Ivan to stop and take a break. The dog sat, his nose toward the scent, waiting.

"Jesus, this is a hike." Rand was out of breath between the

exercise and the altitude.

"They really made some distance." Marshall dug two bottles of water from his backpack and handed one to Rand. "I didn't think they'd've gotten this far." He wasn't as out of breath as Rand, but his words came out heavy.

Rand opened the water and chugged. It was cold going down, but he hadn't realized how dry his throat was until it was washed by drink.

"How high do you think we are?"

"If the GPS was working I could tell you, but my best guess is above seven thousand, maybe eight by how thin the air feels."

"Jesus."

"Didn't plan on going over a mountain pass today?"

"Definitely not on foot."

Ivan whined.

They both glanced down at the dog. His gaze was precise on a gap between the spruces ahead.

"I think he wants to go," Rand said, and swallowed another gulp.

"You ready?"

"Yeah."

Snowflakes filtered through the trees, landing on Rand's nose and cheeks. It sent a shiver over his skin and down his arms.

"Okay." Marshall secured his pack and told Ivan, "Jít," and they set off again.

The spurt of travel lasted about a hundred feet as snow fell harder and the ground became blanketed in white. Ivan stopped and whined, pawing at the white as if blaming it for his trouble. He sniffed a tree, a bush, taller debris peeking through the ivory veneer, then turned to Marshall and barked.

"Try again," Marshall said. "Najděte to."

Ivan darted from tree to tree, sniffing. He whined, making

wider and wider circles around the area.

"Trouble?" Rand watched the dog, getting the sensation that they had run out of luck. An unrecognized parallel formed in his mind—losing ATVs, walking through the woods, losing their way—but it was a clouded idea whose only recognizable aspect was a sinking feeling in the gut.

"The snow's making the trail fade."

"He looks frustrated."

"He is."

Ivan crisscrossed a dozen trees, his lead winding around their trunks.

"Shit." Marshall followed the lead, untangling the mess from behind while Ivan weaved through brush and saplings, only his nose leading him. The dog had created a twisted series of pretzels by the time Marshall yelled, "Ivan, stop!"

The lead stretched stiff from both sides, and Ivan and Marshall were held in place. Ivan pulled and whined. His eyes darted from tree to bush to shadow. His eyes were wide, and his legs shuffled below him as he fought to move.

"Ivan, stop!" Marshall left the end of the lead wrapped around a low bough, stepped over the intertwined netting the dog had created, and kneeled beside Ivan.

The dog growled and twisted and snapped at the lead.

"Ivan!" Marshall grabbed Ivan's collar.

"What's going on?" Rand said.

"Klid, klid," Marshall told the dog.

Ivan looked up at him, taking a deep breath. He let out a whine and sat.

"It's okay, boy." Marshall ran a hand down the dog's side and unclipped the lead from his collar. "Come here." He gestured at Rand.

"Yeah." Rand came closer, but not too close. There was something happening here he didn't want to get in the way of.

"Hold him."

"I don't—"

"It's fine. He's calm now, but I need to untangle his lead before we can move on."

"I don't know his commands." Rand came slowly closer.

"And you shouldn't. It's okay. Just tell him klid. It'll calm him down."

"Klid? What is that? German?"

"Czech. Just hold the handle on his vest."

"Okay..." Rand reached over and took the handle between the dog's shoulder blades. "Klid, Ivan, klid."

"Good."

Ivan glanced up at Rand, then Marshall, and Marshall began backtracking through the tangles.

"Klid, Ivan. Good dog." Rand looked down at the animal.

Ivan watched Marshall, then stared into the woods. A low growl rumbled from his chest. Rand could feel it through the nylon loop.

"Klid, Ivan. It's okay." Rand looked into the woods, following Ivan's gaze. He saw tree trunks and shadows, darkened shapes of overlapping pine in the dimming evening light. Some, he noticed, looked like things, like people. He felt an icy spike as he wondered if it was them, the fugitives, but the limbs were too long, the bodies too big. The snow thickened, forming a screen, and the shapes seemed to move.

A heavy feeling swelled inside Rand. It begged him to run before whatever it was set its grips into him. He told himself that it was nothing more than his brain making shapes out of the shapeless, like seeing resemblances in the clouds. He wanted to believe that.

Ivan whined and jerked the other way. His claws kicked up

snow, and the jolt sent pain up Rand's wrist.

"Ivan, no!" Rand shouted.

Marshall turned their direction. "What's going on?"

"I don't—"

Ivan spun and sunk his teeth into Rand's shin.

It was more pressure and shock than pain at first. It was like someone had hit his leg with a bat. Then the sharpness, then the fire.

"Ow!" Rand let the dog go and jumped back, dropping on his ass.

Ivan darted into the trees. After twenty feet, he was invisible through the shower.

"Marshall!" Rand grabbed his leg.

Marshall was already running over. He kneeled and looked at the wound. He turned and screamed, "Ivan!"

"Ivan!" Marshall screamed, all the possible consequences circling in his mind. They already risked reprimand for going off on their own. Now, he could get suspended or fired for losing his dog. He could get lost in these woods in the downpour of snow and catch frostbite or worse. He could lose his friend.

It was a tidal wave of fears he pushed down as he followed Ivan's tracks in the snow, careful not to move faster than Rand could follow.

Rand was another one. Another growing fear. The bite wasn't deep, but there was bleeding, and blood loss meant heat loss. As the temperature dropped and the snow rose, that got dangerous, especially when he had no idea where he was going.

"You see him?" Rand shouted from behind. He was limping—quickly, but limping—trying to keep up with Marshall.

"No." And he feared he never would again. "Ivan!" The tracks were shallow now, more dimples in the snow than recognizable footprints. He cursed Rand for holding him back and cursed himself for having Rand hold the dog. He should have held the dog and asked Rand to undo the lead. He wanted to run ahead and leave Rand to watch out for himself. He wanted to race after his friend before the storm separated them forever.

He couldn't do that. Rand was a human and his responsibility, especially after the bite.

"Ivan! Přijít! Ivan! Přijít!"

The trail was gone. Not a print, not a dimple, nothing but a smooth sea of white in the midst of... Marshall noticed the trees around them. They were different. Still thick and old, but the branches had no needles. They were skeletons of a forest, like beetle kill or the result of a fast-moving fire. It was eerie, and it only made his worry worse.

He kept moving, but he slowed so Rand could catch up. "The trail's gone." He pointed ahead. "I think he went that way, but I can't be sure."

Rand looked in the direction Marshall pointed, then around. "Are we anywhere near where we think Betty and his crew went?"

"No way to know. We have no scent and no trail to follow." He gestured to the fading light above. "I don't even know what direction we're going at this point. All I can think to do is try to cut our losses and hope to find Ivan."

"Jesus. We may be out here all night in this."

"Yeah. But I have some emergency stuff in my bag and my radio, so we may get reamed for it, but we can call for help if we absolutely need it."

"Last resort."

"Yeah."

"I hate to say it, but I think you're right." Rand looked at the snow underfoot. "I'm sorry I lost him."

"Yeah."

Beside their path, one after another, the skeletal monoliths appeared broken. They were cracked in their centers and fallen on one another. They lay on the ground, lumps under the piling snow. They made enormous structures of dead, withering trunks and limbs in jagged, blackened shapes and low fields of rotting, jutting wasteland.

"What happened here?" Marshall pointed.

"It's like the entire forest died and crashed in on itself."

"Have you ever heard of something like that?"

Rand stared, speechless.

The death was silent beyond the patter of flakes over woody corpses.

"I don't like this," Marshall said. He felt like a fool saying that to another cop, another member of this brotherhood where men didn't admit their fears or say no to challenges. But he said it anyway, because somehow he knew this was different. This situation was getting more severe by the minute, and everyday bravado would be more dangerous than truth. "I want to get out of here."

He screamed into the wall of white. "Ivan! Come here, boy!"

Neither said anything about the shadows.

Part IV

29

S TEVIE'S HEAD THROBBED IN waves with his heartbeat. His skull could have been broken for all he knew, but when he realized he was back in the waking world, his first thought was how much he wanted to go back to sleep.

Then he remembered his dreams; at least, he thought they were dreams. But they weren't. They were his mind rehashing his memories, ones he would rather forget.

They were taking that little ranch from the girl and her family. Dad told them not to move, and the crippled guy went for his gun. That didn't work out so well for him.

Then he was with Honey in the bedroom, having a good time. Then he was in the living room, and the dead guy was back, but he wasn't right. Slimy living things dripped from his body. They came after Mom and Dad and Honey. They came toward him, and he ran.

Stevie didn't want to sleep anymore, so he opened his eyes.

The room was dark and cold. His hands were tied. There were whispers to his right.

"Yeah, he's waking up," one said.

"Shit." He was with the goddamn hostages. *He* was a prisoner now. But why? Was Honey?

He saw the moms and kids. Why the fuck were they even out here? They stared back at him, waiting for something. He didn't see Honey. She was with *them* now, he knew it, probably bouncing on Shamus's lap as he sat here.

Shamus… "Stop him," the Irish prick's words rang in his mind.

He saw those bodies, the blood, the reason he ran. It was all a delusion, right? Something weird from the cold and stress and lack of sleep? It had to have been. Maybe if he just explained that to Shamus, they would untie him. If not, he'd untie himself and kill them all. Especially Honey, that traitorous bitch.

"Shamus!" Stevie's head ached as soon as his voice started. The word echoed with pain around his skull.

There was light below the door. A shadow crossed it.

"Shamus! Get me out of here!"

The shadow nearly filled the gap, and the door opened, letting firelight spread into the room. It was Nick. "What do you want?" He held a silver camping cup in his hand, and Stevie was sure he smelled coffee.

"I want to talk to Shamus. I shouldn't be in here."

"Shamus's resting right now. I'll be sure to pass along your displeasure when he awakens." Nick began pulling the door shut, a smirk on his lips.

"Wait! Let me out of this. This ain't right."

"Shamus wants you here. This is where you stay." Nick's brow was tight, like he was explaining to an idiot and had exhausted all his patience.

"I know I was acting crazy. I'm better now."

"Yeah." He pulled the door.

"Where's Honey?"

Nick opened the door, his smile wider. "Oh, I think she's *resting* with the boss. You'll have to get in line, because me and Perry get to *rest* next."

"Fuck you!"

Nick snickered and slammed the door.

"Let me out of this!"

The fuzzy-headed bastard didn't return this time.

"I'll kill all you fuckers!"

Stevie huffed and yanked on his bindings. The bed behind him squeaked and thudded against the floor, but the fabric didn't tear.

"Looks like you're one of us now," the black girl said.

"Fuck you."

She shook her head.

Stevie looked closer at them all: the redheaded kid, the blond kid, the white woman, and the black one. Fuck 'em. He didn't have to talk to them. He'd get out of this. He would kill them all and get back on the road. He'd find a new girl and more money.

A vision passed through his mind of Shamus in that other bed, leather sheets and Honey on top. She straddled him and rocked her hips, and that Irish prick smiled like a goddamn moron.

"Fuck," he grumbled.

Fuck her. Fuck all of them.

"What was all that?" Perry asked from his seat beside the fire.

"That asshole's awake." Nick took his seat.

"Yeah, I figured that. What was that shit about Honey?"

"I wanted to fuck with him." The sneer on Nick's face became a gaping smile.

Perry shook his head.

There was a beep, and Nick and Perry turned to the corner where Tony was playing some game on one of the kids' Nintendo. His expressionless rat face was lit in a blue glow.

"You think we should light a fire in there?" Perry said.

"Why would we do that?"

"They're hostages, right?"

"Yeah."

"Hostages aren't any good if they freeze to death."

Nick rolled his eyes. "I suppose you want to feed them too? Give them back their sleeping bags and—hey Tony, we need to give the kids back the video game you got there."

"Shut the fuck up."

"You shut the fuck up. Why you being soft on these assholes?"

Perry held his tongue and stirred his cup of horrible coffee.

"Yeah, I guess if it gets *too cold,* we'll make a little fire in there. But that's it."

Perry nodded.

"But I'm keeping the goddamn sleeping bags." Nick stared into the flames inside the wood stove. "Slept like shit last night."

Out of habit, Perry pulled his phone out of his pocket to see the time. The window had become flutters of white over black, and he was sure it was night now. But his phone was as unhelpful as the last time he looked. Battery dead. No image, no time, no nothing. He was tempted to slam it into the wall, useless piece of crap. He slid it into his pocket, and there was scratching behind the walls again.

There was a sense that it was later than it felt. Something rolled around in his mind, telling him that as much as Nick was complaining, tonight could end up worse than last night despite the roof over their heads and the sleeping bags.

From the darkened corner of the room, something agreed.

Tony could feel the eyes on him. Not Perry's or Nick's, but the others. The things obscured in the gloom. They crawled, and they scratched in the corners and cracks and crevices as they waited and watched. He liked it.

He pressed button after button, racing go-carts and building crap in Minecraft. None of it mattered, but he got the idea they liked watching him do it. Like they were learning from him—not how to play Minecraft, more like they were learning who he was. They had their fingers in his brain, and he enjoyed the feeling.

They were interested in him. They wanted to be his friend.

He remembered turning eight, at the park, and the three kids that came to his party—not his friends, he didn't have any; they were his mom's friends' kids—and they all played with each other on the elaborate playground that looked like a medieval castle. They raced over pathways and slid down slides and swung, and each time he tried to join them, they ran away.

The others liked this memory.

He thought of asking out Shawna Stevens in middle school and how she said no, and later that afternoon he got a phone call. It was a girl's voice, saying she was sorry and really did want to go. She prodded him for compliments, asked what he liked about her, and promised to sit with him at lunch the next day. When the next day came, the whole school lunchroom, and he sat alone.

It was a prank. She was on the phone, but so were four of the biggest douchebags in school, the ones who chanted *Rat Face, Rat Face, Rat Face* at him daily.

They really liked this one.

The memories would have made him sad. They made him want to drive his car into the river and kill himself more than once. But this time, they didn't bother him. He was entertaining his friends now.

He would keep doing that, entertaining them. It made everyone happy, after all.

30

S HAMUS STRETCHED OUT, THE leather sheets gliding over his bare skin. They were soothing, feeling more like silk than what he knew they were made of. They had told him, after all. Not that he was sure if it came from his dreams or a whisper or the sort of extra cognition/connection he'd felt since walking into this place.

Connection. He liked that idea. More than any other feeling going through his mind was the sensation of *home*. He was home now. It was an idea he had scoffed at in the past. He had said the word but not really felt it since childhood. Home then was Mom. But since her throat was slit and her blood ran cold, he never really thought he would have a place like that again, a place where he felt like he belonged—connected.

As the stitched quilt of human skin and hair contoured his muscles, he knew he had that now. His need to keep running had faded. The need to get out of the woods to a safe house was gone. This was his safe house. This was where he would live and die. He was sure of that. What he wasn't sure of was his crew. Would *they* connect?

Flip a coin. It was up to them. Either way, though, they weren't leaving this place. That's what he had been told, and he agreed. If they didn't want to accept the gift they had been given, it was on them.

"*Yes*," they whispered.

His stomach clenched in on itself. He'd gone so long since eating, then slept, he could feel his body atrophying. It was time to find some nourishment.

Shamus stood and slid on his pants and shirt, opened his bugout bag, and grabbed his hunting knife. He slid his belt through its loop so it hung at his side like some medieval warrior's sword.

Shadows danced and parted as he passed the dresser, nodding at the pictures as if they were old friends and glancing down at the gap in the floorboards beneath the dresser. The floor shook with his heavy steps, and he grabbed the lantern as he pulled open the door.

"Boss." Nick laid his cards face down on the table.

"Boss," Perry repeated, cupping his cards to his chest.

Tony glanced up from his game and nodded.

"You want some food, boss?" Nick gestured toward the bags of freeze-dried survivalist stuff and the other snacks they discovered.

There was a moment of stillness in the room. Only the fire moved as it crackled and popped and shed embers into its ash.

Shamus looked around the cabin and raised his hands. "Where's the girl? The hot one?"

Nick shook his head and sucked air through his teeth. "She ran. Not sure why. She was making some food, went out for some snow—to melt into water—and she just took off. Don't know what to say, boss."

Nick and Perry stared at him, waiting. Shamus looked at the door, and his head tilted as they whispered into his ear.

"You know, it's all right." Shamus walked to the table's edge between Nick and Perry and set the lantern beside the deck of cards. "I mean, if she got picked up, she could tell the cops where we are. But I don't think that's going to happen." He grabbed Nick and Perry by their necks and slammed their heads together. There was a crack as skull met skull.

"Fuck!" Perry shouted. Nick stayed quiet. Their faces grimaced, but they dared not move.

"Still, though," Shamus released their necks. "You two should have known better." He strolled to the pile of food and scanned what was there, then leaned in and picked up a chocolate bar. The rest had no appeal. He was hungry, sure, but nothing there looked satisfying. The chocolate would be tasty, even if it didn't fill him up.

He opened the wrapper and sat at the table, opposite Nick and Perry. They watched him. Perry rubbed his bald head. It was obvious Shamus had something on his mind. They would just have to wait for him to get to it.

"You want me to cook you something?" Nick said. "Any of those meals look good?"

"You serious? They look like crap." He took a bite of chocolate and chewed it with his mouth open. Brown saliva rimmed his lips.

"What are you thinking, boss?" Perry said. The side of his head glowed red. "About the plan, I mean. How long do we need to stay here?"

"You in a rush to leave?" Shamus swallowed and took another bite.

"I—I don't know. Get back to a bed, to some real food. I'd like to get to those."

"My friends..." Shamus opened his arms wide. "We have everything we need here. Let's not rush ourselves. Last thing we want is to rush out there and get nabbed by the cops. We're safe here, for now."

"Yeah," Nick said. "I get ya."

"Safe." Perry nodded, though his eyes seemed to be searching the cabin for answers or other solutions.

"Safe indeed." Shamus shoved the rest of the chocolate in his mouth and gulped it down. It had done nothing for his hunger, only postponed it.

He turned to his nephew. "What do you think, Tony? Are you in a rush to leave?"

Tony shook his head. "I'm good here."

"So, we're in agreement, then. We wait here a bit longer." Nick and Perry nodded. "So, how about we celebrate with some real food then?"

"Whatever you say, boss." Nick tapped the table. "They even got some booze over there."

"First things first." Shamus pulled the knife from his belt. He leaned across the table and sat it in front of Nick. "Go cut us a few steaks for dinner."

The men were silent as Nick looked around the room. There was no side of beef or even a fridge with meat. His forehead wrinkled. His lip curled. He squinted, searching for what he must have missed until his eyes scanned past the blood stains on the floor. Then, he froze.

"You don't mean..." Nick's voice faded as he spoke. His gaze went to the front door.

"I mean, we need steaks for a room full of hungry men. Go get 'em."

Nick stared into Shamus's eyes, expecting his straight face to crack a smile, burst out laughing, and say it was all a joke. He glanced at Perry, whose mouth was slightly opened, a controlled expression as he waited for the same. When he saw Nick looking his way, he nodded down at the knife.

There was no choice here. The boss was serious.

Nick reached over the table and took the knife in hand. A rock formed in his gut as he felt its heft. It was heavier than he expected, with a long, thick blade. It was a knife that cried to be used, that seemed like it would only feel proper when slicing through meat. He wanted to drop it but felt something cold pushing his fingers to tighten around it.

"So, Perry, you want to give me a hand?"

Shamus gathered the cards on the table and motioned toward Perry that he wanted the pile in front of him as well. "No. Perry's going to sit with me and play." Perry slid the stack over, and Shamus straightened the cards and started shuffling. "You got this."

"Yeah, I got it." Nick nodded. He really didn't want to do this. He didn't mind killing so much, but truth be told, he had a weak stomach for the cleanup.

Nick headed to the door and took a last breath of warm air before he stepped out into the blizzard.

I got this.

Luckily, he didn't have to go far. A few feet to his right, the corpse of the woman Shamus had killed leaned against the log wall.

Nick had to brush away three inches of snow to see what she looked like, blue and stiff. If you didn't look at the ruptured eye socket, you might have thought she fell asleep and froze sitting against the side of the cabin.

He lifted her arm. It moved, but he could feel the hardened skin and the resistant muscle.

"Fuck."

How was he going to do this? He couldn't believe he was here trying to figure this out. Shamus must have lost it. Whether it was the snow or the stress of being on the run, he wasn't sure, but he was positive that if he didn't come back with what he was told to, he'd be lying in the snow next to this bitch.

He glanced into the wall of white. Every few seconds, he could see the skeletal trees through gaps in the downpour.

He could run like that chick had. He could say *fuck it* and take off.

The frozen body in front of him argued otherwise. Honey was probably dead. They all would have been dead if they didn't find this place. They got through last night okay, but there wasn't a never-ending blizzard last night. He would turn into a meat popsicle if he went out there.

"Fuck."

The decision came to him; he needed her legs. There was plenty of meat on the legs, and he should be safe from having to make too many cuts. He doubted Shamus would be sympathetic if he came back with vomit-covered meat from spending too much time and letting the act get to him.

He pulled the woman off the wall and laid her beside the house, then lifted her coat and began undoing her pants.

It instantly hurt. His fingers were freezing the moment they touched the snow and her metal snap. He could barely feel what he was doing as he unzipped her zipper.

Nick groaned and shoved his fingers in his armpits, trying to heat them back up. Her fly was open in a V, and he wondered how many times he had undone a woman's pants all by himself. There was Lisa Olson in high school. He'd scared her so badly she didn't move an inch as he did his thing—not until the very end, when he was done. That was when she wiped away the tears.

"Here we go." He tucked his fingers behind the band of her pants and widened them. He jerked on her jeans, and her entire body shifted. The damn jeans didn't move at all.

He should drag her inside and do it there. It would be so much fucking easier. But then Shamus would give him shit, or worse, lose all confidence in him.

No. He could do this.

He grabbed the right side of her body with both hands and pulled. She flipped on her side, and he nodded. This was going to work. He ran his fingers down the waistline and tugged again. She flattened on her stomach.

"Yes." He tucked his fingers back in his armpits. "Rump roast." Why not? That would be easier.

He peeled down the woman's pants and underwear together and paused for a moment, admiring her ass. It was a shame. It was a nice ass. If it wasn't so goddamn cold, maybe.

Nick readied his knife to the right of her ass and smirked as he wondered what the kid inside would do if she knew what was happing to Mommy right now.

Perry wished he had different cards. A pair of jacks, king high, could go either way, and right now, he did not want to win. He didn't know what the hell was going on with Shamus, but he had seen that look in a man's eyes before, and he knew the guy had snapped. It was possible Shamus might pull it back and rejoin reality, but it wasn't going to be before this game was done. And right now, Shamus had a pistol at his side—Perry's rifle was across the room with the others.

"Go on," Shamus said.

There was about ten bucks in the pot after the first round of betting, an amount Perry would be happy to lose if he just folded, but that would look weak. He couldn't afford to look weak. If he lost, that could slide. If he won, maybe he could play it cool enough not to piss off the man. But folding, no. That was the same as giving up.

Perry threw a bill on the pot. "Five."

Shamus fanned out his five cards. His eyes scanned over each of them, and Perry hoped they were good, something to cool the madness blazing from his wild pupils. The boss set down the hand and fished a bill from his pocket. Without even looking at it, he slapped it down on the pile.

"Ten."

A five-dollar raise. *Shit.*

Shamus's eyes twinkled in the lantern light, and Perry debated on calling or raising. Whether to hold a strong front or just match. That twinkle seemed to glow, and Shamus grinned.

Perry threw in five. He matched. Shamus would have called no matter what he raised. That grin—he was ready to rumble.

"Lay 'em down," Shamus said. His hand hovered on his waist. Over his pistol.

Perry took a quiet breath and laid his cards face up. Jack, jack, king, nine, three, all in mixed suits.

"Well, goddamn." The grin widened. Shamus laid his cards out. Ten, ten, eight, eight, five.

"Shit." Perry wanted to leap. He was out a few bucks, but he was alive. Thank fucking God. He reached to pick up the cards. It should be his deal next.

"Leave 'em." Shamus raked in his cash. "I want the deal."

"Okay."

"Go get that whiskey bottle." He nodded at the supplies. "I feel I need a good swig to keep this luck going."

Perry rose and did as he was told. He grabbed the bottle, pulled the cups together, and poured four shots. He wished Nick would hurry the fuck up as he passed Shamus a cup.

Shamus dealt two hands of five, set the cards down, and lifted the cup to his nose. "Smells like shite."

"Bunch of girls. What do you expect?"

Shamus raised his eyebrows and tossed back the shot. Perry did the same. Shamus slammed the cup and picked up the one Perry had intended for Tony and tossed it back as well. Then he grabbed the fourth cup and drank it hard and fast.

"Well, maybe if we drink it fast enough, we won't taste the shite." Shamus laughed.

Perry didn't know whether to laugh or not. He did. He poured four more, and the door swung open, bringing in a gust of snow and cold. Nick marched inside with four big hunks of red meat.

Nick forced the door shut with his back and came to the table. His teeth chattered, and his hands were glowing red. "Got 'em."

Shamus picked up his cards. "Then cook 'em up."

A slow slimy sensation circled Perry's gut as he watched the hunks of meat dangle from Nick's grip, knowing he was going to have to eat one of them. He didn't dare glance at his gun again, but he thought it, and as he did, Shamus pounded on the table.

"Drink!" Shamus shouted.

Nick took his without another thought and headed to the stove. Perry shot the whiskey, gathered his cards, and looked down at his hand. He wanted to puke. A pair of aces stared back at him.

A moment later, the pan sizzled.

31

LIGHT FLICKERED BELOW THE door, the sole illumination clawing its way inside the lodging room. Wanda watched it highlight their male companion's shoes as each adult alternated from struggling for their freedom to resting and repeating.

Wanda's wrists burned so badly she couldn't tell if they were bleeding or just extremely sore. The fabric was still tight around her wrists, maybe tighter, but she thought the cordage was getting longer. She was stretching it or slowly cutting it strand by strand. She couldn't see to be sure, but she prayed it wouldn't be long before the old cloth gave altogether.

Lins hadn't said much at all. She wept softly off and on and was now back on.

Angel focused on her mom. If she wanted to keep her eyes open, there weren't many other options. She could barely see Abby all the way at the far end of the room. Looking at Lins made her sad. She had tried to comfort her friend but didn't know what to say that could help in the slightest. To her left was the man, and beyond him, the eyes. She had found her way to ignoring her gore-soaked surroundings, but she didn't think she could ignore them.

They floated on that side of the room. Their brown and blue irises, their yellowed, cloudy sclerae were here, and they were not. They were close and far at the same time, hard to measure and hard to define.

If it was only their eyes, Angel might have been able to handle them. In the dark lull between the presence of light, it was only the eyes. When the flames flickered brighter into the room, that was when Angel saw more. The blood. The gashes. The cavities in their corpses where someone had removed bits here and there and left the remainder.

Angel couldn't tell if she was seeing the aftermath of blind rage or the meticulous barbarism of a backwoods Dr. Frankenstein hunting for parts, and she didn't want to know. If there was some way she could help these souls, especially the kids, she would have, but tied to a bedpost, there was nothing she could do but weep and fear.

So she didn't look.

Wanda paused every time a voice spoke in the next room. The tones were muffled, and she could only catch every tenth word, but she was determined to learn any piece of information she could. So far, that added up to almost nothing.

She knew the boss was back—not from his words, but from the return of his booming voice. She also knew something had happened to the woman. She wasn't sure if she was in the far room or gone, but the lack of her voice told Wanda something—she just wasn't sure what.

Wanda hoped she was in the far room. As long as another woman was around, the men might not... She shivered as her mind flashed to the house, the bum, his penis inside her, tearing her flesh, his stench pulsing over her as he thrust.

She sucked in air. Tears burned the corners of her eyes and her heart pounded. She fought them both. She envisioned how the house burned as she ran away, how that place was nothing but a charred pile of ash today. She only wished he was in there when it happened.

The thought had occurred to her a thousand times since then:

What would she do if she ever saw him again? Be it in the street, a store, a back alley—in her bedroom. She liked to think she would bash his brains in. She wished she was confident that she would have the strength of will to do it and not collapse in fear.

She never would have doubted herself in the past. She had always been the first one to charge in and tackle a situation, but when that bum hit her on the back of the head, it was more than her ability to fight that he removed that day. It was her confidence that she could ever fight as she wanted to again. How could she know she wouldn't get clobbered on the head again while on patrol? What if some lowlife she pulled over got behind her?

She saw the ceiling rocking. She felt the burning. She tasted the trash left from his spit on her lips.

"Mom?" Angel whispered.

Wanda snapped back into the dark room, questioning whether reality was actually better than her vision.

Yes, it was. Because she was going to find a way out of this—she looked into Angel's eyes and there was no doubt. She had to. She pulled harder, damning the pain and any damage it may bring.

"We're going to get through this," Wanda groaned.

The man huffed.

Angel glanced at the door and back at her mother. "Mom? What's that smell?"

Wanda refused to stop, but as the scent hit her nose, she couldn't help it. It was cooking. It wasn't the rations she'd brought for the hike, but something else, something real—meat. There was an edge to it that reminded her of bacon, then savory smells that made her think of grilling a pork chop.

There was no pork in her bag, or in any of their bags as far as she knew. Not unless Kathy had snuck something as a surprise, maybe? Or maybe their captors had brought it.

"I don't know," Wanda finally said. "They're cooking something."

It made her stomach churn inside its emptiness. Her mouth watered. How long had it been since she ate? Breakfast? They all needed food. Maybe once those bastards had eaten, they would be easier to deal with. She would wait a little, then call them in.

She pulled at her bonds again.

She would free herself, call them in, and give them a surprise.

"Man, I'm hungry," Abby said. She leaned against the bed, her nose in the air, taking in the smell.

"Me too," Lins said.

Angel didn't agree. She was hungry, but something more pressed into her than the hunger. There was something more attached to that smell, and she knew it wasn't right. It wasn't something they should want.

"Let them eat first," Wanda said. "We can ask again for some food once they've had their fill."

"I'm cold," Lins said.

"We'll ask them to light this stove, too, sweetie." The chill had been getting worse since the lights had gone dim, but Wanda hadn't wanted to admit it. Not yet—another problem to deal with. The danger, the death, the hunger, the cold. It was never-ending. "Try to hold on, Lins."

"You having any luck?" Abby asked, her arms taking turns going forward and back, pulling her cords against the bed frame.

"I don't know," Wanda said. "I—can't really feel..."

"Yeah... We'll get it."

A large, boisterous laugh shook the floor. It was the leader. Smaller, less committed laughter followed from the others.

The man huffed again.

Abby stared at the guy, gritting her teeth as she worked her bonds. "Whether you want to admit it or not, you're one of us now. Why don't you tell us what the hell's going on with your people?"

"They aren't *my* people," he snapped back.

"Then who are they?" Wanda said. "And who are you?"

He shook his head, dismissing the questions.

"What's it going to hurt at this point?" she asked.

"Just talk, man," Abby said. "Why are you here?"

He stared at the roof. "I'm not telling you shit. When this is over, I'm out of here. And if you make it—which, by how Shamus's been acting, I doubt—I don't want you knowing anything about me."

"So you're criminals," Wanda deduced, "and the lead guy's name is Shamus."

He scowled at her.

"So don't tell us about you, then. Tell us about them."

"You know what—fuck it. I don't owe them shit after this. Yeah, the big guy is Shamus, the bald guy is Perry, the big-haired guy's Nick, and the rat-faced guy's name is Tony, I think."

"And the girl?" Abby said.

He gazed down and ground his teeth together.

"It's Honey, isn't it?" Wanda asked. "The other guy, Perry, said it before. She's your girlfriend, isn't she?"

"Fuck her."

"Okay. Why are you here? Why tie us up like this?"

"We're on the run. Cops are chasing us."

"Now it makes sense," Abby said. "So, we're hostages or something?"

"I guess. We were just trying to get out of the snow when we bumped into you."

"So were we," Wanda said. "It was so weird. All that snow out of nowhere."

"We were walking after our four-wheelers died when it started."

Abby hesitated. "It felt like it was pushing us."

"They want us here," Angel said.

Angel watched them swarm from the far side of the room. The eyes glimmered over the dark walls. Their wounds shined and dripped, leaving trails of blood as they hovered inches from the floor. Their mouths moved as if talking. They snapped as if they could bite the air and chew it.

"What do you mean?" Mom said.

Angel's eyes were glued to one of the smaller ones. She heard drips as his blood ran from his gaping gut, down his bare leg, and splashed into the pools below him. He was a child, no more than eight, face nearly black with caked blood—he had no bottom jaw. He had no tongue. But a hiss came from his mouth. Not words, words wouldn't have reached Angel even if he could speak—their words never did—but she could hear the hiss of his dying breath repeating as he moved.

"Angel?" Lins said. Her face was frozen in curious worry.

"What are you looking at?" Abby said.

The boy leaned forward. He reached for Angel with a fingerless hand, only a palm and five bloodied stumps. She shook her head but said nothing. She didn't want what was coming.

His palm touched her forehead.

It was a dark place, a pit. Light came down in slits from the ceiling. Heavy feet walked over boards, and as dust rained over Angel's face, children whimpered.

She could see their faces. Josiah, Beth, Melanie, Hans, Walter, Ansel, Mort. At least three had been taken; she was fuzzy on the numbers. The rest cried, knowing it would eventually be their turn. They huddled over dirt in each other's arms. They hated themselves, knowing what they would do when the trap door opened.

Smells wafted down. It was a soup. Angel had smelled it before—was boiled in it.

There were words above. *She* yelled at *him*. Stomping across the floor.

Blinding light crashed down. A hinge whined. The door crashed into the wall above, and a beast climbed down.

Beth was the first to run to the opposite side, clawing at the dirt wall as if she could tunnel away from fate.

Hans grabbed her and threw her toward the monster of a man. He hugged the wall ahead, and Walter pushed himself against the dirt beside him.

Melanie grabbed Walter's back, pulling herself as close to the far wall as she could get. Ansel tossed her at the man and took her place as she hit the ground. Beth stepped on Melanie and tried to dig her way between Ansel and Walt.

The cries screeched in Angel's ears. There were no words. No arguments. Only grasping hands and clawing fingers.

The Monster seemed amused by the sight.

Josiah stomped on Melanie's face and snagged Beth by the ear. He dragged her, and she screamed. He dug his fingers inside Ansel's nose and ripped him from his spot. He took handfuls of Hans's and Walter's hair and ripped their faces from the dirt.

They punched and scraped. Blood ran down children's skin as fingernails ripped into one another. They forced each other back and punched guts and faces. They dove away from the danger, praying to cling to the dirt for one more second—the crucial second when the man would make his choice.

None heard the thumps. None head the ladder creak. They all stopped and looked back when the trap door slammed shut, strands of Melanie's hair caught in the wood.

She screamed from the top side of the floorboards.

They were repeating Angel's name as she returned. Mom called. Abby. Lins. She didn't talk back. She cried. She looked over each ghostly face and recognized most of the children. There were others in the back who looked on with radiating anger. Others wandered between them in sorrowful glides, unhindered by the living or the children.

"There're so many." Angel couldn't keep her gaze still.

A man with no arms walked past Lins and faded through the wall into the next room. Another with a beard and no legs floated away. The children looked back to the far side of the room, where they had been watching from. Fear hung from their mangled faces.

"So many what?" Lins asked.

"So many people." Angel whimpered and shook her head.

"Ghosts?" Mom said. "Here?" Her usual layer of misunderstanding was somehow removed. "What do you see, Angel?"

"There are ghosts?" Abby said.

"All of them. So many." Angel watched as they all came toward them. They all moved like a swarm, some looking back in fear, some refusing and darting through the walls. The rest passed Angel and Lins, passed Mom, passed Abby.

They were all gone from the room, and the flicker from below the door dimmed. It wasn't that the light stopped, it was still there, but the firelight seemed less potent, its reach less energized.

"Oh no." Angel looked down and closed her eyes.

"Angel, what?" Mom said. Her voice was loud now.

"Shhh." She tried to hush the others. Tears ran down her face. "Don't look." Her words trembled.

The dark side of the room grew dimmer. The blackness folded over the walls and beds and shelves until nothing could be seen. Nothing returned a dot of light. It was an absence that reached to other places, obscure regions where light was scorned. In those places, blackness devoured fear and exhaled towering waves of wrath. The gloom was an endless stretch through nothingness, and an onslaught of malevolence called attention to its advance.

"What?" Mom asked. "What is it?"

From the endless night, a shape crossed the floor. It stepped past the door, and the light fled from each footstep. It was a presence in the shape of a man, darkening the walls as it passed by and slipping from surface to surface like a shadow from another place.

"What is that?" Abby stopped moving. She pressed her back to the bed and held still. She was confused before as they spoke of ghosts. She didn't see those. But she saw something now. She didn't know what it was, but she saw something. And it burrowed into her with a dark, twisting sickness that made her insides tighten and quiver.

The shape was burned into Angel's mind. She didn't want to look up but knew it was there now. It was in the room. It had been allowed from some other place and was intent on harm whether it had the hands and body to perform it or not. It was the thing she felt in her room and in her dreamwalk—not those people, not the man and wife, but possibly the thing inside them. The thing that drove them.

She raised her head to see it.

It was on the wall above Lins.

"Get away from her," Angel said.

"What is that?" Mom asked. Her voice cracked as she said it. It was the sound of fear. It was a trembling pitch that was unmistakable and unavoidable once it took hold.

It stood tall, a man-shaped shadow over the blackness of night. But it was far from a man. It was a thing using the shape as a convenience, as a piece of bait and source of fear.

It leaned down toward Lins.

"What are you looking at?" Lins cried. "What's behind me?"

"Fuck," the man droned.

"Get away from her!" Mom yelled.

"Leave her alone!" Abby joined.

Its arms spread. They stretched from the girl as if threatening the room with its massive breadth. It reached forward, and what had been a foggy blackness attached to a wall came free.

Its long arms were a fuzzy, black manifestation, reaching from the wooden surface into the room. They were a solid patch of shady black gases with long stretching fingers and sharp, pointed ends.

It bent forward, arching down over Lins. Its head came closer, and cold, rancid breath flooded over the room.

"No," Angel said. "You can't have her."

Lins cried. "What's happening?" She tried to follow their gazes and see behind her but couldn't.

"Go away!" Mom screamed.

Abby had lost her voice.

Mom yanked on her bonds. The bed rattled against the floor. "Stop it!"

Its black hands wrapped around Lins's jaw. Its thumbs rested on her forehead. Her tears rolled over foggy fingers and dripped to the floor.

If Angel had had another moment to think, she probably wouldn't have done what she did. The thing in front of her made no sense. It was a thing made of shadows, not a thing of this world. It was a being from somewhere else that had no business in this world and should not have been able to touch Lins, but here it was—the girl's skin indenting where its hands pressed. Her flesh reddening from the pressure and who knew what else. This was an unreal thing which should not be, and yet, here it was.

Its fingers spread Lins's mouth wide. She shook under its touch, too scared to fight as her eyes fell on the dark mass. Its fingers went deeper, holding her mouth in a broad circle, and its unseen face rolled down toward the hole, diving toward it like a swimmer.

"Come here!" Angel howled.

Her voice shook the room nearly as much as the boss in the next. Wanda, Abby, Lins, and the man all recoiled as she spoke. Her words vibrated not just their outsides but within their thoughts. It was a command not to be disobeyed, and though Wanda, Abby, and Lins weren't the target, they wanted to obey.

The shadow beast sprung from its perch over Lins, releasing her mouth and soaring across the room. Its head dove into Angel's mouth, followed by its shoulders, arms, legs, and a wisp of gloom that trailed its essence.

Lins's face bled from burns where the creature had held her. She gasped.

All eyes fell on Angel.

Her eyes clouded black. They bled. Her head draped over her chest, and her eyes shut.

"No!" Wanda screamed.

32

G LOOM GAVE WAY TO light as the door burst inward. Shamus came through the opening more like a storm front than a man, his presence shoving a sickly taste into each mouth and causing a repulsive lurch within each belly.

"Angel!" Wanda screamed. The heavy bed thudded as she yanked and scooted inches at a time toward her daughter. "Get it out!" she yelled at the room. "Get it out of her!"

Shamus hovered over the center of the room, watching. A grin crept up his jaw.

"Let me loose! Let me help her!"

Nick leaned into the room. "All okay, boss?" His mouth was flat, his eyes searching and worried.

"It looks like one of our hosts showed himself." Shamus was focused on Angel now. His head tilted, analyzing, trying to understand what they wanted with the girl. There was something they wanted from each of them, after all. What was it this girl had?

"Let me help her!" Wanda screamed. The bed pounded hard on the floor as she lunged and slammed back into its frame.

As if she hadn't said a word, Nick asked, "Hosts? What do you mean, boss?"

Shamus didn't answer. He watched the mother now. Maybe this was what it wanted? The show? A mother's agony over not being able to help her child—the inner horror of it all.

"Shamus?" Stevie called. "I think we've got a misunderstanding here. Can you let me out so we can talk?"

Tears ran down Wanda's face. She threw herself forward and snapped back. She twisted, lost her balance, and her face slammed into the floor.

Nick took a step back and watched from the other side of the doorway.

Dust clung to Wanda's wet skin as she looked up at her daughter. Tears made muddy streaks across her cheeks. She blinked hard to get the specs from her eyes, and she howled.

"Shamus?" Stevie's voice was calm and controlled. "Come on, man. You gotta let me out of this."

"Let me go, you scumbag!" Wanda shifted her weight, rotating her body back upright. "Let us go!"

Shamus slid forward like a blur, lunging, lowering, his fist raising and crashing into Wanda's chin. Her head rocked back and slammed into the bed frame with a crack.

The room went silent, watching.

Wanda gurgled. She coughed as her head lowered, and she met Shamus with wide eyes. Her mouth spread, and before another sound emerged, his left hook rocked Wanda's head back against the bed again. Blood flowed from the side of her mouth like a faucet.

She coughed and spat. He watched her elusive gaze. When it met his, he jabbed with his right, her nose cracking from the impact. Another faucet of blood ran from her nostrils.

Abby whimpered. She didn't speak.

Lins stared at the floor, breathing fast and weeping.

Stevie held his breath.

Wanda coughed and hitched. She didn't look up.

Shamus nodded and stood. She would stay where she was. She would cry and wish she could kill him. But most of all, she would feel the helplessness she was supposed to, and she'd hate herself for it. And when they were ready, they would kill her. That would make his hosts happy.

Shamus glanced at Stevie, and Stevie took his chance. "Really, man, we can work this out."

Shamus spun, his boot flying. There was a wet crunch as the tip found Stevie's face and smacked his eye deep into the socket. Stevie's head whipped around, and he fell silent.

Shamus turned to Nick. "Bring the black one."

"No, no, no," Abby whispered.

Shamus left the room, and Nick went in.

He kneeled by Abby. "Shit. You have fucked up your wrists." He freed her from the bed and retied her bonds, then yanked her to her feet. "Go." He shoved her from behind.

Abby took a step, then glanced back at Wanda, at Angel, at Lins. She looked at Stevie, slumped over and breathing through shallow breaths. No one met her gaze.

For the first time, Abby cried.

"Don't make me tell you again." Nick shoved her in the back.

When the door thudded shut, the light went with them. Only cold and dark and shivering fear remained.

Perry held down his puke as he watched Shamus cross the main room and go into the bedroom. Nick trailed closely behind, shoving one of the hostages into the room with Shamus.

Perry looked away. He didn't want to know what was about to happen. His gaze skimmed over the plate before him, the half-eaten hunk of human flesh he had partaken in—that Shamus had insisted be served medium-rare—and his stomach leaped upward. He pushed it back down, turning to the fire.

The door slammed shut, and through the walls, there came a scraping noise of wood against wood. A clatter of something banging.

Perry tried not to listen. He wished he had some earbuds or some shit. He wished he had anything to take his mind off this crap.

The woman screamed, muffled but more than audible. It went softer and stopped.

Perry would never argue the fact that he was a violent guy. He would beat up a man in an instant for a stack of cash or if the boss said to. But what was going on here was... well, it was too far.

You don't kill your hostages for no reason. You slap 'em up a little, sure, make sure they know you mean business. As callous as he was, he was never cruel. And this felt cruel.

And eating a dead chick?

His stomach churned and bubbled.

That was just sick. He had swallowed a few bites, yeah, but shit, he didn't want to. Not like Shamus, who gobbled that crap down. Not like Tony and Nick, who seemed like they couldn't get enough. There were rations right there—this wasn't the Alps, and they weren't some soccer team stranded with no food. It was just overkill.

There was definitely something very wrong here, and the more time passed, the more he thought Honey may have had the right idea. Shamus wasn't himself—he was worse than himself on his worst day. Perry expected everyone to be on edge with the cops on their heels, but the look in Shamus's eyes as he stared into that plate of meat—it was unnatural.

A beep sounded from behind Perry. Tony's face was back in that toy.

"Shit," Tony said. "Battery's almost dead."

Perry would have been happy about that—no more beeps and chimes—but the thing was keeping Tony's attention. He was a little concerned with what was going to happen when Tony needed something else to occupy his time.

A muffled scream from the bedroom. Another clunk. A scream again, though quieter.

"You going to eat that?" Tony asked. He was standing over Perry's shoulder, staring at the chunk of that women's ass.

"I'm full, man—after all that dehydrated stuff earlier."

"Mind if I..." Tony's voice rose with eagerness.

"Go for it, pal."

Tony reached past Perry and snatched the bloody hunk with his bare hands. He shoved the whole thing in his mouth and went back to his game, cheeks bulging like a goddamn squirrel.

Perry's gut thrust against his ribs, and he wanted to just let it go, to get this stuff out of him. But there was no way, not without Shamus finding out. And with Nick and Tony acting as batshit as him, he was outnumbered. He damn sure wasn't going to end up like Stevie in there. He was no prognosticator, but as it sat right now, he did not see a good future for that guy.

He had to hold it down. He had have to bide his time. Maybe once everyone was asleep, he could take one of those sleeping bags and a handful of food and try his luck outside.

Maybe.

Wanda felt her brain waver on the edge of consciousness. Spots floated. Her nose burned. Her body was cold and hot at the same time. The back of her skull rang as badly as it did that day five months ago when her law enforcement career was put on hold indefinitely.

She looked at Angel, her angel, her one and only reason for being, and she saw a dark shape with a million fireworks dancing. She wanted to hold her baby's head and run her fingers through her hair. She wanted to tell her it would be okay and—something—there was a reason Angel wasn't talking, wasn't awake, but Wanda couldn't put her finger on it. She needed to help her angel, but why?

She tried calling her. A moan left her mouth.

Fear ran through her. It froze her insides, and vomit gurgled over her lips. This was worse than the West Hemlock house. This was worse than being pinned down and raped. It was worse than that Halloween night. At least those times it was only her in trouble, not her Angel.

Lins said something.

"What?" It came out as a breathy *Wha*.

Some words ran together, then, "Okay?"

Wanda looked at the child. Her eyes shined, and sparkles dripped from her face where tears ran wild. She didn't understand the question. *Okay*, what?

"What?" Again, *Wha*.

"Angel," something, "that shadow?"

What was that supposed to mean? What shadow?

"It'll... alright... sweetie."

The ceiling fell around them. Snow, showers of sparks. Drips of blood. Eyes surrounded them, stared into hers. Blood-soaked children, mutilated, limbs hacked, bodies mangled.

Tears streamed down Wanda's face. They turned red under her nose, and she tasted her own blood. It was filling her mouth and dripping down her throat. It was filling her belly, and over the pain, over the shame and sorrow, her heart ached for her baby girl.

She looked into the eyes of a dozen kids and bearded men,

and all she could whisper was *I'm sorry*.

33

Lins could never explain to Mom just how much she hated her new school. She didn't have a choice of where to go any more than Mom did. Mom was stuck, and so was she. Telling Mom would have made her feel worse, and she already felt bad enough.

The recess before school wasn't that bad if the gym was in cafeteria mode. On those days, she could grab a box of Froot Loops and find a seat on the far side, away from the line, and wait for the bell to ring. On the days when there had been a game the previous night, there was just a table outside the gym doors, and once she had her cereal, she had to take it to the playground. Those days sucked.

Chelsea Wallace was always there early, and it seemed like there was no escaping the girl. She had formed a group out of all the girls in Lins's class—the ones she had deemed worthy, anyway—and unless you wanted to bear the brunt of every other girl's wickedness, you had to play the game.

There was a ritual every day. Standing in a circle, one girl would make a dare, and the next had to do it. Then that girl would make a dare, and so on. But the dares always started with Chelsea, and only on a handful of days did the circle ever make it back around to her.

Dare after dare, day after day, the nature of the taunts varied, but their targets rarely did. They ranged from girls who had turned down the honor of being in the club to those who were never offered membership to the boys that one girl or another had a crush on. The worst thing a girl could do in the group was admit they had a crush, because the next day, that boy would become the target.

As Lins cried for the thousandth time in this cabin, her mind wandered to two days ago, maybe the last day she would ever go to that school, and she wished she hadn't confided in Zoe Carrol that she had a crush on Donald Zimmerman. If that was the last time she was to have seen Donny, she hoped that wasn't what he would remember her by.

She knew telling Zoe wasn't a good idea when it happened, but she had spent the entire time in math staring across the room at him and imagining holding his hand and him telling her he liked her. Her face was red when Zoe popped into her view—there was no way Zoe hadn't seen. Besides, Zoe wasn't as bad as the other girls... usually.

The bell for morning recess rang, and Zoe's lips were pursed, her grin growing and her eyes wide. "You like Donny, don't you?" After a mere half-second of Lins refusing to answer, she barked repeatedly, "You do! You do! Don't you!"

Kids filtered out of class, and Lins tried to get in line to leave, but there was no escaping Zoe. She trailed behind Lins, her voice slowly rising.

"You do. Admit it. You do. Come on."

"Okay." Lins skimmed past the watching eyes as well as those focused on the outdoors, on slides and swings and kickball and rock throwing. "Fine. I do." The words were a hiss.

"I knew it!" Zoe screamed as if it was hard to figure out, as if she couldn't have known by simply watching who Lins was staring at any time over the past fifty minutes.

"Shh." Lins slipped through the door. She was half relieved, having wanted to tell someone for nearly a week, but she was half terrified. "You can't tell anyone."

"Of course not!" Zoe ran her finger over her lips in a zipping gesture. "Not a soul. I promise."

They had barely been on the playground for five minutes when Chelsea started the Dare Circle.

She stared across the circle, taking her time and raising each girl's alarm bells as her gaze passed by. She stopped on Lilly Chapman.

"Lilly, I dare you to go tell Bobby that you heard Hank Peltzer likes him."

Lilly brightened like a giant red bulb on a Christmas tree. Not only was Bobby the boy she liked, but Hank was her brother's best friend—and boys in her school didn't like each other that way. Sure, she had seen boys liking each other on TV, but that didn't happen until high school, at least. Her mom said so.

Regardless of whatever Chelsea was up to, she couldn't tell Bobby that. She could barely speak to him, had a hard time even looking him in the eye. She would just die telling him something crazy like that.

"I—I don't want to," Lilly said.

"You have to," Zoe said. "That's the rules."

"Do it," Chelsea said, "or you're out."

Lilly looked over the group of twelve girls. Her eyes fluttered to the ground as she debated. She only really liked Stephanie and Lins; the rest didn't talk to her very much, but she was part of the group. Not being in the group—being like Suzi Hoffstead or Molly Stubbs, girls who didn't join—would mean total ostracization. Those two only had each other at lunch. The group avoided them. No sleepovers, no birthday parties, no friends at all.

So Lilly had to do it.

She walked over to Bobby. She stared over his head, then down to the slides, and she said the words. She watched Jimbo White slide, his feet splashing in the mud at the bottom of the aluminum tube, and she told her crush exactly what she had been dared to.

He squinted, puzzled at both the message and the delivery. Lilly ran back to the circle as half the group laughed, and all Bobby did was tell Mike Bardi and Saul Essex. The story didn't stop there, because by the end of the day, every boy in the class knew the rumor. On his bus ride home, Hank was forced to sit alone, stared down by the rest of the passengers.

Chelsea wouldn't give it another thought. Torturing Lilly was complete.

When Lilly came back, she was shaking. Her turn was practically wasted, daring Molly to throw a rock at the kids playing kickball. Molly missed, then dared Zoe to run up the slide and get in everyone's way.

When Zoe came back, mission accomplished, she wore a smirk from cheek to cheek. She glanced at Chelsea, who smirked back, and she made no attempt to hide the fact she already knew who she was picking.

Zoe stared into Lins's eyes and pointed at Donny, on the other side of the playground. He was taking turns throwing rocks at the maintenance shed with Barney Hutchins and Cal Erwin.

"I dare you to kiss Donny—on the lips—for three Mississippis."

Lins turned white. How could Zoe do this? How could she have told Chelsea and... Her brain flooded with fog as she stared across the playground. Her heart raced. Donny wound back and threw, and fear gripped her heart and squeezed.

"But..." was all Lins could say.

"You have to do it," Zoe said. "That's the rules."

"But..." She could have never imagined—could she do it? She would fall over dead from embarrassment before she reached him. She'd have a heart attack and die if she tried to kiss him. And what if he refused? If he pulled away? That would be even worse. If she made it out of there alive, she'd have to kill herself after that kind of humiliation.

How could Zoe do this to her?

Lins was shaking as she started across the playground. Her foot caught on a root, and she stumbled under the giant blue spruce where the playground mulch met the grass. It was all she could do not to scream as she fought for her balance.

None of the boys noticed her approach. The circle of girls watched wide eyed, some covering their mouths, Chelsea snarling with glee.

Lins froze four feet from the boys. Barney nailed the shed broadside with a bang, and he, Cal, and Donny all spun at once to see if any of the teachers had noticed the noise. When the adults had been checked and found uninterested, six boys' eyes locked on Lins.

"What?" Barney said.

Cal leaned over and picked up a rock. "What do you want?"

Donny smiled—just a little.

Lins's heart fluttered. She wanted to kiss him—she was grateful for the dare—for three milliseconds. Then she wanted to melt into the ground, into the soil, to slink into the earth and never be seen again.

In that moment, she hated her dad. She hated her mom. Why did they have to break up? Why did she have to live here? Why did Grandma have to live here and subject her to this school? She hated her own guts for taking part in this stupid dare contest.

But she was committed.

Lins remembered the days before the group, when she first started there. She remembered the loneliness, the teasing, the rocks pelted off her head that no one ever took credit for but they all laughed at. Those things didn't happen anymore. She may be miserable now, but that was hell.

Lins darted forward and wrapped both hands around Donny's head.

"Whoa!" Cal shouted.

Barney sneered.

She placed her lips on his, closed her eyes, and counted in her head.

One Mississippi.

His lips were tight but so soft. His breath came gently through his nose onto her face. His body was restricted, startled.

Two Mississippi.

Donny loosened. His lips, his posture; his head no longer pulled away from her. She didn't have to hold so tightly.

Three Mississippi.

"Gross!" a kid shouted from the edge of the kickball field.

"Ew!" "Look!" "Kissing!" They all echoed as Lins lost track of her time and let go. When she opened her eyes, the world was staring at her. Donny was smiling, while the rest pointed or laughed or made squeaky kissing noises.

"Lins and Donny sittin' in a tree," someone chanted. The nursery rhyme spread in an instant, and Lins felt her whole body flush. Her eyes met one, then another, then Zoe and the circle, who all chanted, "K-I-S-S-I-N-G."

How she wished she had never been born.

They were all a blur as she sprinted inside.

They were a blur now.

She shook her head and wanted to wipe her face. The bonds hurt so badly. Her eyes stung from the endless tears. Her heart was hollow and burning.

She never should have thought so badly about Mom. She never should have wished she was dead.

How could she know that only hours later, Mom would be...

Her chest heaved as the tears rushed. She couldn't stop the faucet when she wanted to, no matter how hard she squeezed her eyelids shut.

34

T HERE WERE FEW TIMES in his life when Detective Mark Rand regretted a decision more than he did right now. The snow burning his face. The wind cutting through his clothes as if he was wearing nothing at all. The knowledge that he may lose his toes if this trek went much farther—they had gone from numb to burning to nearly guaranteed frostbite.

In 1995, Rand had been too much of a coward to ask Janeen to Homecoming. She went with Frank Howard, and it started a relationship that lasted the rest of senior year. It would be five years before they were both done with college and back at home and he had the balls to ask her out. Five years missed. Five more years he could have had her by his side, and that never happened because of fear.

He should have asked her to Homecoming. He regretted that.

During his third week on solo patrol, Rand pulled over an old lady who swore her son was a firefighter. She name-dropped the fire chief, the mayor, and two city councilmen, trying to get out of the ticket. When Rand didn't buy it and gave her the citation, and later it turned out she was telling the truth, he got put on nights for three months as well as earning the nickname *Depends* for his hard fight against geriatric disease.

He should have let her go. He regretted that.

In 2022, when Stuart Harrison sat in that bed in Custer Falls Memorial, Rand only checked in a few times. He was on a weird case, a knife-wielding madman who had attacked a couple in their home then disappeared. He was so eager to catch the guy he didn't notice when his friend checked himself out of the hospital too early, went investigating a lead on his own, and got himself killed.

Stuart should have known better. Rand should have known better. He regretted that.

As he lifted foot after foot, fighting knee-high snow and drifts twice as tall, he couldn't see ahead or behind. Not where he was going or where he had come from. Not through the trees or into the sky or even Marshall if the man got too many steps ahead. It was night, and only their flashlights lit the downpour, ten thousand streaks of white and almost nothing else.

He shouldn't have come out here. He should have let the state and the task force do their thing. He regretted that. But regrets weren't going to keep him warm. Only fighting this would. Moving, stepping, searching—as long as he could keep going, he had a chance. It was stopping that would kill him at this point. You stop, you cool down, you freeze to death.

Those bastards had to have gone this way. Even if he couldn't see anything, he could feel it. Sooner or later, they'd have to come across their shelter or their bodies. Then they would at least have an answer.

Marshall had stopped calling for Ivan. The repetition had worn down, his calls stretching further and further apart over time. Five minutes, ten, thirty. It had been an hour since the last one, and Rand hated the silence. When Marshall had been calling, he hated that—the guilt over his responsibility. Now that Marshall was silent, the guilt was a hot knife in Rand's gut.

Rand didn't notice when the trees went bare. No needles and cracked upper limbs. He was watching when the skeletal masses gave way to large heaps of deadfall and the sky seemed to open to even wider blows of white.

There was a moment when he thought of climbing inside one of those deathtraps. Some looked like tepees made of rotted, jutting wood, and he had to wonder if there was any space inside, just a place to get out of the snow and wind for a short while. He may not have spent much time in the woods as an adult, but he knew better than that. They were thousand-pound Jenga sets just waiting for the snow to build or the wind to blow a little harder so the entire structure could collapse.

He thought freezing to death would be better than getting crushed under one of those piles of lumber. But he wasn't sure.

Marshall halted, and Rand stopped just before running into him. A second passed where Rand didn't understand what was happening; then he saw Marshall pointing.

Through minuscule cracks in the white, Rand saw it too. There was a structure ahead, something dark-colored like stained wood, with a single window that radiated firelight.

Firelight meant fire—meant heat. It meant an end to this frozen death. They just had to get in there.

It was a few seconds before he realized the question: whose fire was that? Was it their fugitives or someone else—a lone hermit who managed to eke out a life in this wilderness?

They had to prepare for the worst. Their fugitives had automatic weapons, and he wasn't even sure his fingers had enough feeling to pull a trigger.

Marshall leaned toward Rand. He whispered just over the wind. "What do you think?"

"It may be them. It's definitely warmer than out here."

"Yeah."

Marshall swung his rifle to his front and checked the safety. Rand pulled his service weapon and put his hand on Marshall's shoulder. He held on, and they both moved to the front door.

Perry wasn't sure if he had ever been so bored in his life. His phone wouldn't turn on. He was sick of solitaire. There were no books or magazines. Tony had played the game machine until it died and was now asleep in one of the sleeping bags. And Nick and Shamus had yet to return.

There had been squeals from the other room, and Perry had tried his best to ignore them. He didn't know what Shamus and Nick were up to, and he didn't want to. Not that he hadn't been a little rough with a girl in the past—sometimes he liked it that way; sometimes they would too. But the way Shamus had been acting, the way Nick was following along with every order, it gave him a bad feeling, a feeling he didn't want to encourage. It was bad enough they were trapped in this place together; the last thing he wanted to deal with was being on the wrong side of someone's psychotic break.

He'd let them play with the girl. He'd mind his own business. Hopefully, the goddamn snow would stop and he could sneak out. Either way, he was left with nothing to do while he waited.

Perry tapped his fingers on the table and flicked the cards to the opposite side. He thought of tossing them into the fire just for spite—goddamn things cost him over three hundred dollars playing with Shamus. A slight snore rose from Tony's sleeping bag, and Perry wondered if he should just take this opportunity to grab one of the rifles and silence the guy for good. Then he could walk into the next room and be done with Shamus. But somehow, he didn't think it could be that simple.

There was a sound like a crunch in the snow.

That didn't make any sense. They were alone out here, unless that girl Honey had come back.

He chuckled. Maybe she did. Maybe she got so goddamn cold out there she turned her tight little ass around and piloted it back here.

Now he was smiling. He wouldn't mind looking at that ass. That could break the boredom, as long as she kept her mouth shut.

Perry stood and walked to the door. He took the handle in his grip and pulled.

"Fuck."

Two men stood in the doorway, cops by their haircuts and square faces. One had an AR pointed at his chest, the other a black pistol.

Perry's heart beat twice before he knew what to do. It wasn't like he had been in this situation before, but he could be quick when he had to. He was never the smartest guy in the room, but he was good on his feet at times when others fell apart. It was like someone would hit the slow-mo button and everyone was affected but him. So he went with it.

He slammed the door shut as the men charged forward. By Perry's estimate, they had two steps to take before they touched the cabin, and he had three steps between where he stood and aiming his rifle.

One—he was halfway across the room, his eyes zeroed in on the weapon. They shouted something outside, but it was muffled and he didn't care.

Two—Perry was by the wall, hand over the rifle's grip and raising it up as he spun. The door flung open with a flurry of cold and ice. Flakes swirled as they danced into the room, and the tip of the cop's rifle poked its nose inside.

Three—Perry shoved the stock into his shoulder and aimed down the sights. His finger hovered over the trigger. He wanted to blink. His eyes could feel the cold rushing toward them, and they wanted to soak themselves in saline. He didn't let them.

The lead cop stepped inside, swinging his weapon toward Perry. Perry squeezed the trigger on his AK-47. Three bullets fired from Perry's gun. The cop's clicked.

One, two, three, the rounds hit breastbone, neck, and chin. Bones splintered, flesh split, blood sprayed. The cop's chin cracked down the middle, exposing the hidden, soft insides of the mouth.

As the first cop dropped, Perry took aim at the second. That one was racking the slide on his gun over and over again. Each time, a bullet flipped up into the air, and the cop pulled the trigger again. The gun clicked and did not fire, and he racked the slide once more.

Perry didn't fire. He watched as the cop expelled round after round on the cabin floor, not a single one firing. He didn't know if he was the luckiest guy on the planet right now or if the cop was the worst at maintaining his weapon. He had never seen a pistol misfire so many times or, now that he recalled the rifle in the other cop's hand, two weapons misfiring at the same time.

"Just drop it," Perry said.

The cop nodded and dropped the gun. It cracked against the floor and fell into the swelling pool of blood below his partner.

"You got it?" Tony groaned from inside his bag.

"I got it," Perry said.

35

S TEVIE'S HEAD SHOT UPRIGHT at the sound of gunfire. He didn't realize he had almost fallen asleep. Maybe he'd given up and didn't know it yet. Maybe he just knew his luck had finally run out. First it was Mom and Dad, and now this. Maybe his family's luck had just run its course.

Fuck that.

Scenarios ran through Stevie's mind. Were the cops here? Was there infighting? Had Shamus finally blown his stack and started taking out his own crew? Or—God, please—had Honey finally taken charge and come to rescue him.

Not likely. But he could dream.

Stevie watched the shadows under the door. There was a thud, and he heard the front door slam shut. Heavy boots stomped over the floorboards. A dragging sound headed toward him.

Stevie stared at the door, waiting to see what would happen next.

Nothing.

He was sure the door was going to fly open and either the Irish Rock Perry or Disheveled Hair Nick would have some new issue for him to deal with, but they didn't.

Was his fate to just sit here until morning—until they had the time to kill him before they moved on?

Maybe his family's run *was* up.

He never thought anything could happen to Dad, after all. The man was built like a Greek god and never seemed to have trouble with anything—not until the other night when that goddamn thing came after them.

He remembered being a kid, waiting in the car as Dad beat the shit out of deadbeats and collected money. He watched Dad's fists turn grown men into little, weeping girls. He saw Dad lift a man and choke him to death with one hand once—yeah, that shit you only see in movies.

If only he had inherited his dad's size and not his mother's. If he had gotten Dad's strength, he would have been able to break out of this, he was sure.

Mom was strong in her own way. He could still feel a million stings, one for every slap across the face he took as a child when he was caught doing something he wasn't supposed to. When he talked back. When he got caught watching her dress through a crack in the door.

He was just curious—at least, that's what he told himself. And it was just a coincidence that Honey was almost a dead ringer for his mother, minus twenty years.

There was wetness on his cheeks. Stevie looked up, wondering if there was a leak. Would he soon be sitting in a puddle of melted snow coming from the roof?

Not that he could even see the roof, but he realized it wasn't that, as the sides of his face became streaked. He was crying. But crying for what? It had to be this place, dust in his eyes. He wouldn't cry for Mom and Dad. They were bastards. He had the scars to prove it. He wouldn't cry for himself. He didn't want to die, but he wasn't afraid of it. Right?

But the tears kept coming. His breath hitched. His nose ran.

What the hell was happening to him?

He remembered Saint Louis in his teens, parking a newly

stolen car beside the trailer they were crashing in while Dad prepped for a job. He remembered Dad heating a metal hanger on the kitchen stove and pressing it to his chest—the sizzle as it seared his skin—then Mom handing Dad a beer as Stevie went crying to get rid of the vehicle. She told him to get over it.

He had no reason to feel bad for them or the fucked up way they died, but here he was, crying like a little girl.

"You deserve this," Dad said.

Stevie stared into his father's eyes. They shone with the reflection of the under-the-door flicker. Dad's face was layered in various-sized scrapes and gashes. There was a hole in his cheek where Stevie was sure he could see teeth. Something twitched in Dad's short hair, and a reddish-pink slime dangled from Dad's ear.

"You were supposed to die with us, boy. But you ran like a coward."

"You're not here." Stevie shook his head. "You can't be. Mom and Dad are dead."

"But we're right here," Mom said. She emerged from behind Dad and kneeled on the floor. "It's time for you to die. You're supposed to die."

A layer of blood coated her face. Some kind of bite marks ringed her mouth. The same pinkish slime leaked from her nose and beneath her cloudy eyes.

"Are you ready, sweetie?"

She hadn't called him sweetie since he was six. Not since she found him in the bathroom inspecting a bloody tampon she left in the trash. He was dangling it in front of his face, studying it, smelling it. He'd said he was just curious, that he didn't know what it was and he was intrigued by the blood. But she saw in his eyes; there was something else there. She never figured out what it was.

She pulled a straight razor from somewhere in her belt line. "Are you ready now?"

"No." Stevie shook his head. "No, no."

A red gleam reflected from the blade. It caught his eye and pulled him in.

"It's time, Stevie," Dad said. He pulled a knife from his own belt.

Mom leaned forward, the blade hovering below his chin. "You were supposed to die already. Just go with it."

The aroma of old, sticky blood made his nostrils tighten. It was a smell of rot, of death that clung to the living and urged it near.

Stevie saw the time he had broken into a pawn shop at night, unexpectedly finding the owner in the office. After the scuffle, the owner was dead with Stevie's knife in his chest, and Stevie slipped on the man's gushing blood, knocking himself out when his head crashed into the desk's edge. There was tacky blood on Stevie's clothes and a stiffened puddle below him when he awoke eleven hours later. It smelled like his mother's blade. The regurgitation on the pawn shop owner's chin and chest smelled like her breath. The cloudy whiteness in his dead eyes was now hers.

The tears ran thicker down his face. He didn't know why. He didn't give a shit about that pawnbroker asshole. Never did. But his eyes staring back at him from his mother's head seemed to cut right through him. They burned into the center of his brain and crushed his conceptions. Those moments when Dad whipped him with his belt, the burning welts and bleeding gashes; those made his heart soar. They were warm and soft in his memory, soaked in a father's love. The pinches from his mother, the pokes in his back from the knife she kept in her purse and shoved into him when he was out of line; those were like butterfly kisses. They were memories of joy and acceptance. He could feel his back opening up, the blood soaking his shirt behind him, and he wondered if his parents were right.

Maybe he *was* supposed to die with them. Maybe he was only prolonging the natural order of things by struggling with Shamus and trying to go his own way.

Stevie stared at the blade, at the crusted edge moving toward his face. There was an overwhelming sensation of homesickness that that blade could remedy. It could wipe it all away and bring him to Mom and Dad forever. It could heal the wounds that separated them in life and allow them to be a family again, like they were supposed to be.

"Let it happen," Dad said.

Through the dim, crimson splotches on the steel, Stevie saw movement. A reflection.

"Sweetie, just say yes," Mom said. The flesh on the tip of her nose shuddered. A crack formed across its bridge, and the lower flesh slid slowly down.

"Say yes," Dad said. His knife hovered by Stevie's side. His right eye drooped from the socket. His entire face tilted right, and the eye bulged, a dark red gap seeping, oozing behind the ball.

But that reflection. There was something there. It shooed him away, but he couldn't help but look. Mom and Dad called for his attention, but this blade, the reflection in it, was something he didn't want to know but needed to see.

Dad's knife pressed into his skin.

"Accept us," Mom said. There was bone in the gap on her nose. The spaces between her teeth widened, and thick, dark blood pooled in her mouth.

Sharp pain in his side; Dad was stabbing him. Warm wetness. But he was focused on the blade. He had to know what that reflection was. It moved as Mom moved, but it wasn't Mom. There were eyes and a nose. There was a wide, gaping smile and a mouthful of oddly-shaped teeth. He saw a glimmer in those eyes and a shine inside that mouth as blood poured free.

It ran over his knees, sticky and slow like red molasses, smelling coppery and dank and moldy. He watched in the blade as it fell from his mother's lips.

It drenched his thighs.

The knife was deeper inside him. The hole was wide and expanding. Dad was circling forward into his gut.

"Let us in," Dad said.

The eyes shined with hunger, and the face came into view. It wasn't Mom in that reflection. It was another woman—the one from the picture on the dresser. The one from his vision—the bodies, the mounds and mounds of bodies.

Stevie's head jerked up, eye to eye with his mother. Her nose slipped from her face. Her cheeks split, and her scalp rolled back over a blood-slicked skull.

"No." Stevie didn't understand. His head rocked back and forth in disbelief.

Mom's face flopped onto his lap, and as the blood parted, he saw her—the woman.

"No!"

"Let us in!" Dad screamed. He jerked the knife up and into Stevie's chest as his eyes dripped from his sockets onto the floor and his face melted from his skull like skin-colored cheese.

Stevie screamed. His belly split open, and his intestines rolled into the lake of blood.

"You're not my family!"

Stevie jerked and rolled left and right, rocking and getting nowhere. He rocked over his insides and screamed at the pain. He screamed at his father—but it was not Big Steve. It was the man from the same photograph.

They lied to him. They got in his head and lied to him.

Stevie turned to the girls, his last chance—maybe they could help.

Wanda was screaming at him. Only her voice was muted. Her face was tense, her jaw moving, but no words came from her mouth.

He screamed, "Help!"

"Just let us in," the woman said.

"No!" He refused to look at her. He felt the man's knife twist in his lung, and he knew this had to be it. You can't live through that, especially without a hospital. They were fifty miles from one of those, at least.

Wanda continued.

"What are you saying?" he shouted back.

He watched the cords flair on her neck, and her words came through like a whisper. "Send them away."

That didn't make any sense. Why would these disgusting people leave just by telling them to?

The knife turned. It ripped and burned inside him. Stevie could feel it aiming for his heart.

He screamed as loud as he could. "Go away!"

"Mean it," Wanda said. Her voice was no longer a whisper, but a dull tone.

Mean it? What the hell could that mean? He was dying here. His guts were on the ground in front of him. He was faint from the blood and the pain. He was likely dead no matter what happened now.

But something was happening. The woman in front of him was farther away. Inches, maybe, but farther.

"Let us in," the man said. His voice was softer.

Stevie dug deep inside himself. This time, he pushed back

the sorrow, focusing on the pain, the anger from each time Dad punched him in the gut. Each time Mom locked him in his room when they went out to the bar, each time they had sex on the other side of the wall and he wanted to wrap his fingers around their throats and choke them together.

"Get! Away! From me!" Stevie belted at the man and woman.

He had barely a breath left in his body, and they were gone. He panted, nodding forward and back. Tears raced from his eyes as he looked down, preparing himself to calculate how many seconds he had left to live.

His guts were gone. His belly was fine. The pool of blood had vanished as if it had never been there.

"What the fuck?" Stevie whimpered to himself.

"You did it," Wanda said.

He did. And he hated himself for doing it. Not that he wanted the pain. But the sorrow—he missed Mom and Dad, as shitty as they were. And part of him wanted the couple to return. Even if it wasn't the real Mom and Dad, did it matter?

36

WANDA KEPT WATCH ON the door, sure that one of their captors would run in to see what all the screaming was about. She saw both entities vanish, yet no one came. There had been two ghosts tormenting that man, ripping into him. They had been screaming, and still no one was here to check on them? It made no sense.

Her head ached but her wounds were clotting. The taste of blood remained heavy on her tongue.

She turned her gaze to Angel. Still out of it. Her heart sank a little lower. She pulled a little harder. She needed to help her baby.

On to Lins.

Lins was staring at her.

"Are you okay, Lins?"

"Why were you screaming at him?"

Wanda had to process that for a moment. She looked at the man, then back to Lins. "You didn't see those people? The man stabbing him?"

Lins's face was wide and worried. She shook her head *no*.

"You didn't see all the people standing over there that vanished when the last two came?"

"I didn't see anyone."

"Didn't see anyone?" Wanda mumbled. They were ghosts, she was sure of that, but while Angel had always seen *things*, Wanda never did—at least not since she was a kid—not since 1992, when her dreams seemed to turn upside down.

Her jaw ached and her nose throbbed. She probably had a concussion. If the guy over there hadn't responded to her, she might have thought she hallucinated it all. But she couldn't have...

There was a vague memory. She must have been four or five. She was on the back porch at Grandpappy's ranch, and Mom was brushing her hair as they sat on the steps. A boy and a girl played in a tree a dozen feet away. They laughed and shouted, though their voices never came. They poked and pushed each other until they both tumbled from the branches and slammed into the ground. One stopped moving as the other crawled away bloodied before collapsing ten feet away from the house.

Then they did it again.

Laughing, playing, climbing, falling. Dying.

Mom said not to worry about them, and Mom always knew best. But Wanda didn't try to climb any trees after that.

Did she once see the same things as Angel?

Her head pounded, and the man's mumbling called her gaze. Wanda couldn't make out the words. She wondered just how bad it had been for him. They were in his head; she couldn't tell what they showed him, but she was sure it was horrible by the way he was screaming. She was just happy her guess had worked and he was able to send them away.

But was it a guess? She only assumed, but at the time, she was sure Mom had warned her. "Tell them to go away if you have to."

Mom had seen things too? She must have.

She sighed and shook her head. There was more to worry about right now than that.

"We gotta break free."

Wanda leaned forward, pulling on her bonds as hard as she could. She ignored the burning on her wrists until she heard something tear.

"I'll try to break mine too," Lins said, and she pulled her hands apart.

"No, Lins. You'll just hurt yourself." She pulled again and felt blood rushing to her face as she struggled. More tearing sounds. Was it working this time?

Lins grunted as she pulled.

"Lins, you're going to—"

"It doesn't hurt."

"Try it for a few hours."

"Whoa." Lins grinned in a sad, shallow way, bringing her hands to her front. Corded sheet hung from her arms.

"What the—?"

Lins shrugged. "Maybe they didn't tie mine as hard?"

"Get over here," Wanda hissed. "Undo me."

Lins scurried across the floor on all fours. Wanda saw her face almost too clearly when she neared. There was red puffiness around her eyes. The wetness on her cheeks—had this girl stopped crying once? And Wanda's heart broke that she hadn't cried more for her lost friend. She had told herself there would be all the time to cry once she got out of this, but what if they didn't? What if this all ended before she had a chance to say goodbye in her own way?

She warned herself. *No, you can't think that way. We grieve when we can. Now is not the time.*

"Untie me," she whispered.

Lins leaned under the bed behind Wanda.

"As fast as you can. We don't know when they'll be back."

"I'll try." Her little fingers pulled and prodded at Wanda's bonds.

Wanda checked on Angel. She was still out. Red marks lined her face where that thing had grabbed her. Wanda's heart sank deeper and deeper into her stomach the longer she looked.

She glanced at the man. He was whispering something to himself and staring into the far corner. She didn't know if that was good or bad. Was his crazy going to help her or hurt her? He might be good to sic on the other men, or he might scream like a loon and call them in, hoping it would buy his freedom. There was no way to know right now and definitely nothing she could do to address it before getting free.

"Come on, Lins," she whispered.

"I'm trying. It's so tight."

This was Wanda's fault. She had pulled so hard to get free she probably tightened the knots.

"Keep trying."

But it didn't work, not for the next five minutes.

"It just won't come," Lins said. She sat up beside Wanda, rubbing her fingers.

There was a shuffling noise in the next room, and they both stared at the door. A wave of terror ran through Wanda. What was she going to do if they came back and Lins was free? They might take her like they did Abby. They might shoot her in the face like they did her mother for not following directions. No, she had to figure this out. There had to be another way.

"Lins," she whispered, "search the room. Look for anything we could use to cut the rope."

Lins's eyes went to the man. She bit her lip.

"He's tied up. He can't hurt you. Tell you what—" she nodded at the far end of the room where Abby had been. "Start over there."

Lins nodded. "Okay."

Perry yanked on the cuffs holding the cop to the support beam near the rear of the cabin, then he unrolled one of the sleeping bags near the wood stove.

The fire was getting low, so he tossed in two logs before he took a seat on his bag with the rifle and extra magazines. He was about to eject the weapon's mag when the door to the bedroom opened and Nick came through.

"The fuck is this?" Nick pointed at the unconscious cop and shut the door.

"A cop." Perry ejected the mag and compared it to the two others.

"What the fuck is he doing here?"

"He said they were tracking us."

"They?"

"Yeah, there were two. The other one's wasted. I threw him outside." He used a magazine to point at the puddle of blood by the door.

"You question him? Are more coming?"

"You see his face?"

Nick looked back at the cop. Besides being knocked unconscious, his lips were fat, his eyes were almost swollen shut, and half his face was glowing red.

"Okay—so what did he say?"

Perry lowered his project and stared into Nick's eyes. "They were alone, slipped away from their team, got lost in the storm, and found the cabin. Then he passed the fuck out."

"Shamus'll want to question him too."

"I'm sure. But I didn't want to disturb him."

Nick looked down at his bloody hands. "Yeah. That's probably a good idea." He walked toward the front door.

"What are you doing?"

"I'm headed to take a piss, if you have to know. And I guess I'll take a look at the other one."

"Say hi for me."

"Yeah." Nick let a flurry through the door and slipped outside.

Lins found nothing on the first side of the room and headed toward the far end. She crawled over the bed the mumbling man was tied to instead of crossing in front of him. She didn't know what he and Ms. Wanda had been talking about, but he had been screaming like he was dying. And he wasn't. That kind of crazy was more than she knew how to deal with, so she just stayed away.

The far side of the room was more of the same. Just a few beds, a few end tables, and some weird pictures on the walls. The pictures got her thinking.

She took one down and grabbed the nail. It was dry and flaked rust in her hand, and she pulled on it. She wasn't sure if it would work, but nails usually had a point, and a point might cut Ms. Wanda's ropes.

But as she pulled on the thing, she found it stuck. She didn't count on that. At home, nails seemed to just slide out of the wall—but these walls were wood. Was that why?

"There's a nail here," Lins whispered.

Wanda looked and squinted through the gloom. "I don't see anything. Can you get it?"

"Doesn't want to come."

"Try another one? Just keep looking."

The man mumbled again.

Lins went to a picture on the next wall and took it down. The thing was somehow sticky in her grip, and she was glad to get rid of it. She pulled on the nail, and it snapped in half, coating her hand in a layer of powdery rust.

"Hmm." She held the half-inch piece of metal between herself and the door. She wasn't sure if it would work or not.

"What?" Wanda asked.

"Let me show you." Lins crossed behind the man again and kneeled beside Wanda, holding up the scrap.

"It broke. But it might work."

Wanda nodded. "Put it in my hand and keep looking."

Lins placed the nail head between Wanda's wet finger and thumb. She was happy it was dark and she couldn't see why Wanda's fingers were wet.

Lins retraced her steps, searching anywhere she hadn't previously checked. Wanda grunted to herself as she tried contorting her fingers to scrape her bonds with the broken nail end.

The little tables had nothing. Lins looked over the pile of wood beside the stove, thinking maybe a sharply cut stick might work.

She gasped.

"What?" Wanda asked.

"Oh, my god," Lins whispered. She picked the tool up by the handle and slowly walked back to Wanda. "Look."

With two hands, she held forward a dull, rusted hatchet. "It was behind those logs." It was the first time she had really smiled in hours.

"Yes." Wanda dropped the nail. She was on the verge of crying at the sight. "Put it in my hand."

Lins dropped to her knees and did as she was asked. Wanda held the hatchet by the head and sawed at the fabric holding her in place. It ripped more than cut, and the noise was nearly as loud as the man's renewed muttering, but it was working.

New tears formed in the corners of Wanda's eyes—she couldn't hold them back. It was working! They were going to get out of here. And they had a weapon! A dull, rusted weapon, but a weapon.

The bindings fell apart, outer layers dropping to the floor, inner layers sticking to Wanda's bleeding wrists. She put the hatchet on the floor in front of her and rubbed her wounds, removing debris and assessing the damage. She wasn't streaming blood, but it was going to take time to heal. That would be fine as long as she got out of here—got all of them out of here.

Wanda snagged the hatchet and scooted toward Angel. She leaned behind her daughter and started on her bonds.

Lins bobbed up and down as she waited. She flexed her fists and bit her lip.

"There." Wanda sat upright and tucked the bobcat plush into Angel's pocket. Angel was freed. But she wasn't awake. Wanda turned to Lins. "Sit with her while I check things out?"

Lins said nothing. She sat beside Angel, hugging her close.

Wanda crawled to the door, laying her head on the floor so she could see under it and into the next room. She saw the wood stove and the fire burning hot. She could feel the heat creeping into the room, and for the first time in hours, her face wasn't cold. She saw a pile of her stuff. She saw the other door across the room and the bottom of the rustic, splintered table.

She could see none of her captors.

Was that a good thing or a bad thing? Had they left? No, they were making noise a little bit ago. Maybe they were in that other room? Or maybe her view was just too narrow?

Fear spiked in her veins. She was going to have to open the door to know. God help her.

Wanda got to her knees and stood as quietly as she could. She placed a hand gently on the door handle.

"I wouldn't do that," the man said in a soft singsong voice.

Shit. He could give them away to curry favor with the others—or if for no other reason than to screw her over.

She turned and squatted in front of him. "Why shouldn't I do that? Why do you care?"

"Because." He glanced at Angel and Lins, then back to Wanda. "You can't run fast enough."

"To escape your buddies?"

"To escape this place."

He smiled, but it wasn't a happy smile. It struck Wanda somewhere between sick and sinister, and she really wanted him to stop.

"So, what? We untie you and you'll help us get away?"

He chuckled. "No. You untie me, and I'll take that hatchet from you and chop you to bits. Then, I'll chop the rest of them to bits. So at least you'll get a little vengeance." His sibilance seemed to stretch for days.

Wanda shook her head. His voice made the hairs on her neck stand at attention. This guy was not the same guy they tied up with her. Ever since those ghosts... They had gotten to him somehow. And what would happen if they returned?

And what to do with this guy? She examined her ax. She could kill him, but she didn't want to. But if she opened the door and he screamed... The back of the hatchet caught her eye. It was rounded like a hammer. She could hit him with that, try to knock him out. But that was just as likely to crack his skull as it was to put him out.

Then she knew.

Wanda walked to the stove and grabbed a log. The man was chuckling again as she neared and wound back the hunk of wood. There was a hollow thunk as it bounced off his skull. His head sank, and she set it on the ground. He was still breathing, though a trickle of blood ran down his face.

Lins's eyes were glued to Wanda. Her mouth hung open as Wanda took hold of the door handle once again.

She wasn't sure of the best way to open the door without alerting anyone. She went with her gut.

As she pulled the door inward, Wanda put pressure toward the hinge. It opened without a sound, and she stopped it with only an inch gap. That was when she saw them.

She could only see the head from the top, but it was enough. Laying inside Kathy's sleeping bag was the rat-faced one—Tony, she thought. That was good; she could sneak over and hit him with the hatchet while he slept. She saw a pool of blood by the door, and her heart ached—*God, please, not Abby.*

Wanda opened the door to see a little more and froze in place. The big bald one, Perry, was practically facing her. He sat on her sleeping bag with an AK-47 in his lap. He was loading a magazine. Her heart thrummed as it leaped into her throat. If he looked up right then, it would have been a race to plant the hatchet in his head before he raised the rifle and cut her down.

She'd never make it. She knew that.

Shit!

Wanda leaned back and slowly closed the door. She would have to wait a while for him to sleep too. Then she would have a chance.

Nick kicked the dead cop in the gut and watched as his snow-blanketed head bobbed. There was no blood coming from his wounds. No steam. He wasn't frozen yet, but he was on the way.

A moment passed where he wondered what the cop would

taste like. Would he taste the same as that woman? He liked the hunk of her. He didn't think he would, but he was happily surprised. Then he wondered if he could eat part of a guy. *Would that be gay?* He wasn't gay, but something about eating a man seemed a bit gay to him.

But then again, meat was meat. That had gone through his mind while he gnawed on the medium-rare slice of ass. If it was just meat, it wasn't sexual—not as long as he didn't eat the guy's dick or fuck the dead body like he heard Dahmer used to.

He wondered if he should strip the guy and start cutting before he froze too much. But then again, there was so much left of that woman—they should probably finish her off first. But—he always heard hunters field dressed their kills and removed the guts so they didn't spoil the meat. He should probably at least do that to protect the meat—after he pissed.

Nick put out his right hand and glided it along the cabin, past the other corpse to the corner. The wind was at his back here; that would keep it off his dick.

He unzipped and pulled it out. The rush of urine was almost immediate, cutting a hole in the snow and wafting a steam trail ahead until it was carried away by the wind.

"Ah." He waved it around as he went and, with a smile on his lips, started writing his name in the snow. He hadn't done that since he was a kid.

He had no problem with the N or the I, but as he started the C, his stream began to die. At the start of the K, he was all out of piss.

"That's a shame," a woman said from behind him.

Nick pictured the dead woman standing back there like some kind of frozen zombie. She was pissed that he cut her up and was taunting him before sinking her teeth into his jugular.

He spun, one hand shoving his dick back inside his pants as

the other reached for the hunting knife. He had finished neither by the time he saw who it was.

Honey.

She stood with one finger over her bottom lip and her hand on her hip. Her eyes were on his crotch.

She smirked. "Don't put it away yet. I was hoping to see you finish."

Nick's grip fell away from the knife. His other hand was locked in position. Thirty-plus years of society had taught him to keep himself covered, but this woman—she made him want to keep it out.

He looked behind her, at the door, into the snowfall, the woods. They were alone now. Her man was tied up inside. Everyone was inside except them.

He could have her out here, regardless of whether she wanted to or not, regardless of the cold.

Before he could work out the plan, she stepped toward him. Her upper hand unzipped her jacket while her lower one reached for his crotch.

He didn't need a plan. He understood now; she wanted him. She always had. She was just held back by her piece of shit boyfriend before. He put both of his hands on his hips and let her do her thing.

"You see, don't you?" she whispered in his ear. She stuck her hand inside his underwear as he slipped one under her shirt, under her bra.

He squeezed gently around her breast, harder on her stiff nipples. She took his penis in her hand and stroked it as he became a rock.

"Oh, I see," Nick said. He dug his other hand under her jeans, around the back, and squeezed her ass. It was a perfect ass. It felt exactly as he knew it would, perfect in his grip, perfect tone, perfect shape for him to roam down and around and skim the lips of her pussy with his fingertips.

She tugged harder on him, massaging as she pumped. "Will you let me in?" she whispered.

"I'll let you do anything." His breath heaved, pushing clouds of steam from their grinding rhythm.

She pulled back, and his hands slipped from her skin. The funny thing was, as she moved, she became colder as if she was becoming hypothermic by the second. He even felt it on her hand around his penis. It was soft and working, but it was cold and getting colder.

"What?" His eyes met hers. She was smiling, but her skin had turned as white as the snow. Her eyes were glassy as if frozen and clouding over while he watched. Her lips were blue and spreading to talk.

"Thank you," she whispered.

There was a flash of white and a flash of red. She held the knife, his knife, in her free hand, and it was dripping sheets of crimson.

That can't be.

Nick looked down. A line of blood steamed in the snow. Blood pumped from a strange dark area in his waist. A bloody line over his midsection—

She giggled.

Nick gasped, and a sharp pain cut his breath short. The knife was in his chest. It glided to the left, slicing a gap in his lungs.

"Thank you," she repeated.

Nick fell back against the cabin and slid down. She pressed her lips against his as he drifted into the snow. When he sank as low as he could go, she did a funny thing.

Her freezing hands dove into the cut. They pried back his ribs.

He couldn't scream. No air moved in or out.

He couldn't seem to push her away. She was like a rock, and he was like a wet noodle.

He howled inside as the gap in his lungs stretched and tore to the size of baseball, as bones cracked and flesh slurped. She crammed her head inside him.

Part V

37

T HE CUFFS ON RAND's wrists were too tight. He tugged quietly against the post, pretending to sleep and hoping not to alert anyone as the metal dug into his skin. He wasn't sure what these scumbags were doing in this cabin, but he knew they were cop killers.

(The memory of bullets ripping through Marshall replayed in his mind—the guy never had a chance.)

The last thing he wanted to do was provoke them, especially while he sat so vulnerably. He assumed he was being held for leverage, but that would only last for so long.

One of the assholes had just gone outside; two were in the room. There was a guy in a sleeping bag, while the other sat on top of one, counting his ammunition and reloading his rifle. When he was done, he rested the rifle against his chest. Rand was watching through squinted eyes, but it looked like the guy was planning something.

The big guy leaned forward and back, his upper body swaying. His eyes closed slowly and dragged as they opened back up. He looked like a kid falling asleep at the dinner table. As if guided by some unseen force, he drifted backward and settled on the sleeping bag with the AK resting on his chest.

Rand couldn't believe it. It was too good. With that guy asleep—both the guys asleep—he might find a way out of this. If he could get free of the post and fish the key out of that guy's pocket, he could get the rifle. He could get out of this.

Rand pushed his back against the post. Maybe he could find a way to stand, and then—

Rustling from the other guy's direction. The rat-faced one sat up, unzipping his bag.

Shit.

Rand relaxed his body and closed his eyes to slits.

Rat Face gazed around the room. His head lolled when he changed directions, as if the weight of his skull was too much to hold it up straight.

There was a moment of panic when Rat Face's eyes passed over him. It was an unexplainable fright, a feeling that something could see through his deception, that it was looking into his thoughts and soaking them up. He felt slimy and wet on the back of his head, and goosebumps raised on his arms and legs. And as if it hadn't happened at all, Rat Face turned toward the center of the room and rose from his bed.

He walked with a heavy sway, more than how his head had moved. His entire body leaned to one side as he slowly shuffled toward the table. He reached for something, and a dark feeling slithered over Rand's shoulders. There was something on that table that would change the atmosphere in this room for the worse, and Rand prayed for it not to happen. He felt his heart pound and hoped to God he could keep his chest from rising and falling any faster—he was supposed to be unconscious, and his heart was racing like he was in a goddamn marathon.

When Rat Face turned, his head lolled to the opposite side, and his body shifted to follow. He took a step from the table, and shining in his grip was a blade.

No. This was going to end badly. Rand knew it. The guy was going to come over and stab him. He was going to cut Rand up and use his insides for a hat or some other sick shit.

He fought the urge to cringe into himself, to curl his fingers into fists and jump and pound at the post holding him in place.

He could see Rat Face more clearly now, and the man had a strange, blank look. His eyes were only halfway open, and his jaw hung wide and to the side with his lean.

The man kept rotating. He faced away from Rand and took a step. He was walking toward the wood stove. Then he adjusted his direction again. He was walking toward his friend.

A rising wave of anxiety gripped Rand's insides. His stomach was like ice, and his gut turned. It was like a wreck he could see coming, only he had no idea how bad it was going to be.

Rat Face gently lifted the rifle from the big guy's chest and set it aside. He kneeled beside his partner and scanned the large body, lolling one way toward the feet and another way toward the head. He leaned in, and the big man exhaled a wet clicking sound and a soft snore.

The knife sent golden sparkles across the ceiling as flames reflected and sputtered. Wood popped and hissed in the stove, and the knife descended.

Rand shut his eyes completely. He couldn't watch this. Part of him wanted the guy to wake up and defend himself so this wouldn't take place just feet from him. He was a detective; he was supposed to show up after the crime was over, not be a witness to the horror.

The other part of him wanted this to happen—not this specifically, but for these guys to turn on each other so when (if) he got free, it would be easier to escape and take them down.

But it didn't matter how either part of him felt. It didn't matter that he wanted to keep his eyes closed, because without his will, somehow, his eyes were cracking open once again. He was like some prisoner of war or lab rat, a victim in an experiment with his eyes taped open. Though they were only forced open a hair, they were forced nonetheless, and he could not close them.

Rat Face had a hand on the big man's face. With his thumb and index finger, he held open the sleeping man's right eye. It jerked left and right as REM sleep overpowered whatever his pupils were taking in.

The knife went between the eye and the socket wall. Back. Deep. It levered up, and the eyeball lifted from the socket just a bit. He levered more, rotated the blade around the cavity, and the entire eye rose above the big man's face. With his other hand, Rat Face gently pinched the ball and held it as he sliced the nerve clean.

Rand's stomach lurched, and he felt vomit rising in his throat. That couldn't happen. He couldn't give himself away. Any noise at all would bring that maniac's focus to him. It made his stomach grip harder, the vomit push harder. He felt tears burn the corners of his eyes, and he fought them. He clenched his throat, holding his breath, forcing it back.

His nose made a noise, a brief nasally exhale, and every muscle in his body tightened.

Please, God, please. He didn't hear that. He didn't—

Rat Face rose, holding the bloody eye in his palm. He walked toward Rand. Rand could see into the depths of the light brown eye as it rocked in the nutjob's hand. He saw what it had seen. Days of playing as a child. A first date as a teen. Crime and murder as an adult. Himself, across the cabin, as it floated in the hand of a madman.

Then he turned. Rat Face gingerly set the eye in the center of a skillet on the table.

Rand's stomach lurched again as the truth set in of what this psycho was going to do. He was going to eat it. He was going to cook it and eat it.

A new wave of chills washed over him. A new wave of panic.

A new realization of just how bad this could all turn if he didn't fool the guy now and escape soon. The thought of his own eyes in that pan, of his own flesh being separated from his body, of pieces of himself being removed forever—not being reattached after the result of some freak accident—gone forever and digesting inside someone's gut. It may have been the worst thing he could imagine. First, parts of him gone, then all of him gone—without a trace—and then ending up as a pile of shit.

But the psycho didn't turn to him. At least not yet. He turned back to the big man on the floor, lolled in the other direction, and wandered over.

He kneeled, and Rand thanked the heavens his view was blocked this time. Then he wished he couldn't hear either.

He pictured it as the sound forced itself into his ears. The fingers holding back the other eye. The knife sliding in and around the wound as the eye was elevated from the socket. The flick of the blade as the nerve was severed. Then Rat Face stood.

Back to the table. Back to the pan. Lovingly setting the organ in place. And then he was beside his friend again.

Rand wanted to weep as his mind rocked inside his head, wondering just what this maniac was doing now. Was he after another piece of meat to go in his pan? Or was it something worse that he couldn't even comprehend?

Rat Face squatted by the big man's head. The big man gasped and snorted and sputtered, then settled. His chest rose and fell, and Rand couldn't help but hope the guy was having a nice dream. He was a murderer, a cop killer, but no one deserved this. No one.

A cold breeze washed over Rand. It was like the fire wasn't even going. It was like he was out in the snowstorm and flakes were pouring into the back of his coat, down his back, and frosting his skin.

A thing skittered in the walls behind him, then in the roof above. Mice, maybe? Whatever it was amplified the chills in his back and crawled over his spine, making him shiver in a way he was desperate to hide.

Rat Face lowered the blade over Big Man's throat. Blood sprayed as the knife dove into the side of his neck. It settled into a pulsing wave as the steel opened a line across his throat to the other side. Blood washed over his neck in a rippling tide, and the bald man's hands raced, fingers wild, feeling toward his throat. They clutched at the wetness and felt along the contours of his neck and then wound. He said nothing, made no noises except gurgles. His bloody fingers walked up his face and touched the gaps where his eyes should have been.

Then he went limp with his arms at his sides. A belch of vomit sputtered from his throat, then lips, then nose.

Rat Face's expression didn't change. He stood and shuffled to the table. His head flopped, and his body leaned over the ancient surface. He pointed the blade at himself, and before Rand understood what was happening, before he had a moment to wonder what the fuck this crazy bastard was going to do next, Rat Face's fingers held back his eyelids, and the steel tip drove into his socket.

Tears ran down Rand's face. There was no stopping them. They weren't from sadness. He didn't know what they were from other than the pure terror at the knowledge that he wasn't getting out of this. He had hidden that fact from himself under a veneer of hope and bravado, but under it all, he knew he was doomed. He knew the next minutes were his last, no matter what his fantasy plans of escape held. He was going to die in here. It was going to be bad. And it was only a matter of time.

The coldness swallowed him.

Rat Face set his eye in the pan, held back the lids of his other one, and went to work again.

Why was Rand watching this? Why couldn't he close his eyes? He wasn't sure if it was a stress reaction or fear or if he was having a complete mental breakdown. Why couldn't he squeeze his lids closed and pretend he was anywhere else? The lake with Janeen? At home watching *Gunsmoke*? The lake on a summer's day? Anywhere but here.

He was imagining her, overlaying the thought in his mind as if he could use it to wipe away the scene in front of him. He caressed her hair. He rubbed her back. He held her close as they stared into the natural beauty of a snow-capped mountain on the opposite side of the lake.

It didn't work.

The psycho came away with his other eye and broke every thought in Rand's mind. He set the organ with the other three and bent over the pan. His jaw hung left and flopped right as he leaned with no discernible reason or logic. Then, he plunged the blade into his own throat.

Blood gushed. It landed in the pan with a splash across the table and slowly filled the steel container. Rat Face hung deeper forward. Lower. His body slumped, and he braced the table with his bloody hands.

Like some inanimate object being shooed away, the man leaned back and toppled to the floor.

"*Fuuuuuuuck*," Rand whined. His eyes were open now. The tears ran. He was doomed. He was cursed. They would do the same to him. Maybe worse.

He found himself staring into the far corner. It was the darkest place in the room, nearly untouched by the fire's light. He stared into the darkness as if it had answers. As if it was his getaway from this horrid place.

It gave him one response. And that froze him completely.

From the depths of the blackness, an arm reached. Then a foot. Then a body.

A black, fuzzy shape, a being made of pure shadow, walked across the room toward the front door. It was like a person was walking through the room but only his shadow could be seen. The was no one there. No one to make this shape, no object in the room that could trick the light and create this.

A thought went through Rand's mind that this person was in some parallel universe, and for some reason, his shadow was showing here. Or maybe it was a memory, a recurrence of energy like some ghost hunter shows would recite to explain the supernatural—someone had walked that path long ago, and this was just an echo. But Rand knew that wasn't so. As strongly as he felt the ice clawing at his back, he felt the presence in front of him. That thing was real, and it was here right now.

It strode with confidence, something almost cocky in Rand's mind. It reached the door and paused. Its head changed shape just slightly like it was turning. And Rand knew it was looking at him. It was watching him as he watched it.

Only a second passed, but Rand felt his heart pound a lifetime's worth of beats, and the shadow slipped into the crack between the door and the frame.

Rand's chest heaved. His mind was numb. There was no more energy in his core to process what was happening in this house. But he could finally close his eyes.

That was when the door opened.

38

WANDA SAT IN FRONT of the girls, hatchet in hand, ready for anyone to come through the door. She had seen shadows pass on the other side, but no one had come in since they had gotten free. Only strange sounds that she couldn't place passed through the entrance.

When she heard the front door open and close, she held the hatchet tighter. She was sure any minute now they would come for her. But they didn't.

The waiting gnawed at her insides. She needed to know what was happening out there. She needed to get these kids out. She needed to help Abby. Waiting was doing nothing to help. The only positive was that those ghosts hadn't returned.

She knew it may be a rash decision, but she had to know more—she would look again.

Wanda raised a finger to her lips, and Lins nodded at the gesture. She crawled to the door and put her head against the floorboards. Her hair draped over the cracks between boards, and a horrifying image filled her thoughts of something beneath her, grabbing strands and yanking her down. It was silly, but she saw it, and the feeling struck that it was more than a worry. There was something down there, below the cabin, that was dangerous.

As she focused on the gap into the next room, she ran her hand under her head, scooping up her hair.

She saw a man on the floor beside the table, and her heart skipped a beat. He was facing her.

Fuck! She was sure he could see firelight flicker in her eyes' reflections below the door.

Then she noticed his eyes—or lack thereof. His stillness. His blood pooling on the floor and leaking through the cracks.

Who would do that? His eyes?

A moment of revulsion preceded a moment of relief. He didn't look much older than a teenager—but he was one of them.

The rest of her view was calm. She saw none of the criminals. Not the ones that took Abby and not the one that was loading his gun.

Did he do that to his friend? If he did, she really needed to look out for him. For all of them. What the hell had she gotten them all into?

She didn't want to do this, but she had to.

Wanda trembled as she rose to her knees. She glanced again at the guy in the room with them—still out cold. She glanced at Lins and again motioned with a finger over her lips. Lins nodded, and Wanda grasped the handle.

She trembled. The door shook under her hand. She pressed her other hand against the wood to settle it, and she pulled.

There was a whisper-like whine as the door moved, and it rang in her ears like a siren. She glared through the crack as the door widened, praying every second that she would see no one, that this would be their chance.

Wanda saw Perry on his back. He was asleep—no, he wasn't. Blood soaked her sleeping bag. She couldn't see his face, but she saw his throat. It was wide open, so far that she saw split muscles and reddish-yellow tissues bulging out. Someone had killed him. The same person who had killed the other one, probably.

Her eyes scanned the room. Every corner, nook, and shadow,

anywhere within the narrow slit of vision she could spy. Nothing. She pulled the door farther in. Leaned out.

The front door was shut. It called to her. It was only across the room, but the gap between her and it felt like miles. She'd have to pass two dead bodies and a floor coated in blood—doable, but there was a killer on the loose, and she had two children to escort. That small gap between here and there could mean their deaths if they were spotted.

She knew then what she had to do. She would need to carry Angel and guide Lins and race across the room and out the door. She hated herself for thinking it (and planning it), but she'd have to leave Abby behind. The kids were more important and easier—she had to get them to safety first, then come back for her friend.

It was a shitty choice, but she had to do it. And she was sure if Abby were in her position, if one of the kids was Abby's, she would make the same choice. And Wanda would want the kids saved at her expense if it had to be. She tried to think Abby would agree.

But first, she had to check the rest of the room.

Wanda leaned farther into the room. She saw the other bedroom door. Her eyes bounced over cluttered objects: old cans, beer bottles, her own supplies that had been piled up, and a body—another body? But this one she didn't recognize until his eyes opened.

"Higgins?" he whispered.

"Rand?" His face instantly clicked in her mind—Detective Rand. She knew why he recognized her; she was the daughter of the old radio operator, Rhonda Higgins. But why was he here? Did that mean backup was coming?

Another quick pan around the room, looking for danger, and she rushed to him.

"Are you okay?" She looked him over. His wrists were bright red, and his face was bruised and blue with a black eye. His arm was covered in dried blood. "Is backup coming?"

"No." He shook his head, and Wanda could feel the embarrassment radiating from him. "We're on our own." He nodded at the giant on her sleeping bag. "He's got the keys to the cuffs in his pocket. Grab 'em quick."

Wanda glanced at the bedroom door she had come from, at the other bedroom door, and then the front. A second passed where she feared what would happen if she didn't just get the kids and go. What if using this time to free Rand got her caught and ruined their escape?

No, she had to help him. He was right there. The key was right there. But then they had to run.

Wanda's heart raced. She ran to Perry, set down her hatchet, and pulled at his pocket, squeezing her hand inside the gap. She looked at the AK-47 on the ground beside him and knew she had to take that with her. That was her safety; that could be her insurance policy.

She pulled out a handful of change, a Bic lighter, a wad of crumpled paper, and a pen. No key. Wanda reached across the body, trying not to look anywhere above his chest or touch the pooling blood, and dug into the other front pocket. She felt a keyring and a phone and pulled. The phone came out, but the keys stuck to the inside of his pocket and refused to move.

"Come on!" Rand hissed.

"I'm trying." She stuck her hand back inside, and the front door blew open. It whacked into the inner wall.

Wanda jumped back.

Frosty wind and snow gusted across the room. It thrust into the open space like an angry rhino, raining crystals and frost over floorboards and icy wind that pierced like daggers into

Wanda's flesh. Wanda had to squint beyond the flakes battering her eyes, and she jerked to look through the opening.

No one was there but the night. It was dark except for the thousands of white flakes dancing in the wind.

"Wanda!" Rand whispered.

She leaned forward again, using two hands to open the pocket and pull out the keys.

The ring jingled, and she tossed it aside. She was sure he hadn't taken the time to put a key to Rand's cuffs on his ring. She felt inside the pocket again, and she was sure she felt it—skinny and round, down deep at the edge of the seam. She wrapped her fingers around it.

The door banged viciously against the inside of the cabin. It was loud, a deep sound that sent terror through her body. That sound was going to call the others. It was the sound of alarm, and she had to stop it.

Bam! Bam! Bam!

Wanda jerked the key from the dead man's jeans and held it tightly as she hurried toward the front door.

"Higgins! Come on!" Rand's voice was buried by the wind and slamming.

Bam!

Wanda reached for the door. As much as she wanted out, right now it needed to be closed. She saw bony tree stumps. She saw a field of white; escape. She saw the vast beyond and ached that she was trying to seal this instead of rushing out into the open, into freedom.

Wanda's hand touched the edge of the door, and the door flew toward her. It cracked her in the middle of the forehead as it swung, and she rocked backward. Blood leaked from a gash, stars fluttered, and as the door slammed shut, she hit the floor and saw the wide grinning face in the corner.

It was *her*—the ghost from the other room. Her salt and pepper hair flowed as if blown by an invisible wind. Her face was white and cracked, dead skin drying and decaying in a grave. Her eyes were clouded over, but they broadcasted hate and hunger as she stepped toward Wanda. She reached for her, a knife in her hand. She exposed blackening, yellow teeth below her desiccated lips.

Wanda screamed and turned and bounded on all fours. She passed the dead guys, her hatchet, the rifle, and the table.

"The fuck?" Rand shouted.

Wanda raced back into the room. She had to get back to Angel. She had to protect her baby.

"Wanda!" Rand's voice trailed as she slammed the door.

The door jumped inward, and Wanda braced it with her shoulder. Her weight slammed it shut, but it only lasted an instant. The door flew in a few inches and slammed shut again. The noise was deafening. It rang in her ears as it banged under her weight again and again.

"Stop!" Wanda cried. How was this happening? This couldn't be happening.

The door jutted open, and a knife stuck through. It traced the edge of the opening up and down, scraping as it searched for anything to slice.

Lins screamed, huddling beside Angel, her arms and legs sucked into her body. The man at the end of the bed jerked awake.

He grinned at Wanda and laughed. "Let her in! Let her in!"

"Shut up!" Wanda yelled.

"Let her in!" His face was mad. His eyes bulged and his cheeks flared. His wild smile was manic and unrestrained. "Let her in, bitch!"

"Shut up!"

Lins screamed again, then shouted, "Wanda!"

The door slammed shut, then open, then shut.

"Let her in!"

"Wanda!"

She turned to the child. Lins was pointing to the far side of the room. Wanda turned to look as the door rocked behind her.

A man stood in the darkness. He was nearly as tall as the ceiling and as wide as a bear. His face was pale, cracked, and angry—the other ghost from before. He took a step toward Wanda, and the floor boomed. The walls creaked. There was a scraping sound as things moved in the ceiling.

"No!" she howled.

"Let her in!"

What was she supposed to do? She should run. She had to run. But as soon as she let loose the door, the woman would be after her. Did she even have a choice? Have both monsters inside this dead-end space or get killed by one while stopping the other?

She turned to Lins. The poor child. She was shuddering place. At the end of bed, Angel shook with her as she rocked and cried.

"Get over there!" Wanda pointed to the far corner, between the head of the bed and the outer wall, as far away as she could get from the creeping giant. "Drag Angel."

The girl didn't move. The door shook and banged.

"Let her in, goddammit!"

The noise vibrated her being. The man stepped closer.

"Go!" Wanda screamed.

The child wouldn't move. Fear pinned her in place.

Wanda tightened her fists as the door slammed into her. She pushed and howled again. The knife scraped. The man came closer, and she could smell his rot.

"Let her in, you fucking bitch!"

She could feel the coldness in his breath. She knew it was now or never.

The door banged shut, and Wanda sprang toward the children. She dove and scooped an arm around Angel, pulling her close, and took Lins by the hand and dragged her along.

The door flew open and banged on the inside wall. The woman knew just where Wanda was and tracked her with her decaying eyes. She pointed her blade as they ran.

Wanda searched the room for the thousandth time as she rushed to the corner. No windows, no other doors. No way out. As she studied the corner, the likely place of their deaths, she spotted something: a small person.

She slowed as her mind took in the sight. It was a little girl, maybe seven. She wore dirty, tattered clothes stained with something dark, but her face bore a sympathetic frown. She waved Wanda toward her, and she crawled under the bed.

There had been no children in this room. They had been alone until those ghosts came. Unless…

"Yes!" the madman screamed from across the room.

Wanda couldn't trust this, but what else could she do? She followed.

She dragged Lins and pointed under the bed. "Go, go!"

Lins fell in the corner. She looked up at Wanda. It was like she had been broken and didn't know how to move.

"Under the bed, Lins, go!"

Lins cried and turned, and she must have seen something under there, because she vanished into the darkness.

Wanda dropped to her knees and pushed Angel's head under the bed. She glanced at the couple. They were at the foot of the frame, only feet away, and their darkness reached out with an icy wave as they moved in.

Angel jerked from Wanda's grip, disappearing under the bed.

"Angel!"

It was a shock to Wanda's already fractured mind. It was like something had sucked her out of Wanda's grasp, and she was gone into that darkness.

"Angel," she whimpered and dropped to the floor. She reached below the bed. She was about to be attacked—she knew that. Those evil things were going to grab her, but she wanted to know Angel was under there and not just gone, not just sucked away into another place like it felt. It was an irrational idea, but she had to know where her baby was.

The floor boomed as they closed in. The icy air stung Wanda below her clothes.

Something seized Wanda's hand. Then something else. Another one. Hands. Tiny hands were wrapping around hers. And they were cold—so cold.

Before Wanda knew what was happening, as the angry giant and the foul woman reached, she was jerked under the bed. Those hands pulled.

She slipped into a gap between the floorboards. She was dragged down under the house. Frozen dirt sprayed her face. It scratched her cheeks and hands as she went fast, too fast, under the house and into a tunnel she barely fit through. It was dark and tight on her shoulders and hips, and she knew she would be stuck there forever if those little hands let go. If they decided to stop pulling, this would be her end. And the fear inside her was unsure if it wanted to see where she was being taken or left in that cold, tight place to find her own way.

This is a path for children, she thought. She pictured little ones crawling and digging and hoping to find escape from the torment and death in this house. She blocked out the images of spiders and worms crawling in the empty darkness, taking advantage of these children's ingenuity. She blocked the worry of where this was going—they were ghosts, weren't they? It was likely a place for death.

She burst through an opening and into a small room.

Light trickled down through the cracks in the floorboards above. The room was dirt and old boards with an uneven floor, only a few feet tall; not really a room at all, more like an abandoned earthen cellar—or a hidden place where—

A match lit. It was Lins. She lowered it and placed it over a candle. As the space illuminated, Wanda saw bones coating the floor, small children's frames and older adult pelvises and shoulder blades. Fingers and feet and skulls. Limbs and ribs and—there were thousands, things that were once alive and now were in a pile of—someone's trash.

Wanda saw the fear in Lins's expression as the child took in the space. She saw Angel's face wince and grimace behind her dreams, and she sank and pulled both kids in close.

She heard Abby scream through the dirty plank wall.

39

A NGEL WAS NOT ANGEL. She was a dark thing in a dark place. A cave, maybe? Light filtered through the trees above and hurt her eyes. She knew if she left the dark and touched the distant light, it would burn, so she remained. Hungering. Waiting. Something would come.

The light faded, and night came, and she wandered the darkened forest. She occupied and consumed the voles and mice from the inside as they passed. Their blood sustained but did not fill. The deer no longer came to this side of the forest, nor the elk. They had learned and kept their distance now. Humans, though, they seldom learned.

The night waned, and as false dawn approached, the light hurt. She hurried back to her cave, leaping from shadow to shadow, from tree to tree to bush to rock, careful of the distance and the light, careful of being trapped away from her cave.

Then she waited. She stared into the gloom of her sanctum and waited. She thought she may have slept, but she didn't, couldn't. Not for eons had she slept, not since the Earth was under a blanket of night for years and the food was so scarce that pain and hunger were all she knew. Then she slept. Until life came back and her hunger could be calmed—calmed, but never satisfied, never satisfied after that.

The next night was the same. Voles, mice, ground squirrels, the occasional bird that landed too close to the ground for the night.

The next day was the same. In the cave, in the dirt, in the darkness until it was safe.

Another day. Another night. Another day. Another night.

A human came. She plunged inside him and ate every part.

Another day. Another night. Another day. Another night.

A bear cub wandered close. Its mother nudged it and snapped at it. It ran closer. It tasted good. Its mother tasted better, her loss on her mind.

Another day. Another night. Another day. Another night. Another year. A dozen more.

It was day, and a girl came. Angel thought she looked a little older than herself, thirteen or fourteen, maybe. Her hands were red with dried blood when she entered the cave. Her clothes were torn, and her groin bled.

She set a knife beside her, leaned against the rock wall, and stared into the woods. Her eyes were bloodshot, and her belly was empty, and though it would hurt her eyes to keep looking, Angel did. She moved closer, hugging the rock, invisible to the girl unless she watched very closely. She didn't usually feed in the daytime, but this chance was too good. The girl was drenched in sorrow, anger, and pain. It was as if the old ones had sent an offering.

As she loomed over the girl, she heard her thoughts, saw and pictured what she remembered and feared.

Florence was done crying. Ma's blood was thick on her hands, but she was glad Ma was gone. That was the last time she took a man for Ma, the last time any man put his pecker inside her without asking—without paying *her*, not Ma.

She felt the coin purse she'd taken from the old hag on her waist as she watched the woods. No one was coming. She'd been running from camp for a half day, and if the train wanted to make it over the pass before the snow fell, they wouldn't waste their time tracking down a whore for stabbing her missus.

Either way, she'd wait 'til morning before heading down the mountain and back toward that last town. She was sure there was enough in this purse to buy a ticket east, and if not, she could ride a few peckers there or rob a miner or two to get what she needed.

She was free now. That was all that mattered.

Her breath under control, she opened her satchel and found a cigarette and a match. She was about to light it when a cold gust sank over her shoulders and ran down her back. It brought with it the smell of death, and she winced from the onslaught of sensations.

Florence's skin prickled, and she stared into the cave. It occurred to her she hadn't looked for lion or bear scat. Had she wandered into something's den?

There was movement, but not a thing. It wasn't a bear or a cat. It was something she'd never seen before, a black man-like shape moving across the shadows, over the rocks, along the wall, toward her.

Florence's legs went numb, maybe from the cold, maybe from the rising tide of fear that enveloped her body.

What she was seeing wasn't natural. Shadows didn't move like that. Shadows only came from objects; they were dark spots from people or animals or things. They didn't move on their own. They didn't walk. They didn't charge across a cave at someone.

Florence leaped to her feet, and the shadow was on top of her. It was freezing cold, burning to the touch, and while she felt it over her, it did not feel like flesh. It was thick and heavy but not solid. It wrapped around her chest and moved up toward her face.

Florence pushed, but her hands went through this thing. She screamed and ran, and as her fingers threatened to touch sunlight, she felt her feet leave the hard rock floor, and she was yanked deeper into the cave.

"Let go!" Her face burned from the cold. Scratches moved toward her mouth. But she felt more than just cold and burning as it moved over her—she felt hunger. She felt desolation. She felt a need to be free, and she recognized how similar that feeling was to her own.

She clawed at the ground, back toward the cave mouth. She pushed with hands and feet, and the burning seared her lips, prying open her jaw.

Angel was barely inside the girl before she saw everything that had ever happened to her. The dirt-floored shacks, the booze, the rapes, the blood of her father in her mouth. The blood of her mother on her hands. The men—so many men. If Angel had a body of her own, she would have wept.

It was a string of five thousand movies, a different one for each day the girl had been alive, and each one held moments of evil. She poisoned her brother with lamp oil in his milk. She smeared her lunch on her father's clothes, hoping something wild would take him when he went trapping. She was forced to lay with Pa. She was forced to lay with other men while Pa was away, and none of them paid her. They only paid Ma.

She had a lock of Ma's hair in her satchel and Pa's knife at her waist. Both were there to remember their deaths, not their lives.

It was then that Angel's host decided not to eat the girl just yet. This human had something to offer.

Angel/Shadow/Florence dusted herself off and walked out into the woods. As Florence had planned, she was going to see what more she could take from town.

Shamus climbed the ladder into the bedroom, leaving bloody handprints on each rung. He pulled himself into the room, passing the ghost woman, and stretched his arms upward behind his back and neck from one side to the other. He had worked himself tired, and the hunger growing in his gut was unimaginable.

He should have Nick slice off more of that woman outside. She would complement the taste on his fingers.

The ghost gestured for him to cross the room, toward the bed.

"I'm not tired," he growled. "I'm hungry."

She gestured again.

He thought of the delays: telling Nick what to do, Nick doing it, waiting while it cooked. Ugh, that would take so long, and he was starving.

A whimper rose from the basement, and Shamus slapped the trapdoor. It slammed down with a crack.

He took a step toward the main room and the ghost was gesturing again.

"What the fuck do you want?" he shouted.

She scowled at Shamus and marched toward him until she was standing right in front of the man. Her wispy arm swung from her side to slap; her hand slid right through him.

Shamus chuckled. If she were real, that would have stung like a bitch. Then, he understood something of what she had been trying to say. Not entirely, but a drive pushed him across the room as if it knew.

He stood at the shelves, facing a few dozen jars. Their insides were black and gooey, and Shamus couldn't discern at all what was in there, but he knew what he wanted to do with it.

Shamus grabbed the closest jar and held the base stiffly with one hand, the lid with his other.

He twisted, and the jar didn't budge. It creaked inside his grasp.

It was taunting him.

He gripped the lid harder and twisted. That fucker wouldn't turn. He squeezed harder. It was all a matter of grip. He just needed a better grip.

Shamus looked into the black contents as he pressed. The blackness was wet and sliding very slowly around as he moved. He watched it like one would watch a steak on the grill. There was a turning in his belly. Saliva gushed in his mouth. His teeth rose and fell as if they were eating.

There was another creak and then a tink as the top of the jar shattered and twisted away from the bottom.

Shamus yanked away the lid, the top of the jar clinging securely to the ring. A scent of spices and meat and aged tenderness reached his nose, and he dropped the lid to the floor.

He reached between the jagged jaws of the jar and pinched a piece of the black substance in between his thumb and index finger. He pulled it from the container, and the thick, gooey object unfolded into an eight-inch, glistening hunk. It smelled like a savory, heavily-salted meal but also pungent with earthen spices. Below that was the odor of old meat that should have been cooked days or even weeks ago. But the scent was far from repellent. It sang to him to take a bite.

Shamus lifted the thing over his face and opened his mouth.

A drop of black fluid fell on his tongue, and he tasted years of aged perfection. He lowered it into his mouth and bit into what he was sure was a piece of meat, a tongue, he thought.

The meat was tough, but only for the first chew, then it softened and melted in his mouth. The back of his head tingled, and the rush ran down his back and his arms.

He took another bite, and another. He gripped the meat in his hand, holding it tightly, feeling its juices run over his knuckles as he squeezed and licked it from his skin, thrilled at this new taste mixed with fresh blood.

He had to know how to make this.

He ripped another mouthful with his teeth.

He did know how to make this. He had everything he needed in the basement. And the ghost woman would help him. She wanted to help him.

Shamus shoved the remaining chunk into his face and seized another jar.

Angel/Shadow/Florence was coated in dust and grime by the time she found town. The night was cold, and lanterns lit half the windows in the small western camp. The shack, loosely referred to as *Jack's Saloon,* was the loudest, and the hunger inside her small body drove her there.

Four men sat at two round tables, three of them drinking, one with his face on the rough wood surface, passed out. At the long, high table they called a bar there were another four men. One stood behind it with a bottle in his hand. One was on the end, the largest in the room, and he watched the other three with a hand on his whiskey glass and the other on the butt of his revolver.

The room went silent when the bartender set eyes on the girl and pointed.

"You, get out of here, girl." He shooed with the back of his hand.

Angel looked from man to man, gauging them, wondering which would make the best meal.

"Go on," the bartender shouted.

"I'll help her home," one of the men at the table said. He stood with a wobble and braced himself on his chair. "I'm done for the night anyway."

"Good." The bartender nodded and checked the volume on the whiskey bottle he was holding.

The rest of the room resumed its ruckus as the stranger took Angel by the arm.

"Let's go, little lady. Show me where you live."

She glanced around the room again and then met the man's gaze. He would do.

They walked into the night together.

"This way." She pointed right, and they strode down the boardwalk. After a shack labeled *Hardware*, she pointed into the darkness. "Our tent's that way."

He stared up the hill into the gloom, swaying. She could tell he didn't want to go, that he was ready for his bed, which was likely only a few shacks down.

"Please walk me, sir," she said. "It's awful dark." His eyes blinked one after the other. She pulled on his arm. "Please? I'm sure Ma'll give you two bits for your kindness."

"Fine, fine," he finally said.

She led, and he followed up the incline and along a path that stopped at the base of a massive spruce. A ring of rocks surrounding a pile of cold coals was all that remained from her company's campsite from last week. A dozen empty cans cluttered the bushes to the side.

"Oh, no," Angel said. "I hope they haven't gone on without me."

The drunk looked at the dead fire ring and around in a circle. "Left you? I think—"

When his gaze made it back to her, she was holding his collar in one hand and plunging the knife into his belly with the other. He looked down, then into her eyes as his hot blood ran over her fingers. There was a sadness in his gaze, a look of regret.

She expected him to say something else, to fight. He did neither. He dropped to his knees, and Angel pulled back the knife. She placed her lips on his and inhaled his last breath as she slid the blade across his throat and soaked in the hot, red spray that coated her clothes.

She followed him down as he fell, then she undressed him and began the process of removing each organ and setting them neatly on a nearby rock. When she got to the kidneys, though, she just couldn't hold herself back and bit into one as she carried it to the others. She was removing the man's pants to get at his legs when a stick snapped on the path toward town.

Angel spun toward the sound. Her teeth clenched, and her grip tightened around the blade.

The giant man from the saloon stepped into the clearing, his pistol pointed at Angel. His eyes went from the dead man to the pile of organs to the cold fire ring to her bloody mouth. His expression stood firm.

As the giant moved closer, there was a gleam in his eyes that Angel recognized. She smiled at it, then dropped the knife on the ground and put her hands on the sides of her dress. She bunched the fabric in her grip, pulling the hem up her ankles and over her knees. She sat on the ground and leaned back, spreading her legs, and the giant holstered his pistol.

40

D ETECTIVE MARK RAND PRESSED his back into the support beam and pushed with his legs. The wood groaned and cracked, and dust trickled down from the ceiling. He thought about Higgins leaving with that key, and he was scared to death that some cracking and dust was all he was going to get before being stuck here forever.

His wrists ached. His back and legs burned. He hated himself for not figuring a way out of this. He was a detective, after all; he was supposed to be able to see the big picture, look at situations and find the solution. He just couldn't find one here.

He pondered breaking his thumb to make his hand small enough to slip through the cuffs. He didn't think it would work, though, not as tight as these things were. He had been trained to leave enough space around the wrist so detainees wouldn't get hurt or even bruised—that spelled a lawsuit. If these cuffs were that loose, he was sure a broken thumb would do the trick, but here—as tight as that asshole had made these things—he feared he would be disabling himself for nothing. But as the beam failed to move, he knew he might have to try that, regardless.

And what if pushing on the beam worked? Maybe he could get the thing to slide off its foundation and fall, and maybe he could slide the cuffs off the top or bottom of the log, depending on how it landed. But what if the goddamn ceiling came down on him? It was a nearly two-hundred-year-old place, not a modern cabin built to code.

He didn't know, but he had to keep trying things.

Rand closed his eyes and groaned as he gave the log another heave. It groaned back. He felt a splinter crawl into the back of his neck. His face flushed bright red, and his muscles screamed. The log shifted a hair, enough that he felt it. And little enough that he knew using every bit of his strength was pointless.

He exhaled and rested his legs. When he opened his eyes, there was a face beside the far wall, watching him. It floated in the gloom, a bearded stare with angry eyes. Its lips slid left and right as if the man was grinding his teeth. His stare met Rand's, and the face moved toward him.

Rand pressed himself against the post, not trying to move it but more instinctively, as if his subconscious knew to get away—as if he could slip around to the other side of the post and close his eyes, hiding, and this thing would be gone.

It wasn't that simple, and he knew it. That woman's ghost had banged on the door and swung a knife. What might this one have?

The rest of the head came into view as the thing drifted closer. Then came its shoulders and arms and massive hands and waist and legs, all fading slowly into existence.

Rand's body stopped listening to him. His legs pushed toward the side of the post as if running away. His heart climbed into his throat. His arms fought against the handcuffs, splitting his skin and causing him to bleed.

"Go away," he whispered.

It came closer. Its feet dragged across the floor as it floated. It descended to Rand's eye level, its lower body fading into nothing as it touched the floor. It studied Rand's face, and then it reached for the detective.

"Go," Rand told it. "Go away." The words were just noise. They meant nothing and came from nowhere. He didn't know what to say or if the thing could even hear him, but the sounds came out nonetheless. "Leave me alone." It was a terror in his heart that lacked any modern thought or intellect—in his face was pure horror.

The ghost grabbed Rand by the jaw, icy fingers inside his mouth and a thumb below his chin. They burned with cold, and his throat hitched as the thing pinched tighter. Closing tighter. His tongue arched away. His teeth ached. Panic seized Rand, and he trembled under the enormous monster's touch.

Air refused to pass through Rand's mouth. Every molecule that entered his nose carried the putrid stench of rotting death.

The thing gazed hard into Rand's eyes, and Rand felt himself sinking.

"Go," Rand croaked out. It was all he could manage.

Surprisingly, the thing backed away. Only, as it moved, it pulled Rand's jaw with it. It was an ice-cold stone hand, and it was yanking half of Rand's face from his body.

The inside of Rand's bone felt cold and brittle as the tension mounted. His teeth screamed in pain from their tips to their roots. There was a cracking sound as his jaw muscles reached the end of their elasticity, and his joints burned.

Frozen fire scorched his mouth as Rand tried to form words. Nothing more than a low squeal made it from his lips.

He tasted blood. He envisioned his mouth ripping from his face and flying across the room as if he was in some B-grade horror flick, and his squeal turned into a high-pitched howl.

He felt it throughout his body. The pain was electric. It was convulsive. It made him cry in a way nothing else ever had.

The thing clamped harder and grinned. Black teeth exposed themselves over cracked blue lips. His eyes delighted in every rising decibel of Rand's pain.

The doors vibrated in their jambs. Cups shook on the table. Chairs danced across the floor.

Spots hung in Rand's vision. He thought he'd felt pain before, but this circled his body and stabbed into his skull. It was like the back of his head was on fire, and his melted brain was leaking down his throat. It had to stop. God, it had to stop!

Rand realized he was hovering, stretched over the floor from the post to the ghost as it pulled. There was a tearing sound in the left side of his face, and the pain consumed his mind. The room flashed, and the ghost became two—the entire room became two. Double-vision and flashing lights filled everything in front of Rand.

The right side of his jaw emitted the same tearing noise. He barely heard it over his screams. It was the last thing he heard before the pain took him away.

Abby imagined herself in some medieval dungeon, the way the shackles held her suspended over the dirt floor. She didn't know an inch of her body that was not in pain. She didn't know if her body even worked.

Blood dripped from her chin down her bare chest. It was the one warm thing she had. When they stripped her naked and hung her by her wrists, her fear was rape. When two strange men drag you away and undress you, that's what you're trained to expect as a woman. She wished it had been that. Not this. Not the big one explaining to the other one how she needed to be "tenderized."

Tenderized?

She wasn't a piece of meat. God, she didn't want to be.

But punch after punch on her bare skin, the two taking

turns—she didn't know if an inch of her body was unbruised. She didn't know how many broken ribs she had or if her feet could support her. She had cried herself dry, passed out, and came back so many times. She wasn't much more than a hanging bag of bruises at this point.

She would have never wished for death on any other day, but today, even after they had taken a break and left her to *cure*, she may have welcomed it if given the choice.

An end to the pain. The throbbing, ceaseless agony. An end to the cold. The prickling, frozen tendrils of winter that dug into every inch of her flesh. An end to the shivering, which over her bruises and broken bones hurt almost as bad as their blows.

Abby wished her brother Miles was with her right now. He wouldn't have let this happen. She wished she hadn't left Georgia. It was a stupid idea. What was she thinking, coming out here?

She coughed, and hot blood warmed her chest as it ran over her breast. Her entire torso shot waves of pain for the jolt.

She wanted to cry but mashed her eyelids closed as the thought of her brother returned. He wouldn't cry here. He would stay strong. He was the most hardheaded, stubborn person she knew, and he wouldn't cry. He wouldn't give up until he was dead in the ground—

(or in their bellies)

She shuddered.

No. She wouldn't do that.

Abby pulled on the shackles. Dust trickled down from the wooden beam above. She thought of heroes in movies doing pullups and freeing themselves. That wouldn't happen here. The hanging had worn down her shoulders. Her arms were more bruise than muscle. Her chest felt like a thousand swords in her lungs just by that small tug. Even if it was possible to unhook her chains, there was no way she could physically do it.

Her only escape was a key on a nail ten feet away. It hung over a table, over an arrangement of bones and dried-up meat. Wax mounds signified the remains of burned candles circling what she believed was an altar, and dried blood streaked the wood in sheets.

There was no reaching that key. But goddammit, she had to find a way.

Wanda listened closely. Rand quieted above, and she felt the handcuff key in her pocket, wishing she could release him. Abby coughed on the other side of the wall. Lins whimpered and sat on the pile of bones, hugging Angel. Angel's eyes twitched back and forth as she fought whatever was happening inside her head.

There was so much she wanted to do, and she felt frozen in place and ashamed that she couldn't do any of it: free Rand, help Abby, wake Angel, get Lins out of there.

She sat on a pile of bones and hated every part of this. There were maniacs and ghosts and who knew what else—what was the thing that crawled inside Angel's mouth? And she was even deeper inside the house—under the house—on some kind of mass grave or trash pile. She had known the legend of travelers disappearing, but this... it was unreal.

What happened to bring her here was unreal. As her eyes swept over the mound of bones, she knew for sure—those were children's hands that had grabbed her and pulled her here, saved her, saved all three of them. They were the hands of ghost children.

The empty eye sockets of small skulls stared at her. They held gashes, chips, and cuts from blades. All the bones did. That realization made Wanda's blood run cold.

She didn't want to but found herself looking closer. Small bits of dried tendon clung to bones. Cuts in hips and femurs were stained with dried blood. The larger skulls were cracked open, with similar gashes inside.

She wasn't just on a mass grave; she was on a heap of cannibal refuse. Those children had been eaten.

She wanted to puke, but the idea of vomiting on the remains held her back.

This was worse than horrific. It was worse than anything she saw in that house on West Hemlock, worse than that man and the assault (the rape); this was evil on a level she found impossible to comprehend.

There was another cough from the other side of the wall—from Abby.

The sound vibrated in Wanda's core. Her friend was so close. She could practically see her right on the other side of that bare wood. She was sure she could just reach out and touch her if that board wasn't in the way.

Wanda extended her arm and placed her hand flat against the wood. It was rough, and she could feel the splinters tease her palm. She pressed against it, and the wood bowed under her weight.

She wanted to jerk her hand back. What if they were in there with Abby? She didn't hear them in there, but that didn't prove anything.

Her hand trembled. She wished she had a gun. She wished she had the hatchet—shit, anything more than her fists alone.

Lins shuffled, and the bones below her rattled. Wanda stared at Angel, at Lins, saw them on those bones, and she saw their future if she didn't do something. Her and these kids' bones would be decaying atop the rest. Their ghosts would reside in this house with those kids and that couple. Whether she was scared or not, whether it was risky or not, she had to make a move, and she only knew two ways to go. She damned sure wasn't going back through that tunnel.

Wanda pushed harder against the bowing board. It creaked under her pressure. Splinters broke free while others arched out from the top and bottom. It cracked, and she pushed harder, faster.

She panicked—someone in there could see her coming, hear her coming—she had to move faster and take them by surprise.

Wanda threw her weight forward. The ancient board crumbled under her, and she tumbled through the wall, down three feet, and crashed on another dirt floor. She spun, taking in the room as fast as she could.

A packed dirt floor. Walls of the same thin board. A lantern hanging. A pile of clothes in one corner. A table in the other corner with an arrangement of items she didn't have time to study. In the center, Abby looked the other way. She was naked, hanging from chains like some torture victim.

Wanda's hand shot to her mouth as the swollen body of her friend revealed itself. Her arms, legs, back, and waist all puffed out inches more than they should. Blood dripped from her toes, soaking into the hard earth. Her breath was labored and low, and Wanda prayed she wasn't too late.

A weight fell over the room, a thickening of the atmosphere as it cooled into a blanket of icy air. The feeling was too familiar, and Wanda jumped forward to check on her friend before it was too late.

Abby's eyes were barely open. Her lids fluttered as Wanda stood in front of her.

"Abby," Wanda whispered. The word hitched as tears burned the corners of her eyes. She reached up and felt the chains as she examined them. They were old but tight and working just fine. She needed a key to get Abby out. "Abby, I'm going to get you down. Do you know where the key is?"

Abby groaned and winced. Her eyes widened, and she mouthed the word *there* as she stared across the room.

Wanda turned. A rusty shard of metal hung on the wall by the corner.

"Hang on, I'll get it." Wanda darted across the room, stretching for the key before she understood what she was reaching over.

The bones made a circle, and a strange design was piled inside. Each bone was small, smaller than those of the children in the mass grave. Wanda could have assumed they were from some small animal, but she knew deep within they were human. Each one was covered in carvings in a language that reminded her of old, dead tongues. And below the center mound were dried pieces of meat—pieces of a child.

"My god." Wanda shuddered backward, her heart sinking and her hand still open, the key still hanging. "It's..." She turned to Abby. "They murdered..."

She saw her friend again, and it sunk in what those men wanted, but worse than that, appearing in the air between Abby and the hole in the wall was the face of the woman, the ghost that chased her under the bed, and the knife was still in her hand.

Wanda spun, reaching with intention this time, and snagged the key from the wall. She grabbed a long knife from the table beside the bones, a knife that looked strangely identical to the one hanging from the ghost woman's hand.

"Go away," Wanda demanded. "Leave us alone. Now." Her voice was soft and deep. She spoke as sure as she could, trying her hardest to mask the fear on the tip of her tongue. Fear for Abby and herself, but even more than that, fear that the ghost would turn around and go after the kids. She would have had no way to stop it.

"Leave," she repeated.

The ghost bitch smiled and raised her knife. She floated toward Abby and let the blade rest on Abby's shoulder, then ran it slowly down her side.

"Don't you—" Wanda started toward Abby. She didn't know what she would do when she got there, but she had to close the gap and help. She had to get closer to this thing to stop it from whatever it was planning.

The knife floated just below Abby's rib. The ghost shook her head left and right. There was no sound, but Wanda was sure she heard a woman's voice in her head saying, "No, no, no."

Wanda stopped at an arm's length from her friend. Abby looked Wanda in the eyes. They were pained, pleading eyes, and they drilled into Wanda's heart, crying for help.

"What do you want?" Wanda asked the ghost. Thinking only of the silly paranormal shows she'd seen on TV, she asked, "Do you have some unfinished business? I can help you."

She took a step forward and the coldness was oppressive. It sank through her clothes and into her skin and burned.

The ghost gave no answer. It pushed the tip of its blade into Abby's side.

"Stop!"

Abby whimpered. It seemed like all she could do.

The blade hung there, an inch inside Abby's skin, fat, and muscle. A line of blood escaped the wound and ran to Abby's thigh, where it paused then traveled down her leg.

"You don't have to do this. Please?" Wanda begged.

She watched a grin cross the ghost's mouth, and its arm flexed, preparing to skewer Abby and end the confrontation.

"No!" Wanda raised her own knife and jutted forward. She

thrust the blade around Abby's side, planting it deep into the ghost's waist.

She had no idea if it would work, but she had a hunch and she did the only thing she could.

The ghost darted backward, clutching her side, a scream on her lips and an unearthly ear-piercing sound shrieking through the room. She shot across the pile of bones, across the kids, and into the opposite dirt wall. The scream faded with her.

Wanda wanted to collapse on the floor right there. She couldn't believe that worked. There was no time for resting, though; those men may have heard the screams.

She shoved the key in one manacle's lock, and Abby's hand dropped free, leaving her suspended from one arm. Wanda climbed under her, lifting while she freed the other hand.

Abby trembled. Tears burst from her eyes as Wanda set her on the floor. She squirmed in every direction, whimpering and shifting, searching for any position at all, even existing, without causing herself pain. She found none. She ground her teeth together and held in the screams as Wanda gently slid clothes over her swollen flesh.

Above them, footsteps walked across the wood toward the ladder down.

41

ANGEL LIVED WITHIN FLORENCE, behind the shadow, as a year passed before her eyes. She watched a thousand evil things and did a thousand evil things that no child should ever bear witness to. She cried within herself. She felt the fears and thrills, the hate and the needs of each being from inside Florence's head.

It had been just over a year when Eustace led the wagon with pregnant Florence into the mountains. She was balancing in back over a bed of blankets when they stopped at the cabin in the woods.

Eustace climbed down from his seat, and John Garret walked from the side of the house with a hammer in his hand. The old-timer wore suspended pants over his long johns, sleeves bunched up over his elbows. His short, gray beard was sweaty and dripping, as were the man's arms.

"Help ya?" he asked. He watched as Eustace took Florence by the arm and braced her as she climbed from the wagon. He waited for each of them to turn and face him. "Am I right that you two need a bed overnight? We don't get many this time o' year, but I see you're in a motherly way, so I reckon you could use a bed instead of a night camping."

Eustace didn't speak. He rarely did. He found it boring, and conversation tried his patience.

"A bed for the night would be agreeable," Florence said. "And a meal if you could spare it."

John Garret nodded and pointed to the cabin door. "Go on in and tell Selma what you need. I'll be followin' ya in shortly." He stared up into the darkening clouds. "I've got a few shingles that need replacin' before that storm hits. Last thing you want is a drip on your face while you're catching forty winks." He smiled wide.

"That'll be perfect." Florence nodded and turned. "Eustace, bring our bag."

The giant reached into the wagon, gathering a large leather suitcase. As he and Florence walked toward the door, John Garret went around the side of the cabin.

Angel could smell the scents of huckleberry and cinnamon as Florence reached for the door. The wood stove was bright and warm, steaming pots on top, and Selma Garret was stirring. She looked Florence over, and a smile bloomed over her weathered face.

"Aren't you a pretty young thing! I heard voices out there and started working on a batch of bread, but I had no idea a doll like you'd be joinin' us." She marched across the room and planted her hands on the sides of Florence's belly. "You are just about ready to pop too! No wonder you need a bed."

Selma stepped to the side and ushered Florence toward the table, gesturing at the closest chair. "Sit, sit. I'm sure that young'un's ready for a snack." She turned to Eustace, who was closing the door, and pointed at the guest room. "Go ahead and put your bags in there—any bed you want."

When she turned back, her mouth gaped. Her eyes rolled back into her head. Angel could see the knife through her open smile as Florence drove it up under her chin and into her skull. There was no blood at all until she yanked out the blade, and the woman crumpled to the floor. The blood ran over the floorboards into the earth that would later be tossed out back, making room for the pit.

John Garret opened the cabin door, wiping sweat from his brow. "I think it'll hold back the rain, 'suming the wind isn't too bad. Can never tell what's gonna happen when that wind gets blowin'."

He froze with one hand on the door and the other by his side. His eyes were set on the bloody floor, then moved to the table. He locked onto the red, skinless carcass lying on the table, not much more than a torso now. He didn't spot the cast iron sizzling on the stove or Eustace in the corner to his right.

"What that hell?" He stumbled forward. "Where's Selma?" His voice was weak. He suspected—more than that, he knew the bits and pieces—but refused to add it all up.

He reached toward Florence, wading through the savory scented smoke. "What did you—" He stopped as she looked at him. Her delicate frame, bulging yet strong, the knife in her hand, and the eyes that spoke of hunger; the gears clicked inside his head. She chewed something and spat on the table. His eyes followed the chunk as it landed in blood beside a stringy cut of red flesh. It unfolded.

When he recognized the ear, his legs gave. There was a thud as his knees hit the floor. His hands caught him before his face hit the wood, before Eustace's rifle stock crashed into the back of his head.

It took five days for Eustace to dig out the first basement room. By the time he was done, little more than bones with clingy shreds of tendon remained of Selma. Not much more than that clung to John as he cowered in the corner, hands tied and mouth clogged with a rag.

They had tried to feed him. Florence even shoved a hunk of meat down his throat. The damn fool puked it back it. That was the last time.

He begged them to kill him. He wept as he watched them slowly devour his wife day after day. They weren't about to do that, not until she was completely gone and they were ready for him.

Now, though, the day was here. It was the day of days. The day the shadow had said was coming. They might not have much food left, as skinny as John was, but the future held a basket o' plenty ready to overflow and tip in their direction. All they had to do was follow its plan.

John Garret screamed into his gag as Eustace dragged him across the cabin and dropped him through the trap door he'd built into their bedroom floor. He hit the earthen ground below with a thump, and four of his ribs cracked.

Eustace climbed down the ladder, then supported Florence as she descended. She kneeled with Selma's knife in hand, and she pulled the gag from John's mouth.

"I want to thank you for this wonderful place," Florence said. "It's been my dream for a long time to have a place like this."

She was lying. Angel watched her lie and knew what was coming. She knew every gruesome detail of the shadow thing's plan, and she wanted out. She wanted back to her world more than anything she had ever wanted. So much of the past year had been futile—she'd used her will and pushed to overcome it, and it never worked. She had wished and prayed and cried in the back of Florence's mind. She had been forced to watch tragedy and depravity and screamed inside herself. But what was coming in this basement was too much. It was more than she could stand, and she knew either she had to find a way to escape or it was finally going to drive her mad.

"What are you gonna do with me?" the old man croaked. Blood ran over his lips as he coughed and winced.

"We're gonna set you free," Florence said. She could see his eyes on Selma's knife. There was no getting over on him. He knew the end was coming, that the blackness was in her and there was no hope for him. But still, she smiled as if she had made some joke and he should be laughing.

"Light the flames," Florence said. Her eyes didn't leave John's.

Eustace struck a match and lit three candles on the corner table he had hauled down from the bedroom. In the center of the candles, Selma's rib bones, carved and prepared, made a circle, awaiting something in the middle.

"Good." A contraction squeezed Florence's womb, and she leaned forward and kissed John on the forehead. "Thank you," she repeated.

Selma's blade ran over her husband's throat, and his steamy blood pumped onto the dirt floor.

Florence dug into the earth as the blood flowed. She gouged a path, leading it in an arc around the room until it came back on itself, forming a circle.

Another contraction grabbed hold, a strong one, and she led the crimson stream from the outside into five distinct shapes, led by the shadow. She didn't know what they were or what they meant, but she did it. It wanted it. It was going to give her exactly what she wanted, so she would do the same.

The next contraction was larger, collapsing her to the ground in the middle of the awkward circle. Another one, and she screamed.

The baby was coming. Her body, the shadow, the dark essence driving them all, all wanted it out.

Another contraction. Another scream. She pushed.

"Get ready," she howled at Eustace.

He hugged the wall like a statue, waiting.

Florence pulled up her dress, exposing a crowning head between her legs. She howled like a wild animal and pushed again.

The candles flickered. The room dimmed. Inhuman voices crossed through the walls. The bloody trench around Florence hummed, and what looked like red fire ignited above it.

A nose, a chin, a neck poked out. She pushed again, and the room went dark as a tiny being and a splash of blood slid out of Florence and into the flickering light of the basement.

Florence screamed. She sat up and lifted the child. She wiped its face, and as it started to cry, she looked into its small, black eyes.

It was her, and it was hers. It was Eustace, and it was a new, clean soul, ready to live its own life.

A boy.

She saw all the things it could do with its life: grow, play, love her, marry, make more life, and bring more souls into the world—this damned sorrowful world. This hellish place that only existed to torture souls and drag the good ones like her down.

No. She couldn't let that happen to her baby.

She pushed again and felt the rest of her womb clear out. She raised the boy above her head.

Eustace grabbed the child, its cord and placenta swinging. He carried it to the table, placing all of it in the middle of the ring of bones.

The room went black as he raised Selma's knife.

Angel screamed. She pounded on the edge of her confined reality with only the strength of her will. She cried for help and, this time, felt a bulge in her pocket back where her body was, and she knew just what it was. It was warm and it was not just hers, but it was also Grandma's. Betty Bobcat was in her pocket, and more than that, a connection was with her—a connection to a warm, loving place that filled her with the hope and power she needed.

She had seen too much on this demonic ride-along—more horror than a person should see in a lifetime. Murders, rapes, cannibalism. She had gotten by by telling herself this had all already happened, that she was merely witnessing the past and there was nothing she could do to stop it. She could not witness this. *No!* What was about to happen was too much.

The candles flickered, making no light. The ring of fire burned around Florence/Shadow/Angel, and it cast no rays, made no shadows, but the things on the other side of the walls refused to stay still. They chanted in words unknown to the Earth. They screamed for the blade to fall. They howled for their freedom—and so did Angel.

The blade came down, and the infant's scream dwindled to nothing. The room burst into a brightness that blinded them all. Angel exploded into a weeping rage, and as the lights faded, a dozen shadows crawled on small spidery legs from the infant's mouth, and Angel found herself propelled through a blackness of time and space from the basement of that retched cabin. She traveled among the stars through light and energy, past visions she could not comprehend.

She opened her eyes on a pile of bones with a spider made of shadow racing from her mouth.

42

ABBY TRIED TO STAND and collapsed into the dirt. She cried out as her bloated muscles thumped against the ground. The trap door over Wanda's head whined back, and a rush of air flooded down with the salty scent of fried meat.

Both women shivered.

Wanda's fingers flexed around the knife in her grip. She knew this might happen—that it would probably happen. She wasn't getting out of this without confronting these animals, no matter how much she wished they could just slip out the front door.

Size thirteen boots led the way down the ladder, and Wanda prepared to leap forward. Then the worst thing that could have happened did: Angel called from the gloomy pit of bones.

"Mom?"

Wanda turned. Her baby was back. She had already concluded she would have to carry Angel out of this basement, up the stairs, all the way through the woods, to the car, to the steps of Custer Memorial Hospital; but now she was awake. She was awake!

Boots thumped on the dirt. A pair of huge hands seized the back of Wanda's neck, and before she understood what was happening, she was flying face first toward the broken plank wall.

Abby screamed and climbed to her feet. Her fists flailed before she was all the way up, and she barreled toward Shamus, limping and wobbling like a train on oval wheels.

Wanda crashed into the wood wall inches from the hole. Colored blobs filled her vision as Angel screamed. She slid down the plank, splinters lodging in her cheek. She felt the knife slide from her hand before her knees hit the soil.

"Mom!" Angel's voice beyond the spots.

There was a moment when Wanda saw nothing but knew everything. She knew Abby's fists collided with Shamus's chest and the man barely moved. She knew Angel was rushing over the sea of bones toward her as she wished her child would stay back and stay safe. She knew the ghost woman was still there, even if unseen, as was the giant man, the shadow things, and dozens of others. They were watching, like her. They were waiting to see what would come of this because no matter the outcome, they won.

Wanda saw a glow within the space behind Shamus. Another in Angel's hand. There was a sensation surrounding Angel that Wanda hadn't felt in a long time, and something about it gave her a slight sense of hope—

But as the spots faded into a double-visioned view of Angel picking up the knife and Abby screaming, that hope vanished.

Angel ignored Lins for now. Her friend could cry in that corner if she wanted to; it was probably the safest place for her while this was all happening. She climbed over bones, ignoring the ghostly bloody soup and decaying flesh rippling with each move. She ignored the wetness on her knees and the slime on her hands as she made her way through the broken panel and into the altar room.

Abby was up against the wall, gagging. Shamus held her there, his hand around her throat. Her eyes were bulging—her whole face was bulging.

Angel wished there was more she could do, but right now, Abby was doing her job whether she knew it or not, just as Angel had to do hers.

Ghosts lined the room as Angel leaned down and lifted Florence's knife. The scared little ones only showed their faces through the cracks in the walls. The older trappers and travelers hugged the edges. The shadows lingered by the ceiling. They knew what Angel was up to, but she didn't think they could stop her, not now anyway. Florence and Eustace were near, but she wasn't quite sure where—they were coming, though.

Angel slid her bobcat from her pocket. It was a soft, warm thing, just like Grandma. It brought Grandma's scent into the room. It lit the path ahead, telling her where it wanted to go. She hated that this was the way it had to be, but she was sure now it had to go this way. That's why Grandma had to come—why Betty had to come. If only she had figured it all out sooner.

Abby reached out for Angel. Her swollen eyes locked onto her as she approached quietly, sneaking across the room. Abby spotted the knife, and Angel could see the thought in her head. *Stab the bastard! Save me!*

It wouldn't work. Angel was sure. The man was too big, and there was a shadow inside him. Abby had to do her job. That was how this worked.

Angel slipped behind Shamus. She was six feet from the altar, six feet from ending this if she did it right.

She raised Betty Bobcat in one hand and the knife in the other. She took another step, bracing for the impact of what was to come.

"Please, Grandma," Angel whispered, and took another step.

Abby gurgled behind her. Mom shifted and rolled over. Lins

huddled against the dirt wall in the pit, spying through the gap in the wood and weeping. A century and a half of ghosts watched.

Another step, and Florence's hands burst through the left wall. She raced at Angel, her knife high and coming down.

Angel clutched Betty Bobcat to her chest, the scent of lilacs brushing away the stench of this basement and the acrid smell of burning meat upstairs. She thrust her blade up.

The ghost's knife stabbed Betty Bobcat where it hovered over Angel's chest. Angel's knife sliced up into the ghost. Both knives slid loose. Betty glowed orange through a gash in her fur. Florence staggered backward, her mouth open in a silent scream and her chest gushing with black blood.

Florence glared at Angel with a look of knowing. She recognized her—the voice that was in her head for a year so long ago. She darted toward the child, her bony hands forward and clawing, her mouth misshapen, teeth turned to fangs, eyes drenched in black, hair blowing in rage.

Angel turned and ran to the altar. She grabbed the pile of bones, scooping the child and its shriveled insides into her hand.

She heard then, for the first time, the voice of a ghost.

They were always silent. Their words weren't allowed to reach the living. That was just how it was. Their time was over, and they weren't supposed to be here. But this voice was unmistakable. It was a voice silenced too long ago and never allowed to rest. It was a voice that had only been heard once by the living and had been crying to be heard again ever since. And Angel was going to do what had to be done to hear it.

She set the baby boy on the ground, calming it.

Wanda watched as if it were all a dream, because there was no way this was real.

Abby's eyes went blank as she hung from Shamus's grip. The woman ghost was charging at her baby. Angel was setting a pile of bones on the ground as if it were something precious.

It was surreal. It was unreal. It was her brain playing tricks on her after the concussion. But she had to do something, regardless.

Wanda climbed to her feet as the ghost's hands touched Angel's shoulders. Shamus dropped Abby and turned toward Wanda. Wanda struggled with what she could do—could she even fight a ghost? She had to get it off Angel, but Shamus was turning toward her; she had to deal with him first.

Angel stood, ignoring the hands on her shoulders. Wanda cranked back her fist and dropped to her knees. The ghost's hands stiffened, but as they tried to stop Angel, something amazing happened.

Every ghost from the walls and every kid inside the cracks lunged forward like a gust of angry wind and seized Florence. One bearded trapper grabbed her knife and used it to carve a slit from her belly up to her throat. Another took her by the head and wrenched back her skull. Another grabbed her hands, another her arms, and they twisted them behind her. Children reached into her open chest, their tiny fingers gripping decayed flesh and bone, and they ripped the hole wide, spilling her insides out.

Wanda waited, not blinking, ignoring the rest of the chaos, as the massive man came near. She unleashed her fist like a rocket, uppercutting Shamus in his balls. His fist came down on the side of her face, and while he tumbled over her, she crumpled into the dirt.

Angel didn't look at any of them. She wanted to help Mom. She prayed that Mom and Miss Abby would be okay, but she had to finish. It was the only way.

Tears streaked her cheeks. Her hands trembled.

Angel set Betty Bobcat on the altar in the center of Mrs. Garret's bones. She wasn't sure how this was supposed to work, only that Grandma would lead the way.

The ghost knife had cut her furry, her grandmother's essence, stabbed into the bright light of Betty's insides, but as Angel's fingers slipped free, it glowed even brighter. It lit the room in a new orange hue, and the circle Florence had drawn in the dirt all those years ago lit up again. The ceiling brightened, and a dozen shadowed things with long, spindly legs scattered into the cracks of the floorboards and the holes in the dirt.

"It's time," Grandma said, and Angel turned back to the child in the dirt.

Wanda rolled past Abby's body, hoping to God she had enough time. The room got brighter, and what she could only describe as a ghost brawl tumbled back into the walls, dozens of spirits dragging the woman out of sight, leaving a knife on the floor. She needed that knife.

The handle was cold in her hand, as if it had been in a freezer. There was a sound of rhythmic thudding, like a horse's gallop, and Shamus was on her, his grip on her shoulder, flipping her over and slamming her on her back.

She saw Angel as she spun. Her daughter was digging a hole in the basement floor—another surreal vision that was quickly ripped away as her spine slammed into the dirt and her eyes fixed on him.

Wanda smelled disgusting trash. It was the thick, sour scent of mold and decay. She smelled blood. She saw the first floor's floorboards above Shamus—she saw the roof of the house on West Hemlock, where she had stared helplessly while being attacked. That's what she was smelling—not something here, not this place—she was smelling that bum. She saw his face in Shamus's as he hovered over her, placing his giant mitts on her throat.

She was frozen in place. She had been hit in the head back on West Hemlock, but here she didn't know why she was helpless. She could feel the knife's handle in her palm, just as she had felt the broken springs in the mattress in that derelict house, but her hands wouldn't act.

He huffed over her. She rocked as his grip shook and squeezed. His eyes bulged with rage. She felt raw burning in her gut and a numbness in her limbs, a blurring of the world as the room grew hazy around her—around Angel!

It hit her like a bolt of lightning. Her eyes darted to Angel. Her baby. She was lowering bones into the ground, and a single truth held itself aloft in Wanda's thoughts. If she didn't act right now, Angel would be next.

There were no other thoughts.

The next thing she knew, hot blood ran down the knife from Shamus's gut. Wanda yanked it out and stabbed him again. And again, and again.

Wetness soaked into her clothes. His hand softened but didn't relent. She stabbed again in the side of his chest.

Her vision cleared. She raised her arm and rammed it into his neck. There was a gurgle in his throat as she twisted, and a gap that reached across his neck opened up.

The big man collapsed on Mom as Angel shoved loose dirt, filling in the hole. A flash of light consumed the room as Betty Bobcat bursts into flames.

"No!" Angel screamed and jumped to her feet.

The fire reached the ceiling, scorching the wood above them. But it wasn't a normal fire; Angel could see that. It was tinted orange gold, and as the altar smoked, she knew this had to be.

But that didn't stop the tears. It didn't stop Angel from feeling Grandma's fingers running through her hair and massaging her scalp or the memories from flooding through her mind of giggling together on Grandma's couch, cooking in her kitchen, drawing on her dining room table, hugging and breathing in lilacs and vanilla and love. It was all there in that fire, and Angel wished with everything inside that all those memories wouldn't burn away with the flame.

The baby finally fell quiet. Asleep.

A sense of relief hit Angel, however momentary.

Mom was on top of Abby, pounding on her chest and breathing into her mouth, but that was the most mundane thing in the room.

Shadow things shot from the holes in the walls. They twisted like frantic insects, their thin, creepy legs swatting at the air as they flew into the altar's blaze. They came through the cracks. They melted up from the dirt. One crawled from the mouth of the dead man on the floor, and they were all sucked into the fire.

Abby gasped and coughed, and the ceiling burned.

From the walls around them, ghosts walked into the room, for the first time with smiles on their faces. Their wounds and their missing limbs were healed. Their faces were clear of blood and pain. They came toward Angel as if by some duty, and as she met their gazes, they flashed and disappeared, and her heart thumped with a joy she wasn't quite sure she understood.

"Lins!" Wanda called into the pit. "Come on! It's safe now. We have to go."

Safe wasn't a word she would have used to describe this at any other time, but she had to get the girl moving. The walls were burning. The fire was creeping closer to the ladder. There was no telling how far the fire had spread upstairs, and if they didn't move immediately, they might end up trapped under this fiery hell.

Lins refused to move.

Angel stepped between her mother and the hole in the wall and reached into the darkness. "Come on, Lins," she said calmly. "It's time to go."

Lins closed her eyes and bit her lip. She took a deep breath and crawled forward.

Wanda guided Abby to the ladder and braced her as she started up. Abby groaned. Her feet shuddered every time she put weight on them, but she climbed. When Abby was up, Wanda told Lins to go. Then Angel. Last was Wanda.

The bedroom they surfaced in burned from one side to the other. The bed smelled like burning hair. A chair was ablaze beside it, and looking through the flames, Wanda was sure its frame was made of bone.

"That way." Abby pointed to the door and hobbled toward it. She leaned on the wall as she pulled it slowly open, peering carefully into the next room even as this one heated like an oven and smoke filled the ceiling.

She pushed it aside and staggered through.

Rand was collapsed against the same pole. On the stove, a cast iron skillet smoked with two pairs of charred, black balls inside it. Fire ran up the walls, and the smoke on the ceiling was lowering by the second.

"Get the kids outside," Wanda yelled. "I'm right behind you."

The girls slipped under Abby's arms and supported her as they staggered toward the door together.

Wanda dug into her pocket and found the key. She kneeled beside Rand, and then she saw his face. His jaw hung from his skull like some depressed marionette. His face was black and blue, bloated from every angle. Blood ran from the corners of his mouth, and he didn't seem to notice she was even there.

She felt his neck, not sure if it was better for him to be alive or dead. His pulse was strong.

Sweat ran down Wanda's face as she fumbled getting the key into the cuffs. The room brightened as sleeping bags and firewood caught. Smoke gnawed at her throat until, finally, she slipped the key in place and Rand's right hand dropped free.

She didn't bother freeing the left one; they could do that later. She slid the key back into her pocket and kneeled beside him, pulling his arm over her shoulder.

The ceiling cracked, and wood crashed onto the stove. Sparks showered the entire cabin, and smaller fires burst to life on the pile of Wanda's supplies.

"Fuck." He was heavy, and she had to move. She yanked, and he groaned, and they stumbled steadily toward the door. She saw the AK-47 and wanted to grab it, just in case. She saw the hatchet and kept going. There was no time. She just couldn't get either. She would have to hope the knife she slid into her waistband would be enough.

"Come on!" Angel yelled from the doorway.

There was a sliver of brightening sky out there, and Wanda thrust herself and Rand toward it. "We're going to make it. You hear me?" she told him. He groaned in response.

They fought through the doorway, and Angel pulled them out into the dawn. They all collapsed on the ground ten yards from the cabin into two feet of snow. The cabin creaked and whined until it caved in on itself with a bellowing crunch. It burned in a crackling goodbye, and Wanda stared up at the pink morning sky, a final wave of relief surrounding her.

It wasn't snowing. They had no supplies, but they were alive—most of them. It would be hard, but they were going to make it off this mountain.

She believed that even as footsteps neared from the woods.

Abby cried as she stared into streaks of clouds and the blue sky beyond. The snow on her back and limbs was the first good feeling she'd had in hours. She wanted to die from the pain, but more than that, she was determined to live. And she wasn't sure if the tears were from her agony or her hope.

Angel sat beside her friend. This time, she was the one providing the comfort. She watched the logs spit and crackle, and deep inside herself, she was sure she would see Grandma again no matter what strangeness was inside that altar. Yeah, she was sure.

Wanda took a breath. She glanced at Abby and dwelled on Rand. She had to get them to the hospital, and soon. Resting for a minute was good, but then they needed to get going.

She stood and looked into the forest, hoping she could figure out the way back to the main trail system. She saw the sun peeking over the distant ridges and recognized Mount Custer to the north. She could do this.

"Come on, guys. I know it sucks, but we need to get moving."

There was a crunch in the snow from behind and Wanda spun,

grabbing for the knife.

Nick was lunging at her, but the look of him didn't make sense. He looked... dead. His skin was blueish white. His pants were drenched in icy blood. If she didn't know any better, she would have thought his eyes were almost frozen in place. But here he was, a knife in his hand, swinging.

Lins screamed.

Wanda barely had time to pull the knife from her waist when a growling blur of black and tan crossed in front of her. It crashed into Nick and took him to the ground.

It was a dog—a K9! It ripped into the guy's throat, but his arm raised, a knife in hand, almost like he didn't feel it. He turned the blade toward the dog, and Wanda jumped forward. She aimed her knife and plunged it into Nick's chest.

At first, he reacted no differently than he had to the dog bite. It didn't bother him at all, and Wanda's heart skipped a beat as his blade moved toward the K9. Then she shoved harder, deeper, and felt the steel enter his icy heart.

Nick's face stilled in a frozen rictus.

When he stopped moving, the dog stopped fighting. Wanda ripped the knife free and tossed it into the snow, shedding the disgusting thing and relieved to be rid of it.

She found that she was crying.

Angel, then Lins, then Abby wrapped their arms around her. After a while—once they had gotten their breaths and the dog had calmed—they stood and slowly prepared themselves for the next step: the hike down the mountain. They knew it was going to be a long, hard task, but, God, they were ready. Except for one thing.

Angel took a moment as the others watched silently. She lifted Florence's knife from the snow and wandered to what had been the cabin's entrance. She took a breath, and she heaved. She tossed it over a cracked and smoking carving, a cursive G beside a sleeping bear, into the smoldering pile of logs. Something told her it belonged there amidst the wreckage it had wrought.

Wanda watched her baby rejoin the group and lead them into the trees with Lins by her side. The thought occurred to her as she hefted a dreary Rand over her shoulder and began down the path:

It was all about an angel.

Epilogue

W ANDA SET DINNER ON the table, a variety of Chinese entrées for herself and the girls and the easier-to-chew fried rice for Rand.

"Dinner, guys!"

She had spent a lot of time at Mark Rand's house since he got out of Custer Memorial, and she saw herself spending more there if things kept going the way they were going. It wasn't just that he needed help, though she wondered more than once if she had acquired some kind of Florence Nightingale Syndrome by helping him. But it was more than just some shared endorphin release from escaping the woods together or a shared tragedy. They laughed together. They seemed to understand each other almost immediately. They felt value in each other's company, even if there was almost a ten-year difference in their ages.

Mark had given her and Angel the spare bedroom to use when they stayed over, and more and more, she had been sneaking out while Angel was asleep, though she always returned before morning. She wasn't ready for that, and she wasn't ready for Angel to see that. Though she didn't think it was too far off.

Wanda spread out four plates and forks and called down the hall, "Angel! Lins!"

"Coming!" Angel shouted back.

She sat, and the view from the dining room window caught

her eye. There was Mount Custer. Beside it, Mount Lobo. And on it, the trail to that ruined cabin. She could still see the smoke rising in her mind, the smoldering, ashy logs, the snow-covered deadfall that reminded her more of massive tombstones than some natural occurrence.

She shivered.

It had taken them most of the day to find one of the dozen search teams that were out looking for Shamus and his crew, then another hour for a medevac chopper to pick them up and get them out of there. The questions while they waited, more when they reached the hospital, seemed endless. And most she didn't know the answers to.

How did they get from a trail on Mount Custer, where the falls are, to Lobo? Where was Officer Marshall? They had his dog, after all. How did they manage to escape?

She was still trying to figure that out.

Wanda knew a big part of it was Angel. Some part of it felt like her mother, but she was sure she was just projecting that. There was a vague memory of ghosts and strange lights, but she knew that was due to the head injuries and stress. She hadn't believed in ghosts since she was a kid, and she wasn't going to start that again. No, they made it. That was all that mattered.

She had been praised after bringing Mark down the mountain and been cleared to return to duty the next week. There was no reason to push for deeper answers. Not now, anyway.

The search teams found the cabin based on Wanda's directions, and after digging through the snow, recovered Kathy, Marshall, and one of the suspects. Thanks to Wanda's report, the others were marked dead, though the bodies were never recovered. It was a real letdown to the search team—so many were ready to return shot for shot, each bullet that had taken Wazowski, Braden, McNeil, and Harris—they were never given the chance. Regardless, the law enforcement community around the county was glad for it to be over, and through the last month, the town overall seemed to be more at peace.

Mark took the seat beside Wanda. "Thanks." It was a whisper, but stronger than yesterday, and she assumed tomorrow would be even better. He smiled when the pain was low enough to let him—and she suspected often when it didn't, just for her benefit.

She nodded and turned to the hallway. "Girls! Come on!"

"Angel! Lins!" Mom shouted from down the hall.

"Coming!" Angel shouted back. She could smell the sweet and sour chicken, her favorite, but she had to finish this drawing first. It was a bobcat in the woods, and it was important to get all the details right before she walked away and lost her place.

"I like it," Lins said from her right. She was finishing her drawing of an anime character she had come to like recently. She was alone a lot more these days and watching a lot more TV because of it. Sure, her grandmother was in the house and even asked constantly if Lins wanted to do things with her, but she almost always said no.

Her grandmother reminded her of Mom, and every time she thought of Mom, her eyes burned and it took all she had to hold back the tears. Sometimes it didn't work. Sometimes, the tears just came down and felt like they would never stop.

TV helped, but Angel helped more. Lins would ask almost every weekend to go to Angel's, and her grandmother never said no. Grandmother would make the drive to drop her off, regardless of how long it took. She and Angel would draw and play with her stuffies. They would play video games and build elaborate cities where animals ruled the world and people were their servants. They would talk about the future, and with Angel around, she actually felt like one was possible.

On those weekends, Mom only came to her in her dreams, not all day long like she did at her grandmother's house. And when she woke up crying, Angel was always close and ready to offer a hug. Lins only hoped that one day the dreams would stop altogether. Maybe one day she could forget Mom completely and it wouldn't be a problem anymore. Maybe one day she would find her own cabin in the mountains, and she could be in control of who came and went and lived and died, and the sadness wouldn't hurt any longer.

"Girls! Come on!" bellowed from the dining room.

Lins stood. "You ready for dinner?"

"Go on," Angel said. "I'll be right there."

Angel watched Lins head out to the dining room, then studied her work. The woods were bright. The trees were happy and green. The stream fed flowers and a deer. Betty Bobcat sat in the sun, enjoying the rays.

She wished it was that way for Grandma. Deep inside, she knew it wasn't, despite what she tried to tell herself. She wanted Grandma to be safe and enjoy the afterlife, not trapped in that dark place with the creepy, crawling shadows. She wanted to feel Grandma nearby when she needed her, and that was gone right now.

It had been hard coming to terms with the way things were—the loss of Ms. Kathy, the pain in everyone around her, being at Mark's house so much—but she found it worked best to keep a smile on her face. Everyone seemed happier that way, and when everyone else was happier, it made her happier.

But as she looked at Betty Bobcat in the forest, she couldn't help but see shadows in those trees. She knew there was a smoking pile of logs somewhere beyond those beautiful evergreens that she'd have to go visit one day. As much as she wanted to look into Betty's hazel eyes and smile, look at her peppered white fluff and be happy for her, Angel knew she would have to rescue her one day.

She was the only one who knew. The only one who could.

The voices never seemed to stop talking to Stevie.

He thought he was on fire at one point, then crushed. He had felt the chill of cold soil, and then he was jabbed by bones in his back and arms and legs. He'd heard voices and was so, so hungry, and someone had given him jars, and he ate. But all the while, someone was talking.

It was Mom sometimes. Sometimes, it was Dad. Sometimes, it was Honey. The voices changed, but the message was always the same. "Eat. We're stronger together. Eat. We're always together. Eat."

The bones didn't bother him so much anymore. The pokes in his flesh were almost reassuring, reminding him that he was safe and sound, right where he belonged. It was when the voices changed that he sat up, concerned.

Ash coating his face and hair, clothes drenched in his own waste, he twitched and glared in each direction. It was daytime, he knew that from the light coming down through the cracks in the floorboards above and the smell of sunlight in the air.

"Time for you to go," Dad said.

Big Steve was on his right. Dad's square chin was as strong as always; it didn't matter if the flesh was cracked and his eyes were rotting inside their sockets. It was Dad. And Dad was invincible. And Dad was always right.

"You need to go now," Mom said. She leaned on Dad's shoulder. A beetle scurried from her nose, down her chin, and into her hair.

"But I don't want to go," Stevie whined. "I want to stay here forever."

"And you will," Dad said. "When you get back."

Stevie shrugged. "I don't get it."

"Stevie." Dad's voice was firm. He bore his blackening teeth.

"Fine." Stevie stood and pushed on one of the boards above. It creaked and rose, dropping soot into the pit. Stevie gripped and pulled on the next board, lifting himself from the hole. When he was out, he pushed the loose board back into place, catching a glimpse of Mom as he did.

His stomach was tight. He would have cried if he didn't think Dad would have burst through the floor and smacked him for it.

Stevie climbed over half-burnt logs and rubble, out into the forest of deadfall, his eyes focused on the distant trees and the valley beyond.

"Bring back a good one!" Dad called.

"A pretty one," Mom added.

Acknowledgments

Garrets Lodge was a lot of work, through countless long nights and innumerable weekends. It would not exist without the effort and kindness of many people. I thank you all and regret those I may have missed. This is just a token.

Christina Hitz — Thank you for sacrificing time together, encouraging me, and picking up all the pieces I missed through my absent-mindedness. Thank you for being there when I needed you.

My kids — Thank you for believing in me and giving me the space I needed to work, especially when you wanted to write your own words into the pages.

Melinda Parrish — Thank you for reading my work over the years, believing in me, and pushing me to put it out there.

My Editor: Heather Ann Larson, your keen eyes and attention to detail really helped to pull this book together. Thank you.

My Cover Designer: Don Noble, your art brought this thing to life for readers. Keep strutting that massive talent.

About the Author

D.W. Hitz loves the outdoors and enjoys making it a background character in his work. He devours stories in all mediums. He enjoys writing in the genres of Horror, Supernatural/Paranormal Thriller, and Science Fiction/Fantasy. He aspires to tell stories that thrill the heart and stimulate the imagination.

When not writing, D.W. enjoys spending time with his family, hiking, camping, and playing with the dogs.

More from Fedowar Press

Bloodtooth by D.W. Hitz, a small-town coming of age horror compared to Needful Things crossed with A Nightmare on Elm Street with strong IT vibes:

After nightmares begin in the small town of Custer Falls, Montana, in 1992, it'll be thirty years before they end.

Available now from online bookstores or signed from Fedowar.com.

Uncanny Valley Days by C.J. Sampera

Rocked by grief and recurring apparitions of her dead brother, Olivia is losing her grip on reality and may have inadvertently invoked a cybernetic, serial-killing slasher demon. Or is it all in her head?

Available now from online bookstores.

The Frightful Tales of Louis & Lovely by Noelle Strommen

Louis and Lovely just moved into their new house. When they find a mysterious treehouse nearby with a new book waiting for them inside, they are unprepared for what awaits them.

When they start reading, and things go terrifyingly crazy, they want to restore the world around them and keep their family safe, they must survive the dark twists and turns of all six stories within the Frightful Tales.

Available now from online bookstores.

Dear Creator by Ast Geil

The apocalypse has come, and the Dear Creator is behind it. But what can humans really do in the face of godly injustice?

Available now from online bookstores.

Camp Slasher Lake: Volume One, winner of the 2023 Spatterpunk Award for Best Anthology.

A tribute to the glorious slasher movies of the 1980s, Volume 1.

Featuring stories from: John Adam Gosham, Gerri R. Gray, Patrick C. Harrison III, Carlton Herzog, D.W. Hitz, Derek Austin Johnson, J.D. Kellner, Brian McNatt, Nicholas Stella, & Vincent Wolfram

Available now from online bookstores or Fedowar.com.

Camp Slasher Lake: Volume Two

Another tribute to the glorious slasher movies of the 1980s, Volume 2.

Featuring stories from: Jay Bower, Justin Cawthorne, Kay Hanifen, D. W. Hitz, Brett Mitchell Kent, Aaron E. Lee, Kevin McHugh, Carl R. Moore, Daniel R. Robichaud, Darren Todd, & Mark Wheaton.

Available now from online bookstores or Fedowar.com.

Cody Was Here and Other Stories by D.W. Hitz

Cody Was Here and Other Stories is a chilling collection of works. They range from tales within Hitz's town of Custer Falls, known well from his novels and novellas, to stories of Sci-Fi Horror, Folk Horror, and even a ghost story.

Available now from online bookstores or Fedowar.com.

Gods are Born by D.W. Hitz

This is not the world you know. When aliens crashed on Earth, everything changed. Humanity has been decimated by predators and plague. Electromagnetic waves render most technology useless. The survivors are afflicted by strange mutations—some troubling, others amazing.

Gods are Born is a mature sci-fi read with elements of horror and graphic violence that follows the paths of seven extraordinary beings as they struggle to survive, find peace within themselves, and ultimately, defeat the King and something far worse than they can imagine.

Available now from online bookstores or Fedowar.com.

Thank you for reading